SUNDRY CREDITORS

SUNDRY CREDITORS

BY
NIGEL BALCHIN

THE REPRINT SOCIETY
LONDON

FIRST PUBLISHED 1953
THIS EDITION PUBLISHED BY THE REPRINT SOCIETY LTD.
BY ARRANGEMENT WITH WM. COLLINS, SONS & CO. LTD.
1954

*So it is not strange to mourn the passing of
a man whom we would in no wise have
alive again* — MONTAIGNE

PRINTED IN GREAT BRITAIN
BY R. & R. CLARK, LTD., EDINBURGH

I

An hour earlier a stream of cyclists would have been turning into the main gate of Lang's. Now, at five to nine, an occasional one branched off there. The rest, a mere trickle, went on another fifty yards to the office entrance. Lawrence Spellman changed down and edged the car among them at a walking pace.

Humphrey Peart looked at the jumble of buildings and said: 'There is a certain sort of red brick that time cannot assuage. When was all this built, Lawrence?'

'Built?' said Spellman vaguely. 'It wasn't built. At least, not for us. It was just here.'

Moira Peart said: 'What's that rather intriguing bit that looks like a disused chapel?'

'A disused chapel, darling. It's still called "the chapel". We use it as a sheet metal store.'

The car nosed cautiously through the big iron gates. Lawrence said: 'This house straight ahead is where old William Lang started. It is now the offices. Then he bought a bit more and a bit more until he ended up with this bloody muddle. Those saw-tooth sheds at the back are the only building on the place that was ever designed for its job. We had an American here once to see if he could help us to improve the layout. He went round the place and then came back and said: "Gentlemen, what this place needs is a few charges of dynamite and a clean start".' Spellman slid the car neatly into one of the white parking rectangles outside the offices. 'They say in the works that during the war Gustavus Lang used to go to chapel on Sundays and pray for the Germans to pop a bomb down on the place. Then we could have built a proper factory.' He sat for a moment looking at the irregular jumble of buildings.

Peart said with mild disbelief: 'And you come here every day?'

'That's right, Humphrey. Every day. Except

5

Saturday, Sunday and any other day when I can find some reason not to.'

As they climbed out of the car, a shining four-and-half litre Bentley drew up twenty yards away. Lawrence waved a hand vaguely towards it and the driver flapped in reply.

'Is that somebody very important?' said Peart. 'It's a very important car.'

'Jim Talbot-Rees. Sales Director. He's like that.'

Talbot-Rees had jumped out of his car and was hurrying ahead of them towards the main office door.

'Observe,' said Lawrence without malice, 'the brisk walk. The Burberry. The hat at precisely the right angle. The brief-case. It reminds you of that American advertising campaign for whisky . . . "Men of Distinction". Wouldn't you rather place an order with that, than with some scruffy little man out of a pre-war Austin Seven?'

'No,' said Peart briefly.

'Nor would I. But we're not representative.'

There were a lot of puddles in the yard. Moira Peart picked her way carefully between them. She had been uncertain whether a visit to a factory was Town or Country, and was glad now that she had plumped for tweeds and flat-heeled shoes. Moira looked up at the big gilt letters over the main office entrance and said: 'Why does Mr. Horseman get such a raw deal?'

'Does he?'

'Yes. It says "William Lang, Sons and Horseman" here. Outside it says "William Lang Sons", and over the factory it just says "Langs". *Is* there a Mr. Horseman?'

'No. Horseman was old William Lang's first partner in the days of bows and arrows. Drank himself to death as soon as he'd made enough money to buy the liquor. I've often thought he had the right approach to industry.'

Humphrey Peart said: 'You know, darling, I don't believe Lawrence is happy in his work.'

'Nonsense,' said Spellman. 'I live for nothing else.' He nodded as the commissionaire touched his hat. 'Come up to my office and drop your things.'

There was a big hole in Hilda's stocking, and underneath the knee was swollen and reddish blue. Miss

Warner said: 'That's a nasty bruise. How d'you come to fall off like that?'

Hilda said: 'It was on the tram-lines, nurse. They was slippery and it slid away under me.'

'Why didn't you come in straight away?'

Hilda blushed and said meekly: 'I—I thought it'd be all right, and then it got stiff and started to hurt and Miss Stark . . .'

Miss Warner said: 'All right. Well, take your stocking off, dear, and I'll bathe it. Shan't be a moment.' She picked up the box of elastic dressings and hurried into the next room. The big dark workman was holding his hand in the bowl of antiseptic. Miss Warner took the hand by the wrist and looked carefully at the cut running across the ends of three fingers. 'Weren't wearing your gloves, I suppose?' The man grunted. 'You boys in sheet metal, I don't see how you reckon to have any hands left the way you go on. You'll have to have three dressings, one for each finger. Better than a big bandage. 'Morning, Mr. Spellman.'

Lawrence said: 'Good morning, Miss Warner. More cut hands?'

'Yes. Not too bad, this one.'

Lawrence turned to the Pearts. 'We get a lot of this. It's handling sheet metal. Filthy stuff for cutting yourself, and you have to watch the cuts, or they go wrong on you.' He nodded towards the inner room. 'Can we go in, Miss Warner?'

'Oh yes, Mr. Spellman. There's nobody in there but a girl that's fallen off her bike.'

Hilda pulled her frock and overall down hastily. Lawrence said: 'Hallo 'Rene. What have you been doing to yourself?'

Hilda blushed and said: 'I fell off my bicycle, Mr. Spellman.'

'What did you want to do that for?' said Lawrence, with automatic fatuity. He turned to the Pearts. 'This is the girls' first-aid room and that's the men's.'

'Beautifully fitted up,' said Moira.

'Oh yes. This whole welfare section is the Chairman's pride and joy.'

'How do you divide in numbers between girls and men?' said Peart, taking a solemn interest.

'Oh—let's see. About half and half. Counting the offices. About a thousand of each.'

Moira said: 'I'm very ignorant, but is that *big* for a factory?'

'Medium. It's big for this district. But of course you get places running up to ten thousand and more.' As they passed Hilda, he said: 'I expect you'll have to lose your leg you know, 'Rene. You should be more careful.'

Moira smiled brightly and said: 'Good morning.'

When they were outside Peart said: 'I hope she doesn't. They were rather nice legs.'

'Yes. Pretty little codger, isn't she?'

Moira said: 'Do you know them all by name, Lawrence?'

'Lord, no. Why?'

'You called her 'Rene.'

'I always call all the girls 'Rene. About four out of every five *are* 'Rene.'

Peart said: 'I love Lawrence's jovial manner. The very essence of the *faux bonhomme*.'

'That's what's known as the human approach. This place is a shrine dedicated to the human approach. Old William Lang didn't worry much about it. He just made a quarter of a million out of sweated labour. But son Gustavus, who's Chairman now, read somewhere in a book one day that workers were human beings, and he's never forgotten it. We never have a board meeting without the Chairman reminding us that workers are human beings.'

Moira said: 'Well, aren't they?'

'Yes, dear. And so we have a welfare department, and proper seats for the workers to sit on, and hot water in the cloakrooms, and a good pension scheme, and a democratically elected Works Council, and we're just one big happy family.'

Humphrey Peart said: 'I don't quite see what you're saying, Lawrence. Surely all that's a good thing?'

'It's an enormously good thing, Humphrey. And I'll tell you another thing—it shows a hell of a good profit.

It's the only form of practical Christianity I know that pays at least ten per cent.' Lawrence's whole body suddenly sagged as he walked. 'Don't take any notice of me, my dears. It's just that I work here.'

The big presses were ranged down each side of a wide gangway marked by white lines. The service men moved along the gangway with their heavy jack-trucks, bringing a platform full of blanks and taking away a platform full of pressings. The air was full of a heavy rumble, overlaid with a squeaking and clanging.

Lawrence leant close and said through the noise: 'As I told you, this is the only bit that's properly laid out. One-way traffic. Blanks come in—pressed—pressings go out. It's a good press shop, as press shops go.'

Moira said: 'What are they making?'

'I don't know. We're mainly fabricators. We make some finished things of our own, but most of it is making bits of things for other people to assemble.'

Jack Partridge glanced up for a moment from the pit in front of the big press at the three figures above him. His hands went on slipping the blank into place. He stamped on the pedal and the heavy press began to rumble down. As the die struck the blank there was a squeaking crunch. The die moved up and the ejector pushed out the bowl-shaped pressing.

Humphrey Peart said: 'The whole thing is obviously an act of worship—of sacrifice. The press is the obscene idol. The light down there by the jaws is its eye. The man crouches in a pit below and feeds it, and that noise as it crunches its food is the death cry of the sacrifice . . .'

Lawrence said: 'There'll be another sort of cry in a minute if that young fool doesn't use the guard.' He stepped forward and said something to Jack Partridge. The young man looked up sulkily and then reluctantly untied a piece of flex.

Lawrence said: 'He'd got the guard tied back. He could be fired for that. You see, when the press comes down, the guard comes across so that he can't get his hands squashed. But it gets in the way slightly, so he ties it back and takes the chance. They all do that if they're not watched. We spend thousands of pounds on safety devices here—guards and goggles and gloves and so on. And nobody uses them if they can get out of it.'

'Stupid but understandable,' said Moira.

'Workers are human beings, my dear.'

'But really,' said Humphrey. 'But *really* it is an act of sacrifice. Look at it. The one-eyed god . . .'

As they moved away, Jack Patridge glanced up again. His eyes followed Moira's close-fitting tweed skirt with appreciation. Catching the eye of the man working on the next press he raised a thumb and an eyebrow.

Lawrence was saying: 'Jack Partridge ought to know better than to work without a guard. He's on the Works Council, and anyhow he's second generation here. His father's a pattern maker. Been here since the flood.'

'Have you got many like that? Two generations?'

'Oh Lord, yes. If people come here they stay for life and bring their children. I tell you it's just one big happy family.'

Jack Partridge paused for a moment in the steady rhythm of his work, picked up his piece of flex and carefully tied back the guard. But instead of knotting it he secured it with a bow, so that a single quick tug would bring the guard into action again.

It was not really necessary for Hilda to go through the press shop to get from the Welfare Section to the assembly room, but it was a possible way. Hilda was a shy girl, and if Jack had been working and had not noticed her, she would just have gone past without speaking to him. But he was still fiddling with the guard and saw her. He said: 'Hallo. Where you been?'

Hilda half paused: 'Been to nurse.'

He nodded, uninterested.

Hilda said: 'It was to-night you meant?'

'That's right. Odeon. Half-past. O.K.?'

'Yes.'

Jack nodded again and turned to his work.

Hilda said to his back: 'I must get on.'

Lawrence said: 'Would you like to see the casting shop?' It was a silly question. He knew that they could hardly say no, they didn't want to see the casting shop.

He could take them there, or he could just leave it out and they would be none the wiser. But it was a part of his private internal war to make the suggestion, knowing it would be accepted and hoping to the last that it would be refused.

Humphrey Peart said: 'We are in your hands, Lawrence. We'd like to see anything that's good for us.'

Lawrence said: 'It's across the yard.'

As they neared the door the cold shaking fear came to him as it always did. To help it he said carefully: 'They may not do it as Moira's with us. But usually when the boys are pouring metal they manage to slop a bit by your feet if you're a visitor. It's their favourite joke.'

'The object being to make you jump?'

'That's it. If you take no notice you've won. Of course, they never *do* burn you but—some people find it alarming.'

Some people do. Some people who've had a tank brew up under them—some people who can remember tugging at little Billy Hart in the driver's seat, and finding his legs were jammed, and seeing the flames coming up round his feet and legs. . . .

Humphrey Peart said: 'I shall probably scream and jump a mile.'

'That will give great pleasure,' said Lawrence from a dry throat.

There were plenty of times when they weren't pouring in the casting shop. There had been plenty of times when he had stopped outside and squared his shoulders, and gone in and found that they were not pouring, and said a silent prayer of thanks. But it wasn't so to-day. Lawrence stopped just inside the door and said quietly: 'Well, here we are—you make a solid pattern out of wood, like this. Then that's moulded in sand in two halves. Then the two halves are put together so that there is a space in the middle the shape of the pattern. Then you pour the metal in, wait for it to set, knock away the sand, and there's your casting.'

Moira said: 'How d'you get the metal in?'

'You have a hole for it.' Lawrence hesitated for a

fraction of a second and then said steadily : 'Come over and see them doing it.'

The two men with the pouring bucket on a pole were working their way along the line of moulds. The last few that had been poured were still smoking, and in places little rivulets of metal had run over on to the sandy floor and solidified, and now glowed a dark and dirty red. There was plenty of room in the gangway. The hot metal was three feet away as you walked. At least three feet away. Lawrence flicked his fingers across his damp forehead. He fancied that Moira looked at him oddly. He smiled at her with an effort and said : 'Hot job.'

The two big men who were pouring glanced up but only for a second. Otherwise they went on as though the visitors were not there.

'God, isn't that beautiful !' said Moira, as the bucket tilted and the heavy incandescent stream gurgled into the mould.

They were pouring expertly, cutting off at the exact moment, so that scarcely a drip was lost. The blue flames played round the top and sides of the filled mould.

Moira said : 'I want to look in the bucket. Can I ?'

Lawrence nodded. She stepped forward. The men paused for a moment and grinned. She was right beside them and the glow from the liquid metal was on her face.

'Lovely, lovely stuff,' she said. 'God, the heat from it is terrific, Lawrence.' She made a little gesture that half suggested that he should join her, but he stood there, six feet away, and swallowed and said : 'Yes.' They had to move her back slightly when they poured the next. But they didn't play the joke on her. They liked her because she wasn't afraid of their metal.

Humphrey Peart said : 'Do they ever get burnt ?'

There were thirty girls in each conveyor assembly team, but they worked in three groups of ten, and by the time the job reached Hilda's group it was only a question of tightening down the six screws that held the upper ring, slipping the cover cap over the projecting spindle and the holding bolts, tightening them down, and wiring on the instruction tab. As number two, Hilda's job was to tighten three of the screws with an electric screw-driver. Madge, as number one, would already have tightened the other three. When everything was going smoothly Hilda would start to tighten her first screw when the assembly was well to her right, get her second finished as it was nearly opposite her, and finish her third just before the conveyor took it out of reach. It wasn't a bad job now because they had slowed the belt down. When the job first came on, the belt had been much too fast, and you were always rushing and missing ones out.

Hilda worked with a slow rocking movement from right to left. If you did that you could follow the job as it went along the conveyor, and besides it was soothing. Everybody rocked—even Jean, who was putting on the cap and really didn't need to follow along.

Jean and 'Rene always talked all the time. 'It said, one pair of nylons if you got two ordinary, and I thought, well that's not bad, because the ordinary's all I want for here, so I wrote up, but it was shocking stuff; looked all right, but you get it on. Short, hardly covers your knee.'

'Rene said: 'I had some like that. Reg gave me them for Christmas.'

''Course they get them in at Gage's, but they're all gone in ten minutes, and it's always in the morning. Doesn't give you a chance if you've got to work.'

'Phil Lewis says her mother goes and queues for her. I asked Ma if she would get me some but she wouldn't. I might get my sister.'

The frock was of white stuff—tulle. It was right off the shoulders and then it fitted tight in the bodice and had a big wide skirt. As Hilda came down the stairs she held the skirt forward and up slightly, so that the silver shoes were visible. Robert Taylor was standing in the hall waiting for her. He was in evening dress and he had a small moustache and a ribbon round his neck with a medal on. He stood there with the fur coat over his arm ready, smiling up at her. Hilda stopped for a moment half-way down the stairs and they stood for a moment, she looking down and he looking up, just smiling at each other. He said: 'Gee, you look swell.' She didn't say anything for a moment, but just came slowly down some more stairs, still holding her skirt in that lovely way. Then she said: 'Well, you don't look too bad yourself.' Her voice was husky and thrilling and she looked at him and raised her eyebrows. He put the coat round her shoulders very gently, only it wasn't a coat of course but a cloak, and came right down to her ankles. He said: 'Come on, honey, let's go,' and she could hear the love in his voice, and they went out to the car, which was one of those huge ones that are the same at both ends. Madge said: 'Take mine a mo', dear,' and slid off her seat and went off with her queer splay-footed walk rather like a duck. It wasn't till she was gone that Hilda realised what she had said, and she missed two assemblies. But after that she started to do number one as well as number two, which was quite possible as long as you stood up and followed along beside the thing. But you wouldn't want to go as fast as that for long. She forgot to call to Jean not to cap the two that she had missed, but unless they happened to be picked out for inspection nobody would know.

Madge came back and said: 'Thanks, duck.'

Hilda sat down and went back to doing number two. The chauffeur was in a dark green uniform and he held the door of the car open and touched his hat.

Moira said: 'How on earth many of them are there in here, Lawrence?'

'About two hundred. It's the biggest single department.'

'It looks like more than that.'

Peart said: 'And they go on doing this all day and every day?'

'Oh Lord, no. As Walter Lang will tell you, that's the great difficulty—to get long runs on a single job. As it is, they're probably changing over to a different job every day or two.'

'But always working like this with things going by them on a belt?'

'Yes.'

Humphrey Peart said : 'Again, clearly a religious ceremony. The female acolytes swaying in the ecstasy of worship. There should be a low chant.'

'There often is. If you wait a minute they'll probably sing "Clementine".'

Moira said : 'Queer, that rocking movement. I wonder if they—if they *mind* the job?'

'Why should they? Comfortable, scientifically designed seats. Air-conditioning. Rest pauses. After all, it's only eight hours a day, five days a week for the best years of their lives. If you were nineteen, would *you* mind?'

Humphrey Peart said : 'I think you can over-estimate what people *want*, you know, Lawrence. You wouldn't like it and nor should I, because we want to *think*. But plenty of people don't. A simple manual job that gets a living. . . .'

Lawrence said : 'When I was young I saw a man—a labourer—get his hand crushed. When I cried my aunt said : "Never mind, dear. You must remember they don't feel pain as we do." It's a useful concept.'

Moira said : 'Oh, there's your 'Rene—the one who'd hurt her knee.'

Mr. James Talbot-Rees took a cigarette from the gold, engine-turned, initialled case and flicked the lighter at the end of the case into flame. 'I realise Production's difficulties,' he said in a beautiful round, musical voice. 'But to ask me to sell an appliance—and an appliance with a seasonal use—on a nine months' delivery date . . .' he spread out his hands.

Walter Lang sat and stared at him for a moment and then turned to Martin and said : 'Nine months is bunkum, George. We must get it better than that. It oughtn't to be three months at the outside.' He stared unwinkingly at Talbot-Rees again with the heavy sullen face, that looked angry even when it wasn't, and said : 'Would three months be all right for you?'

Talbot-Rees leant forward with a hand dramatically extended, palm upwards. 'Walter—you've got an excellent appliance. You've got the best medium-size sprayer in the country. Give it to me on three months' delivery and I'll put the Parker spray and the Cleanwash off the market. I'll . . .'

Lang said : 'What d'you think you could do with it if you had a clear run ? '

'Given a few thousand pounds in the agricultural papers, I could do six times our present output. And that's conservative.'

Lang said : 'Six times ? I want twelve times.' He smiled the sudden brief beautiful smile that flashed on and flashed off again, leaving no trace behind it on the sullen face.

'Well—that's not impossible. I was being conservative. . . .'

George Martin stirred uneasily in his chair and picked at the top button of his white coat. He said : 'I don't doubt we could sell the job if we could make it. But there it is, Mr. Walter—we haven't got the stuff.'

'Well, what is it that's holding us up,' said Lang irritably.

'Mostly steel rod for the carriages,' said Martin patiently. 'That and angle.' Lang had asked him this question and been given this reply about four times a week for the last year.

'Well, we can't have the whole job held up for a few tons of steel rod. Can't young Lawrence get on to the stockholders and say it's urgent ? God damn it, we do enough business with them, don't we ? '

'Mr. Lawrence is on the telephone to them every day.'

'What's the good of that ? He ought to go down and see them. Take lorries down and not come away until he's got it.'

Martin shook his head. 'I really don't think they've got it, Mr. Walter. Steel's very short all round. Everybody's in the same boat. What with re-armament and . . .'

'Then leave out the stockholders and go straight to the mills and . . .'

'But they haven't got it either.'

Lang gave a snort of disbelief.

Talbot-Rees said gently: 'It's not my pigeon, but—well I know steel's short, but I sometimes wonder whether we do as well as we might in getting it out of people. . . .' He smiled at Lang confidentially.

'Yes,' said Lang. 'It's no good young Lawrence just sitting on his behind and telephoning. He ought to go out and get the stuff. . . .' He turned to Martin with the air of one reasoning gently with someone being stubborn and unco-operative. 'See, George, I've told you what I'm trying to do. I want to get shot of these damned fabricating jobs and concentrate on our own products. I don't want the factory full of a lot of bits and pieces that barely pay their overhead. Now if we could get going on three or four jobs like this sprayer, and no more, we could plan production properly, get decent length runs . . .' He rambled on into the lovely dream—the dream in which there were no shortages, no restrictions, no licences, no jumble of old buildings, infinite capital and a staff capable of doing three men's work each. Martin had heard it all a hundred times before. It would never be done in his lifetime, and probably not in Lang's. It was a phantasy. But he knew that the drive for that phantasy, day in and day out, week after week, year after year, was the motive force behind the business. 'Mr. Walter,' as he had often said, 'gets things done because he goes on so that you have to do *something* for peace. You can't do what he says, because it isn't possible. But you usually find you can do *something*.'

'So there you are,' said Lang, getting up. 'That's what we've got to aim at. So don't you talk to me about nine months' delivery, George.' He had talked himself into a good temper again. He turned to Talbot-Rees. 'Don't you worry, Jim. You go on and book the orders. We'll produce the stuff. Four months' delivery. You hear, George?' Martin smiled dubiously but said nothing. It was all right. Talbot-Rees was no fool. He would come along later and between them they would agree the shortest delivery date the factory could manage. Talbot-Rees had only come to Lang first to safeguard his own position—to make sure that when the optimistic sales figures were not fulfilled, nobody could blame him; that,

and perhaps to have a back-handed slap at Lawrence
Spellman. Martin decided calmly that he would suggest
eight months' delivery and settle for thirty weeks. That
would keep Talbot-Rees quiet, and it was just possible,
if steel got no worse.

Lang said : 'Meanwhile I'll have a word with young
Lawrence. Maybe I'll have to go and see Geoffrey
Bander myself and talk to him straight about this steel
position.'

It was as easy as that. One went and saw Sir Geoffrey
Bander and talked to him straight, and a national shortage—a world shortage—a deficit of civilisation—must
disappear before the absolute necessity that William Lang
Sons & Horseman should make more spraying machines.
The fact must yield before the urgency of the wish, as it
has seemed to do often before.

Lawrence said : 'I'm very sorry about this coffee. The
problem of the coffee we get in these offices baffles science.
It is made from the finest freshly roasted and ground
beans, by the most approved methods, but it always
comes out tasting like this.'

Moira looked round the office and said : 'This is a
nice room. Are all the directors' offices done like this?'

Humphrey said : 'Darling, I don't suppose they *all*
have Degas drawings on the walls. Otherwise it would
come a bit expensive.' He carried his coffee over to the
drawing above the fireplace. The nude girl's legs and
thighs were meticulous. Her torso, and the fact that she
was washing, was slashed in with a sort of miraculous
carelessness. Peart said crossly : 'I don't see how it's
done. I never *do* see how he does it.'

Lawrence was saying : 'The fact that I have all my
own stuff in my office causes deep suspicion. The Chairman won't even have a carpet on the floor. Walter has
one armchair for visitors, but you're not supposed to sit
in it unless you *are* a visitor. There's a general feeling
that no executive can really *work* unless he's thoroughly
uncomfortable. Odd, because Gustavus is always preach-
ing that people in the factory can't work unless they're
comfortable.'

'When are you coming to town?' said Peart, with his back to them.

Moira was sitting back in the big leather armchair with her legs crossed. Lawrence's eyes met hers and they both smiled slightly.

Lawrence said: 'I don't know, Humphrey. Soon, I hope.' He pursed his lips and made a silent kissing motion towards her. Moira shook her head reprovingly.

Peart turned and said: 'Well, let us know in good time and we'll beat some people up.'

Lang opened the door without knocking, put his head in and said: 'Oh, sorry,' and disappeared again. Lawrence rose and called: 'Come in, Walter. . . . I want you to meet Humphrey and Moira Peart . . . Walter Lang, our Managing Director.'

Lang switched on the traffic-light smile, shook hands, said: 'How d'you do?' and switched the smile off again. Lawrence said: 'I've just been showing them round the place.'

'Oh yes?'

Moira said: 'It's awfully interesting. You know it's perfectly disgraceful but I've never been in a factory before.'

'I have,' said Humphrey. 'When I was fourteen. We were taken over a tyre factory from school.'

'Dunlop?' said Lang, with a flicker of interest.

'I think it was. Not far from here.'

'Dunlop.'

'You're probably right,' said Peart gravely.

There was a moment's slightly discouraged pause. Lang turned to Lawrence and said: 'Well, don't let me interrupt, but I'd like to see you for a minute when you're free.'

Lawrence said: 'I'll come along.'

Lang smiled briefly and said: 'I want to know where my steel is.'

'I want to know where it is too,' said Lawrence, smiling back at the steady stare.

Lang gave a grunt and turned away. 'Well, we've got to do something about it.' He nodded to the Pearts: 'Good-bye. Glad to have met you.'

When the door closed, Moira said : 'That's a rather disconcerting character.'

'I hope you caught the implication,' said Lawrence, lighting a cigarette. 'That I ought to be looking for this steel—which by the way is non-existent—instead of sitting drinking coffee.'

'It's rather a good head,' said Peart. 'But something's gone wrong with the mouth.'

'With the heart, Humphrey, with the heart.' Lawrence shook his head. 'Poor old Walter,' he said reflectively. 'He lost his wife a year ago. I don't think he ever noticed she was there much when she was alive, but it's made a lot of difference to him. When Jean was alive, Walter was almost human at times. But he's completely lost the knack now.'

'Is he the Chairman's brother?'

'Half-brother. Gustavus was old William Lang's son by his first wife and Walter by his second. He's twenty years younger than Gustavus.'

'And Walter really runs the place?'

'Runs is the word. He runs it ragged. He gets here at nine, never leaves much before seven, and expects everybody else to do the same.'

Peart said : 'Is he good?'

Lawrence hesitated. 'I don't know,' he said slowly. 'He's not my kind of man and I'm not his, so I'm not evidence. He's certainly successful in terms of the Profit and Loss Account. . . .' He paused and then added almost to himself : 'He'd better be.'

'Why do you say that?'

'Because I've never seen quite what would happen to him if he wasn't, darling.'

Moira said : 'You hate him, don't you?'

'What, *me*?' said Lawrence. 'Hate dear old Walter? Walter who's our mainspring? Walter who keeps us all on our toes? Walter who has a genius for leadership? Walter who's even got a heart of gold somewhere or other? My dear girl, you must understand that the cardinal principle of this place is that we're all devoted to Walter. Poor bastard.'

II

Gustavus Lang took off his pince-nez, put on a pair of bi-focal horn-rimmed spectacles, and looked at the Works Council gathered round the big board-room table with a slight frown.

'Before we start,' he said, in the gentle, slightly puzzled voice, 'I don't like this habit we have got into of arranging ourselves with the members from the works and the members from the executive side opposite each other. This isn't a—a Parliament with a government and an opposition. Can't we re-arrange ourselves so as to—to express the spirit of this Council?' He glanced at Walter and said almost apologetically: 'It's a small point, but these things matter. . . .' The members of the Council looked at one another rather sheepishly. Miss Bell, the Welfare Worker, whose job consisted almost entirely of dealing with Gustavus's small points that mattered, rose and said to Jack Partridge: 'I'll come over that side, Jack, and you come here.'

'That's right,' said Gustavus. 'And Ryan, you come over next to Mr. Walter; and George, you go over by Miss Bell. Mr. North as Secretary stays on my left, and Mr. Walter of course on my right . . .'

The chief shop steward's eyes met Walter's as he took the chair vacated by George Martin. Lang said quietly: 'Is there anything much to talk about? I don't want to be here all the afternoon.'

Ryan said: 'I don't think there's much, Mr. Walter. Not that we can't settle outside. Unless the Chairman's got something.'

'He will have,' said Lang briefly.

'That's better,' said Gustavus with the bright, almost boyish smile that had stayed with him for seventy years. 'Now North, if we could have the minutes . . .'

Forty years ago, as a man of thirty-three, Gustavus

Lang had explained to his father that if you trusted
people they never let you down. The essence of democracy was an elected assembly, representing those who
elected it. There must be a Works Council representing
all points of view, in which all would speak with an equal
voice.

Old William Lang was not by nature a democrat, but
he understood more about the uses of democracy than
his son. A properly constituted Works Council, he decided, could do no harm, might be useful in some ways,
and would keep Gustavus happy. The first Works
Council of William Lang Sons and Horseman met as
early as 1913. It had done no harm, been useful in some
ways, and kept Gustavus happy ever since. It was irre-
verently known in the factory as the Soft Soap Department, or Gus's Circus, in spite of which, to be elected as
one of the factory representatives was a highly-valued
honour.

Indeed, it was an honour that fell to few people. Old
William Lang had bargained for a 'properly constituted
Council,' and had made sure that from his point of view
it *should* be properly constituted. It consisted, in theory,
of three members appointed by the management and
three by the workers, with a neutral Chairman. Henry
Spellman, Lawrence's father, had been one of the management representatives since the Council was founded. The
others were Walter and George Martin. As Managing
Director and Factory Manager they could not very well
be left out. A secretary was necessary and this could
hardly be anybody but North, the Company Secretary.
In 1913, a Works Council was such an advanced concept
that nobody saw anything curious in the neutral Chairman being Gustavus, the promoter of the whole idea,
and in forty years no flicker of doubt about his own
impartiality had ever crossed his mind. In practice,
therefore, five senior members of the management staff
confronted three representatives of the workers, of whom
one, Ryan, the Chief Shop Steward, was an ex-officio
member and the other two were elected annually. When
it was pointed out to Gustavus that this was not altogether
a democratically elected committee on which all points

of view were equally represented, he had proposed that
the Welfare Worker should become an ex-officio member,
in order to strengthen the representation of the workers'
point of view. The proposal, like a good many of Gustavus's Works Council proposals, had been accepted
without comment.

'Right,' said Gustavus briskly. 'Then it is agreed
that a notice shall be posted in the canteen drawing
attention to the loss of china and cutlery and pointing
out the inconvenience it causes. Action with you, Miss
Bell.' He ticked off the item on his agenda. '"Earning
on some conveyor assembly processes." Whose is that?'

Clarice Sloan, a thirty-year-old woman in glasses who
was the women's representative, flushed and glanced
rather nervously at Ryan. 'I put that on, Mr. Lang,
but Mr. Ryan thought . . .'

Ryan said composedly: 'I explained to Miss Sloan
that things to do with rates were really for Mr. Walter
and Mr. Martin and me to talk about rather than for
the Works Council.'

'Yes,' said Gustavus. 'Yes. That's true in general.
What was the particular point here?'

Lang sighed audibly. Ryan sat back and began to
draw idly on his blotting-paper. Miss Sloan hesitated:
'It—it was only that the girls had been complaining about
—when we start it's too tight and then . . .'

George Martin smiled at her and said gently: 'I think
I can explain if Miss Sloan will let me. Sometimes when
we start a new job we get the rate too tight, and then it's
very difficult for people to earn their money. It's happened twice lately. That's it, isn't it, Miss Sloan?'

'That's right,' she said gratefully.

'Well, that's bad, isn't it?' said Gustavus, frowning
and shaking his head. 'It's a thing that ought to be dealt
with. We can't have . . .'

Martin said: 'We always deal with it as soon as we
know it's tight . . .'

Jack Partridge said: 'Yes, sir, but while it's being
found out, the girls can't make their money.'

It was not usual for workers' representatives to speak
on matters outside their own department, and certainly

not new and very young representatives. Lang and Ryan both looked up. Lang said rather grimly : 'I think we should remember that a new rate is also sometimes set too slack, so that everybody cleans up a packet of money before it's corrected.'

Old Henry Spellman opened his eyes and said : 'The cancellation of errors, or two wrongs making a right.'

Jack said : 'Yes, Mr. Lang, but the management set the rates. The workers don't.'

'What's that got to do with it?' said Lang curtly.

'Well, sir, if the management makes a mistake and has to pay for it, that's fair. But if the management makes a mistake and the workers have to pay for it, that isn't.'

The handsome rather snubby twenty-three-year-old face returned Lang's sullen stare with a beaming smile. There was a moment's rather awkward pause.

Gustavus said : 'You know, I think that's right, Walter. I think he—uh—Partridge . . . I think he's right.'

Lang's face hardened. He looked away with a slight shrug.

Ryan said doggedly : 'Well, I think this is a thing for Mr. Walter and Mr. Martin and me to talk over . . .'

Gustavus said : 'Yes. Of course, on wage rates Mr. Ryan is the official representative. . . . But you were quite right to raise it, Miss Sloan. Quite right. That's the whole value of a Council like this. Anybody can raise anything and either the Council can discuss it or— or delegate it to others with instructions that it shall be dealt with. Right. Action with Mr. Walter, Mr. Martin and Mr. Ryan. Now we come on to the chief item on the Agenda. The Works Party. Last time Miss Bell was going to ask people whether they'd rather have only dancing. Now, Miss Bell . . .?'

Henry Spellman heaved his eighteen stone out of his chair and said : 'I hope you'll forgive me, Mr. Chairman. I have to go. But if this issue comes to a vote, mine would be for the entertainer, for reasons which will be obvious to you.' He waddled towards the door amid general laughter.

'Well, Mr. Chairman,' said the Welfare Worker, 'the majority seem to agree with Mr. Spellman . . .'

'Though not all for the same reason,' said Gustavus, smiling.

'People seem to think an entertainer would be nice. It was enjoyed last year.'

'It's the older ones that want an entertainer,' said Jack Partridge. 'The younger ones . . .'

'Could we hear Miss Bell?' said Lang pointedly. He did not look at Jack, but his tone made the slap almost audible.

Gustavus said: 'Yes—I think we'll have Miss Bell's report first, Partridge, and then people can put their points of view.'

The boy went bright crimson and muttered: 'Sorry, sir.'

Miss Bell said: 'It's quite true that some would rather dance all the time, but as there'll be dancing all the evening except this half-hour . . .'

Jack Partridge was staring down at the blotting-paper before him. The flush was fading, leaving his face unusually pale. Once he glanced quickly at Lang, but Lang was leaning back in his chair with his eyes closed.

Gustavus was saying: 'Well, that seems a sensible compromise. Now what was your point, Partridge?'

Jack said sullenly: 'I haven't got one, sir, except what I said. I was going to vote for an entertainer anyway.' He looked across at Lang again with smouldering anger.

Lang opened his eyes and said to Gustavus: 'Well, that's settled then, isn't it?'

As they walked back towards the press shop Ryan said: 'See, you ought to have kept quiet when I gave you the tip. You never want to talk about wages or anything like that at these meetings.'

Jack said: 'Well, then, what's the good of going?'

'It's all right as long as it keeps on little things that nobody cares about,' said Ryan reasonably. 'But when it's a question of handling Walter, and getting something out of him, you leave that to me. See, he didn't like what you said, and you know what he is. If he takes to you, you're made. But if he gets his knife into you, you can't do anything right.'

'Well, I don't want to be one of his pets,' said Jack sullenly. 'Anyhow, I was right, wasn't I?'

Ryan said: 'Listen, son—I've seen a lot of men lose their jobs through being right at the wrong time. You ask your dad. He's seen it too.'

*   *   *   *   *

It was a quarter to seven when Lang turned his car down the road marked 'Private. No Through Way.' The big solid houses, most of them built at the beginning of the century, stood well back in their large gardens, each with its sweep of gravelled drive, its lawns, with a big cedar or a clump of rhododendrons, and its climbing roses or honeysuckle. When they had been built they were the last houses before the open country. It was half a mile away now.

Rosamund came into the hall and kissed him and said: 'Hallo, darling. Had a good day?' It was one of the formulae that she had taken over when Jean died —the coming into the hall, the kiss, the question; one of a dozen things like putting out a clean handkerchief, and warming his shoes on cold mornings and pouring out the tea. She had been seventeen and a schoolgirl of whom he was vaguely aware and vaguely proud and vaguely fond. And then Jean had died. For a fortnight he had been without these things, and then they had been there again.

He kept his arm round her waist as they went into the big square drawing-room. Rosamund said: 'Sherry?'

'Just time for one,' said Lang, glancing at his watch.

'You are dressing for the Spellmans', aren't you? I've put your dinner jacket out.'

'Yes.' He took his sherry. 'You want some?'

'Please,' said Rosamund. She looked critically at the half-filled glass he handed her. 'That's a measly drop.'

'Plenty for little girls.' Lang leant back and looked at her with his curious unwinking stare. 'I suppose I might have taken you to the Spellmans' if I'd thought of it. What are you going to do this evening?'

'Oh, this and that. Who's the man you're going to meet?'

'Sir Francis Proudfoot. Head of the Richmond Glenn

group. They control Lovats and Beal Carter and United Agricultural and God knows what. I suppose this man's one of the biggest operators in light engineering in England. Or in the world.'

'Isn't that the man who keeps giving people a million pounds?'

'I don't know about a million, but he's given a lot away. He's a pal of Henry Spellman's.' Lang took a sip of his sherry and frowned. 'You know, Roz, this steel business is getting serious.'

'Really?' said Rosamund, gazing at him with large solemn grey eyes.

'I mean, here we are talking about nine months' delivery on the sprayer, simply because we can't get ordinary half-inch rod. Mind you, I don't believe it's true. There must *be* the stuff. But of course young Lawrence just sits on his behind and drinks coffee and says, well, he's rung up and they say they haven't got it and . . .'

Young Lawrence. Not so very young now. Not as young as he was coming back in 1943, very handsome in his major's uniform and the black beret, and with his arm in splints. One had been nine then, and had a long plait, and he had liked pulling the plait. He had had six medal ribbons, and Daddy had said that the ones at the beginning of the row—the red and blue one and the white and blue ones—were the good ones. Daddy had got out a bottle of champagne and he and Mummy and Henry Spellman had drunk Lawrence's health; and when he went away, Daddy had shaken hands with him and smiled at him in an odd way. But now he wasn't trying hard enough to buy half-inch rod.

Rosamund said: 'Darling, you ought to go and dress. It's after seven.' When he had gone she uncorked the sherry bottle and added enough to her untouched glass to fill it. Leaning back in her chair she sipped the wine, savouring the acid unpleasantness of it. It was a nastier taste than white wine, but not as sickeningly foul as gin.

* * * * *

It was raining slightly and most of the queue outside the Odeon were sheltering in shop doorways.

There were about thirty people packed into the entrance of Boots.

Jack was saying: 'So I said, "Wait a minute Mr. Lang. You set the rates, don't you? So if you make a mistake you ought to pay for it. Fair's fair".'

Hilda said: 'You said that to Walter?'

''Course I did. I'm not afraid of him.'

'What did he say?'

'He didn't know what to say. He just went red and looked mad. And then old Gus said: "Well, *I* think he's right"—saying that I was right, see? By God, you should have seen his face—Walter's. Ryan said afterwards: "He was angry about that. You oughtn't to have said it." So I said: "Let him be angry. I'm not afraid of him if you are." You know it strikes me Ryan's too "Yes, Mr. Walter, and No, Mr. Walter," with him.'

Hilda said: 'They ought to be out soon now.' She shifted her weight uneasily.

Jack said: 'How's your knee?'

'All right. It aches a bit.'

He put his arm round her and grinned. 'Like me to rub it for you?'

Hilda blushed and gave a slight giggle. 'You know it was awful to-day. See, I was in First Aid, and nurse said take your stocking off and I'll bathe it, and just as I had my skirt right up undoing my suspenders Mr. Lawrence came in with some people and . . .'

'I'll bet he did. I wonder he didn't offer to do it for you. He's a lad. You know Fred Boxall? Well, his sister Nellie's in the stores and he told me Lawrence came in there one day and his sister was up the steps getting something out of the rack and . . .'

There was a sudden stir around them.

Hilda said: 'They're coming out now.'

*   *   *   *   *

Lang came to the head of the staircase and shouted: 'Roz!'

She came out into the hall. 'What, darling?'

'Come and tie this for me. I can't get the bloody thing to stay.'

The black tie was crumpled and limp. Rosamund said: 'This one's rather a mess. Here's another. Stand still, darling. . . . Now let's see, how does it go?'

Lang fidgeted and said: 'Look—I'll show you how it goes and then . . .'

'No. It's all right. I've got it. But stand *still*. . . .'

Her short, shining black hair was just on a level with his eyes and only about a foot away as her fingers worked against his neck. She was frowning effortfully, and a tiny bit of tongue showed between her lips. Lang swallowed and said: 'That's all right. I can do it now,' and pulled away.

Rosamund said: 'No—wait a minute—I've nearly got it. Just . . .'

'It's all right. I'd rather finish myself, anyhow,' he said almost roughly, turning to the mirror. 'It's only tying the knot that always foxes me.'

'Oh, all right,' said Rosamund, rather hurt. 'But don't blame me if it slips round behind your ear. I never knew anybody who made such a fuss about standing still for half a minute.'

He finished the tie and grinned at her and squeezed her hand for a moment in passing.

Rosamund said: 'You'll want your white scarf.'

Lang put his head out of the car window and said: 'I don't expect I shall be very late, but don't wait up for me.'

Rosamund said: 'All right, darling. Good night.'

She watched the car turn out of the drive, with the thick drizzle showing in its headlights. She shivered slightly as she went in and shut the door. Only the centre light was on in the drawing-room and the fire was low. The room looked gaunt and depressing. Rosamund stood for a moment feeling the profound silence of the house. She had sent Mr. and Mrs. Dart, the married couple, out for the evening just to produce this silence and aloneness, and now here it was—that blank silence, like a blank sheet of paper ready for the writing. Turning, she went out into the hall and stood looking up the wide polished oak staircase, and said aloud one of her charms:

> ' Or thou art summoned to the deep,
> Thou, thou and all thy mates to keep,
> An incommunicable sleep . . .'

The hall was a good place to say it, because it was bare and echoing. But it needed a man's voice. One's voice was always too thin and high for the words. She said sharply: 'What's your name, girl?' and then softly: 'Rosamund Lang.' It was a nice name. She had always liked her name. She said again: 'Rosamund Lang,' very gently and demurely.

Her watch said quarter to eight, but it was a bit slow. She was not hungry, but unless she had supper the rest of the evening couldn't begin. Mrs. Dart had left the tray all ready for her on the kitchen table. A glass of milk and some tomato sandwiches and some meat sandwiches and some cheese and biscuits and an apple. Mrs. Dart's alarm clock had a loud, tinny tick that seemed to fill the whole kitchen. Dart's gardening boots were in the corner.

Rosamund took the tray and carried it along the corridor. Halfway along she raised it carefully, so as not to spill the milk, and balanced it on her head, keeping only one finger on the side to steady it. She went to the drawing-room door and looked in. But the fire was almost out and the used sherry glasses and the bottle were not attractive. She switched off the light and went upstairs, bolt upright to keep the tray balanced.

Sitting on the floor in her bedroom in front of the electric fire, Rosamund reflected that this was one of the times when it would have been nice to have a dog. The poodle question must be reopened with Daddy. She ate the tomato sandwiches and the apple, but the meat sandwiches were too dry, and had to be washed down with milk, and made you feel as though they were going

to give you hiccups. She took the last two and threw
them out of the window so that Mrs. Dart shouldn't be
hurt. Mrs. Dart was always hurt if anything she provided was not eaten. If one had had a dog one could
have given the spare sandwiches to him. It was still
raining outside. She put the tray outside on a table in
the corridor and was glad to be rid of it. Apple cores
were always unpleasant. It was only just after eight, and
that meant that going to bed could take two hours, or
even longer. Rosamund switched on the small portable
radio set beside her bed. A comedian's voice—you could
tell he was a comedian by the voice—said: 'Honesty
may be the best policy, but I'd rather have one with the
Pru myself.' The audience laughed with improbable
heartiness. Rosamund sighed and switched off again, and
began slowly to unhook her dress. Crossing her arms,
she pulled it off over her head and went and stood before
the long mirror. The brassière and panties covered the
only white bits. The rest of her skin was still faintly
brown from last summer. There was always something
odd about being in your underclothes with shoes with
heels. With your shoes off it was just undressing. With
them still on, it wasn't. Rosamund decided that there
was a little too much hip and thigh in comparison with
the top. But that was partly because the mirror was
tilted. There was a mirror in the hall that tilted the
other way and that was much worse, because it made
you look short-legged and dumpy as though you had
been hit on the head with a mallet.

Her dressing-gown was lying on a chair. It was the
blue woollen one she had had at school, and very shabby
now. But nobody ever saw you in a dressing-gown, so
it seemed a waste of your allowance to buy another.
Rosamund sat down on the end of the bed and crossed
her legs. The blue dressing-gown parted to show them.
Lawrence had said she had pretty legs. He was always
talking about people's legs, and when a woman passed
him you could see his eyes go down every time. But it
was all right about hers. That was a thing that had
always been all right. Smiling demurely but provoca-
tively wasn't really anything to do with the smile at all.

It was the way you held your head. Holding her head like that Rosamund said another of her charms:

> *'With a host of furious fancies*
> *Of which I am commander,*
> *With a spear of fire and a horse of air*
> *To the wilderness I wander.*
> *By a knight of ghosts and shadows*
> *I challenged am to tourney,*
> *Ten leagues beyond the wide world's end*
> *Methinks it is no journey.'*

III

EVER since his sister had begun to keep house for him, thirty years ago, Henry Spellman's hospitality had been rather peculiar; and now that Miss Spellman was seventy, anything might happen. But this was one of her better evenings, and apart from a large artificial rose fixed exactly on the crown of her head, she seemed normal.

Even so, it was an odd-looking party, oddly arranged. Old Henry was a huge, bald old man, rather like a good-humoured, slightly sleepy sea-lion; while his chief guest, Sir Francis Proudfoot, was a dapper little grey man about five foot three in height, with a large head and a sharp pointed nose. Characteristically, Spellman had put Sir Francis on his right and Lang on his left, leaving Lawrence and his wife to sit on either side of his sister at the other end of the table. There was a marked air that the head of the house had asked two guests to dinner, and that the family should interrupt as little as possible.

Sir Francis said: 'Personally I find it difficult to *see* the French Impressionists apart from the aura created round them by French art dealers and Chicago meat packers.'

'If it comes to that,' said old Henry with a grin, 'I can't see your Italians at all for house dirt and Berensonian scholarship.'

Lang frowned slightly and shifted in his chair. 'What's going to happen in Lancashire?' he said curtly.

'Lancashire?' said Sir Francis politely.

'When Japan gets going?'

'Oh—textiles?' Sir Francis shook his head. 'I don't know a great deal about the textile industry. But . . .'

'Of course, the fascinating thing,' old Henry said in his bass tuba voice, 'is that if you lose a war and all your plant is destroyed you start with a clean sheet. You've *got* to have brand new plant to start at all. But the chap who wins still has all his old stuff.' He chuckled, wobbling slightly all over with the vibration of the chuckle.

'Precisely,' said Sir Francis. 'Though I don't think that applies to Japan.' He shifted rather wearily, like a bored tiger dutifully preparing to jump through an accustomed hoop. 'But take the Ruhr. What's going to happen there . . .?'

As the entrée was removed, Laura Spellman took out a cigarette and lit it and said to Lang's left shoulder: 'How's Rosamund?'

Sir Francis paused for a second almost hopefully.

Lang turned slightly and said: 'Oh—she's very well, thank you, Laura.'

'Why didn't you bring her?'

'Well, it isn't really her sort of party. . . .'

'Between ourselves,' said Laura softly, 'it isn't mine. What does she do when you go out like this? Stay at home by herself?'

'Yes.'

'Rather dull, Walter, when you're eighteen—particularly when you're as beautiful as that.'

Lang smiled back at her smile. Dark red hair, greenish eyes, and looked as though you couldn't cut her with anything softer than a diamond. Lang did not like Laura as Laura, but he liked handsome women. He said: 'Oh, Roz is all right. She rather likes being alone.'

'I must ring her up and get her over to us sometime.'

'That would be nice for her,' said Lang, not very enthusiastically. The combination of Lawrence and Laura was not one that he would have chosen for Rosamund.

'Like Burton and Swinburne,' said Miss Spellman suddenly.

'Who? Dad and Sir Francis?' said Lawrence at once. He was used to his aunt. 'Yes, they are, rather.'

'Henry will have to carry Swinburne downstairs under his arms,' said the old lady firmly.

'Not necessarily,' said Lawrence. 'Burton didn't *always* carry Swinburne downstairs. Or even usually.' He caught his wife's eye across the table. Lang's left shoulder had come round again and he was asking Sir Francis about American capital investment in the Far East.

Laura made a tiny gesture of resignation and squashed out her cigarette.

'I can't remember what the sweet is,' said Miss Spellman in a sudden panic.

'Never mind, dear,' said Lawrence reassuringly. 'Wait and see what they bring.'

*   *   *   *   *

Mr. Gene Kelly's feet performed their facile miracles, to the obvious surprise of Mr. Kelly's face; which was fine in its way, but not what Jack wanted just then. He glanced at Hilda. Her face was a pale shadow in the darkness, but curiously, he could see her eyes clearly enough. They seemed to reflect the light from the screen. Her lips were parted slightly, and she was half smiling as she gazed rapturously at Mr. Kelly. It was a strange feeling to be looking at somebody's face as closely as he was looking at hers, without their knowing they were being looked at.

Jack shifted slightly so as to bring his knee and thigh against hers and pressed gently. There was an immediate and frank answering pressure and the hand in his gave his fingers a little squeeze. But she went on looking at the screen, and suddenly Mr. Kelly did something funny and she laughed out loud, so that for a moment he was slightly startled. Jack gently withdrew his hand, and fumbled for and lit a cigarette. He reclaimed the small, rather rough little hand that had remained lying on his thigh where he had left it. It welcomed his back with another gentle squeeze, but the eyes never turned and the rapt little smile never altered. He felt again that slight irritation that he had felt so often before in these circumstances. It was all right. It was fine. But in half an hour now it would be over, and it would be raining outside, and anyhow Hilda got into trouble if she was home late, so that would be the end of the evening. With a little sigh he turned to the screen. The hard-boiled blonde was handing Mr. Kelly a drink, with a seductive smile. Mr. Kelly said: 'Thank you,' contriving to get into it all the wariness of a man walking the tight-rope. The blonde sat down and crossed her

legs. Mr. Kelly's face showed a faint flicker of alarm.
The audience giggled happily.

It was all right but it wouldn't do. Jack shifted again
in his seat and put his arm round Hilda. She half turned
her head, and for a moment positively looked at him.
But only for a moment. She leant forward slightly, so
that he could get his arm comfortably round her and
then settled back with her head resting lightly against
his shoulder. He shifted his hand up and put it firmly
on her breast—quickly and firmly so that there was no
doubt about it—so that she couldn't fail to notice. Her
eyes came round at that all right, and for a moment she
looked at him in mild, good-tempered, slightly abstracted
inquiry. Then she was back with Mr. Kelly. She slowly
raised her hand and laid it gently over his as it held her
breast. Mr. Kelly was running down the stairs from the
blonde's flat. As he came down to the last flight he leapt
neatly on to the banister, shot down it at high speed,
landed in the hall with a prodigious bound and vanished.
The audience laughed. Hilda laughed with them. Still
laughing, she gently moved his hand down from her
breast to her waist.

*   *   *   *   *

It was easier now that the ladies had withdrawn, and
there was no longer any need to make conversation at
the lower end of the table. Lang said : 'I suppose you
are finding this steel shortage pretty serious too ?'

'My people tell me it's getting tighter,' said Sir Francis.
'And it will be tighter yet. A great *deal* tighter.' He
smiled : 'Of course we have certain affiliations that help
us there. . . .'

'I wish we had,' said Lang rather bitterly. 'Do you
find you can get rod ? That's our chief difficulty.'

'I'm afraid I don't know,' said Sir Francis apologetically. 'You see, nowadays I'm not much concerned with
—with details. Such knowledge that I have is more of
the general economic and financial picture.' He looked
at Spellman. 'I take it that you are purely fabricators,
Henry ?'

'Almost entirely.'

'Oh come!' said Lang indignantly. 'How about . . .'

'Well, say we're almost entirely fabricators with ambitions not to be.'

Lang said: 'We do a lot of fabricating now, and we shall go on doing so just exactly as long as we must to keep the plant fully employed. And not a day longer.'

Sir Francis was looking at the end of his cigar. 'Where have you got surplus capacity?' he asked casually. 'Press work?'

'Mainly. Some in the foundry occasionally. It depends what you mean by "surplus" of course. The place is always full up. But not with the sort of work we want.'

Sir Francis suddenly poked his sharp nose at Lang and said: 'What have you got *against* fabricating work? What's wrong with it?'

'Oh, it's a miserable business,' said Lang contemptuously. 'No length of run. Prices cut to the bone. No product of your own that you can take and build . . .'

Old Henry said: 'There's nothing wrong with fabricating. It's just that there's something wrong with Walter. He's got big ideas.' He chuckled, wobbling.

'It's a good job somebody in that outfit has ideas of any kind, Henry,' said Lang rather bitterly.

'In my group,' said Sir Francis, 'we have several concerns that are purely fabricators. I wasn't aware that anybody particularly *despised* them.'

'I suppose you haven't got any steel rod lying about that you don't want, sir?' said Lawrence with a grin. Lang frowned impatiently.

Sir Francis looked slightly startled. 'I tell you, my dear boy, I don't know anything about steel rod.' He stared again at his cigar ash, his face suddenly and curiously expressionless.

Henry began: 'I heard the other day . . .'

'. . . The man you would have to talk to about that,' Sir Francis said precisely, 'is my Mr. Falk. He is responsible for steel supplies to the group.'

Lang sat up sharply. He was staring at Sir Francis excitedly. There was a moment's dead silence.

Lawrence said: 'But—but *could* I talk to him? I mean is there any chance . . .?'

'I see no reason why you shouldn't have a word with Falk,' said Sir Francis calmly. 'I can't say whether he can help you, but he ought to be able to. I believe our steel position is—fairly satisfactory.'

Lawrence said: 'Well if you don't mind, sir, I should certainly like . . .'

Old Henry chuckled and said: 'Francis, this generosity is unlike you. I thought you never gave anything away but money.'

'It's just that I am getting old and silly,' said Sir Francis with a slight smile. He turned to Lang. 'I should like to come and see your place sometime if I could.'

Lang said: 'We should be delighted. Any time . . .' He hesitated. 'Forgive me—but about this steel. It's a vital matter to us. Can we go and see your Mr. Falk and say you suggested it?'

'I'll drop him a line saying that Lawrence will be coming to see him.'

'I'll go myself if . . .'

'No,' said Sir Francis gently. 'Lawrence can go. After all, *he* had the impudence to ask me, so it's only fair.' He took out his diary and made a note.

Lawrence said: 'And then you tell me I'm not enterprising enough, Walter.'

Lang was smiling like a small boy who has been promised a bicycle. 'Maybe. But I've never said you hadn't got plenty of damned cheek.'

*   *   *   *   *

The bath had been very hot; too hot, so that when Rosamund got out, she felt rather sick. She went back to her bedroom and lay down on the bed for a while with her eyes shut until the sick feeling passed. It would have been easy just to get into bed properly and go to sleep. But the show must go on. With an effort she got to her feet and put on her pyjama trousers and

brassière. She was still rather giddy, and putting on
pyjama trousers was quite tricky. She looked at herself
in the mirror and frowned slightly. The effect was not
really very oriental. The trousers should have been
much more baggy and the brassière should have been
gold and less like a brassière. Moreover, she was not at
all sure that trousers and a bare tummy was the right
sort of oriental for Egypt. She went to the chest of drawers
and sorted out a belt with a big gilt clasp and bound it
round her head. That undoubtedly improved matters.
'Give me my crown,' she said quietly. 'I have immortal
longings in me . . .' She gazed for a moment at her
reflection and it looked back at her with big, grave eyes.
Rosamund frowned crossly and said: Im*mortal* longings,
you little fool. Im*mortal* longings . . .'

The lighting was always a problem. There were only
two lights in the room—the centre one and the reading
one over the bed. Together they made the room bright
and brisk and cheerful, and very nice for a drawing-room
comedy. Separately, they left it coldly dim or warmly
dim, neither of which was right. Going to the chest of
drawers again, Rosamund found a dark red blouse, and
standing on tiptoe, draped it over the centre light. The
effect was rather good. It left a pool of bright light in
the middle, almost like a spotlight. 'Haste, haste, good
Charmian, the bright day is done, And we are for the
dark . . .' On that Cleopatra could move slowly into
the shadows. And then the death scene could be played
on the bed with the reading light tilted away slightly. . . .

Rosamund went slowly over to the door and stood for
a moment with her back to the room and her face in her
hands. Antony—Antony. She had loved him. But she
had betrayed him. She had been afraid and run away.
And now there was nothing but shame and loss, and the
feeling of waste, and the necessity of death. But she was
not afraid of death now. She was one with death, and
could take the asp and clasp it to her.

> '*Oh eastern star . . .*'
> '*Peace—peace*
> *Do you not see my baby at my breast . . .?*'

Rosamund turned, drew herself up to her full height, and walked slowly into the central pool of light. The queen gazed back at her with grief and courage.

* * * * *

When the bus did come it was nearly full, and only two more from the queue were let on. Jack said: 'Oh, come on—let's walk. It's not all that much.'

'All right,' said Hilda rather doubtfully. The rain was pattering on the roof of the shelter. She put the hood of the plastic mackintosh over her hair and took his arm.

It was difficult to walk fast arm in arm, and after a few moments they let go by mutual consent.

Hilda said: 'I like her—what's her name—Leslie Caron. But she's not really *pretty*.'

Jack said: 'She'll do as she is for me.'

'She's got a lovely figure.' Hilda slowed down slightly. 'I'm sorry—I can't go quite as fast . . .'

'Your knee hurting?'

'Only a bit. It isn't anything.'

'I wish there was somewhere we could get a cup of coffee,' said Jack moodily. 'You'd think it was worth while for somebody to stay open, wouldn't you? Not much more than half-past ten and it's like the grave.'

'Well I couldn't, anyway. You know what dad is.'

They hurried on for a moment in silence. Jack said: 'We don't always have to go to something—the pictures and so on. One time we ought just to spend an evening by ourselves, so that we don't have to rush all the time.'

'Yes. That'd be nice,' said Hilda rather vaguely.

The rain was getting heavier, and when they got to her door there wasn't anything to be done except to say good night and go. Just as he had known it would be. He hugged the wet mackintosh to him and kissed the cold, damp little face. The soft lips pressed hard against his with good will but without knowledge. He turned away before the door was fully closed, and heard its soft thud behind him as he set off for home.

His father was sitting at the table with pen poised over the football coupon. The fire was nearly out.

His father looked up and said: 'Hallo, son,' in his gentle way.

He said: 'Hallo. Mum gone to bed?'

'Yes. There's some cocoa there if you want some.'

Jack said: 'I don't want any.'

'Raining out?' said Mr. Partridge.

'Ah. Pouring.'

Jack walked across and looked over his father's shoulder. 'You don't have to write all that out. You just put perm four. Like I showed you.'

His father said: 'Ah,' and went on writing with the scratchy pen.

'Villa to draw with Arsenal is just silly,' said Jack. 'They don't stand a chance. Not away.'

He took out a stub of cigarette, lit it, and sitting down, gazed moodily into the fire.

Mr. Partridge carefully signed his coupon. 'How was your Council meeting?'

Jack said: 'Well, if you ask me it's a lot of nonsense and bluff.'

'You don't want to talk too much at it,' said Mr. Partridge gently. 'Not when you've just been put on it.'

Jack did not reply but smiled bitterly at the fire. Of course it had gone straight back to Dad, what he'd said to Lang.

He threw the cigarette end into the hearth rather viciously and got up. 'I'm going to bed,' he said. ''Night.'

*   *   *   *   *

Slowly Rosamund took the belt off her head, put it back in the drawer, and started to unbutton the brassière. But her chest was still heaving with little sobs, and it was difficult to undo the button when one was wobbling about like that. She stood and fumbled for some time before she got it off and dropped it on the chair. She put on the pyjama coat and sat on the bed gazing straight in front of her. Her nose was running. She put out a hand blindly and found her handkerchief and blew her nose.

'*Oh Eastern star . . .*'

B 2

Rosamund got up and went slowly across to the
dressing-table. She picked up the green leather handbag
and dug about in it listlessly. The packet of Cadbury's
Peppermint Filled Block was half eaten, but there were
still some sections left. She broke one off and ate it
slowly. The sobs had stopped now. She hesitated, and
then broke off another section and put it into her mouth,
blew her nose again, and then slowly climbed into bed.

Lang put the car away and hurried through the
drawing-room into the house. The light was on in the
hall but everything was very quiet. He took off his coat
and went into the drawing-room. The Darts were obviously back because the electric fire was on and the whisky
and soda was on the table. He poured himself out a very
small whisky and filled the glass right up with soda, and
sat down by the electric fire. This was where you missed
it—coming back when something good had happened
and you wanted to tell somebody about it. It had been
fine when he left the Spellmans; and then all the way
home in the car it had drained out of him because there
was nobody to share it with. Jean had never even pretended she knew about it. She would have smiled at him
and said : 'That's lovely, darling. Now you'll be able to
play with your sprayer.' Rather mockingly. And he
would have said : 'Yes, but you see if we *can* get the steel
from Proudfoot it alters the whole situation. . . .' And
the fact that she didn't know about steel and didn't care
wouldn't have mattered, because she cared about him
and had only ever cared about him and nothing else.
Not even herself.
  The pain was almost physical and he got up, leaving
the whisky untouched and put the fire and the light out
and went upstairs. There was a light under Rosamund's
door, and for a moment he half-hoped she would be
awake and could help. He opened the door of her room
very gently and went in. She was asleep but her arms
were outside the bed clothes and both the lights were on,
as though she had just fallen asleep without meaning to.
Very gently, Lang pulled the clothes up round her
shoulders. She was lying in a queer, rather uncomfort-

able-looking position, half on her back and half on her side. Her lips were slightly parted and her lashes were very long and black. As he looked he suddenly realised that her eyelids were slightly swollen and that there were faint marks on her cheeks, and there came to him as a cold shock the realisation that she had been crying. Laura's green eyes looking at him in that cool, thoughtfully appraising way, 'What does she do, Walter, when you go out like this . . .?' Lang hesitated and passed a hand over his eyes. For a moment he wondered confusedly whether to wake her up—to make her tell him why she had been crying—to hold her closely and tell her it should be all right. . . .

He switched out the bedside light and turned slowly and wearily towards the door. There was something odd about the lighting of the room, and looking up, he saw that something was draped over the centre light. He took down the red blouse, looked at it with vague surprise and then dropped it with her other clothes on the chair and went out, switching out the light and closing the door very softly behind him.

IV

ROSAMUND poured Lang out his second cup of coffee, took a deep breath and said : 'Daddy . . .'

There was a long pause. Then Lang lowered his paper and said : 'What, darling?'

'I've looked at my frock, and it won't do for the Works Party. I'm sorry, but it just won't. After all, I've had it since I was sixteen.'

'Grown out of it?'

'Lord, no. Grown into it. I'm miles smaller now. Don't you remember—I was like a balloon then. Anyhow it's too—too maidenly. It was all right as a first frock but . . .'

Lang said : 'You don't want to dress up too much for this thing.'

'I know. But this won't do. Honestly.'

'All right, darling.' Lang smiled at her. 'Any of your allowance left?'

'Eight pounds,' said Rosamund carefully.

'Eight pounds?' said Lang, surprised and gratified. 'You'll be quite all right then.' He picked up the paper again.

Rosamund hesitated. 'I don't know whether I can get anything for that,' she said desperately. 'But I suppose I can try.'

'That's right,' said Lang helpfully. 'Have a look round.' He glanced at his watch. 'I must be off, pet. What are you going to do to-day?'

'Go and look for this frock, I suppose,' said Rosamund rather sulkily.

He nodded. 'Well, don't go and get anything too grand. Remember most of the girls in the factory haven't got much to spend.'

'Then I won't go to Paquin,' said Rosamund. 'I was going to, but now I won't.'

He didn't even seem to hear, and if he had it wouldn't have meant anything to him.

It was nine-fifteen, but Lawrence's secretary said he hadn't arrived yet. Lang told her curtly to ring back when Lawrence came in, and sent for George Martin. Lang beamed at him and said: 'Well George, I've got your steel. Now how about it?'

'Where from?'

'Richmond Glenn. I saw Sir Francis Proudfoot at Henry Spellman's last night, and they're going to help us out.'

'How much with?'

'I don't know exactly. But it can't mean anything to them. They've got huge stocks.' Lang smiled happily. 'Now then, suppose I can give you all the steel you want. *Then* what's your delivery time?'

'Well, of course, it'll still be seven or eight months for the rest of this year. After that . . .'

'What d'you mean, George?' said Lang sharply. 'Everybody's told me it's only steel that's holding us up.'

'Well yes, Mr. Walter. But we've had to fill the place up with other work and it'll take several months to get clear of it.'

Lang slapped his hand on his blotter. 'Listen, George —I want that delivery time down to two months and I want it quick. And I don't care what you throw out to get it. See?'

Martin said: 'Oh yes. I see. But . . .' he shook his head dubiously.

Lang's telephone rang. Lawrence's voice said: 'Morning, Walter. Want me?'

Lang said: 'Yes. When are you going to see Richmond Glenn about the steel?'

'I thought probably the middle of next week.'

'Next *week*? Why not to-morrow?'

Lawrence said gently: 'Because if you remember, old Proudfoot's got to write to this chap, which he easily may not do for a couple of days. And after that I've got to ring and get an appointment.'

'Well look, Lawrence, I want that stuff delivered just as soon as may be. So for goodness' sake don't go to sleep on it.'

Lawrence said : 'Walter—let's get this clear. We've no promise of anything. Proudfoot's only agreed that I should go and see his man. . . .'

'Oh bunkum,' said Lang curtly. 'He wouldn't have said that if he didn't know you could have the stuff. Anyhow, you go right ahead on that assumption. And the sooner the better.' He put down the telephone.

Martin said : 'By the way, Mr. Walter—didn't you ought to have Barker in on this?'

'Why?'

'Well, by the time most of it happens I shall have gone. It's only a few months now.'

Lang sat and looked at him for a moment in silence. He said : 'I always forget that.'

Martin smiled shyly : 'I do myself. But there it is. I'm sixty-five the twenty-eighth of April, see. I've been thinking several times lately that really it's Barker you ought to be talking to about these things.'

'Hell !' said Lang. 'I don't want to think about it, George. It won't be the same without you.'

'No,' said Martin gently. 'It'll be a sight better. Barker's a good man. Very able, level chap . . .'

'Yes. . . .' Lang was staring at him with that sudden brilliant smile. 'You won't know what to do with yourself, George,' he said with real affection.

'Oh yes I shall, Mr. Walter,' said Martin. 'I shall have a rest. I've earned it.'

'Well, I shan't know what to do without you.'

'You'll be all right with Barker, Mr. Walter. Long as you don't fluster him. He's a bit nervous, but as long as you give him a chance . . .'

'You mean as long as I don't jump down his throat?'

'That's right.' Martin smiled. 'See, it's different with me. I'm used to it.' After a moment's silence he added : 'Don't you think you ought to have him in?'

Lang hesitated. 'I suppose so,' he said heavily. He pressed the bell. 'Get Mr. Barker, will you, Maud?'

When the secretary had gone they sat in silence for a while, not looking at each other. Then Lang got up and went and stood looking out of the window with his back to the room.   An epoch came to an end in silence.

*   *   *   *   *

Beale's had quite a lot of evening frocks for eight pounds or less.   There was even one for five, but that was a peculiar shade of bluish pink, appeared to be intended to fit somebody with a forty-inch bust and thirty-two-inch hips, and had lipstick marks on it in three different shades. Most of the rest were just dull, and the only two occasions when they had any interest, they turned out to be about fifteen pounds instead of eight.   After a time they seemed to grow progressively worse, and Rosamund went back to the beginning and started to go through them again rather dispiritedly.   There was one that fitted rather well but was covered with large pink flowers, and there was one that was a pretty shade of greyish blue, but was undoubtedly too big.   Both were extremely modest in cut. The saleswoman came back and said : 'Then there's this. It's reduced from fifteen.   I'm not sure whether it'll fit you, but being jersey . . .'   The frock was bright yellow and left her shoulders bare.   The silk jersey material clung close from her breasts to her knees.   Behind, from the tight waist, were two flying panels, which was just as well. Whatever else it was, it was not dull.

Rosamund looked at herself and said : 'That's certainly more fun.   I'm not sure whether it's a possible garment but . . .'

The saleswoman said : 'It's lovely on you.   Of course it's a different class of thing . . .'

Rosamund turned sideways, picked up one of the flying panels and lowered it again quickly.   She said : 'It *is* a bit tight . . .'

'Ah well, you see, madam, it's supposed to be snug fitting.   Being jersey . . .'

When she was outside the shop Rosamund was seized with a sudden panic and started to go back and change it for the bluish-grey.   But the bluish-grey *was* too big, and there wouldn't be time to get it altered, so she went on and went to Fuller's and drank coffee and ate a cream slice, and only just had enough money to pay for it, because the yellow frock had been nine pounds and she had had to use her pocket money as well as the eight pounds left in her clothes' allowance.

Going home in the bus she could not remember whether it was the gold sort of yellow or the greenish sort of yellow, and had to open the box and tear a little hole in the tissue paper to see. Looked at like that, it was the greenish sort of yellow and rather alarmingly bright. Rosamund replaced the lid rather soberly and decided firmly that it was enormous fun in a queer sort of way.

*   *   *   *   *

Lawrence said: 'We don't need to go for half an hour yet. Have a drink, darling. You'll need it.'

'I don't think I will,' said Laura. 'And I don't think you'd better—in view of what happened the last time we went to this party.'

'Is it kind to bring that up?'

'Well, if you do it again I shall just come home and leave you. I don't care how you behave, but I will *not* be sympathised with about it by Amy Talbot-Rees.'

Lawrence grinned and said: 'I was only being democratic and all boys together. That's what a Works Party is for.' He looked at her reflectively. 'You are a handsome piece, aren't you? It's a pity you haven't got a nice nature too.'

'Well, I don't *feel* handsome. I feel about fifty and very cross, and I wish we hadn't got to go to this bloody thing.'

'Never mind, darling. We needn't stay long. Can I kiss you or will it spoil your face?'

'What for?' said Laura sulkily. 'You don't have to.'

Lawrence got up quickly and taking her in his arms, kissed her hard. He said rather breathlessly: 'Now I *have* spoilt your face. I've put your lipstick all over your cheek.'

Laura turned to the mirror and began to repair the damage in silence.

'Personally,' said Lawrence, 'I always rather enjoy this show. As a party it may not be very bright, but as

a social phenomenon . . . Anyhow, Gustavus is always
worth the money.'

'Is Walter bringing Rosamund?'

'I suppose so. Why not?'

Laura said : 'Somebody ought to do something about
that child. I think perhaps I will have a drink after all.'

*   *   *   *   *

The frock certainly was uncommonly yellow and not
at all maidenly. The top was all right, what there was
of it and she had nice shoulders anyhow. But from the
waist down it was perhaps a bit much. Rosamund looked
at her reflection rather uneasily and flipped at the merciful
flying panels. The trouble was that when you walked
they tended to drift away slightly, and then it was undoubtedly a bit much. She realised that she didn't want
to go out and join Lang without something over it—and
anyhow, what on earth could you wear over it? Her
blue coat would be impossible.

She went to the door and called : 'Daddy?'

'What?' said Lang from his bedroom.

'Do you think I might use Mummy's fur cape?
haven't got anything to go over this frock.'

There was a long pause.

'I should think so,' said Lang slowly. 'Why not?'

'Sure you don't mind?' she said uselessly.

'No. That's all right.'

Most of her mother's clothes had gone. They had
gone within a few days of her death. Rosamund had
often wondered what Lang had done with them. But
the long dark ermine cape with the Bradley label was
still hanging in the wardrobe. For a moment she hesitated, but it was that or the blue coat, and the blue coat
wasn't possible. Rosamund took the cape down, slipped
it over her bare shoulders and looked at her reflection
with a sigh of relief. Now that really *was* something. The
only curious thing was that instead of making her look
older, it seemed to make her look younger.

Lang was standing in the hall when she came down.
A dinner jacket always suited him, and his tie looked
more stable than usual.

Rosamund said again: 'I say, it *is* all right for me to wear this, is it?'

'Oh yes. Of course.' Lang put out a hand and touched the fur. 'It's a nice coat,' he said, smiling faintly.

'It's gorgeous. Do I look all right?' She parted the cape a little so as to show the yellow dress, and looked at him rather anxiously. But he only went on smiling a little and said: 'You look very nice.'

'Not too . . .? You see it hasn't got any top at all.'

'Ought it to have?'

'Oh no. But I thought you might say it was too dashing.'

He was still looking at the cape. He said: 'I gave that to her in 1939. You wouldn't think it was as old as that. But of course it hasn't really had much wear.' He turned away. 'Come on then, darling. We ought to be going.'

*   *   *   *   *

The Works Party always took place at the Palace Hotel—mainly because it was the only place in the district with enough room. Even at the Palace it meant taking over practically the whole of the ground floor. There were no rules about dress. Gustavus always wore a lounge suit; Talbot-Rees was in tails with a carnation in his buttonhole. Apart from that, gentlemen who had dinner jackets wore them and gentlemen who hadn't didn't. Gustavus had once asked the Works Council to consider whether, in the interests of true democracy, it would not be better if all forms of evening clothes were prohibited. The suggestion met with strong opposition from the workers' representatives, and was withdrawn. On the other hand, such few ladies as had any choice in the matter were carefully restrained. Laura, for example, wore a black dinner dress from Balmain that could hardly have been simpler, thereby simultaneously making a sisterly gesture towards the factory girls and aiming a shrewd blow at the Honourable Amy Talbot-Rees.

The Honourable Amy herself, being no respecter of persons unless they were very rich or had titles, went the whole way and displayed a great deal of sallow skin and a lot of diamonds above, and a great deal of wine-coloured velvet below. It was the arrival of the Talbot-Reeses at one Works Party that had caused Gustavus to murmur to Lang: 'Well, I always say the business ought to be able to afford *one* gentleman.'

The guests were received in the entrance hall by Gustavus, supported by the Works Council. Gustavus stood and beamed at the arriving swarm and repeated: 'Hallo. Hallo there. Good evening. Nice to see you,' and the Works Council stood in a group just behind him. Jack Partridge had wanted a dinner jacket ever since he was eighteen, and when he was elected to the Works Council he had gone and cashed some of his Savings Certificates and bought one. This was the first time he had worn it in public, and he stood there shifting from one foot to the other and grinning sheepishly at acquaintances. His tie was much straighter than Lang's and his wavy dark hair was shining with brilliantine. Some vulgar female person let out a low wolf-whistle as she passed him, and there was a burst of giggles. Jack went bright crimson and continued to grin.

'What was that?' said Gustavus, turning.

'Somebody admiring Jack's suit,' said Martin.

'So they ought,' said Gustavus, putting on his pince-nez and looking carefully at Jack with the fourteen-year-old's grin. 'It's a very nice suit. I wish I'd got one like it.'

Amy Talbot-Rees came over to the Spellmans and said: 'Hallo Lawrence. Hallo Laura. You're looking very beautiful.'

'My dear, you make me feel positively dowdy in that dress. What is it?'

'This? As a matter of fact it came from Genoa, of all places.' The Honourable Amy looked round at the arriving throng without pleasure. 'I trust and hope,' she said in her loud, high voice, 'that this year there's a special loo for the Directors' wives. I told Jim to try to arrange it, but I don't know if he has.'

'Would that be in the proper democratic spirit of the party?' said Lawrence.

'I don't know, Lawrence, and I don't care. It's not a

thing I feel democratic about. Last year all that side of it
was a shambles. Have you seen George Martin's collar?'

'No.'

'My dear, the poor old man cut himself or something
and there's a large smear of blood on it.' She looked at
a passing crowd and frowned. 'Where do these working
boys get the money to buy dinner jackets? It's funny
how they never look like gentlemen whatever they wear,
isn't it? Something about their mouths. Well, good-bye
for the present. I shall go and see about my loo.' She
went away with her ungainly rolling walk, the dark red
velvet clutched in one yellow hand.

Laura said: 'I hope she gets her lavatory. All to
herself. In the public interest.'

Lang had had to arrive early to support Gustavus at
the reception. Rosamund had been hanging about for
half an hour, but so far it had not been essential to leave
the dressing-room, or even to take the cloak off. But the
moment was coming now. She stood in front of one of
the mirrors in the large, clean, green-tiled ladies' room
and pretended to be making some minute adjustment to
her hair. Her hands were trembling quite ridiculously.
The place was a milling crowd of women of all ages and
shapes and sizes, and already it was very hot, and the
air had a curious sweet, rather sickly smell. She could
see the curious glances being cast at her, and the admiring
ones at the ermine cloak, but so far she had not seen any
of the half-dozen people in the Works whom she knew
by sight. A little of the yellow frock showed through the
open front of the cloak. It looked more yellow than ever,
and she suddenly realised that standing like that, with one
thigh slightly in advance of the other, one could positively
see a lump where her suspender came. But people were
queueing up to use the mirrors, and sooner or later one
had to make the plunge. Rosamund drew a long rather
jerky sigh, walked over to the counter and slipped the
cloak from her shoulders.

Traditionally, the Works Party had no formal design.
It began at eight and the keen dancers usually carried it

on till two. But a sit-down meal was out of the question, and apart from half an hour from the entertainer, there was no fixed programme. There were two huge buffets, one at the end of the ballroom and one in the big reception room. The band played. People danced or ate or drank. Old stagers went into the smoking-room and played whist; and a very large number sat or stood round the ballroom just watching. At some point in the evening silence would be called, and Gustavus would explain that this was an informal occasion and that there would be no speeches, and then would make one. That was all.

Laura suddenly said: 'Good God. . . .!' and laid a startled hand on Lawrence's arm. Rosamund had just entered the ballroom and was edging round the wall. She wore an agonised smile, as her eyes searched desperately for Lang. The flying panels were floating treacherously. The Honourable Amy Talbot-Rees had seen her and was advancing on the left flank.

Laura said: 'No—that I *will* not have,' and went quickly across with Lawrence following.

Laura said: 'Why, hallo Rosamund. I was wondering where you were.'

Rosamund turned and said: 'Oh, hallo—hallo Lawrence,' with relief.

'You're looking very beautiful and very dashing to-night.'

Rosamund looked down at herself doubtfully and said: 'D'you think it's all right? I was afraid it was a bit much. It didn't look quite so—quite so much in the shop.' She gave a hysterical giggle.

Lawrence said solemnly: 'No no, Roz. Whatever else you could say about it, it *isn't* too much. Anyhow, you look very pretty.'

The Honourable Amy joined them and said: 'Good evening, Rosamund.' She looked the yellow frock over slowly and carefully and glanced at Laura with a little smile. 'I'm glad somebody else has come with bare shoulders. I was beginning to feel rather out of place.' She returned to the careful scrutiny. 'What fascinating stuff. Where did you get it?'

'At Beale's.'

'Oh—I see. At Beale's?'

Laura said: 'That's a very good dress department, isn't it?'

'Is it?' said the Honourable Amy with careful interest. 'Do you go there?'

'Constantly,' said Laura, her mouth like a rabbit trap. She had bought a head scarf there, one rainy day in 1941.

The reception was over. Gustavus was pottering round the room with a beaming smile, stopping every few yards for a word with this group and that. The grey lounge suit seemed too big for him and his knees gave a little as he walked, but he looked very happy. He came up and said: 'Why isn't anybody dancing? Never saw such a lazy lot. Come on Rosamund, my dear. Let's show them the way. Come on Lawrence—come on Laura.' He put his arm round Rosamund and clutched her right hand with his fingers carefully entwined in hers. The band was playing a waltz. Vigorously, though a little precariously at the knees, he whirled her out into the vast, empty, shining spaces of the ballroom floor. The flying panels flew.

Amy Talbot-Rees closed her eyes and said: 'My dear . . .!'

Laura turned to Lawrence and said: 'I'd like to dance, please.'

As they circled the floor she said through clenched teeth: 'I'd like to murder that bloody fool Walter.'

'Of course,' Lang was saying, 'we've got to remember that part of the demand comes because other people are short of materials too.'

George Martin nodded. 'That's what I've always said to Talbot-Rees. "You're not in competition. Not real competition. And you won't be until the steel shortage is over. Then you'll have to watch out".'

'Though mind you, George, I can't see when it's likely to be over.'

Martin shook his head. 'Not in my day, Mr. Walter. And maybe not even in yours.'

'Come on, Walter,' called Gustavus as he passed, still

vigorously waltzing Rosamund. 'None of that now.
Dance!'

Lang raised a hand and smiled. Martin said: 'Is
that your daughter? My word, how she's grown up in
the last year.'

Lang said: 'Yes. She's a big girl. Well—I suppose
I ought to go and circulate. See you later, George.'

As soon as he had gone Mrs. Martin came up and
hissed: 'George!' He looked at the horrified face in
surprise. 'What, my dear?'

'You've got blood on your collar.'

'Have I?'

'Yes. A big smudge. I never noticed. You must go
and . . .' She hesitated. Her eyes were big and worried
behind her glasses, and she dabbed in a frightened way
at her white hair.

'Doesn't matter,' said Martin calmly.

'But you can't go about like that, and I don't know
what'll get it off. . . . I tell you what, I'll go and borrow
some powder off one of the girls and put that over it.'
She hurried away. Old Henry Spellman waddled up.
The front of his low-cut black waistcoat seemed a good
two feet in front of the rest of him. He said: 'Hallo,
George. You're not a dancer either?'

Jack stood at the buffet with a group from the press
shop. Everybody was drinking Pale Ales. Fred Boxall
nudged his arm and said with a grin: 'Hey—Jack—Mac
says if she had a pimple on her behind you could see it.'

Somebody muttered in a high voice, 'Oh Gustavus—
you dirty old man,' and there was a general titter.

Jack's eyes never left the figure in the yellow frock.
He was grinning broadly. 'Quite something,' he said.

'Sister, has anybody ever told you you're priddy?'

Mac said: 'She's only a kid, too. No more than
eighteen.'

'That's old enough for me, brother. Just right and
done to a turn.'

Talbot-Rees came up. He was smoking a cigar in a
tortoiseshell holder with a golden band. He said:
'Hallo chaps. Make room at the bar for a thirsty one.'

They grinned at him sheepishly and moved aside. Talbot-Rees said: 'Scotch and splash, please.' He took out a slim gold cigarette case and gave cigarettes to Jack and Fred Boxall, but not to Mac.

'Well, you can say what you like,' he said with a wink, 'but we've got some damned pretty girls in this outfit. Who's that fair one in the pink dress?'

There was a moment's pause. Mac kicked Jack sharply on the ankle. Somebody tittered. Fred Boxall said: 'That's Hilda Pinner.'

'And very nice too,' said Talbot-Rees.

'That's what Jack reckons,' said a voice from the rear.

'Oh,' said Talbot-Rees. 'Like that is it? Sorry, Jack. Don't let me intrude.'

Everybody laughed without great certainty as to who was laughing at whom. Talbot-Rees said: 'Well, I shall now go and do my duty by dancing with Mrs. Spellman.' He waved a hand and moved off. Their eyes followed him with derision. Mac said: 'Hallo chaps. Have a cigah?'

The band struck up a rumba. Jack finished his Pale Ale, put the glass on the table, walked over to Hilda and held out a hand. She got up and smiled at him. The fair hair was close to his face and it smelt rather pleasantly of lavender. Jack said: 'I just been told you're pretty.'

'Me? Who by?'

'Lord Duke Talbot-Rees.'

Hilda giggled slightly.

Jack said: 'You are, too.' Her hand tightened on his shoulder but she didn't say anything. Hilda never talked when she was dancing. Behind her, Rosamund was just getting up with Lawrence. Rosamund was saying: 'I'm not absolutely sure I can do this. I can do either the rumba or the samba but I can never remember which.'

Lawrence said: 'Darling, I can't do either of them.'

Jack's eyes followed them as the yellow frock jerked rhythmically away. She was a hot-looking little bit all right.

The entertainer was a dissipated-looking man with a long, pointed red nose and spectacles. He came up to the group at the bar and said: 'Forgive my ignorance, but who the hell *are* all these people? Put me in the picture. Who's the little old gent? Is he Mr. Lang?'

Mac said: 'That's right. Mr. Gustavus.'

'Is he called Gus or Gussie behind his back?'

They grinned and said: 'Gus.'

'Gus,' said the entertainer, making a note of it. 'And what is there about him?'

Fred said: 'He's the boss.'

'Well, is he?' said Mac.

'Well, the chairman then.'

The entertainer said: 'Yes, but what is there about him? Does he play the banjo or fish or . . .?'

Somebody said: 'He keeps pigs.'

'Ah,' said the entertainer. 'Pigs.' He made a note of it. 'And the fat old boy over there? Who's he?'

'Henry Spellman. He's a director.'

'Does *he* keep pigs?'

'No. He buys pictures. Got a lot of pictures.'

'Pictures,' said the entertainer thoughtfully. 'Ah well . . . There's a little chap with a wooden leg. Can't see him now . . .'

'Billy Peace,' said Fred and Mac in chorus. 'He's on the lift.' They grinned at one another.

Somebody said: 'Ole *Billy* . . .!'

'Well?' said the entertainer.

Harry said: 'He's got the dirtiest mind you ever heard. *Stories* . . .!'

'Fine,' said the entertainer. 'Now some girls.'

After about a quarter of an hour the entertainer said: 'Well, thank you, gentlemen. I think that does it. Have a drink. Don't hesitate. Just mention my name and they'll throw you out before you know where you are.' He picked up a pint of beer that belonged to somebody else, wandered away into a corner and sat down with his notebook on his knee. He studied it for a minute and then closed his eyes, took his head in his hands and sat quite still for a long time, his lips moving silently. At the other bar, Gustavus, amid cheers, had just ordered his annual half pint of beer. He always had half a pint at some point in the evening, and it always upset his digestion for days.   But it was an essential feature of the Party.

It ought not to have been difficult to meet anybody you wanted to meet, because practically every other dance was a Paul Jones, but after four of them Jack had never been nearer than two away from the yellow frock, though Mac had danced with her.   On the last occasion, despite his best efforts, Jack had found himself unmistakably and unavoidably opposite Amy Talbot-Rees.   He had forced himself to smile at her, but she had not even looked at him.   She had edged firmly to the left and paired herself with Lawrence Spellman, leaving him with Mrs. Sayer, one of the assembly forewoman.   The wave of furious anger had left him trembling.   Not that he wanted to dance with the bitch.   But who the hell did she think she was?

At nine-thirty the band played a loud chord and the entertainer climbed the bandstand.   He wore a very small straw hat attached to his head by elastic under the chin.   He looked sadder than ever, and immediately began to sing at great speed a song about a disastrous visit to the seaside.   He made some effort to get the audience to sing the chorus, but without much help from anybody but Gustavus.   As the song ended the entertainer turned to Gustavus and said: 'Thank you, sir,' and then to the audience confidentially: 'I can always depend on Gus.' There was a roar of delighted laughter. '*Oh* yes,' said the entertainer. '*Oh* yes. I can always depend on Gus. Of course me and Gus is like *that*. Went down there the other day. Maid said: "He's out looking at the pigs." I said: "I'll go out and find him." "All right," she said. "You'll know him. He's the one with the hat on." Now a few days after that I was in a picture gallery and who should come in but Mr. Spellman. You know—Mr. Spellman, senior, the little one. So I said: "Why hallo, Henry . . ."'

Lawrence said: 'It never fails, this. People always love it.'

Laura said: 'Can we go after Gustavus's speech?'

'Soon after, I should think.' Lawrence finished his

drink and took another. 'You know, Rosamund really makes me feel my age. There she is—pretty girl—friendly —laughs at my jokes and I begin to think : "Spellman— you're doing well." And then I suddenly realise that she thinks of me as a sort of uncle.' He shook his head. 'Very sad and discouraging.'

Laura gazed across the room without reply.

Lawrence said : 'Come on, sweet. Cheer up. Have another drink.'

'I've had enough. And so have you.'

'Ah,' said Lawrence solemnly. 'Now *that's* where you're wrong. That's where I join issue with you, darling. . . .'

'Cut it out and listen to Gus.'

The applause for the entertainer's final encore died down and picked up again as Gustavus mounted the bandstand. To some this was the end of the evening, to others its beginning; for after Gustavus had made his speech he would go, and a little while after, at decent intervals, the other directors and their wives would go ; and then the duties and courtesies were over and a man could just dance with his girl, or even somebody else's, without being stared at by Mrs. Talbot-Rees.

There was no doubt that Gustavus's grey suit was too big for him nowadays, and he looked very small and old. But his face was glowing and his eyes sparkled behind his spectacles as he looked round with the small-boy's smile.

'Ladies and gentlemen—you all know what I'm going to say. This is not a formal occasion and . . .' A chorus of voices added '. . . there will be *no* speeches.' Gustavus smiled more widely. 'That's right,' he said. 'No speeches. And what's more—*no talking shop.*' He turned to Lang. 'Hear that, Walter ?' Lang grinned back amid general laughter.

'This is an evening,' said Gustavus, 'when we put off the cares of business and come here to relax and enjoy ourselves, and to meet one another on an equal footing as good friends and good companions.'

'Hear, hear !' said Talbot-Rees, flicking the ash off his cigar and smiling round him with goodwill to all.

'So I shan't make a speech,' said Gustavus. 'All I want to do is to welcome you all most heartily on my own

behalf, on behalf of the Board and on behalf of the Works
Council, to whom we are indebted for the excellent
arrangements they have made.'

'Hear, hear!' said several voices.

'I can remember these parties now for thirty years,
and one thing about them never fails to impress me—that
we at Lang's have really got something that is rare in
business—a sense of pulling together—of being a team
with a single objective towards which we are all working,
in whatever capacity.'

The small-boy smile had disappeared now and had
been replaced by the curious half-puzzled, serious look
that they all knew so well. It was as though he was
pleading with them to agree—to see themselves as he had
seen them over many years—as he had seen them first
as a young man, and had gone on doggedly seeing them
ever since; despite opposition, despite laughter, despite
disappointment, despite failure.

He said: 'A group of people working together—not
just to make money for the shareholders—not just to get
a living—but for something higher and finer. To fulfil
in our little, insignificant way, our duty towards God and
towards our neighbour.'

Everything was silent now. Lang was staring down
at the floor. Jack Partridge shifted uneasily from one
foot to the other. He caught Fred Boxall's eye and gave
him a quick wink. Amy Talbot-Rees gave a slight cough.

'Much has happened in industry since I came to
Lang's nearly fifty years ago. The whole position of the
worker is different—and I thank Heaven for it. Many
of the things that we started then—and were laughed at
for starting—are now the law of the land. Decent working conditions—a fair wage for a fair day's work—shorter
hours—proper pensions—consultation between management and workers—profit sharing . . . All these things
are commonplace to-day. But there's one thing that I'd
like you always to remember. . . .' Gustavus began to
bounce slightly from the knees. 'There is no law that
can replace goodwill. There is no law that can replace
a sense of personal responsibility towards our fellow men.
There is no law that can be a substitute for love. That

is what I think we have always realised at Lang's, and what I hope we shall always realise.' He paused.

'Hear, hear!' said Henry Spellman quickly.

Gustavus smiled. 'Now I'm going home,' he said. 'I'm an old man and it's time I was in bed. Now you young people can get on and dance as long as you like and nobody will interrupt you. Enjoy yourselves. Good night and God bless you all and thank you for coming.' He nodded and turned. George Martin put out a quick hand and helped him down the steps of the stand. The handsome black-haired band-leader was smiling a very white-toothed smile and clapping vigorously.

Through the applause Lawrence said: 'I don't think I've ever heard anybody who can put nineteenth-century paternalism more beautifully in a nutshell. And he believes every word of it.'

Laura said: 'It's not a bad thing to believe.'

'Oddly enough, there are people who'd disagree with you, darling. I am now going to dance with that little girl in pink.'

Laura looked at her watch. 'Look, Lawrence, I'm going to give it half an hour and then I'm going. See?'

'All right, sweetheart. I'll be ready by then.'

'And I shall take the car.'

'All right, all *right*. *Take* the car. But stop nattering.'

Laura watched him with an experienced eye as he walked away. It was about an even chance whether there was going to be a debacle like last year. Amy Talbot-Rees came up and said: 'I always like to see Lawrence at this Party. He does enjoy it so, doesn't he?'

Laura said: 'Yes. He likes dancing.'

The Honourable Amy reached for a lemonade. 'I find Gustavus very trying,' she said. 'Very trying. I never know where to look when he talks about God.'

Lang and Henry Spellman called 'good night.' Gustavus waved from the back of the pre-war Austin as it drove away. As they turned back into the hotel Spellman said: 'The old man's looking a bit tired now, but I think he's enjoyed himself. How very good he is at this sort of thing.'

Lang said: 'Oh yes. Get Gustavus on the higher purpose and he's happy.' He shrugged. 'Ah well, he enjoys it, and I suppose it's harmless enough.'

'Rather more than that, Walter, I fancy.'

'Is it?' said Lang indifferently. 'I don't know. It's not much in my line. But you may be right. I can never really believe that people swallow it.'

'Swallow what?'

'Oh—all the pious duty-towards-thy-neighbour and so on.'

'Why not?' said Henry.

'Because they know that business is a straightforward matter of bargaining. It's the management's job to make a profit and the worker's job to get a fair price for his labour. There's no reason why it shouldn't be a fair and honourable bargain, but I don't see that we need always be dragging God into it.'

'My knowledge of God is limited,' said Henry calmly. 'But in my experience He tends to come into these things without being dragged. Anyhow, without a bit of the higher purpose, it all becomes a bit objectless, doesn't it?'

'Why? The job's worth doing for its own sake, isn't it?' Lang was staring across the room with a curious smile. 'My God, Henry, haven't you ever stood in that press shop when it's in full blast, and really *felt* the place working? . . .' He stopped. 'Anyhow,' he said abruptly, 'it's as much as I can manage to do my job. Maybe some of the rest of you have got more time for higher thought.'

'His favourite music was the sound of presses. His favourite picture was a rising sales curve. His favourite reading was last month's production figures. . . .' Henry chuckled. 'You know, the trouble with you, Walter, is that you've no capacity for childish amusements. Like Ucello, you're so immersed in the mathematics of your art. . . .'

'You get young Lawrence to get me that steel and I'll amuse myself all right. Anyhow, I'm going home. Where's that daughter of mine?'

'Won't she want to stay and dance?'

'I don't know,' said Lang vaguely. 'I shouldn't think so.'

Lawrence said: 'You don't mind my talking all the time, do you 'Rene? You see I can't dance, so I have to talk all the time, otherwise people notice that I can't dance.'

Hilda said: 'You dance quite nice.' It was the first thing she had said.

'Thank you,' said Lawrence. 'Kind girl. Now that encourages me, which will probably be fatal. I shall now do my feather, but I shall have to hold you very close for that because my feather is very difficult to follow. Do you mind being held close, 'Rene? After all, what's dancing for if not so that you can hold pretty girls close to you? That's what I ask myself.' He let go of her left hand and put both hands behind her shoulders, hugging her closely. 'Forgive me,' he said carefully, 'what I seek is not romance but stability.'

Jack was dancing with Fred Boxall's sister Nellie, a slant-eyed girl with dyed blonde hair and a reputation as the factory's bad girl.

She nudged him and said: 'What price Hilda, boy?'

'I know,' he said disgustedly. He looked across at Hilda and Lawrence with sullen anger. 'Wonder what he'd say if I started bunny hugging about with his wife?'

'Lawrence always does that. Remember him last year? I said to him once: "Hey, steady on. You'll get us turned off the floor," I said.'

'They make me sick,' said Jack suddenly. 'Him and Talbot-Rees and Lang and the whole lot of them.'

The dance ended and Nellie made for the cloakroom. He went back to the bar and ordered another Pale Ale. It was his fourth and they were making his head ache slightly. Hilda had disappeared or he would have gone and talked to her and told her to tell Lawrence to go to hell if he asked her again. If he wanted that sort of thing why couldn't he get Nellie or Jill Mead or one of the girls that like it, not a shy kid like Hilda?

Laura was saying good night to Miss Spellman. Lawrence came and stood behind them, leaning against a pillar, and passed his hand over his eyes. He suddenly felt very tired and hopeless. As Laura turned he said quietly: 'I think that's probably enough of that, my dear. Let's go home.'

She looked at him with the wide green eyes thoughtfully but without emotion. 'As you like,' she said indifferently. 'I shall go after the next dance anyhow.'

'No. Not after the next dance. Now.'

Laura shrugged. 'All right. I'll go and get my coat.'

Hilda was in the ladies' room. She was talking in a low voice to Nellie Boxall and giggling. They stopped talking when Laura came in. She made herself smile at them and they smiled back and Hilda blushed. Laura went over to the counter and asked for her coat. If this was all—if he would really come home now—it hadn't been too bad. Nothing like as bad as last year.

The band played a loud chord and the black-haired leader with the white teeth called in his toastmaster's voice: 'Ladies and Gentlemen—the next dance will be . . . Ladies' Choice.'

There was a flutter of laughter and excitement. Mac said: 'Well, come on, girls. Here I am. Come and get it.'

Fred Boxall said: 'I'll bet our Nell asks Lawrence.'

Jack said: 'Well, she can have him.' He looked round for Hilda. She would certainly ask him. But she still hadn't reappeared from the cloakroom.

As the band started Rosamund muttered: 'Oh gosh . . .!' and looked round rather nervously. The obvious person was Lawrence, who was leaning against a pillar with his eyes closed. But as she moved towards him a little slant-eyed girl with blonde hair went up to him. Lawrence opened his eyes and looked down at her uncomprehendingly for a moment. Then a wide smile spread over his face and he opened both arms very wide and put them firmly round her. That was that. Rosamund went up to Lang and said: 'Will you dance with me, Daddy? Or will someone nicer come for you if you don't?'

He smiled and said: 'Of course I will, darling. I'm

flattered.' He put his arm round her and took her into the dance in his firm, decisive, slightly stiff way. He said : 'Enjoying yourself, Roz ?'

'Oh yes. It's fun.'

'Let me know when you want to go.'

Rosamund said : 'Well look—don't stay about because of me, darling, if you want to go.'

'Oh—no hurry. Whenever you like.'

'Look at our Nell, the little bitch,' said Fred Boxall with affectionate pride.

Mac said : 'Walter dancing with young Rosamund. That's a waste now.'

Jack said : 'He'd see she didn't come and ask any of us, chum. We're all equal at the Party, eh ?'

Mac said : 'How about going up and excuse-me him and take her off ?'

'Go on, then,' said Fred Boxall, grinning. 'I'll watch you.'

'Why not ?' said Jack. 'Christ, who's he that you can't dance with his bloody daughter ?'

'Go on, then, Jacko,' said Mac. 'Go and take her like I said.'

'I'm not afraid of him,' said Jack sullenly. 'I would if I wanted her.'

There was a general laugh. Jack looked round and said : 'All right—who's betting ?'

'Twenty Weights you don't,' said Mac.

Jack hesitated for a moment. His eyes were on the yellow frock. 'O.K.,' he said rather huskily. 'You're on.' He squared the big shoulders and walked quickly on to the floor.

'Jesus !' said Fred Boxall. 'Ole Jacko . . .!'

Lang did not feel the first tap on his shoulder. It was Rosamund's face that made him pause and turn. 'Excuse me,' Jack said again. His face was beetroot red.

'What ?' said Lang, puzzled.

'Excuse me,' said Jack helplessly.

Rosamund said : 'Oh . . . it's a sort of dance . . .'

C

Jack said croakily: 'In a Ladies' Choice you can say excuse me and then I dance with her.'

'Oh,' said Lang, rather startled. 'All right . . .' he slowly released Rosamund. He was smiling but rather bewildered. 'Then who do I dance with?'

'You go and excuse-me somebody else.'

'I see,' said Lang. 'All right. Carry on.' He nodded and turned away and threaded his way through the dancing couples to the sidelines.

Mac said: 'I wouldn't have done that for Twenty Weights.'

'Nor me,' said Fred Boxall, shaking his head. 'Not with Walter. Bloody fool.'

'Jacko's Bolshy,' said somebody. 'That's all it is.'

'Well, that won't have done him no good at all.'

He was drenched in sweat and he could feel the wet shirt clinging to his back. The hand on her back was trembling absurdly. Once they got out of step and she said: 'Sorry,' contritely.

'All right,' he said harshly. Then, after a pause: 'You go to dances much?'

'Not very much.'

'Why? Don't you like dancing?'

'Oh yes. I'm not very good though.'

'How can you be any good if you don't practise?' he said roughly.

Rosamund said: 'Do you dance a lot?'

'Fair bit.'

'You're on the Works Council, aren't you?'

'That's right.'

'I thought you were. I saw you when we came in.'

He felt a sudden spasm of anger. It was all so cool and friendly. He hadn't walked across the floor and taken her away from Lang and maybe put himself in wrong for good, just to be talked to about being on the committee. He said suddenly: 'That's a nice frock you've got on,' and stared down at her face with a fierce grin.

'Well, that's the trouble,' said Rosamund calmly. 'I'm not sure whether it *is* a nice frock.'

'What's wrong with it?' he said with a sneer. 'If you've got anything good to show, why not show it?' That worked better. She didn't blush but she looked away and didn't reply. Over her bare shoulders he could see Lang talking to George Martin. Lang wasn't looking at them. He hated Lang and he hated her, and he felt a fool and ashamed. He tightened his arm and pressed her against him pointedly and almost savagely.

After a while Rosamund said: 'Who's the little man with the wooden leg?'

'Billy Peace,' he said through set teeth, and slipped his hand down her bare back to the base of her spine.

They had faded down the main lights, and apart from one spot-light that kept changing colour, the floor was in semi-darkness. He smelt of sweat and brilliantine and he was pressing her tight against a big body that was as hard as iron. It was not like dancing, because held like that you became part of the rhythm of the waltz. It moved you without your volition, as though you were lying on one of those rafts in a gently heaving sea. Rosamund realised that she felt slightly sick, that her knees were weak, and that she was afraid the band would stop. But it played on and on, and now they were in the semi-darkness and the hand on her back was gently moving up her bare spine. Somewhere miles away there was the reflection that there was nothing to be done about it without making a fuss, and all you could do was to go on talking and pretend you hadn't noticed. She heard her voice talking coolly and steadily about George Martin, and the fact that he was going to retire. But neither the reflection nor the calm voice had any reality, and she was keeping the music going now by the sheer force of her will. . . .

He said curtly: 'You ever go to the pictures?'

She started and only just repressed a slightly hysterical giggle, and looked up at him and deliberately said: 'Sometimes,' with no excuses at all.

He said: 'Well, how about coming with me some time?'

Rosamund hesitated. Now she had stopped willing it to go on, the music was coming to a long-drawn, agonised end. For some curious reason she had a vision of throwing the two uneaten sandwiches out of the window of her bedroom.

'That would be very nice,' she said, in exactly the same tone and the same words as she had used earlier in the evening when Miss Spellman had asked her to tea.

When the band stopped they were close to the door of the Ladies' Cloakroom. Rosamund said: 'I'm going in here. Goodbye and thank you.'

He nodded and said: 'Thanks. See you again some time,' and walked slowly back to the bar to the startled, envious, admiring grins. He walked with a slight swagger and grinned back at them. He picked up a Pale Ale and said: 'How about my Twenty Weights?'

Mac said: 'You can have 'em. Did you see old Walter's face? Rather you than me, chum.'

Jack said: 'I'm not afraid of him.' He grinned savagely. 'Wouldn't like to have another twenty on something else, would you?'

In the Ladies' Cloakroom, Rosamund locked herself in a lavatory and was slightly sick, after which she felt much better. She said: 'Well, well . . .' to herself, and then giggled slightly, powdered the sides of her nose and then, with decision, went to the counter and collected the ermine cloak. While they were getting it she said: 'Well, well . . .' again under her breath, and then went to look for Lang. He was still talking to George Martin, but he was very willing to come home.

*   *   *   *   *

The old Austin's springing was usually soft and comfortable, but to-night it seemed to grow harder and harder, so that every little bump in the road sent a jar through his whole body. Once Gustavus nearly told Marsh to stop—to let him get out and rest from the intolerable vibration. But he knew it was not the car, and that the only thing to do was to get home, and he huddled into a corner and pulled the rug tighter about him and shivered in the deadly cold—the cold that seemed to come from inside rather than from outside. His father's grudging voice was saying: 'All right, Gus, if you want to. I suppose it can't do any harm.' All through fifty years there had been grudging voices—allowing, permitting, suspecting, but never really believing.

Except for Miss Bell. And old Bertram Stevens, dead now for twenty years. And Henry Spellman in his way—the way of laughing and saying the cynical thing and then being on the side of the angels when it came to the point. And George Martin who was a simple, good man. . . . It was not good to feel that one had fought alone, when there had been so many who had fought nobly alongside. And now it looked won, and there was no longer master and man, or so they said. But it was not won. It was only that the war was between more equal forces. And it would not be won till there was no war and all were members of one another—until one could smile at a man and see the smile returned unfrightened, unwary, trusting and knowing his worth, and knowing yours.

It was not bumping and jarring any more but it was colder. Marsh's voice was saying: 'Here we are, sir.' Marsh was holding the door open. He had a struggle to get out because the rug was round his legs and Marsh had to help him, and going up the steps he stumbled and if it had not been for Marsh's arm he would have fallen.

Gustavus said: 'My keys . . .' but Mrs. Poulton had opened the door and he was in the big hall and Marsh was taking his coat off. Mrs. Poulton said: 'A little drop of brandy because it's cold outside.' Gustavus smiled and said. 'No, thank you,' and then Marsh was saying: 'Come on, sir, do you good.' Gustavus did not want the brandy, but he sipped it to please Marsh and Mrs. Poulton, who had taken the trouble to bring it. After a while Mrs. Poulton said: 'How did the party go, Mr. Gustavus?' He said: 'Very well. Very well indeed. Excellent. I think everybody enjoyed it.'

Marsh was still there and Gustavus said: 'There's no need for you to stay, Marsh, thank you. I'm going to bed now. Good night.'

They were upstairs outside his bedroom door. The

fire was on inside but it was still very cold. Marsh was still there and he said rather irritably : 'No, no. Not the slightest need. Good night, Marsh.' Mrs. Poulton said something about a hot drink and he said : 'Yes. Thank you. Very nice,' to get rid of her, and went into his room and shut the door in their faces and started to undress. His hands were very cold and it took a long time to undo his waistcoat buttons.

It was necessary to get to the bed and he gave up the buttons and leaned against the wall for a moment to get his breath. He could hear himself panting, but the breath did not seem to be going into his lungs and he knew he must get to the bed quickly because he wasn't well.

He was down on the floor and the carpet was rough against his face and his eyes were so close to it that it was a brown blur. He knew he must not lie on the floor like that or he would catch a chill. He tried to call Mrs. Poulton but there was no air and no sound came out except a sobbing grunt. He was very frightened and there was dust in the carpet and it was stifling him. He fought the dust and then suddenly it was quieter, and he was not afraid and there was no longer any urgency. He lay there and smiled to himself in sheer relief at the calm that came from the passing away of fear and urgency. But there was the General Confession. He should say the General Confession.

'Almighty and most merciful Father, we Thine un-worthy servants do give Thee most humble and hearty thanks for all Thy goodness and loving kindness to us and to all men . . .' Vaguely and unworried he knew that it was not right, but it would do.

'We thank Thee for our creation, preservation and all the blessings of this life. But above all for Thine inestimable love in the redemption of the world by Our Lord Jesus Christ . . .'

The dust was coming again but he did not mind it now. He looked round at the big ring of faces smiling up at him and said : 'There is no law that can replace goodwill.'

'Hear, hear !' said Henry Spellman.

V

ROSAMUND said: 'What does "in trust" mean exactly?'

'It means that you get the interest on the money, but you can't touch the capital until you're twenty-one—at least, not unless the trustees agree.' Lang kicked off his slippers. 'Where are my shoes?'

'Behind you, darling. Who are the trustees? You?'

'No, thank God. Henry Spellman and North. Let's see—on £5000 you'll probably get about two hundred a year.'

'And then when I'm twenty-one I get the five thousand?'

'Yes.'

'But you get your five thousand right away?'

'Yes. I'm considered to have reached years of discretion.'

Rosamund said: 'It seems rather awful to be dividing the poor old boy up like this, doesn't it? I mean, it will be very nice to have another two hundred a year, but if I go and buy myself a silly hat or something it will be rather ghastly to think that it's a bit of Uncle Gus.'

'Oh, I don't know,' said Lang indifferently. 'It's no good to him any longer. Anyhow, if he'd been a different sort of person he ought to have left you the lot.'

'I'm rather glad he didn't. How much will there be to go to the Benevolent Fund?'

'I don't know. A lot of it will go in death duties. But the main question is what they'll get for his shares in the Company.' Lang smiled rather grimly. 'And that's where the fun begins.' He took out a pencil and turned over one of the envelopes from the morning's mail. 'It's rather an interesting situation. There are only two hundred thousand ordinary shares. Gustavus had about eighty thousand. I've got sixty thousand. Old Henry and his family have got about twenty thousand. The other forty thousand are in bits and pieces between four or five other people—old Mrs. Horseman and so on. So

71

if I can buy another forty-five thousand of Gustavus's lot . . .' he spread out his hands. 'Bob's your uncle.'

'Why? I don't see?'

'Because that would give me a hundred-and-five thousand, which would be a controlling interest.'

'Meaning what?' said Rosamund.

'Well—I shall have complete control of the Company.'

'Haven't you now? You're managing director?'

'Yes darling—but *financial* control. If it ever came to a show-down, the person who's got the majority of the ordinary shares can outvote everybody else—and say what's going to be done.'

'And you can do that—get the other forty-five thousand?'

'Who's going to stop me? Under Uncle Gus's will they'll have to sell the shares to *somebody*. If I'm prepared to offer the proper market value, then as the son of the founder I've obviously got a right to demand that they shall be offered to me first. As a matter of fact, some people would say that Gustavus had no right to leave the shares outside the family like that. But if he wanted the money to go to his beloved charities and wanted to make me buy the shares, I don't care.' Lang glanced at his watch and finished his coffee. 'It'll be a sizeable operation of course. Those shares are worth something over two pounds each. The forty-five thousand I want will cost the thick end of a hundred thousand.'

'A hundred thousand *pounds*?'

'Yes.'

'But darling, have you *got* a hundred thousand pounds?'

Lang grinned. 'Not actually in my pocket, honey. But that's what banks are for. What are you doing to-day?'

Rosamund said : 'Oh—this and that. I think I shall borrow Mrs. Dart's machine and do the landing curtains. I like machining.'

When he had gone Rosamund poured herself out a cup of rather cold coffee and picked up Lang's pencil and envelope. There were fifty-two weeks in the year and so it was fifty-two into two hundred. She wrote down two hundred and put fifty-two underneath it and then brought the two hundred into the right position to be divided. The extreme tip of her tongue protruded between her lips with concentration of mathematical effort. It came to 38·46 and a bit. But it couldn't possibly be £38 a week. It must be shillings, and yet one was working in pounds.

Ten minutes later it was sorted out, and it was £3 : 17s. a week, which seemed less than two hundred a year ought to be, but would still be nice. Suddenly she remembered that they had found him lying on the floor. He had died by himself with nobody to help him and his glasses had fallen off. Her eyes filled with tears and she said chokily : 'The damn fools—the *damn* fools—leaving him alone like that.'

* * * * *

The Board Meeting was called for ten-forty-five. Lawrence was on time, but they were all there before him. His father and Lang were talking quietly in a corner. North, Talbot-Rees and George Martin were in a group at the window. Lawrence suddenly realised that he was the only one not wearing a black tie—and to make it worse he was wearing a rather bright red one. He went over to the group at the window and said : 'Good morning,' and saw Talbot-Rees's eyes go at once to the red tie. Lawrence said : 'Who takes the chair now ?' Talbot-Rees and North both looked away. Martin said : 'Mr. Walter, I suppose. Or your father.'

'It doesn't really matter,' said North through his thin pointed nose. 'This isn't a business meeting, is it ? It'll have to be settled later on, won't it ?'

Henry Spellman looked at his watch and said : 'Well I suppose we ought to start, eh Walter ?' He gestured Lang towards the head of the table. Lang repeated the gesture. They smiled at one another and Lang said : 'Gentlemen, may I move that Mr. Spellman takes the Chair ?'

There was a murmur of approval. Old Henry said : 'Well, I'm not sure that that's right, but I don't suppose it matters.' He eased himself into the big chair at the end of the table with a loud grunt and looked round at them for a moment in silence. He said: 'Well, gentlemen, this is not our normal Board Meeting. It has been called, as you all know, because of the lamented death of our Chairman, Gustavus Lang. At eleven o'clock it has been arranged that a two minutes' silence shall be kept throughout the factory as a tribute to his memory, and I think we all felt that the proper place for the directors to pay their tribute was here in the board-room, in which he sat for over forty-five years as a director, and for over thirty years as Chairman.' He removed the heavy horn-rimmed spectacles and began to polish the lenses with his handkerchief, peering at them carefully.

'I'm not going to pronounce a funeral oration on Gustavus,' he said slowly. 'It's not the sort of thing he would have wanted. But as one who knew him and worked with him for forty years I should like to say this: I never knew a humbler man; I never knew anyone who worked harder or more selflessly for what he believed in. If there is such a thing as a good man he was one. Now he's gone—suddenly, and while he was still in harness, which is the way he would have wished it. For my part, I'm glad that he should have gone home to die from the Works Party, which was a thing after his own kind heart, and which I know had left him happy.' Henry Spellman put on his glasses again. 'That's all I've got to say, gentlemen.' He glanced at his watch. 'Now in a few seconds the hooter will blow, and we will all rise and stand in silence for two minutes in memory of Gustavus Lang, late Chairman of William Lang Sons & Horseman.'

The hooter started its rising cry of pain, and settled to the long sad note of ancient loneliness. As it died away the distant rumble of the factory died with it. It was a rumble that one only noticed when it ceased. Standing facing the board-room window, Lawrence could see a bald man with a jack-truck. He had been half-way across the yard when the hooter had sounded and he had stopped, and stood now beside his truck with head bent. There was a strong wind and it was blowing his

soiled white apron against his stomach. A lorry went by
in the road outside, and for a moment Lawrence was
surprised. But it wasn't Armistice Day, and it was only
in Lang's that there was this stillness. He started to count
down, as he always did on these occasions, like a rowing
coach counting off the seconds before the starting gun for
his crew. 'Five—and—four—and three—and—two and
—one—and one—and one—one . . .' The hooter blew
again. As soon as it started the man with the jack-truck
raised his head, took the handle and plodded on across
the yard. But the directors, by a common instinct, stood
on in silence until the wailing ceased. Henry Spellman
said : 'I suppose there ought to be a formal resolution of
regret for the Minutes. I believe Mr. North's prepared
a draft for us to consider.'

Old Matt Wright said : 'Well, you can say what you
like, he was always very nice to me.'
'*I'm* not saying anything against the man,' said
Herbage. 'Anyhow, he's dead, isn't he, and there wouldn't
be any call to say anything against him. All as I say, is
that I got a bit tired of it. 'Nother five bob a week and
less talk about all being equal would have suited me.'
'Well, you won't get that talk from Walter, mate.
Nor the five bob neither.'
Little Marks said : 'What'll happen now, anyhow?
I reckon there'll be changes. Big changes. After all,
Gus was the one with the money, see.'
'I don't reckon he was,' said Matt Wright. 'I reckon
he give it all away.'
'Don't you believe it,' said Herbage.
Marks said : 'I reckon he was a millionaire. Why,
the old man left near half a million and it was a lot
smaller place then.'
Matt Wright said : 'Well, you'll find it different with
Walter. He's more like the old man. Hard. That's
what Walter is.'
'He's a good man of business,' said Herbage. 'And
he don't talk so much of the smarmy stuff.'
'Though, mind you,' said Marks, 'Gus did some things
that was good. I reckon you got to give him that. When

it was bad in 1931 it was him wouldn't lay people off when all the rest wanted to. I know because Ryan told me. "No," he said. "I'm not going to sack a man or a girl. We're going to find them work if we lose money on it." That's what he said.'

'You wouldn't catch Walter saying that, mate,' said Matt Wright. 'I reckon Gus was a good boss, and there's plenty'll miss him now he's gone.'

'Jesus Christ,' said Herbage. '*I* got nothing against Gus. He's dead, ain't he, poor old sod? All I say is I don't want favours from Langs or anybody else. I reckon it's for the Union to stand out for the workers' rights without a lot of fiddle-faddle and fancy talk. The boss is on one side and you're on the other and what's the use of pretending not?'

'I don't reckon old Gus was on the other side from anybody,' said Matt Wright doggedly.

'Listen,' said Marks, waving a hand, 'I reckon it's like this. Say he was a good boss. With a good boss it's all right. He wants to treat you fair. Don't matter whether he gives it you because he wants to, or the Union makes him, you get it and that's fine. But supposing he ain't a good boss?'

'He was,' said Matt Wright.

Marks said: 'You don't see what I mean, Matt. Supposing it was somebody else different . . .?'

'You don't see what you mean yourself, Ikey,' said Herbage, moving away.

Marks said: 'I'm making your point, Jimmy. About how it ought to be the Union does it because if it's left to the boss, when it ain't a *good* boss . . .'

'Well, he was all right,' said Matt Wright sullenly. 'And it won't be long before you're all wishing he was back and there was a few *more* favours going.'

*   *   *   *   *

Henry Spellman took off his glasses, put them on his desk, gave them a slight push and shook his head. He said: 'I'd rather not, Walter. It's nice of you to suggest it but . . . I don't think I want it.'

'Why not?' said Lang.

'I'm too old for one thing. And too lazy for another. If I take it on, in three years you'll want *another* Chairman.'

'So much the better. Anyhow, Henry, you're the senior director.'

Spellman said: 'Why don't you want to do it yourself? You're your father's son and . . .'

'Plenty of time for me later. Anyhow, I don't think anybody can be Chairman *and* Managing Director. And Managing Director's more my job.'

'I see,' said Spellman with a grin. 'What you want's a King Log, eh? Takes the chair at meetings and doesn't interfere?' He picked up the spectacles. 'All right, Walter. I'll think it over and tell you later. I don't suppose any of our colleagues are likely to disagree with whatever we suggest. . . .' He smiled.

'I wouldn't think so,' said Lang smiling back. 'Right. Now then, something more important. What're you going to do about Gus's shares?'

Spellman glanced at him quickly and hesitated. 'I don't know yet. Haven't had time to think about it.'

'They'll have to be sold?'

'I suppose so. Under the terms of the will.'

Lang said: 'What d'you reckon they're worth?'

'Don't know exactly. Been no market in them for years.'

'Two pounds a share?'

'Something like that.'

'And it's eighty thousand altogether?'

'So I'm told.' Spellman hesitated again. 'You want to talk about this now, Walter?'

'Yes. I do.'

'Then we'd better have North in, hadn't we?'

'What for?' said Lang frowning.

'Well—he's trustee with me.'

Lang said: 'Oh damn that. North'll do what he's told.' He lit a cigarette. 'Look Henry—I want to put in a bid for those shares—or at least for forty-five thousand. I don't want any favours. You get a proper valuation, and then all I want's first refusal at that price.'

There was a moment's silence. Spellman said: 'Well,

of course, Walter, you'll realise that as executors and trustees it's our job to do our best for the estate. . . .'

'Yes?'

'. . . which means selling at the best price we can possibly get.'

'Oh I dare say,' said Lang impatiently. 'But if I'm ready to match any offer you get from anybody else you're all right aren't you?'

'Yes . . .' Spellman shook his head rather doubtfully. 'Of course this is a pretty important thing, Walter. I'd have to talk to North, and think it over before . . .'

'Think what over?'

'Well—there's a principle involved, isn't there?'

'What's involved,' said Lang shortly, 'is that you've got to sell and I want to buy.'

'Oh, wait a minute, Walter. This wouldn't be just selling you the shares. It'd be selling you control of the business.'

'What about it? I'm the son of the founder.' Lang was staring at him with his peculiar unblinking gaze.

Henry Spellman shifted uneasily in his chair. 'Yes, but what you've got to remember is that I'm not acting for myself. I'm acting as Gus's trustee. . . .'

'And you've got to do the best you can for his estate. You said that before.'

'. . . Yes. And what's more, I've got to consider . . . well—the interests of—of everybody. Of the business . . .'

Lang's face had gone deep red. 'Look here, Henry,' he said quietly. 'Are you trying to tell me there's going to be some fuss about selling me the shares I want? Because if so . . .'

Spellman said: 'I'm not saying so. All I'm saying is that I'm not in a position to promise you can have them, over this desk at five minutes' notice.'

'I don't see why not,' said Lang with sullen anger.

Henry Spellman's mouth suddenly shut tight so that his lips were very thin and pale coloured. 'I'm sorry about that, Walter,' he said carefully. 'But I *do* see why not.'

There was a moment's silence.

'It's none of my business,' said Henry, 'but what d'you want financial control *for*? You're managing director. Now Gustavus is dead you'll be far and away the biggest shareholder on the Board. I can't remember a time when the Board's stopped you from doing what you wanted to. . . .'

Lang said: 'Well, it's paid them, hasn't it?'

'Of course it has. That's why they've done it. But if everybody agrees that you're the boss, why not let it alone?'

'I want to know where I am.'

'How d'you mean?'

'I don't want to work my guts out and then, if it came to a showdown, know I could be out-voted by a bunch of people who've made no contribution and know nothing about it.'

'But that couldn't happen unless the whole bunch of us were unanimously against you. And if we were, surely there'd be a fair chance that you might be wrong? What you're asking for is a situation where everybody else is a cipher, and nobody's opinion but yours matters a damn.'

'Well, *somebody's* got to be able to make a decision.'

Spellman said: 'There were three times when Gustavus could have had absolute financial control of the business, and he turned it down each time, precisely because he didn't think it was a good thing for there to be a boss that nobody could stand up to.'

'That's because he wanted to be told what to do,' said Lang with a crooked smile. He slapped his hand on the desk. 'Well, there you are, Henry—I'm making you an offer. How about it?'

Spellman said: 'Supposing we sell you thirty thousand. That'd give you practically a fifty per cent interest . . .?'

'No,' said Lang quietly. 'If I'm going to run this business I'm going to run it.'

Spellman shrugged his shoulders. 'All right. Then the only thing to do is to put your offer on paper and I'll have to talk to North and—and see what can be done. But I think you're wrong, Walter. Wrong in principle.'

Lang got up. 'Maybe you're right, Henry. But I like to make my own mistakes in my own way.'

*   *   *   *   *

The man who had been telephoning picked up his brief-case and came out of the box, but Jack walked on past it again. Even if he did get Lang himself it was all right. He'd only have to say: 'Can I speak to Miss Lang, please?' and if they asked who it was he would give any name. 'Mr. Parsons.' And if she brushed him off or pretended she didn't remember, what did it matter? She could go to hell. 'Howy'doing? This is Jack Partridge. . . .' He went back to the telephone box and looked up the number. There were about a dozen Langs and it was the last one. 'Lang, Walter S.' It didn't ring for a long time and he was just going to dial again when it started. It was a slow, lazy 'brr-brr,' and it only rang three times before the voice answered. He thought it was her voice but he wasn't taking any chances, so he said: 'Can I speak to Miss Lang, please?' and it said: 'Speaking.' He took a deep breath and said: 'Hallo, how y'doing? This is Jack Partridge.'

'Who?'

'Jack Partridge.'

There was a slight pause and then the voice said: 'Oh . . . hallo,' and after that he knew it was going to be easy.

He said: 'Get back all right the other night?'

'Oh yes, thank you.'

'Might've said good night to me.'

'You were dancing and—and I had to go.'

He said: 'Well, how about our evening out?'

There was a long silence—so long that he thought the telephone might have been cut off and said: 'Hallo . . .' The voice said: 'Hallo.' 'I said what about our evening out? You ever seen any dirt-track riding?'

'No.'

'Well, how about it if we went to that? To-morrow?'

'I can't to-morrow.'

'Well it's Tuesday, Thursday or Saturday. Say Thursday. You know Phillip's corner?'

'Yes. By the Queen's.'

'That's right. Meet me outside there at seven. O.K.?'

She suddenly said: 'Look I'm sorry, but I've got to go now . . .'

'Well, Thursday at seven then?'

The voice said: 'Good-bye, and thank you,' and there was a click. He said: 'Hallo,' but she had rung up. He looked at the receiver with a frown and then jabbed it down irritably. The old game, trying to leave you guessing.

Lang was hanging up his coat as Rosamund put down the receiver. He said: 'What was that?'

Rosamund said: 'Laura. Wants me to go to tea.'

'Laura . . .?' Lang's head came up. 'Well look, Roz—I think perhaps you'd better get out of it. There may be going to be some fun with the Spellman family, and I don't want to cross any wires.'

She said: 'I've told her I can't, anyway.'

Her hands were shaking so that as she poured out his sherry the neck of the bottle rattled against the glass, and she had to use both hands to steady it.

Lang was saying: 'If Uncle Henry Spellman thinks he can play about with me, he'll find himself in a lot of trouble.' He took his sherry. 'You don't want any?'

She shook her head and smiled. It was fantastic to feel so wobbly just because somebody rang you up on the telephone and asked you out. She sat down opposite Lang and smoothed the frock down over her knees. Thank God he was going to talk, and all you had to do was to sit and be talked to.

Lang said: 'I've always played ball with him. I've offered him the chairmanship, and I've carried Lawrence, who's damn all use to anybody. But if we're going to have a lot of talk about "matters of principle," and "consulting his colleague," and so on, then two can play at that game.'

He was looking at her with that heavy sullen expression

which always reminded her of a cross child. This was
the only thing that she hated—this sullen bragging about
what he would do if anyone opposed him. She looked
away and said lightly: 'I don't suppose the old boy
knows what it's all about.'

'Oh, doesn't he? He's sharp enough when there's
money in it. Of course it may be that he's playing hard
to get just to push the price up. But if so, he's got another
think coming.'

She found with a shock of surprise that she could
hardly remember the face at all—that she couldn't even
be sure that she would know him if she met him in the
street. He was tall and broad and he had wavy dark hair,
and he had a gruff, rather rude way of speaking, and he
smelt of brilliantine and sweat. But he had no face.
Except that his bottom teeth were uneven and he showed
them when he spoke.

Lang was saying: 'If it came to that I'd have Lawrence out in ten minutes. And he knows it.'

Rosamund said: 'Don't do that, darling. Lawrence
is nice.'

'I don't care whether he's nice or not. He's no damn
good, and never has been and never will be.'

'He was some good in the war,' she said, irritated.

'Maybe. And he's lived on it ever since.' Lang
handed her his empty glass. Her hands were shaking less
now and she could fill it using one hand.

'Well, what happens now?' she said vaguely.

Lang smiled. 'That's up to them, darling. I shall
put in my bid and then we'll see what cards Uncle
Henry's got in his hands.'

'And in the meantime you don't want me to go to
tea with Laura?'

'Better not. They probably only want to pump you.'

She wanted to say: 'Don't be silly, Walter.' Mummy
would have said that, and that was what Mummy could
do for him. But one was no good to him—no good. She
looked at him and suddenly she wanted to cry. Oh,
darling, I love you, and sometimes I despise you and
sometimes I almost hate you, but I love you really, and
I don't want to go to Phillip's corner and I'm frightened,

and I never would go if there were anywhere to stay but there isn't, and I can't do it for you.

Lang said: 'I don't think he'll get much change out of North. North's a pretty slippery customer, but he knows which side his bread's buttered on.'

Rosamund said: 'When you've drunk that I want you to come up and see the landing curtains. The pelmet's a bit skew-wiff but the rest's all right.'

VI

As soon as the train started, George Martin took his brief-case down from the rack and pulled out a large file of papers.

Lawrence said: 'What on earth's all that?'

'All the things I haven't had time to read this week.' Martin flipped at the thick wad. 'I always reckon to catch up with a bit of it when I go up to London.'

'But what *sort* of things, George? You always make me ashamed—you and Walter and the rest of you—with your papers. At the board, everybody always comes in carrying about half a hundredweight of stuff. *I* never have anything to bring.'

'That's because you don't do any work,' said Martin with his gentle smile.

'Or because I don't care whether I look over-worked or not?'

'Maybe that's it.'

Lawrence said moodily: 'I don't understand business. I never have. You've got to earn a living—you've got to do a job. O.K. But this game of taking it home with you and eating it and talking it and taking it to bed with you . . .' He shook his head. 'Damn it, George, if Langs fell down to-morrow, just what would it *matter*? We should all have to go and get jobs somewhere else, and people would have to get someone else to do their fabricating. So what?'

Martin smiled. 'You'd better not tell that to Mr. Walter.'

'I have. In those exact words. I've told him that I'm prepared to do my best at it. But I'm not going to pretend that it's my whole life because it isn't. And I've also told him that I think the place would run a damn sight better if he took a day off occasionally and went and played golf and stopped badgering everybody.'

Martin was looking out of the window. 'It's different for you,' he said slowly. 'You've had education and—and opportunities to see things. I started work when I was thirteen and it's been my hobby. It's had to be.' He turned over the top sheets in his file. 'There's three memorandums here from Mr. Walter,' he said with a sigh, 'asking when we're going to see Mr. Falk.'

'Well, I've had four and a telephone call every day. That's the way to be a busy man, you see, George. I told him days ago that we were coming up to-day and going to see Falk to-morrow, but that wasn't enough.' Lawrence stubbed out his cigarette viciously. 'What would be funny is if Falk can't let us have any steel anyway. Which is quite likely.'

'Funny?' said Martin. 'It'll be mighty serious. A few weeks and we should have to stop production on the sprayer.'

Lawrence settled back in his corner and closed his eyes. 'Well, well,' he said. 'Like you, I'm going to catch up with a bit of back-log.'

Martin turned back to his file. After a few minutes he got out his fountain pen and began to make marginal notes in his precise small writing.

When the train stopped at Banbury Lawrence woke up, lit a cigarette, and promptly coughed until his eyes were full of tears. He said: 'It's damned hot in here. This train is always either the Christian hell or the Norse hell—too hot or too cold. You are coming to this party to-night, aren't you?'

Martin said: 'I don't know. It's very nice of you, but it's not much in my line. . . .'

'Oh, you must come. It's nothing exciting. Just a few people coming in for drinks. But I'd like you to meet the Pearts. He's an art director in films. Nice chap with a very nice wife who designs hats.'

'You see,' said Martin, shifting rather uneasily, 'I've got nothing to *say* to people like that. I don't know anything about films. Or hats.'

'Well, they don't know anything about fabricating metal. Except that they found the factory rather exciting.'

'Oh, they've been up there?' said Martin, rather cheered.

'Of course they have. You'd certainly better come, George. At least it'll be better for you than sitting in the hotel looking at last week's production figures.'

*　　　*　　　*　　　*　　　*

North stroked the long, red, shiny nose and said: 'Of course, in a way it would be the natural thing for the shares to stay in the family, wouldn't it, Mr. Walter?'

Lang said: 'Of course it would. As long as I pay the market price, I consider I've right to first refusal. But Spellman's got it into his head that I want to be a—a dictator or something. Of course you understand that I'm speaking to you in confidence, North. . . .'

'Of course, Mr. Walter.'

'. . . but if Spellman *did* refuse to let this deal go through, he might be starting something he couldn't finish.'

North shook his head. 'I can't believe Mr. Spellman would want any unpleasantness, Mr. Walter. After all, that wouldn't do any good, would it?' He smiled at Lang confidentially. 'Of course, you know as well as I do Mr. Walter . . . Well, I don't want to say anything disloyal, but Mr. Spellman's an elderly man and he was a great friend of the late Mr. Gustavus and . . .'

Lang said: 'Oh yes, I know all that. But we can't let that stand in the way of—of the proper arrangement. That's why I wanted a private word with you.'

'Yes. Well, of course, Mr. Walter, you'll understand that—that I'm very much junior to Mr. Spellman. I imagine I was only appointed executor and trustee because of the legal side, and being a trustee of the Benevolent Fund and so on. But if Mr. Spellman says anything to me, you can depend on me to—to put my view to him. After all that's my plain duty, isn't it? I can only say what I think.'

'That's right,' said Lang. 'Well, thanks, North. I don't think there's anything else.'

Talbot-Rees slid the gold cigarette case shut and tapped the cigarette hard on the desk.

'Not on your life,' he said emphatically. 'Not bloody likely! Don't you part, Henry, or God knows where it'll land us.'

Henry Spellman put his glasses on his desk, pushed them away from him and then pulled them back again. 'It's a bit awkward,' he said. 'If the man can't see for himself that it's undesirable, it's a difficult thing to put to him.'

'But it'd be intolerable. Damn it, Walter treats the rest of the board as though they were messenger boys *now*. If he once got control, life wouldn't be worth living.' Talbot-Rees shook his head. 'No, Henry, you and North must just be firm. It's essential.'

Spellman's chair creaked as he wriggled irritably. 'It's all very well to say that, but what exactly can I do? He puts up a bid for the shares at independent valuation and asks for a first refusal. . . .'

'He's got no right to a first refusal.'

'All right. We find somebody else who'll put in a bid and Walter promptly outbids him—which he probably would, being Walter. What justification have I got for refusing to sell to him as the highest bidder?'

'Simply that you don't think it's a good thing, or in the interests of the business, or in line with what Gustavus had in mind.'

'It'd mean a hell of a row.'

'All right, then there'd have to *be* a hell of a row. . . .'

In the corridor outside, Talbot-Rees met North and said: 'Hallo, North,' almost affectionately. He went on along the corridor to his own office and sat at his desk for a few moments in thought. Then he reached for the telephone and dialled Lang. He said: 'Walter? This is Jim. Amy and I were saying this morning that it's high time you came to dinner. We never seem to see you nowadays. How about coming out one day next week and having a quiet meal? And bring that charming daughter of yours, eh . . .?' Twenty-eight years ago he had begun his career in an insurance office.

In Spellman's office, North rubbed the side of his nose and said: 'I don't want to betray any confidence, Mr. Spellman, but we all know that Mr. Walter's a very

impetuous man, and I think I ought to warn you that
what he said—well, it was practically a *threat*. Naturally,
I offered no opinion, but I made it clear that there was
no question of my seeking to—to sway your judgment . . .'

'God, these chaps who like power . . .!' said old
Henry wearily. 'Why can't the man read his Lord
Acton?'

*   *   *   *   *

Humphrey Peart's studio was not large, but there were
at least fifty people in it and it was stiflingly hot. Peart
was wearing a brown Harris tweed suit, with a hard wing
collar, and his tie threaded through a large amethyst ring.
He was slightly drunk. He shook hands with George
Martin enthusiastically and said : 'Ah, the missing Horseman. Why d'you want to bring this fellow Lawrence
here, Horseman? He only makes love to my wife.'

Lawrence said : 'That's exactly what I've come for.
Where is she?' He saw Moira in the distance, fought
his way across to her, and kissed her firmly.

'There you are,' said Humphrey Peart. 'And so it
goes on. Here's your drink. You're not *really* Horseman
are you?'

Martin said : 'No. I'm George Martin.'

'Of course you are. Lawrence said so. Horseman
died of drink, didn't he?'

'The one that was in the firm? Yes.'

'Well, I'll tell you what,' said Peart. 'Go thou and
do likewise.' Somebody grabbed him by the arm and
he drifted into the ruck.

George Martin sipped his drink. It consisted almost
entirely of acid water with a very faint flavour of gin.
A girl not more than five feet high with long dark red
hair, dressed in slacks and a sweater, came up to him
and said very politely : 'I take it that you will be somebody's uncle?'

George Martin smiled and said : 'No. I'm not anybody's uncle. Why?'

'You look like somebody's uncle. An uncle of the
best type.'

He said : 'I'm several people's grandfather.'

The red-haired girl said: 'Are you really? What a terrific thrill. Tell me about it?'

He thought she was laughing at him, but she wasn't. She said: 'How many grandchildren have you got?'

'Three. Two boys and a girl. The girl's about the same age as you.'

'As *me* . . . ?' She grinned at him. 'And how old's that?'

'She's nearly nineteen.'

'Bless your sweet heart,' said the red-haired girl, 'I'm thirty-two. What's that drink you've got there? Is it one of the ones Humphrey . . . ?' She seized it and tasted it, leaving an arc of scarlet lipstick on the rim. 'Yes. It is. You can't drink that muck. I'll go and get you a proper one.'

Lawrence was saying: 'Whenever it becomes necessary to go out into the kitchen to get more drinks, I should be obliged if you'll let me know.'

Moira said: 'It won't *be* necessary. As soon as I knew you were coming I brought all the drinks in here.'

'But it will be necessary to go and get ice, darling.'

'No, Lawrence. No kitchen to-night.'

'Then I shall be forced just to kiss you here before the gaping public.'

Moira said: 'No—listen—the old Hump is slightly on his ear about it, so don't play the fool.'

Lawrence said: 'If you ask me the old Hump is tight.'

'That's all the more reason why he might get nasty.'

Lawrence said: 'I know a place where there's a level crossing and a notice that says "Beware of Hump". Can I have another drink? This is a very poor party from the drinks angle.'

The alert-looking young man with very large ears said: 'But you'll agree that the whole position of management is changing? With materials controlled both in price and quantity, a seller's market, and full employment, management becomes purely a matter of *leadership*—of dealing with people rather than things.'

George Martin said: 'Yes.'

'The understanding of the human factor—of what one might call the anthropology of industrial life, if you follow me . . .' The young man shook his head. The vast ears quivered slightly. 'I find the whole thing so fascinating,' he said. 'So very fascinating.'

'You're in business?' said Martin.

'Not actually. I'm with the Institute for the Study of Strategic Management Problems. I went there straight from Oxford.'

Martin said: 'It must be very interesting work.'

'It gives you an overall view of the thing that practically nobody else gets. These people here . . .' the young man waved a hand at the room. 'It's startling to think that they barely realise that Industry exists. No idea of the problems . . .'

The red-haired girl came back and said: 'Try this, uncle. It tastes more like a drink and less like washing-up water.'

'Take her,' said the young man, pointing to the red-haired girl. 'What does she know of a factory girl's life?'

'Have you ever worked a centre lathe?' said the red-haired girl briskly.

'I haven't actually worked one, but . . .'

'Well, I have. For three years.'

Martin said: 'Have you really?'

'Sure. During the war. Why? Does it mean anything to you?'

'I have to look after a machine shop.'

'There you are,' said the red-haired girl. 'I knew we'd got a lot in common. Come and sit down and tell me about it.'

The young man with the large ears had drifted away looking hurt. The red-haired girl led Martin across to a window seat on which two young men were seated. She said: 'Move over, louts. This is my uncle. He's got a machine shop. Roy Plumett and Herbert. One of them writes and the other's a hanger-on in Wardour Street, but I can't remember which is which.'

Herbert said: 'You're not in this awful film racket, sir?'

'No,' said Martin, smiling, 'nothing as exciting as that.'

Herbert said : 'Exciting.'

Roy Plumett said : 'I don't want to tell tales out of school, sir, but there are one or two things about your niece that I feel it my duty to tell you.'

At about ten o'clock Martin worked his way across to Humphrey Peart and said gently : 'I'm sorry to bother you, but I think perhaps I ought to find Mr. Lawrence and . . .'

'What's that, old man,' said Humphrey, seizing him by the arm and swaying a little. 'Lawrence? Sure. He's about. Outside. Somewhere outside. He's about there somewhere.'

There were two doors in the corridor outside. Both were closed. Martin tried the first one and went into the kitchen. It contained Lawrence and Moira Peart. They were kissing one another very vigorously and did not notice him. Martin withdrew.

When he got back to the studio the party was showing signs of thinning. The red-haired girl was going off with a very tall man to whom she had not spoken during the evening, but who now appeared to be her husband. She called good night to Martin. Lawrence came back into the room. There was a smear of lipstick on his collar. Martin went across to him and said : 'Don't you think perhaps we'd better be going?'

'What for?' said Lawrence glassily.

'It's getting fairly late.'

Lawrence said : 'You've no capacity for enjoying yourself, George. No capacity for enjoying yourself. That's your trouble. That's Walter's trouble. All of you.'

Martin said : 'Not at all. I've enjoyed myself very much. But it's getting on towards my bedtime and . . .'

Lawrence sighed. 'All right,' he said. 'You go, George. I shall stay on for a bit, but don't let me keep you. Between ourselves the whole thing's a bloody bore, isn't it?'

'I thought it was very interesting. Some very nice people.'

'All right. You go, George. Don't worry about saying good-bye. Hump's as tight as a coot, anyhow. So's she if it comes to that. I'll be seeing you.'

Martin had only had two drinks, but they had made him wakeful. It was half-past ten when he reached the hotel but he did not feel at all sleepy. The hotel lounge was empty and rather cold, so he went up to his room, put on the slot-meter electric fire and undressed. It was really surprising that the little red-haired girl was thirty-two, though when you came to look at her closely you could see that her skin wasn't a girl's skin, and she was thickening slightly under the chin. He was a little worried about Lawrence, but it was probably best just to come away and leave him.

His brief-case was lying on a chair. Martin opened it, got out his file, took his pen out of his jacket, and settled down in the small fire-side chair.

*   *   *   *   *

The appointment with Mr. Falk was at ten-thirty. Martin had been sitting in the lounge for nearly an hour when Lawrence appeared. Martin said : 'You got back all right, then ?'

Lawrence said : 'Oh Lord, yes. I wasn't even late.'

'I was sorry to come away but . . .'

'Not a bit. You didn't miss anything. That ass Humphrey got frightfully drunk and started to be very offensive to everybody, so the party broke up.' Lawrence's hands shook a little when he lit a cigarette, and occasionally he closed his eyes for a moment, but otherwise he seemed normal.

Martin said : 'Have you had breakfast ?'

'I never have anything but coffee.' Lawrence glanced at his watch. 'I suppose we ought to go.'

Martin said : 'Do we know what we're going to say to this chap ?'

'It rather depends what he says to us,' said Lawrence with a shrug. 'Can he let us have any steel ? If so, what, how much, and when? That's all it really amounts to, doesn't it?'

Mr. Falk's office was panelled in walnut and his chairs were upholstered in green leather. His windows, high up in the big building, looked out on the river from two angles. Mr. Falk himself was a hunch-back, and when he sat in the big arm chair, the top of the back of it was above his head. It was not clear whether he was angry about this interview or merely angry all the time.

Falk said: 'So there it is, gentlemen. It's no easier for me than it is for you. You want steel—I want steel. Everybody wants steel.' He huddled back in the chair and gazed sulkily out of the window.

Lawrence closed his eyes tightly for a moment and then opened them and said: 'Of course, we fully realise the difficulties. But Sir Francis did rather suggest . . .'

'It's all very well for Sir Francis,' said Falk irritably. 'But where am I supposed to get the stuff? I don't make steel. I only buy it. And if anybody'll tell me where to buy any more, I'll be obliged.'

Martin smiled and said: 'Of course, by your standards, the quantities we're talking about would be very small.'

'I dare say. But it's all extra, isn't it?' Mr. Falk suddenly whipped round and stared at Lawrence with apparent dislike. 'And what's more,' he said, 'I tell you gentlemen frankly, I don't see why we *should* do this.'

'Nor do I,' said Lawrence with a grin. 'I never have.'

'Oh,' said Falk rather blankly.

There was a moment's pause. Martin began: 'It may be . . .'

'I suppose the truth of it is,' said Falk bitterly, 'that somebody took Francis out and gave him a decent bottle of wine and a good meal and after that he'd offer anything.'

'And a rather good glass of brandy,' said Lawrence. 'I was there.'

'Oh, were you?' said Falk. He stared at Lawrence for a moment, and then suddenly smiled rather grimly. 'Ah well, then we know where we are.' He thought for a moment and then frowned and shook his large head.

'You see the trouble is, gentlemen, even if I could find
you a ton or two just to carry you on, I couldn't guarantee
to do it again. In a month's time I may be better off.
I may be worse. I just don't know.'

'But even that ton or two would make all the difference
to us,' said Martin quickly. 'We only need about three
tons a month at our present output. You see we use steel
only in the carriage of the thing. Most of it is brass.'

'Three tons a month,' said Mr. Falk reflectively.
'Well of course that isn't anything much. Mostly rod,
eh?'

'Rod and angle.'

There was a long silence. Falk picked up the letter
from his desk, looked at it and sighed. 'Well, gentlemen,
Sir Francis seems to have liked your brandy, and he's
the boss, so I suppose it's up to me to help you *somehow*. . . .' He gazed out of the window for a while in
silence. 'I tell you what I'll do,' he said at last, not
looking at them. 'I'll find you three tons from somewhere.
God knows where, but I'll find it. That's a month's supply.
Meanwhile, I'll look round and see if I can possibly con-
tinue that month by month. But . . .' his eyes came
round to them, flickering from one to the other, '*but*—
after the first month it's got to be understood that there's
no promise. I'll do my best but I can't guarantee it.
That's the most I can do, and if it's any good to you,
you're welcome. Otherwise . . .'

Martin said: 'It'd certainly be most helpful.'

Lawrence hesitated for a fraction of a second and said:
'It would indeed.' He looked at his cigarette end. 'And
you think there's a reasonable chance of being able to
go on?'

'A reasonable chance but no promise.'

'And how should we know if you could go on?'

Falk spread out his hands. 'You'll simply have to
write to me or come and see me and find out. I'm sorry,
but there's nothing else for it.'

*   *   *   *   *

'Three tons?' said Lang. 'That's a fat lot of use,
isn't it?'

Lawrence said: 'It's just three tons better than nothing.'

'And no promise that it'll go on?'

'No. It's a month's supply . . .'

'Oh, bunkum! It's a month's supply on what we're producing now, but it wouldn't be a week's supply if we gave the sales people their head. Surely if he was going to give us anything, you could have got a bit more than that out of him? After all, it means nothing to them.' He shook his head. 'I wish to God I'd gone myself.'

'I share your regret,' said Lawrence carefully.

Martin said: 'Well, Mr. Walter, there was a time when I thought we weren't going to get anything at all.'

Lang turned to him. 'It really *was* sticky, eh?' he said as though to confirm, from a reliable source, an otherwise improbable story.

'It was. I thought Mr. Lawrence did very well to get anything.'

'Yes,' said Lang without enthusiasm. He shrugged. 'Well—there it is. We shall have to limp along as best we can.'

'Personally,' said Lawrence, lighting a cigarette, 'personally I was never afraid that we weren't going to get anything. What worries me is something quite different.'

'What?'

'I don't like the fact that our production, month by month, will be dependent on them.'

Lang said: 'Nobody likes it. But . . .'

'I don't think you quite get what I mean, Walter. What I don't see is why Proudfoot ever did this in the first place; and why, when he had, it amounts to three-tons-and-more-if-we're-good. You can't get things out of a man like Proudfoot by giving him a meal. And if he really wanted to help us, Falk could certainly have given us twenty tons in one go and left it at that.'

Martin said: 'Perhaps Proudfoot wanted to help and Falk didn't.'·

Lawrence smiled slightly. 'I'll bet you that Falk had instructions in detail as to exactly what he was to do. Proudfoot's like that.'

Lang was staring at Lawrence unblinkingly. 'You think they want us on the end of a string?'

'I think it looks like it.'

'What good does that do them?'

Lawrence spread out his hands. 'I don't know, Walter. I only think it needs watching.'

There was a pause. Lang continued to stare blankly and silently at Lawrence for some seconds. Then he gave a slight grunt and turned away. To him, the value of any idea was always closely connected with who produced it.

Lang said to Martin: 'Well, just to add to it, while you've been away Barker's been in, and he says the new sprayer nozzles are playing up.'

Martin shook his head and said: 'I was afraid of that, Mr. Walter. You remember I told you . . .'

'Yes, I do,' said Lang with a grim smile. 'You told me that I couldn't afford the hand-made ones and that the machine-made ones probably wouldn't work. Well it seems they don't. So I've told them to go back to hand-made.'

Martin said: 'You know what it does to your cost sheet?'

'Yes. It means that there never was any margin worth having, and now there's even less.'

'I shouldn't be surprised if there's a nett loss, Mr. Walter. There's a difference of near ten pounds . . .'

'All right, George—there may be. But what the hell's the use of selling a job that isn't right. You can't build a business on that, can you?'

'Well of course I agree with that,' said Martin. But what're we going to do then, Mr. Walter? Put the price up?'

'No. We're going to get the production cost down without lowering quality.' Lang suddenly gave a loud chuckle. 'Don't look at me like that, you old misery. Go and talk to Barker about it. I've told him and Englefield about six ways of doing it. They say they're all quite impossible and I've told them to go away and do it. Come on now. . . .' Lang flung out a hand towards Lawrence in high good humour. 'Here's

Lawrence who's got you the steel you've been moaning about. You want it all done *for* you, George.'

As they walked down the corridor, Lawrence said: 'I take it that this is now one of three jobs where we only have to sell enough to land in the bankruptcy court?'

Martin said: 'Oh, I expect we shall manage something.'

'Well, if you can get production cost down as soon as Walter tells you to, why didn't you get it down before?'

Martin hesitated for a moment and frowned. 'You don't understand about Mr. Walter,' he said slowly.

'No,' said Lawrence. 'That's quite right. I don't understand about Mr. Walter.'

Martin shook his head. 'I always like to hear him laugh like that,' he said with a smile. 'Sort of chuckle he's got. I always like to hear him do that when he's on to something tough. It always means trouble for me, but I like that.'

D

VII

HE could have rung up to make sure she was coming, but he wasn't going to run about after any little bitch, and certainly not Lang's daughter. In fact, on Thursday morning he had practically decided not to go to Phillip's corner at all, and then if she did come she would just find herself stood up, which would teach her not to try to keep chaps guessing. But by Thursday evening there wasn't anything else to do, and he decided to go to the dirt-track anyhow. He would have to go by Phillip's corner, and he would just look to see if she happened to be there at seven, but if she wasn't, no waiting about or anything like that.

It hadn't occurred to him that she might come in a car, and when he saw the little Morris across the road and somebody waving a hand to him, he was puzzled for a moment, because apart from anything else she had a hat on and looked quite different. He went across and she smiled at him and said: 'Hallo.'

Jack said: 'I didn't know whether you were coming. I nearly didn't come myself. You'd have looked fine then, wouldn't you?'

She said: 'Why did you think I wasn't?'

'Well, you cut off so sharp on the telephone without saying. How was I to know?'

'Somebody came in and I had to stop. But you'd said here at seven.'

He tapped the running board of the car with his toe and said: 'What d'you want to bring this thing for? We don't need it.'

'Well, I'd got to get here and back, hadn't I?'

He said: 'I suppose you don't go in buses.'

'You try to get from home to here in a bus,' she said calmly. 'You'd better get in, hadn't you? I'm not supposed to park here.'

He hesitated for a moment and then went round to

the other side and got in beside her. The little car was
very shiny and new. He said : 'This your own ?'

'Not really. But Daddy's always using the other, so
I use this. Which way are we going ?'

'Straight across along Leeds Street and out on the
Coventry road,' he said reluctantly.

She drove well for a kid, whipping the little car in
and out of traffic as though she was used to driving a lot.
Several times they were stopped at traffic lights, and he
was afraid someone he knew might come along and see
him being driven in a car by Lang's daughter. He would
never live that down if they did. He said : 'I reckon
you'd catch it if anyone was to see you out with me.'

Rosamund smiled without taking her eyes off the
traffic. 'I expect so,' she said. 'But that's half the fun.'

'Oh, is it ?' he said almost angrily. 'Just a bit of fun
you're having, eh ?'

Rosamund said : 'Anyhow, I've always wanted to see
dirt-track racing.'

She had never seen it before, and when they had never
seen it before it always got them. It was why he had
brought her. He was used to it, and nowadays it was
only the first heat that got him—that first moment when
the lights in the stand go out and only the track is lit,
and engines go up to a roar and the four men go hurtling
into the first bend with the cinders flying and the roar
going echoing away round the track. He had meant to
watch her, but it was a close race, and on the last bend
someone went hard into the retaining fence and took what
looked like a fourpenny one, and he never even remembered that she was there. It wasn't until the third race
that he had time to sit back and look her over. She was
staring at the track, leaning forward. Her eyes were
shining and her lips were a bit apart, and she was pulling
at her handkerchief with both hands. It always got them.
And particularly when it looked like as though someone
was going to break his bloody neck. That was what they
liked. She wasn't as pretty with a hat on—at least not
that hat, which was just a silly bit of velvet that came

down to a point over her forehead. And she certainly didn't look as hot a bit in the blue coat as she had in the yellow dress. But she was all right. There was no doubt about that.

When the first interval came he said: 'Come on,' and led the way up the steps to the bar at the back of the stand. Jack said: 'What'll you have?'

She hesitated and said: 'Do they have sherry?'

'I should think so,' he said, and went and fought his way through the mob and came back with a dubious looking dark brown stuff and a Pale Ale. He jerked his head towards the track and said: 'Well, d'you like it?'

'It's terrifically exciting. I don't see how they get round the corners.'

'The chap puts his left foot down, see, and lays her over and gives her the gun, and that puts him into a slide and he steers into it.' He sipped his beer. 'Not as good as dancing though, eh?' he said with a grin.

Rosamund said: 'Well, of course I don't dance really well enough to get all the fun out of it.'

'You dance all right. Anyhow, it's not as good as that dance you and me had the other night?'

The big grey eyes flickered up for a moment to meet his grin, and then looked away. To his delight she went rather pink.

He said: 'Oh, you can blush, can you?'

'Blush?' said Rosamund, looking puzzled. 'Of course I can blush. Why?'

'Never seen you do it before.'

'Am I doing it now?' she said calmly. 'I don't feel it.'

Someone said: 'Hallo, Jack,' and he turned sharply. But it wasn't anybody from Lang's nor even anybody whose name he could remember. He said: 'Hallo,' and raised a casual hand, and saw the quick glance at Rosamund as the man passed on into the crowd. She said: 'Hadn't we better get back to our seats? They're coming out.'

Dirt-track was all right, and it always got them, but there wasn't much you could do about it while you were there. He put out his hand and took hers, and when he did that she didn't look at him, but looked down at their two hands and gave a little laugh to herself as though she thought something was funny. But she didn't try to take her hand away, and let him take the glove off it and fool around with her fingers. Her hands were soft and smooth, not like Hilda's. But that was because Hilda had to work and she didn't have to, but only had to drive a car around and be Lang's daughter. She wouldn't have another drink, which was all right because the stuff she had cost two bob a go, and anyhow he didn't hold with girls drinking, and certainly not kids like that. She wouldn't smoke either, though when he asked her she said she did sometimes but not much. The trouble about dirt-track was that towards the end you always got tired of it, with nearly every heat being settled at the first corner and hardly ever any overtaking after. But she went on staring at it like that to the end and once she dug her nails into his hand when there was something exciting.

It was a bad car-park with narrow gates and it took a long time to get out. Rosamund said: 'I'd better drop you first. Where's the best place for you?'

He said: 'No—I'll come out with you to your place.'

'But then you'll have to get right in again and it takes hours at this time of night.'

He said: 'That's my worry. I'm a big boy now. I don't have to be taken home.'

They didn't say much driving back into town, except about the racing, and she said she'd enjoyed it and thanked him for taking her. But when they got into town she tried again and pulled up at Phillip's corner and said: 'Look, let me drop you here. It's silly for you to come all out there and then have to come back.'

He said: 'Why should you worry?'

'Well, there's no sense in it.'

He said: 'Afraid I shall ask myself in or something?'

'Of course not,' said Rosamund in a low voice.

'O.K. Then carry on.'

She had always known that this was the bit that might be difficult, but she had gambled on the fact that he would get out in the town, and now the town was behind them and it was going to be difficult, and she desperately didn't want it to be, because she felt sick. Not the same sort of sick that she had felt at the party, but a sick desire not to be touched—to be home and safe by herself. She hadn't liked him much the first time, but all the same she had been terrified that the band would stop. But this was quite different and he was just a big, rather common young man who spoke rudely and grinned at her, but not in a friendly way. She didn't know what he would expect now, or what one did about it, but she knew she didn't want to be touched, and if you didn't want to be touched then you wouldn't let people touch you if you were a decent person, because otherwise it wasn't fair.

They were outside the town now and off the main road. The lights were poor, and she had to use her headlamps. Rosamund said rather unsteadily: 'I have to turn down to the left about two hundred yards on. It's a private road. I'd better drop you on the corner.'

'All right,' he said briefly. 'Pull in here.'

She went on as near to the corner as she dared and stopped. He leaned forward and switched the head-lights off, and as he did so she opened the door on the driver's side and got out and stood beside the car. There was a moment's pause. He said: 'What you getting out for?'

For the life of her she couldn't think of an answer. She said: 'I . . .' and stopped.

'Get in again,' his voice said with quiet anger. 'And shut that door.'

'No,' she said. 'No. I'd rather not. I'm sorry. But . . .'

She could only see his face as a white glimmer in the light from the dash-board. 'Well,' he said quietly, 'you're a nice young lady. With real nice manners. What d'you think anybody's going to do to you?'

Rosamund said: 'It's not that . . .'

'If it isn't that then get back in, and I'll get out.' He said it with all the bitterness of disappointment turned to injury—of one deeply wronged. He said: 'You're treating me as though I was . . .' his voice choked in anger. 'You get back in here and I'll show you,' he said hoarsely. 'And it won't be what you think. Call yourself a lady and treating me as though I was dirt just because I work in a factory.'

Rosamund said in horror : 'It's not that at all. Of course it isn't . . .'

'Oh yes, it is. I watched you all the evening. You think I don't know how to behave because . . .'

She said : 'That's absolutely untrue. I haven't done anything—and I haven't even thought of it.'

'Then what d'you get out for ?'

She hesitated for a moment and then on a sudden impulse got quickly back into the car and shut the door with a bang. 'There,' she said defiantly. 'Now do you believe me ?'

There was a long silence. Jack was staring sullenly at the road ahead. Then he said in a slow crescendo of anger : 'You think you're so much that a chap can't keep his hands off you.'

'I *don't*,' she said in childish indignation.

'Yes you do. But of course, being Walter Lang's daughter with a car and all of it, you don't want to get yourself dirty touching a chap that works in a factory.' He whipped round suddenly so that his face was close to hers. 'Well, I'll tell you something. I wouldn't touch you if you were the last girl alive. I don't let anybody treat me like dirt.' He turned away, fumbled for a moment with the door catch, scrambled out and started to walk back the way they had come with head held high.

Rosamund hesitated for a moment and then called : 'That's the wrong way. It's much quicker for the buses if you go on . . .' But she was in the car and he was already twenty yards away, and if he heard her he did not look back.

Often when she came in after the pictures Lang would be reading or working and would hardly notice, but this evening he came out into the hall as soon as he heard the front door close.

He said : 'Hallo, darling. Where've you been ?'

Rosamund said: 'To the Odeon. I told you I was going.'

Lang nodded and glanced at his watch. 'Bit late, isn't it?' he said mildly.

'Only ten to eleven. It never finishes till half-past ten.'

'Couldn't you go earlier, Roz?'

This was new, and in the circumstances disconcerting. She said: 'But that means going at about half-past five, or else going in in the middle.'

'It's just that I don't much like your driving back at night.'

'Oh come, darling,' she said lightly. 'It's a bit hard if a girl can't even go to the pictures.' She grinned at him: 'You'd better take to coming with me. Be good for you.' Lang's hatred of films was a family joke.

He smiled the smile that he kept for her and George Martin and for nobody else, and moved as though to shepherd her into the drawing-room. But that was too much. Rosamund said: 'I think I shall go straight to bed. I'm a bit tired.'

He said: 'All right, darling,' and kissed her. But he looked a trifle disappointed, and she saw it and hated herself. Lang said: 'There was just one thing, Roz—I've got Sir Francis Proudfoot and another chap coming round the works on Monday, and I'd like to bring them back to dinner. Could you tell Mrs. Dart? That'll mean four of us.'

'Four counting me?'

'Yes.'

'You're *sure* it's only four this time?' Last time it had ended most disastrously as six—not counting her.

'Yes, of course,' said Lang rather impatiently. He had a short memory for his own mistakes.

'All right,' said Rosamund. 'I'll fix it. Good night, darling.'

Rosamund shut her bedroom door and heaved a sigh of relief. But it was a rather intentional sigh. She had wanted to be home and alone, and as she had driven the last two hundred yards and put the car away it had become a crying need. She could have rushed upstairs then, and slammed her door, and thrown herself on the bed and . . . and so on. But now, because Lang had come out into the hall, even a sigh of relief was something of an effort. A few lies to Daddy, she reflected with fine cynicism, could make everything ordinary. But even if you couldn't very well throw yourself on the bed in cold blood, you could reflect bitterly that you were a silly little fool and no good to anybody. He had been hurt—really hurt, and what he had said had been quite true. It was unpardonable to go out with him and then panic in that absurd way when he wasn't doing anything and hadn't intended to. And the awful part was that there *was* something in what he said about being 'a chap who worked in a factory.' Not in the horrible snob way, of course, but because you didn't know what . . . well, what to expect, or what was expected of you. After all, there were a number of possibilities. . . . After a while Rosamund roused herself with a jerk, undressed rather hurriedly and went and cleaned her teeth. It was bad enough to have made a fool of yourself and been hurtful and silly, but then to go home and start thinking things like that was just plain awful. She looked at her reflection and said : 'The trouble with you is that you're not a lady *either* way.' Her reflection seemed curiously unabashed and even grinned slightly.

Lang did not particularly want Henry Spellman to walk round the factory with them, but since Spellman knew Proudfoot and wanted to come, there was nothing to do about it. In fact it worked out quite well, since Sir Francis, who obviously knew nothing about the practical side of factories, could walk with old Henry, who didn't either, while Lang talked to Winter. Winter was a big dark man of about forty-five, who was introduced rather vaguely by Sir Francis as 'My collaborator in these things.' Whether he was a personal assistant, or a director of Richmond Glenn or what, was never clear. He had very thick black eyebrows and a flat nose like a prize-fighter's, and when he smiled, which was very seldom, he simply showed his teeth without anything happening to the rest of the face. He gave an odd impression of being somebody else in disguise, and later on Rosamund, who went to the cinema more than Lang, assumed without hesitation that he was Sir Francis's bodyguard. But whatever Winter was, he certainly knew about workshop practice, and long after Sir Francis and old Henry had tired of it and gone back to the offices, he walked about the press-shop and the foundry watching, and occasionally asking Lang and George Martin detailed questions about outputs or plant. He very seldom made any comment on the answers, or on anything else, except to show his teeth when Lang pointed out the horrors of the layout of the paint spraying, and to say 'Very nice job' when they finally left the press-shop.

Rather to Lang's regret, Winter did not show much interest in the assembly shop, dismissing it with 'Not much in my line.' But what *was* in his line he knew with a certainty and keenness that warmed Lang's heart. 'God, George,' he said to Martin, 'what a joy it is to take somebody round who knows what he's talking about, and wants to know the back-end of everything.'

'He certainly does that,' said Martin drily. 'How much of the back-end d'you want him to know?'

'How d'you mean?'

'Well, he's asking me if he can see some of our costings. Wants to know how we allocate overheads on press work.'

Lang said: 'I don't suppose he wants to see actual figures. There's no reason why we shouldn't show him the methods we use. Nothing new about them.'

'And if he *does* want to see actual figures?'

'Well, it doesn't matter much, does it? We're not in direct competition with any of their outfits. After all, George, they're helping us out. And they're very useful people to be on good terms with.'

'Then I'm to show him everything he wants to see?'

'I should think so. Within reason. Why? What's the matter, George? Don't you take to him?'

Martin said: 'Oh—he's all right. You know he was putting a stop-watch on some of those jobs in the press-shop? Had it in his pocket.'

Lang chuckled. 'Was he really? He's a keen member all right. Well, I hope he liked what he got.'

* * * * *

Mrs. Dart was one of those cooks who don't know their own strength. After thirty years at the job, she could cook an ordinary family meal comparatively calmly. But anything beyond a family meal was a Dinner Party, and a Dinner Party threw her into wild agitation and deep pessimism. In fact, nothing disastrous ever *did* happen. The food was always well-cooked, if not very imaginative. But Rosamund had to spend most of the day reassuring her, and explaining that as dinner wasn't wanted till eight, there was no need to start roasting the chicken immediately after tea.

As soon as they came, Rosamund knew that Sir Francis was going to be easy. The trouble with most elderly men was that they either decided that you were a child, and called you 'little lady,' or else that you were a full-blown hostess, and kept jumping up all the time when you were pottering about and getting cork-screws and things. But Sir Francis at once treated her as an adult, and realised that you had to pop about and do things; and he had one daughter of nineteen and one of twenty-one and who sounded quite possible human beings, which people's daughters seldom did. The man who looked like a body-guard hardly seemed to notice that she existed, and just talked to Daddy all the time. About a quarter to eight Rosamund went out to the kitchen. Mrs. Dart was rushing about, white-faced, uttering little moans, and handing things to Dart and then snatching them away again. But apart from the fact that she had forgotten to boil the onion for the bread sauce, everything seemed to be all right, and the table looked rather nice.

Dinner wasn't too bad, though it was always a mistake to let Dart serve, because he had a way of creeping up behind people and then shoving things suddenly over their shoulders in a most startling way. Once when he had done it to old Miss Spellman she had let out a loud scream and turned round and said: 'Gracious heavens,

my good man, how you frightened me!' Apart from
that, and the fact that Lang was so preoccupied with
Winter that he forgot to give her any stuffing, it wasn't
too bad. But four people at the big table were rather a
long way apart, and though Sir Francis was nice and
talked to her quite a lot, there were times when he was
talking with the others, and one felt rather silly and un-
necessary. They were deeply in it when the end of the
meal came, which was rather awkward, because she
couldn't very well just get up and go without their
noticing, and she couldn't catch Lang's eye. But she
managed to catch Sir Francis's, and he saw at once and
rose as she did, and trotted across to open the door for her
very nicely. Lang and Winter got up when they realised
what was happening and stopped for a moment, and
Lang smiled at her.

Out in the kitchen, Mrs. Dart was washing up, quite
calm and happy now it was all over. Rosamund said
the dinner had been nicer than it had been, and told her
about coffee, and then went back to the drawing-room
and sat and looked at the fire.

Sir Francis said: 'It must have been a great loss to
you, not only personally, but from a business point of
view. I only met your brother a couple of times, but I've
heard him speak at conventions and so on, and he seemed
to me a very fine type of man.'

Lang said: 'Of course he hadn't been so active since
the war, but . . .'

'Oh, quite. But the very presence of a man like that
has an effect on a business, you know.' He sipped his
port, glanced at it rather sharply and put it down. 'I
assume you take over the Chairmanship?'

'No. Henry Spellman will do it for a year or
two.'

'Oh, really? Henry? He didn't tell me.'

Lang said: 'I'm not much good at a lot of the stuff
the Chairman has to do—Works Councils and so on. I
like the practical side of the job.' He smiled at Winter,
who nodded and bared his teeth.

Sir Francis sighed. 'And now,' he said, 'I suppose

you'll be up against this iniquitous taxation that's ruining every fine old family business in the country.'

Lang said : 'You mean death duties and so on? Yes, of course there's all that. Luckily Henry's the executor, not I, so it's his headache.'

'But presumably he'll have to market a substantial block of shares?'

'Oh yes. Under the terms of the will they'll have to sell the lot.'

There was a moment's silence. 'Well, well,' said Sir Francis gently. 'I don't suppose there'll be much difficulty in disposing of them.'

Lang looked up sharply, but Sir Francis was carefully piercing a cigar with a gold implement.

'Oh, they'll be placed privately,' Lang said shortly. 'They won't go outside the family.'

'Which of course only postpones the problem, unfortunately.' Sir Francis shook his head. 'In twenty years' time,' he said regretfully, 'there won't be a genuine family business left.' He applied a match to his cigar. 'What a charming young woman your daughter is.'

'Roz? Yes. She's a nice kid.'

'Any others?'

'No. She's the only one.'

'I asked,' said Sir Francis gently, 'because I wondered whether there was a next generation to take over the business. Of course, Henry has a son. . . .'

'Oh, young Lawrence. . . .' Lang shrugged his shoulders.

'Not very interested I should guess?'

Lang smiled. 'Lawrence was a damned good fighting soldier in the war. Let's leave it at that.'

She had been sitting there for quite half an hour looking at *Picture Post* when the telephone rang.

He said : 'I want to see you.' His voice sounded very close.

She said : 'Oh . . . hallo.'

'I want to see you. I got something I want to say.'

She hesitated and then said : 'All right . . . When?'

'Now. I'm in a box just outside. If you came out to the gate it wouldn't take a minute.'

She was startled and said: 'But I can't. There are people here. I can't come out now. . . .'

'It won't take a minute. I came out specially.'

'But I tell you I *can't*. I can't go away and leave them. . . .'

'Well, later on then? After they've gone?'

'They won't go till late.'

'Well, you can go away for just a minute, can't you?'

She glanced at her watch. It was quarter-past nine. They might come out of the drawing-room at any time now, or they might be another half hour.

'Half a mo' while I think,' she said desperately. She took the receiver away from her ear and looked quickly round the hall. She could hear something that he was saying crackling in the receiver. It was no good. She couldn't risk it. But once they had settled down she needn't stay long. . . . She said in a low voice: 'Listen —I can't come now, but if you wait till ten I can slip out for a minute. Is that any good?'

'All right,' he said. 'That's all right. And I'll be outside in the road. Ten. See you then.'

Rosamund said: 'Yes,' rather breathlessly and hung up. She got back to the drawing-room just as the other door opened and they came through. Sir Francis said: 'What—all by yourself? Never mind. It's better than being bored by a lot of shop.'

She went across and rang the bell for coffee and said: 'Oh, I'm used to that. I quite like hearing people talk about business.'

'Extraordinary taste,' said Sir Francis. He glanced across at Lang and Winter. 'Between ourselves,' he said confidentially, 'it bores *me* to tears.'

It was quite all right. By ten o'clock it was perfectly natural for her to say good night and go to bed. She would have done so anyhow. Rosamund closed the drawing-room door behind her, went quietly across the hall to the cloakroom, and slipped on an old raincoat. The only risk was the Darts, and they would be safe now at the other end of the house. She nearly forgot to leave the front door on the latch, which would have been a pretty mess, because she had no keys. To get to the front gate you had to go past the drawing-room window, and she walked on the grass verge so as not to crunch on the gravel. As she passed the window, Lang's voice was raised saying: 'Ah no . . . wait a minute. It's not so easy.'

He had said he would be waiting on the road, but he was standing among the trees inside the gate, and when he moved in the shadow and said: 'Hallo,' it frightened her for a moment.

She said: 'Hallo. I'm not late, am I? I couldn't get away before.'

They were standing three or four feet apart. He looked very big in the dim light that filtered through from the street lamp outside, and she could just see that he was wearing an overcoat and a muffler. He never wore a hat. Rosamund said: 'I can only stay a minute.'

'All right,' he said, and seemed to hesitate. Then he said rather stiffly: 'I wanted to see you to say I didn't ought to have said that and gone off, but I was mad with you. I'm sorry. . . .'

She said: 'It was my fault anyhow. I don't know why I did it. You were quite right. It was rude.'

'Ah well,' he said with more confidence. 'Let's forget it, eh?'

'Yes.'

There was a moment's pause.

'My word,' he said. 'You're right about getting back into town from here. Took me nearly an hour.'

'Well, you went the wrong way,' said Rosamund with a slight giggle. 'I called after you but you didn't take any notice.'

'It's better to go on down the road?'

'Yes. Miles quicker. You get the bus just at the end.'

There was another silence.

'Tell you what,' he said, 'I've been thinking, if you could get your car, we might have gone out to the Palace at Birdwood one night and danced. It's a fine place, and nobody from the works there or anything, see.'

Rosamund said: 'I don't think I could very well be as late as that.'

'No reason why it should be any later than the pictures. Leave any time we like, can't we?'

She said: 'I suppose so.'

They were closer together now. He said in his rough way: 'Well—would you like to come some night?'

'Yes,' she said, without hesitation.

'All right. Friday. Same place. 'Bout seven. Can you do that?'

'I think so. But can I ring you up in case I can't?'

'No,' he said drily. 'You don't have telephones on presses. I'll ring you up and see. How about wearing your yellow frock?'

'I can't do that,' she said hastily. 'Why? Will it matter just coming in ordinary clothes?'

He chuckled quietly. ''Course not. I was only kidding.'

There was a long silence. Rosamund said awkwardly: 'Well—I must be getting back?'

'O.K.,' he said coolly. 'Thanks for coming out. Good night.'

'Good night,' she said, and turned away. She had gone a few steps when he said softly: 'Hey—Rosey.' Nobody had ever called her Rosey before, and he had never called her any name. She paused and turned. He took three quick steps so that he was standing close beside her. She could see the broad grin even in the darkness. He said: 'You were right about getting out of the car when you did. See?'

'But you said afterwards . . .' she began weakly.

'Otherwise do you know what I'd have done to you?'

'You said you wouldn't have . . .'

He said: 'Well, I would've begun like this . . .' and laughed, and his arms were round her and his body was as hard as a rock and her lips were crushed against her own teeth. After a while he loosened his grip and said: 'Friday then?' and she said 'Yes,' breathlessly, and turned and ran up the drive. He called: 'Good night,

Rosey,' after her softly, but she didn't call back or look round, but ran on up to the house.

Sir Francis and Winter left about eleven-thirty. As the car turned out of the drive Sir Francis said: 'Dull, but otherwise satisfactory.' He sighed. '"Il faut souffrir d'être boss."'

Winter switched on his head-lamps and said: 'I thought you were a bit quick with him. He pretty well tumbled to it.'

'I've handled more men like that than you've ever seen,' said Sir Francis contemptuously. 'Your job's to decide if we want it. Are you sure we do?'

'We want the press-shop and we could do with the foundry. You can throw the rest away.'

Sir Francis nodded and they drove on in silence. Just before they reached the hotel Sir Francis said: 'Most extraordinary, people of that type. I can understand most perversions without difficulty. But to marry sheet metal, and form an emotional alliance with a press-shop . . .!'

'He's not bad at all. Bit out of date in places, but . . .'

'It must be the loss of his wife,' said Sir Francis. 'The daughter struck me as having been begotten quite normally.'

VIII

THE P74 assembly was the one everybody hated, because it was a tall thing and you had to stand up to work on it and lean over the conveyor, which made your back ache. After a day on it you felt nearly dead, and they had been on it now for three days. Moreover, Hilda was doing Number Four, and they had never got the team properly balanced, so that Number Four was always hurrying to keep up and people farther on kept grumbling because there were some that just got by without the washers on. Everybody was in a bad temper and even Jean and 'Rene weren't talking. Madge said: 'If I'd known we were going to be on this again, I'd have stayed away. I didn't ought to be doing it with my veins. The way your legs ache.' But the worst part of it was that if you were Number Four you couldn't think about nice things, because sometimes it was one washer and sometimes two, and you had to look at each one and decide which it was, and that meant the time went so slowly. Hilda looked at her watch, and when it said only twelve o'clock she thought it must have stopped, because it had said ten to when she looked before, which was a long time ago. She held it up to her ear but it was going, and doing that she missed one, and 'Rene said: 'What you doing?' crossly.

It was a fortnight now and he hadn't said a word except once when they met in the yard and then he only said: 'Hallo, Hilda,' and went on. Mum had noticed it and said you never go out now in a nasty way, because she had never liked Jack and said he was jumped up and no good. They hadn't had a cross word that she knew of, and last time he had kissed her good night like always, and at the Party he had danced with her but not much, and she would have chosen him in the Ladies' Choice but she was in the cloakroom, and when she came back he was dancing with Miss Lang. But she hadn't chosen anyone else but just sat out, so it couldn't be that. If there was something he might have told her and not just not have spoken. Hilda could feel her eyes beginning to fill with tears so that everything was blurred, and that made her fumble putting the washers on and 'Rene said : 'Oh come on, duck !' crossly.

There was a bit of sun that day and you could sit on the steps of the canteen. Hilda went out and sat right over by the men's entrance so that he was bound to see her when he came out. It would be all right for her to say hallo even if he didn't, because everybody knew about them and that they were walking out or partly. Madge was talking about her leg and how the doctor said she might have to have an elastic stocking, and then she saw him coming out with Ryan and two chaps. Hilda got up quickly so that she was standing and he couldn't help seeing her. They were talking and she thought they were going straight by. But they stopped in the doorway right by her.

Ryan was saying : 'What some of you don't realise is that if I go fuss-arsing about over every little thing like that, people get so they don't want to listen when there *is* something to say.'

One of the chaps said : 'Frane hadn't got no right to call him a bastard.'

''Course he hadn't,' said Ryan irritably, 'but if I go along and make a fuss about a thing like that Walter'll just say : "Oh Christ—what's this—a girls' school ?" And what do I say ?' He threw out a hand towards Jack. 'You got a Works Council, haven't you ? Here's your man. It's just the sort of bloody silly little thing that's there to waste time on. Let Jack here report it, and then there'll be a nice resolution that charge hands mustn't swear or use bad words. Poor old Gus, it would have been just his hammer. He'd have had Miss Bell put up a notice about it. I don't know whether anyone will, now that he's gone. But anyhow, *I* can't be bothered with it. I got something more to do.'

He stumped irritably away. As Jack turned, Hilda said : 'Hallo,' and knew she was blushing.

He said: 'Oh . . . hallo, Hilda. How's tricks?' But he said it casually and not as though he was going to go on and say something else. She had thought of it before-hand and she said all in a rush: 'You know that thing with Virginia Mayo we saw that you liked her in? When she danced? Well, there's another with her in coming.'

He said: 'Is there?'

'Yes. At the Plaza next week.'

He wasn't looking at her. He nodded slowly and took a stub of cigarette out and lit it. 'Ought to see that,' he said. 'Maybe we will some night.' He glanced at her briefly and looked away again. 'Well, I got to go and see Mac. Look after yourself.' He nodded and went back inside the Men's Canteen.

Sometimes when you had tears in your eyes it made the ground seem close, as though you were short. Madge said: 'What you standing up for? Don't you want to rest your legs?'

*   *   *   *   *

Old Henry said: 'From one or two words he's dropped, he's looking for a row. And the easiest way for him to get at me is through you. So just don't give him an opening. See?'

'All right,' said Lawrence wearily. 'But you know what he is.'

'Of course I do. If he gets his knife into anybody they can't do anything right. But it's very important just now that he shouldn't have anything to bite on to.'

'Christ!' said Lawrence with sudden fury. 'One life to live, and half of it gone, and the best I can do is to spend my time sucking up to Walter Lang.' He got up and walked over to the window, with his back to the room.

'Well,' said old Henry drily. 'Any other ideas?'

Lawrence said: 'How the hell have you stuck it all these years? You don't believe in any of it any more than I do. You've sold your life to them, and what have you got out of it?'

'Half a dozen decent pictures,' said Henry with a smile, 'and a lot of amusement.'

'I give you the pictures. What I don't see is the amusement.'

Henry removed his glasses and began to polish them. 'In my day,' he said reflectively, 'we didn't expect as much as people do now. My father and mother would have told you that this world was a vale of tears through which we pass, if we behave suitably, to eternal bliss. You people want the bliss in advance.'

'You don't believe in eternal bliss.'

'No, m'boy. But I don't believe in bliss on earth either.'

'Bliss?' said Lawrence bitterly. 'What the hell do I care about bliss? All I want is to get away from this place and Walter and poor old George Martin and those poor little bitches in the factory. Christ, I've seen and smelt enough dead people without wanting to live with them.'

Old Henry shrugged. 'All right, then. But if you're going away from something, it means you're going towards something else. What are you going towards?'

There was a long silence. Then Lawrence's shoulders drooped suddenly and he turned away from the window. 'God knows,' he said.

'To me,' said Henry, holding up his polished glasses to the light, 'this has always been quite simple. The Lord didn't see fit to make me able to paint, write, compose music, or do anything of that kind. After that, it really didn't matter. I imagine that the problems of creative work are peculiar. But the problems of every other sort of work are always exactly the *same* problems. I was born into a position where I could become what is called an "executive" and not just a pair of hands. And all executive problems are the same. Whether you're in business, or the army, or the civil service or what. They only differ in scale and in the material you reckon in. Most of the problems are produced by the peculiarities of the people one has to work with. And the range of those peculiarities is distressingly narrow when you come down to it.' He shook his head. 'People like Walter Lang are a human phenomenon, my boy. You don't get away from them by just going somewhere else and finding them called George Jones. And if you work in sheet metal or custard powder it doesn't make any difference.'

'What you don't realise,' said Lawrence, 'is that I don't want to work in either.'

'No,' said his father. 'What you want is another nice war. Killing people isn't a very constructive job : but it can be made to seem so. And it's undoubtedly colourful.'

'There's also the possibility of *being* killed, which is important. At least, to me.'

Old Henry shook his head. 'That's why there *are* wars,' he said moodily, 'because so many people—particularly upper class people—have such a much better time in a war than anywhen else in their lives. No man who's really *fought* in a war is much good after. Except to fight in another. The thing has possibilities, good and bad, that make ordinary life dull.'

Lawrence shrugged his shoulders in silence.

'What's worse,' said Henry, 'the fighting soldier's job is a tremendous over-simplification. Once having been allowed to attack his problems in a tank, he has no patience with attacking them in any other way. Take Walter . . .'

'Why should I?' said Lawrence with dreary flippancy. 'I don't want him. You take him.'

'Considered objectively, Walter's quite interesting. In a very mild way, and on a very small scale, he's not unlike some of the things you were *really* against in the war. Obsessional. Highly prejudiced. Very uncertain, and therefore seeking power to reassure himself. . . .'

'Yes—yes,' said Lawrence impatiently, 'but can't you understand that not being a trick cyclist I don't see any fun in playing Jew to a sort of small-town Hitler? It may be very interesting that Walter should be a mass of prejudices, but I happen to be one of them.'

'You give him too many openings.'

'Only because I know that if I don't, he'll make them for himself.' Lawrence crushed out his cigarette. 'Anyhow it isn't only Walter,' he said sombrely. 'The whole place gets on my nerves.'

There was a long silence. Henry said: 'Well, you don't have to stay here, I suppose.'

'Would you mind if I packed it in?'

'Good Heavens no. Your life's your own. It just happens that this was something I could arrange for you, and it seemed the obvious thing. But I'm too old now to think I can arrange somebody else's happiness for them. I begot you, paid for you to be half-instructed, and eventually I shall leave you enough money to keep you safe from the more crudely unpleasant bits of reality. That's the best I can do. Or the worst. The rest is up to you.'

Lawrence said: 'Of course it may be just that I don't like work.'

'Nobody likes work. That's the only definition of work—something that you don't like doing. Only fools work. The rest arrange to be paid for doing something they like. What I don't know is what you *like* doing?'

'Nor do I,' said Lawrence. 'At least, not anything that they'll pay me for.'

'Well, try and think of something,' said old Henry vaguely. 'And remember what I said about Walter.'

As Lawrence got back to his office, Lang came out. He said: 'Oh there you are. I wanted to tell you, I was dining with Proudfoot last night and from the sound of it, it isn't much good relying on them. So you'll have to find some steel somewhere else. How about these bloody stock-holders? Have you been to see them?'

Lawrence said: 'I go to see them about three times a week.'

'Well, you want to keep after them,' said Lang, as though Lawrence had said 'No.' 'You can't do this job sitting in an office.'

He nodded curtly and disappeared down the corridor. Lawrence went into the office and picked up the papers in his IN tray. The top one was a memorandum from Lang which began: 'I dined last night with Proudfoot and from what he said . . .'

Lawrence tore it up slowly, pitched the pieces into the waste-paper basket, and glanced at his watch. It was just half-past five. He put on his coat, put his head into

his secretary's office and said : 'I've gone.' His car was
parked just outside the window of Lang's office. In
starting, he made as much engine noise as possible, to
ensure that Lang looked out of the window and saw him
go. That, he reflected happily, would give Walter
something to bite on. But what of it? Walter would
have made seeing him go at midnight something to bite
on.

Laura was sitting reading a shiny weekly and listening
to the radio. He said : 'Hallo, honey,' and she looked
up and said : 'Hallo.'

She put aside the magazine and said : 'What sort of
a day?'

'Lovely,' said Lawrence.

'You're early.'

'That's why. I've had Papa on the necessity of keeping on good terms with Walter. As if anybody ever has
been or ever could.'

Laura said : 'I think he must have told Rosamund
that she mustn't come here. I've asked her to tea twice
and she seemed very embarrassed and made very feeble
excuses.'

'Quite likely. I gather he's looking for a row with
Papa over Gus's shares.' Lawrence sat down and said :
'I think I shall have to go up to London for a couple of
days again next week, honey.'

Laura raised the green eyes and looked at him.
'Want me to come?' she said expressionlessly.

'Not unless you particularly want to. It'll be very
dull.'

She took a cigarette out of the box and lit it slowly
and with care. 'Lawrence dear,' she said gently, 'there's
a thing I'd better tell you. . . .' The eyes were still
quite impassive. 'If you start playing about with Moira
Peart again—or go on playing about with her, it probably
should be—I shall leave you.'

Lawrence smiled. 'Now why would you do that?'
he said with interest.

'Not because I'm jealous, or because I have any particularly moral feelings about it. I've told you long ago

—I don't care if you must run after other women, as long
as you don't rub my nose in it. . . .'

'Then why?'

'Because it—it's purely destructive. Destructive on
purpose. It's the thing you do, like drinking, sometimes,
just to make everything dirty and broken. And I can't
watch you do that any longer.'

'I see,' said Lawrence.

Laura was gazing into the fire, the dark eyebrows
arched very high. She said: 'It isn't as though Moira
was a new one. You had her before, and then it was
over, and she married Humphrey, who's supposed to be
a friend of yours. They're very fond of each other in
their way. What earthly point is there in messing that
up, when you don't want her? What can you possibly
get out of it?'

He said: 'I'm very fond of Moira. I always have
been.'

'It seems a poorish way to show it, Lawrence.'

'At least she's always been kind to me and—and
tolerant,' he said bitterly.

'Meaning that I haven't?' Laura shrugged her
shoulders. 'That may be true. I never set up to have
a heart of gold. You say I'm hard. But have you ever
thought what would have happened to me if I hadn't
been?' Laura flicked the ash off her cigarette. 'The
thing that you always resented about me, darling, is that
you can't break my girlish heart.'

'The thing that I've always resented about you is
that you won't try to help,' he said sullenly.

'No? In what way won't I?'

'Listen,' he said. 'You're beautiful. You're faithful.
You're straight. You do your job as a wife so that
nobody's got anything on you. In fact you're just the
sort of girl that any headmistress would like to turn out.
But you've never loved anybody in your life. Never.
And I'll tell you why. . . .' He got up and threw his
cigarette end violently into the fire. 'You've got no idea
what it's like *not* to be beautiful and faithful and straight
and admirable, and not an ounce of sympathy with
people who aren't.'

'I should have said I'd put up with a good deal in our marriage,' she said quietly.

'Put up with it? Of course you've put up with it. Because putting up with it is part of being the perfect wife. But you've had your own back in every look—every word. You've never left me in any doubt that you were "putting up with it".'

Laura said: 'What d'you expect me to do? Throw up my hat?'

'God!' he said, 'God, if only sometimes you could have called me a drunken bastard and—and grinned at me. If only you'd kicked up a darn sight more fuss—and seen why it happened. If . . .'

'. . . if only I'd walked out on you, so that you could have hated yourself and been sorry for yourself, and come and asked me to come back,' she said with a tight-lipped smile. 'I know, darling. I know.' She shook her head. 'But you see I can't do that. I never was any good at amateur theatricals.'

'Amateur theatricals?' said Lawrence in a low voice. 'Well—that's one way of putting it.'

Laura said nothing. 'Well, anyhow,' he said, 'where we've got to is that you'll leave me if I go on with Moira?'

'Yes.'

'Would you rather pack it in anyway, Moira or not? I'm rather in a mood for packing things in, so say if you would?'

Laura said: 'No. I've never wanted us to break up, if it was avoidable. I'm only telling you that we might have to if—if we can't get it any better than this.' She shook her head. 'Perhaps somebody else could do it better for you, Lawrence. I don't know. But I can't. I've really tried, and I think, I'm just not helping. As you say.'

There was a long silence. Lawrence was staring down at the carpet. 'I don't appear to be very popular at the moment,' he said at last. 'What with you, and Papa, and Walter, and one thing and another. . . . Not that I see why I should be, mind you,' he added, leaning back in his chair and closing his eyes.

She looked at him for a moment and then leant forward

and took his hand in silence. Lawrence did not open his eyes but covered her hand with his and said : 'Yes, yes, darling, I know. But it always ends this way, doesn't it? And it doesn't get us anywhere.'

'Need it?' she said quietly.

'You seemed to think so. You say you'll leave me if I don't do this and that. . . .'

She took her hand away without a word and sat staring into the fire in silence.

After a while Lawrence opened his eyes and said : 'My God—I promised I'd telephone Phil,' and got up and went out.

IX

THE Birdwood Palace was a fine new place with a restaurant and swimming-pool as well as a ballroom, and as it was five miles out along the by-pass, you got a nice class there. As they got out of the car Jack looked at the parked motor-cycles and said: 'Reckon I'll have to get a motor-bike. Been meaning to for a long time.' He grinned at her. 'You ever been on the back of a motor-bike?'

'Yes,' said Rosamund unexpectedly. 'During the war. Lawrence came to see us on one—Lawrence Spellman— and he took me a little way. It was lovely.'

'Ah,' he said, slightly disappointed, 'well, you wait till I get my Norton.'

It was a fine place, but it cost five shillings to go in. As they approached the pay-box Rosamund said quickly: 'Look—it's my turn to pay. You paid last time.'

He glanced at her quickly and then looked away frowning. He said: 'When I take girls out I pay for them. What you think I am?'

'But don't you see—if you always pay I—I can't come out with you.'

He hesitated and grinned: 'All right. What's the good of having a rich girl if she doesn't pay? You can pay for yourself if you want to.'

It was a lot easier this time than it had been before. In the car he had still been rough and off-hand, but now, as soon as they were inside he began to smile at her and call her 'Rosey.' They went into the bar, but this time he didn't ask her what she wanted to drink, but just went off and came back with a Pale Ale for himself and some lemonade for her. He said: 'You can have sherry if you want, but I reckon you like that better, don't you?'

'I do, if you don't mind.'

'Why should I? It's only kids that drink for swank.'

As they went into the big ballroom, she saw his eyes flicker round it uneasily, and for a moment she wondered why. Somehow, when she was out with him, the possibility of meeting anybody she knew never occurred to her. She speculated, idly and without nervousness, on who would be the most embarrassing person she could meet, and plumped for the Talbot-Rees'es. But even they, curiously, wouldn't matter. He danced very well—far better than she did, or than any of her male acquaintances like Lawrence. It was all a bit tricky, because something was happening all the time, and you needed to concentrate hard to follow him. Rosamund suspected that it was the sort of dancing that looked rather common and dance-hall-ish. But when you were doing it, it was fun, and not really difficult.

Jack said: 'What d'you do with your time, with your dad out all day and you there by yourself? Must be pretty slow?'

'Oh—I shop and—and do things about the house and so on.'

'Does he ever take you out? Take you to the pictures and things?' He chuckled. 'You know I can't see your father going to the pictures somehow.'

Rosamund said: 'He doesn't. He hates them. But he—he takes me to the theatre.' He had done so just once since her mother's death. Six months ago. Suddenly one night. 'Roz—I've got tickets for the theatre. . . .' They had gone and seen a very bad farce at the Repertory Theatre. Never before and never since. She said: 'And of course we have people in to dinner and things like that.'

He shook his head and repeated: 'Must be pretty slow.'

'It is,' she said with sudden unintentional bitterness. His arm tightened round her slightly. Rosamund added quickly: 'It must be even slower for my father.'

'Ah,' he said quietly. ''Course he works very hard.'

She said: 'Yes,' and they danced for a while in silence.

It was the fortieth anniversary of George Martin's marriage and he had bought Clarice flowers, as he always did. But it was young Bill and his wife who came in and insisted that they should go out to dinner and celebrate. Bill took them in his car and when they got there the table was booked, and the dinner ordered, with a bottle of champagne. Clarice was doubtful about the champagne, but Bill said he thought she could drink a glass on her fortieth wedding anniversary without becoming a drunk, so she did. Bill had always been her favourite, and anything he said or did was right.

There were notices everywhere boasting that the ball-room was air-conditioned, but it was very hot all the same. It was cooler in the bar, and quieter if you wanted to talk.

Jack said: 'It's all right in its way, and I reckon I should find the difference if I was in digs. But you know —sometimes you wish you were on your own. Dad's all right, but mother, she fusses about . . .' He stared at his beer rather moodily. 'I never noticed it till I went away and did my National Service, because I was used to it, see. But nowadays . . . I don't know.'

Rosamund said: 'What do you do at the works? You're in the press-shop, aren't you?'

'That's right,' he said. 'Well, I work a press. You been round?'

'Yes.'

'Well, then you know. An' as far as I can see I go on working a press for ever.'

'Oh come. You're on the Works Committee and . . .'

'That'll do me a lot of good,' he said rather bitterly. He swirled the beer round in his glass so that it frothed. 'Twenty years' time I might be shop foreman. If I'm lucky. An' that's that. Look at Dad. He's been at Lang's thirty-five years. Foreman patternmaker. That's what he is and that's what he'll stay.' He shook his head. 'You don't know what it is, you people. . . .' He paused and then got up quickly. 'Well come on, let's dance.'

When they were dancing he said suddenly: 'You ask your dad about me sometime. Know what he'd say? "Him? He's got too much to say for himself."'

'Why would he?'

He smiled grimly. 'Your dad doesn't like chaps that answer back. Where's the boss that does?'

'But he's easy enough to handle if you know him.'

'Maybe for you. But I'm not his daughter. But to hell with it, anyway.'

Up till now they had just danced, but now it was like the Works Party again, with the big, muscular body pressed hard against hers—hard and bitterly and almost insultingly; exciting but unfriendly. She said quietly: 'You don't have to hold me like that just because you're cross about something.'

He looked down at her in surprise and then laughed. 'All right. Why? Don't you like it?'

'I—I don't mind. But not just because you're angry.'

He said: 'You're a good kid. Listen—I'll tell you something. That first night I danced with you was for a bet, see? They bet me I wouldn't, see? So I did just for the hell of it.'

'But why shouldn't you?'

'What—come and excuse-me when you were dancing with your dad?'

'But that—that's what the Works Party's *for*. I mean —he wouldn't mind. . . .'

He said: 'Well, anyhow that's how it was. I been wanting to tell you.'

Something was expected of her. She said: 'Well, I'm glad you won your bet.'

'You're not mad with me?'

'Why should I be? Unless . . .'

'Unless what?'

'Unless it was—a sort of—a thing against my father. Is that what you're saying?'

He hesitated and then said: 'No. I tell you—it was just a bet. . . .'

'Oh I don't mind *that* at all,' she said with relief.

Jack grinned and said: 'It was that yellow frock you wore. See, I thought . . .'

'My God!' said Rosamund. 'That frock!'

It was nearly ten o'clock when the anniversary dinner

was over. As they passed through the big, space-wasting entrance hall Bill Martin jerked his thumb towards the sound of the music and said: 'How about a turn round the floor to finish up with, Mum?'

Clarice said: 'Not me, my dear, after all that food and champagne and all. But if you and Betty'd like to dance . . .'

'Oh, we're not particular. Fine place though, isn't it?'

They stood for a moment in the little group of people who were watching the dancing through the big glass doors.

Bill said: 'Not as many here to-night as I have seen. Saturday night you can't move.'

Clarice Martin suddenly caught George by the arm and said: 'George . . . look . . .!'

'What, my dear?'

'Over there. Just passing in front of the band. Isn't that . . .?'

They had stopped talking now. He was holding her closely, but not fiercely any more—not angrily. They were waltzing, and she could just feel the lightest touch of his face against her hair. There was no need to concentrate now—to follow those intricacies. It all happened by itself, automatically and smoothly, as it had done in that first dance. Rosamund closed her eyes.

'That's right,' said George Martin calmly. 'So it is.'

*   *   *   *   *

She didn't really fully understand about having danced with her because of a bet, and there was something unpleasant there—something he didn't like and was ashamed of, and hadn't wanted to tell her. But he *had* told her, and she felt dimly that all the roughness and off-handedness had been connected with it, and that now he had told her it would never come again—or wouldn't be quite the same if it did. He was miserable and restless and asking for help, and when he was asking for help it didn't matter if you were only eighteen because he was younger than you. She had said she would be home by eleven, and the drive would only take half an hour, but just after ten she said: 'Come on—let's go.'

He took her hand as they walked very slowly through

the big car-park, but neither of them spoke until they
came to the little Morris. Jack said : 'How about letting
me drive ?   I got a licence.'

Rosamund said : 'All right.'

They had taught him to drive in the Army.   He was
quite good, though rather showy, with too much un-
necessary slick gear-changing.   Out on the by-pass he
said : 'What time you got to be home ?'

'Eleven,' she said steadily.

'Fine.   Plenty of time.'

'Drop off in the town.   You don't want that foul journey
again.'

He said : 'No.   I've had that . . .'   After they had
driven for about a mile he said : 'I'm going to turn down
right after the roundabout.'   It was a question.

'All right,' said Rosamund calmly.   'Then we can go
through Hemming and back that way.'

They did not look at one another for a few moments.
Then they turned their heads and gave a simultaneous
giggle.

Jack said : 'An' I suppose when I stop you'll be nip-
ping out of that door so quick . . .'

There was a moment's pause.   'When you come to
think of it,' said Rosamund suddenly, 'by doing that
before and—and sort of being rude, I've made it awfully
difficult to do *again* if I wanted to.   I hadn't realised that.'

The driver gave a faint chuckle.   'Hadn't you, Rosey ?'
he said gently.

The turning down the right was still a country lane—
one of the lanes that the by-pass had been built to avoid.
Jack drove a few hundred yards down it and then pulled
on to the grass verge and stopped.   He had to ask her
where the hand brake was.   It was easy really, if you
knew about girls.   Always the same.   Go a bit too quick
and let them stop you, and then take offence, and then
all you had to do was wait.   She was Walter Lang's
daughter, and she knew he'd only danced with her in the
first place for a bet with the boys, and she knew what was
coming to her now.   Yet there she was.   He smiled in the
darkness in bitter self-appreciation for the neatness of the
thing, and still smiling, turned to her and said : 'Well—

E

want to get out?' She did not reply and he put his arm round her and drew her closer to him and said: 'Oh Rosey . . .'

*   *   *   *   *

'You got to remember,' said George Martin doubtfully, 'that things are different nowadays.' He stuffed a finger into his pipe and re-lit it.

'They may be,' said Clarice, 'but not as different as all that, I'll be bound. What you think Mr. Walter'd say? He'd be pleased, wouldn't he?'

'For all you can tell, he might know.'

'Don't talk such drivel, George. It's likely he'd let her go about hugging up to Jack Partridge, isn't it? He's no good anyhow, not to any girl, if I know the rights.'

'What's the matter with him?'

'Never mind,' said Clarice darkly. 'But he isn't. And I'll tell you another that'd have something to say, and that's Joe Partridge himself. He's got enough sense for that.'

George said: 'Well, I don't see it's our affair, Clarry. After all . . .'

Clarice smoothed back the wispy white hair. 'George,' she said gently, 'she's got no mother. If she had, maybe it'd be different. But what good will Mr. Walter be looking after a girl that age? Him never thinking of anything but business anyway? I knew when I saw her at the Party. I thought: "Somebody'll have to watch that girl or she'll turn out no good." Well, there you are. It's no place for a young girl out there dancing and certainly not with him. You got a duty to do even if you don't like it. A duty towards God and a duty towards your neighbour. How would you like it if it was a child of yours, and people didn't tell you a thing like that? It's not fitting for her to be with Jack Partridge, now is it?'

'Maybe not,' said Martin in mild exasperation. 'But what you don't see is that if I go and tell her father it'll get young Jack into trouble and her as well. I daresay you're right. I daresay her father *doesn't* know. But where's the harm in two kids going out together dancing,

just because he's in the works and she's Walter's daughter?
You wouldn't say anything if it was a girl out of the
factory.'

'That's where half that's bad and dirty and evil comes
from,' said Clarice quietly. 'From asking "what's the
harm in it?" when you *know*.'

'But I *don't* know,' said Martin stubbornly.

Clarice's lips shut to a thin line. 'Well, I do,' she said.
'You've got to speak to Joe Partridge to-morrow, George.'

*　　*　　*　　*　　*

It was like the last waltz before they had left the
Birdwood—soft and languorous and easy, but unfrighten-
ing and understood; and if one was not exactly in charge,
one was in a strange way in charge of not being in charge.
. . . When he pulled away sharply and suddenly, she
thought for a moment he had seen or heard something.
Rosamund opened her eyes and said: 'What is it,
Jack?'

But he was sitting bolt upright and staring at nothing.
He said hoarsely: 'You're just a kid. Don't know what
you're doing.'

She smiled and said: 'Of course I do. I know just
what I'm doing. What . . .?'

'O.K.,' he said sarcastically. 'Well then, I don't.'

All the bitterness and antagonism was suddenly there
again. 'What'd you mean?' she said helplessly.

He leant forward and started the engine. 'I'm going
to take you back,' he said curtly.

'But you can't just suddenly . . . Did I do something wrong?'

He put out a hand and patted hers—just two brief pats
—and let in the clutch.

Her eyes were full of tears but she said nothing. There
was nothing to say. They had gone a mile before anybody
spoke again. He stared at the road as he drove and said
in a low voice: 'Ah, Rosey . . . don't you see?'

'No,' she said simply.

'Well, I been out with girls before. Plenty of 'em. . . .'

'Yes?'

'. . . and it's easy, see? If you know how. I was

thinking that, even when we pulled up there—thinking
how smart I'd been to get you like that. . . .'

She said : 'I know.'

He turned and looked at her. 'How d'you mean
you know ?'

'Well, we had all that before—at the Party—and when
you came back with me—and even a bit when you came
out and said you were sorry and then kissed me. It was
all part of that. And then this evening it was different
and you stopped hating me. About half-way through the
evening you stopped. And after that I thought you knew
I understood and didn't mind it—if . . .' She suddenly
gulped and said miserably : 'I think it was mean to start
hating me again when I'd understood and you'd stopped.'

'Hating you ?' he said furiously. 'God damn it, why
d'you think I'm taking you home if I hate you ?'

She said : 'I don't know. Why are you then ? You
were angry before when—when I got out of the car and
now you're angry because I liked it and . . .'

He suddenly gave a loud crow of laughter. He said :
'Well, I'm damned. This is a fine turn up if you like.'

He grinned at her and she smiled back with an effort
and said : 'It all seems to have got complicated. It wasn't
before. Not when we were dancing and . . .'

He jammed on the brakes so hard that the car swerved
slightly. 'It's not complicated now, Rosey,' he said
between his teeth.

X

O<small>N</small> his way to the Board Meeting Lawrence was joined by Talbot-Rees. Talbot-Rees was wearing a black jacket and a double-breasted waistcoat and pin-striped trousers with a red carnation in his button-hole. He said: 'I gather that to-day we elect a new member of the Board.'

'Barker? Yes. That'll add to the gaiety of the Board Meetings, won't it?'

'Between ourselves,' said Talbot-Rees, 'I think it's rather a mistake. Barker's a good enough chap, but these production-manager types who started at the bottom never really understand the *strategy* of business.'

'Well, if Walter's memorandum is the strategy of business, nor do I. What d'you make of it?'

Talbot-Rees hesitated and said: 'It's an interesting point of view. What do you feel?'

'I think it's crazy.'

'Well yes. Of course it's not very practical *immediately*. But you know what our little Walter is. He must have his visions.'

The bespectacled thin-faced Barker was waiting in the anteroom to the Board Room. He was wearing a new grey suit and there was perspiration on his forehead. He said: 'Good morning,' but did not enter with them.

Lawrence said: 'Do they keep him out there till he's been elected and then bring him in?'

'It's the correct procedure,' said Talbot-Rees.

'There ought to be some initiation ceremony. Couldn't we break a bottle of champagne over his bows or something? He looked as though he could do with it.'

'Quite frankly,' said Talbot-Rees, 'I don't think he's got the *drive*. . . .'

'All right,' said Henry Spellman thankfully. 'We've elected a new director as per item one and received the

report of the pensions committee as per item two and
reviewed the production forecast as per item three. The
next item is for me to tell my secretary something I've
forgotten. And after that we'll take Mr. Lang's memorandum.' He rose with a loud grunt and waddled off to the
telephone.

Lawrence completed a lightning sketch of Talbot-
Rees's head, looked at it critically and tore it up. 'Have
you had a copy of this memorandum of Walter's?' he
said to Barker.

The spectacled young man started slightly and said :
'No, Mr. Lawrence. I understand that they couldn't
give me one since it was a Board document.'

'But that's bunkum. It concerns you more than anybody else. Or soon will.'

Barker smiled deprecatingly. 'I've seen Mr.
Martin's.'

'Ah—I see. The correct procedure. What d'you
think of it?'

Barker said : 'Well . . . I've got some figures that
I've given to Mr. Martin. . . .'

Henry Spellman came back, lowered himself very
slowly until he was within six inches of the seat of his
chair and then collapsed into it with a crash. 'Right,'
he said. 'Errors and omissions dealt with. Item four.
The managing director's memorandum. . . .' He took
off one pair of glasses, put on another, looked at the
memorandum, took off the second pair of glasses, put
them on the table and gave them a little push. He said :
'You've all seen this. It's a memorandum on the broad
future of the business. Mr. Lang's view is . . . (correct
me if I've got anything wrong, Walter) . . . Mr. Lang
feels that the future of the business lies—or should lie—in
more concentration on our own products, and less fabricating for other people.' He grabbed suddenly at his
spectacles as though they had made an attempt to escape,
and put them on his nose for safety. 'I venture to suggest
that nobody is going to disagree with that.'

'Hear, hear!' said Talbot-Rees heartily.

'In fact,' said Henry, 'I can never *remember* anybody
disagreeing with it, and it's been coming up every so

often for the last thirty years. We all know that these outside fabricating jobs are a nuisance. Nobody in their senses would want them if he could do something else. But the principle's always been that we'd get rid of them when we could see how to make our normal turnover and profit without them. What's new in Mr. Lang's memorandum, as I understand it, is that he wants to get rid of them anyhow, whether we can see immediately what to put in their place or not. That so, Walter?'

'More or less,' said Lang, smiling.

'All right. Well now, gentlemen, I ask Mr. Lang to speak to his memorandum and explain what he's got in mind.'

Lang looked slowly round the table. 'I don't want to talk very much,' he said in his curt voice—the voice that seemed to grudge every word. 'It's all set out here. The Chairman's told you we've wanted to get rid of fabricating contracts for thirty-five years. I'm suggesting that we should get rid of them in the next two—that by the end of 1955 we should be working solely on our own patented products. I've tried to show how that might be done without much loss of profit. But the main thing is the principle that we put this through whether we lose turnover and profit or not.' He leaned back in his chair. 'As long as we can go messing on with the fabricating work there's no real incentive for anybody to get on and develop our own stuff. If our bread-and-butter depends on it, it'll be different.'

Henry said: 'You reckon the best way to teach us to swim is to pitch us into ten foot of water, eh?'

'That's right, Mr. Chairman.'

There was a long pause. Henry said: 'That all you want to say, Walter?'

'Yes. The rest's all down here.'

'Well then, gentlemen, the discussion's open. I've got my own view about this, but I'd rather hear somebody else first.' He looked round with raised eyebrows. Nobody seemed anxious to speak. At last North gave the side of his nose a final polish and said: 'I don't want this to be taken as—as an observation on Mr. Lang's memorandum, Mr. Chairman, and still less as a criticism. But

I've taken out a few figures which might help in the discussion. . . .'

There was an almost audible sigh of relief. North had an invaluable habit of taking out a few figures.

'The average rate of net profit on fabricating work over the last five years,' said North in his catarrhal voice, 'was only 4·7 per cent. On our own products side it was just over 14 per cent.'

'And mind you,' put in Lang, 'that's when the patent side's still about a quarter efficient.'

'I agree, sir.' North turned over a page. 'But on the other side, of the *total* net profit, fifty-eight per cent came from fabricating work and only forty-two per cent from our own products.' Lawrence caught George Martin's eye and winked. Lang's face was quite expressionless. 'I thought the Board might like to have these figures in front of them,' said North. 'The relative turnover figures are about eighty per cent fabricating and twenty per cent own product.'

Henry glanced at Lang. 'You accept these figures?'

'Of course,' said Lang calmly. 'They *are* my case. Twenty per cent of your turnover gives you nearly half your profit.'

Lawrence said: 'Hey—wait a *minute* . . .' at the same moment as North and George Martin said: 'But. . . .'

'George?' said old Henry.

Martin smiled across at Lang rather apologetically. 'I was only going to say that perhaps that's rather too simple a way of looking at it. After all, the fabricating may only show four per cent net, but that's after it's paid eighty per cent of your overheads.'

Lawrence said: 'In fact *without* the fabricating work we should make a sizeable loss?'

'Oh, naturally,' said North.

Lang frowned and shut his eyes tightly. 'Look,' he said, 'this is just what we've been doing for thirty years and what I'm asking you to stop doing. Nobody needs to trot out these figures as though they were a discovery, or to remind me that there are such things as overheads. I don't just see the turnover and margin figures of this business at Board Meetings. I darn nearly sleep with them.' He opened his eyes and looked round the table.

'Yes?' said Henry Spellman politely but pointedly.

Lang said: 'Well, then, can we stop talking about what the business used to be or is now, and start talking about what it's *going* to be?'

Lawrence leant forward. 'Forgive me, Mr. Chairman,' he said gently, 'but I'm getting a bit lost. I understood that the Managing Director's whole point was that he wanted to scrap the fabricating work more or less as—as a matter of *principle*, so to speak?'

'Well, I rather understood that myself,' said Henry. 'But of course . . .'

Lawrence said: 'Then surely Mr. North's figures are extremely relevant? Perhaps they're the reason *why* we've wanted to do this for thirty years and haven't done it? To talk about scrapping the work that gives us eighty per cent of our turnover . . .'

'Oh come!' said Talbot-Rees with a flash of very white teeth. 'Surely we can assume that the Managing Director didn't mean it like *that* . . .'

Lang said: 'I've got the use of my senses, even if some of you seem to doubt it.'

'Quite,' said Talbot-Rees. 'As I read it, this memorandum merely suggests that in order to carry out the changeover we should be prepared, if necessary, to accept some sacrifices.' He smiled at Lang. 'Do I interpret you rightly?'

'Of course,' said Lang contemptuously.

'Right,' said Henry briskly. 'Then the obvious question is, what are the sacrifices likely to amount to? Nobody's likely to object if we reckon net profit's likely to fall by ten per cent for a few years. And nobody's likely to agree if it's going to fall by fifty per cent.'

'Why not?' said Lang.

Henry hesitated. 'Very well,' he said. 'Mr. Lang would consider even fifty per cent.'

Lang smiled. 'In fact, according to my calculations, there'd be very little loss of profit after the first two years, and by the fifth year profits would be back to normal.

And what's more, you'd have a worthwhile business instead of a lot of odds and ends.'

There was a pause. Henry took off his glasses and chased them away a few inches. 'Then what we want to know *now*,' he said, 'is how far the Board accepts Mr. Lang's calculations as approximately correct or likely to be fulfilled. Or possible to fulfil. First of all—can we produce the stuff? George, this is you?'

'Well, Mr. Chairman,' said Martin with his quiet smile, 'I shall be gone, so . . .'

There was a general laugh. Lang looked across at Martin with that almost loving grin that he gave to few other people. Martin said: 'But Barker and I have been through this and we think there are several things the Board ought to realise from the production side. First of all, out of the six patent jobs Mr. Lang mentions, only two are in production, and three are only experimental. Take a thing like the paint-spray gun. We think we're on to something. But we may not be. I certainly wouldn't like to guarantee that we could depend on that as a big line.'

Lang said: 'Don't forget that I'm asking that you have a proper experimental department, George. Not two men and a cat.'

'Even so, sir, we don't *know* it's any good. Then take plant. There's bound to be a heavy capital expenditure tooling up, of course. But how about getting the machine tools? There's plant now that we've had on order for three years. And it's not getting any better. Then we all know about steel. . . .'

Lang said: 'I thought we should come to steel soon.'

'Taking it all in all,' said Martin, 'there's a lot of real headaches here. I don't say we couldn't do it eventually. But I'm afraid it'd take a lot longer than's suggested here.' He turned to Barker. 'You check?'

Barker nodded. 'Yes, sir. I don't think a plan like this could be carried through under present conditions in less than ten years.'

'Oh, bunkum!' said Lang impatiently.

Henry said: 'Well, that's the opinion of the production

side. How about selling the stuff if we could make it?
Talbot-Rees?'

Talbot-Rees placed two fingers in the pocket of the
double-breasted waistcoat. 'Well, sir—I should like to
pay a tribute to the—the quality of *vision* that has gone
into this memorandum. As a salesman it thrills and
challenges me. And I can only say that if the plan is
adopted the sales side will throw themselves into it heart
and soul.'

'Quite,' said Henry. 'But could you sell the stuff?'

Talbot-Rees smiled. 'With respect, Mr. Chairman,
that's hardly a possible question.'

Lawrence said : 'How long is a piece of string? You're
asking him if he can sell something that doesn't exist, at
a price not stated, at some unknown date in the future.'

Lang flushed and said : 'Well, we're asking *him*.'

'Sorry, Mr. Chairman,' said Lawrence blandly.

'I see nothing *impossible* in Mr. Lang's figures,' said
Talbot-Rees. 'But naturally it does depend on so many
factors. . . .'

Lang said : 'I asked you about every one of these
figures before I put them down.'

'You did, sir. And I answered that they were not
impossible given that the article was right, the price was
right, and the state of the market favourable. I stand by
that.' He sat back with the air of a man prepared to
hold rather dimly-lighted ground to the last.

Lang threw down his pencil and said : 'Why is it that
neither production nor sales people have ever got the
courage of their convictions?'

Lawrence said : 'It's just that they haven't got the
courage of *yours*, Walter.'

There was a long pause. Henry caught his glasses
again and said : 'Well, gentlemen—the sense of the
meeting seems to be this. We all accept the principle
behind the Managing Director's memorandum. And
we admire the vision and force with which he has expressed his ideas—as he always does. But on the production and sales side there are a lot of question marks.
We're living in difficult times and we don't know whether
we could do these things, or if so, *when* we could do them.

This is too big a thing to go rushing into in the dark.
We may not be altogether satisfied with the business but
it's sound and it's profitable. As directors we certainly
shouldn't be justified in giving up the substance for the
shadow. But that doesn't mean we want to sit and do
nothing. We must get on with this changeover just as
fast as is prudent.' He turned to Lang. 'So I suggest
that what we, as a Board, say to the Managing Director
is that we support and offer every encouragement to the
principle he has expressed; and that we are prepared
to taper off the fabricating work just as quickly as the
development of the patent products side is able to replace
the loss of turnover and profit, or the greater part of it.'
He paused. 'How about that?'

Lang sat up and said curtly: 'With all respect, Mr.
Chairman, that's no use to me at all.'

'Oh,' said Henry rather blankly.

'It just leaves us exactly where we were.'

'But I said . . .'

'It's no use saying things. We've got to *do* something.
And this is just a formula for doing nothing.'

Henry said: 'I don't agree for a moment.'

Lawrence said: 'Are you still asking the Board to
accept this memorandum exactly as it stands, Walter?
Because . . .'

Lang looked at him for a moment and then turned
pointedly away. The deep cut lines at the corners of his
mouth were harder than ever and his head was tilted
forward in the curious characteristic bull-like way.

'Gentlemen,' he said, 'my father founded this business.
I think I'm right in saying that to-day I'm the largest
individual shareholder in it. I've run the business for
the last fifteen years and what I've done with it is there
on the accounts for everybody to see. When I put up a
considered memorandum like this I don't expect it to
be dismissed after a quarter of an hour's amateur discussion.' Lang's face had gone a deep red. He glared
round at Lawrence and said more loudly: 'There are
some of us here who . . .'

Henry said quietly: 'I don't think we shall get anywhere like this, Walter.'

Lang said furiously: 'I refuse to be impeded at every step by . . .'

'Nobody's trying to impede you.'

'No—and they'd better not!' Lang shut up his folder of papers with a snap, pushed back his chair and walked out. There was a moment's silence. Lawrence continued to draw with a slight smile. George Martin was staring at the table and Talbot-Rees at the window. Barker, looking pale and frightened, glanced at the Chairman.

Henry put on his glasses and said quietly: 'Well—I think we'd better adjourn.'

As they left the room Lawrence said to Barker: 'You mustn't be disappointed if it isn't always as amusing as that.'

* * * * *

Talbot-Rees flung out a hand and said: 'It's quite intolerable, Henry. It's a deliberate attempt to bully the Board. "Do as I want, or else . . ."'

'Or else what?' said Lawrence.

'It's insulting to you as Chairman and humiliating to everyone else.'

Old Henry said: 'You've got to remember he's a hot-tempered man.'

'Well, some of the rest of us here have tempers,' said Talbot-Rees. 'But we don't show them off by insulting our colleagues at a Board Meeting. We should be perfectly justified if we resigned in a body.'

'The only snag in that,' said Lawrence gently, 'is that Walter would be so pleased.'

Old Henry sighed deeply. 'There's nothing so deadly in business as the artist manqué,' he said unhappily.

'Well, there's one thing,' said Talbot-Rees after a pause. 'I should think the trustees of Gus's estate will know *now* whether they want to sell Walter control. Old North's face was a picture.'

Henry looked up. 'Yes,' he said heavily. 'He doesn't make it easy for people, does he? He never did.' The telephone rang. He picked it up and said: 'Yes? Oh hallo, Walter . . . Yes. By all means. Shall I come down to you or . . .? All right. When you like.'

Talbot-Rees said : 'Cooled off and coming to apologise.'

'Maybe,' said Henry. 'Or maybe not. Walter doesn't apologise much.'

*   *   *   *   *

'Frankly, Henry,' said Lang with careful calm, 'I'm not prepared to work my guts out to make a success of this place if I've got to be obstructed by wind-bags like Talbot-Rees and nonentities like Barker. They've no stake in the business. They're purely courtesy directors, and it's intolerable if they're going to meddle with major policy.'

'Well,' said Henry slowly, 'if you appoint a man a director, you can't blame him if he acts like one.'

'All right. Then we must re-organise this thing and not make these people directors.'

'Being a bit old-fashioned, aren't you, Walter? Family Board and so on ?'

Lang said : 'Well, we can't go on like this.'

'No,' said Henry slowly. 'We can't. . . .' He leaned back in his chair, which creaked warningly. 'Look, Walter,' he said gently. 'I took on the Chairmanship because you asked me to. But having taken it on, I've got to do the job. And as long as I'm Chairman, you mustn't treat a Board Meeting like you did that one to-day.'

Lang flushed : 'What d'you mean ?'

'The principle's always been that in the Board Room we're all equal. You talked to-day like the boss talking to a lot of unsatisfactory office boys.'

'I had reason,' said Lang sullenly.

'You had no reason,' said Henry calmly. 'Except that people didn't entirely agree with what you wanted to do. You can't get men there and ask their opinions and then act like that if you don't happen to like what they think.'

Lang shrugged his shoulders in silence.

'I can see it must be damned annoying,' said Henry thoughtfully. 'You get an idea. You know it's good. You can't prove, but—you just know it. And then you have to try to explain it to a lot of chaps who haven't got that sort of vision. . . .'

Lang said : 'If you can see that, why the hell didn't you support me?'

'Because it isn't *reasonable*, Walter. Because there's no real case for it, except to satisfy you. You can visualise something that'd give you more personal satisfaction than what you've got now—that would express you better. That's fine if you're cutting a bit of stone. It's up to you to have it any shape you want it. But you're talking here about something that gives two thousand people their livings. And it's no good losing your temper if you can't do just as you like with it.'

'Look here, Henry,' said Lang. 'If you're looking for trouble with me . . .'

'God help us,' said Spellman wearily. 'I'm not looking for trouble with anybody. I'm only trying to help you. This individualist approach of yours . . .'

'You don't like the way I behave? Well, let me tell you that *I* don't like the way Lawrence behaves towards me. I don't go to Board Meetings to be lectured by him.'

'Well then, you'd better tell him so,' said Henry. 'He's of age.'

There was a long pause.

'It's no good squabbling about like this,' said Lang. 'I've got a proposition to put to you. I want to re-organise this business. If I do, I'd rather do it my own way and risk my own money. You've got twenty thousand shares. I'll buy them from you at five shillings over an independent valuation, provided you'll also sell me twenty thousand of the Trust's shares.'

Spellman said : 'Walter—we've been through all this before. I've already told you that in my opinion it wouldn't be in line with Gus's intentions to sell you control.'

'And why the hell should you think that, except that it suits your book to think it?' said Lang angrily.

Spellman hesitated for a moment and then sighed: 'Well, if you must know,' he said, 'because he told me so.'

There was a moment's dead silence. 'Gus told you

you weren't to sell the shares to me?' said Lang in a low
voice.

'He didn't say I wasn't to sell any of them to you.
He said I wasn't to sell enough to give you complete
financial control. He didn't think it'd be good for the
business. Or for you.'

'I don't believe it.'

'Please yourself about that, but it's true.' Spellman
spread out a hand. 'I'm sorry, Walter. I didn't want
to tell you that, but you left me no option.'

'It'd have been straighter if you'd told me before,'
said Lang bitterly. 'Does North know that?'

'He does not. Nobody else knows it.'

'Except Lawrence, eh?'

'Including Lawrence.'

Lang stared at him for a moment in silence. Then he
got up abruptly. 'All right, Henry,' he said with a slight
smile. 'Then I shall have to find another way. There
always *are* other ways.'

*   *   *   *   *

That was always the longest bit of the day, between
the tea-break and the end bell going. It was only just
over an hour, but the electric drill got so that it seemed
to weigh a ton and your wrists ached. But it hadn't been
a bad day because Hilda had been doing Number Three
and Number Three was the easiest number on Pressure
Tank R.B. Not like Number Two, which was too quick
and Mollie kept missing. But Hilda had been able to
help her with Number Two and Mollie had had some
gum sweets that her Dan had given her, and Hilda had
gone on thinking about being on a switchback at the
Pleasure Grounds right up till the bell went, whereas
usually after the tea break you were too tired to think
about nice things. She had been on the switchback and
gone on and on; sometimes it was Robert Taylor with
her and sometimes Lawrence Spellman, but younger,
like he used to be in the war. And once Jack had come
and asked her if he could, and she had said: 'No, thank
you very much,' and turned her back. And it had gone
on and on and there was always that moment just before

it went down the slope when it seemed almost to stop, and then go rushing down so that you screamed even if you hadn't meant to.

She was so used to going to the bicycle racks that she went all the way out there before she remembered that she hadn't got her bicycle because it had a puncture that morning and she had to come by bus. It was a nuisance having to walk right up to the bus and then walk again at the other end, but there it was, and if she walked slowly the first lot of buses would have got off, and it wouldn't be so crowded, though the Greengates bus always was.

Lawrence said: 'Well look, Ted, whatever else you do with it, *don't* let them put it down in the chapel, or somebody'll come along and stack it with the rest and we shall never find it again. Put it in West Store. O.K.? Right.' He hung up the receiver and turned to his secretary. 'Now, May . . .?' The tall pale, freckled bespectacled girl put the letters and cheques before him. ('Having May as a secretary,' he had once remarked, 'is the only gesture towards respectability that I have ever made.') Lawrence scribbled his signature to the letters and looked at the thick wad of cheques. 'Look, sweetheart,' he said, 'it is now nearly six. My union won't like it if I stay and sign all these. Bring them in to-morrow morning.'

Talbot-Rees's Bentley and Martin's Vauxhall were still in the car-park, but his father's car and Lang's Daimler had both gone. He could never before remember leaving after Lang, and decided not to let it occur again. One must not fall into careless habits of industry.

It took a long time for people to come in the morning, but precious little time for them to get away at night. It was only five to six, but the road outside was practically clear. He took his hands off the wheel for a moment and lit a cigarette. The question now was whether to go straight home or stop off at the County for a drink. The girl in the green coat up the road in front had uncommonly pretty legs. In fact she was an uncommonly pretty shape altogether. It was the sort of back view that nearly always went with spectacles and spots when you got abreast. Lawrence slowed slightly and glanced sideways just to confirm the guess. Then he looked hard and pulled the car in to the pavement. 'Why, hallo, 'Rene—want a lift?'

Hilda blushed and hesitated.

Lawrence leant over and opened the door. 'Come on—hop in.'

She said: 'Thank you very much, Mr. Spellman. If you could just drop me off at the bus stop . . .'

Lawrence said: 'Where d'you live?'

'Greengates, Mr. Spellman.'

'Well, that's all right. On my way home. I can take you down to Market Cross.' He let the clutch in. 'D'you always come by bus?'

'No, Mr. Spellman, but I had a puncture this morning.'

There were a lot of people still waiting at the bus stop. They looked at the car as it passed and Hilda blushed and didn't look out. Ten minutes or so later quite a number of people saw Lawrence's car stop at Market Cross. Hilda got out and walked away towards Greengates and the car went on.

*   *   *   *   *

'All right,' said Jack off-handedly. 'So I took her out dancing. So what?' Standing there with his father sitting at the table was too like being a defaulter before one's company commander. He turned away and threw himself into a chair defiantly.

Joe Partridge said: 'Birdwood Palace. Very nice too. How d'you get there?'

Jack hesitated. 'She's got a car.'

'Oh,' said his father. 'She's got a car. Who paid to go in?'

'Who d'you think?'

Joe said: 'Well, I should think she did, son. You certainly couldn't afford to go. . . .'

'Well, she didn't.'

'Then you're a bloody young fool.'

Jack said: 'I don't ask you how you spend *your* money, do I?'

Mrs. Partridge came and stood nervously in the kitchen doorway and said : 'Jack . . . !'

He said : 'Oh, for God's sake, don't you start too.'

'Don't you speak to your mother like that,' said his father quietly. 'Have you been out with Miss Lang before ?'

'Yes, I have.'

'Well then, it's got to stop. D'you hear ?'

Jack said : 'Who says so ? If I like it and she likes it, what the hell's it to do with anybody else ?'

'The trouble with you is you're crazy,' said Partridge. 'What d'you think'd happen if Mr. Walter got to hear of it ? You'd be out on your backside in half an hour.'

'Well, what if I was ? There's other places beside Lang's, isn't there ? You and your "Mister Walter . . . !" I'm not afraid of him if you are.'

Mrs. Partridge said : 'Jack dear . . .'

Joe Partridge took a deep breath. 'Now listen, son,' he said quietly, 'there's no call to shout about. And it's not a question of being afraid. A man who does an honest job needn't be afraid of anybody. But you know as well as I do it's not right for you to go running around in cars with a girl like that.'

'Why not ?'

'Well . . .' Joe spread out his big hands. 'Haven't you got any pride, boy ?'

'I don't see where pride comes into it.'

Mrs. Partridge said : 'She's not your class, dear. You must know that. We're only working people and . . .'

Jack sat up sharply. 'All right. We're only working people. And what's she ? Walter Lang's daughter. And what's Walter Lang ? His father's son. And his father was just a working man who happened to strike lucky and make money out of other people's work.'

'You better get a soap box and get out on the street corner,' said his father drily. 'That's what you'd sound like. Hot Labour man.'

'Well, what the hell d'you expect me to be ?' said Jack violently. 'You make me sick, some of you old ones. You're worse than the boss class itself. You *like* licking their boots and saying they're a different class from you and . . .'

Joe Partridge rose slowly to his feet. 'Sonny,' he said, 'I never licked any man's boots in my life. . . .'

Mrs. Partridge said: 'But your dad's done his duty in that state of life that it pleased . . .'

'. . . but when I was your age,' said Joe, unheeding, 'I wouldn't have reckoned myself much of a man if I'd gone sneaking round after the boss's daughter without his knowing—a kid of eighteen with no mother. Or let myself be taken riding in his car.' He smiled slightly. 'What you reckon they'd say about you in the shop if they knew? Know what you'd be called?'

'What the hell do I care what they'd say?'

Mrs. Partridge said: 'Why don't you never see Hilda now? She's a nice girl. . . .'

Joe moved a hand to silence her. 'Anyhow, what you got in mind, eh Jack? Going to marry her, eh? Or maybe you reckon her father'll do something for you, so's you can just live on the Langs' money? My God, you talk to me about boot licking. . . .'

Jack jumped up. His face was yellowish white and his whole body shook slightly. 'You got something wrong,' he said quietly but rather thickly, 'I'm not a kid of ten. You don't keep me. I earn my living and I pay my whack. If you don't like what I do, you only got to say so and I'll get out, see? And not come back. Otherwise, for Christ's sake, mind your own bloody business.'

He turned and went out. Mrs. Partridge said: 'Jack . . .' feebly. The front door slammed.

In the silence Joe Partridge sat down slowly and heavily. Mrs. Partridge said: 'Joe—you don't reckon he meant that—about going away?'

'Not he,' said Partridge bitterly. 'He knows when he's well off.' There was a long pause. 'Damn young fool,' he added.

'What you going to do about the other thing?'

'I don't know,' he said rather helplessly. 'Unless I was to see Mr. Walter.'

'I don't see why you should,' said Mrs. Partridge rather unexpectedly.

'Why not?'

'Well, it's putting Jack in the wrong, and I don't

reckon it's all his fault. Why does she go with him? She doesn't have to. A girl like that—it's putting tempta-tion in his way.'

'She's only eighteen.'

'Some of these girls of eighteen know what's what. I saw her at the Party and I thought that she looked a fast little thing. I reckon she must've encouraged him. It's Mr. Walter's job to look after her, and if he doesn't do it I don't see he's got the right to blame a boy like Jack. . . .'

'All right, all right,' said Partridge wearily. 'Your Jack couldn't be wrong, could he? But you can bet your bottom dollar if I don't tell Mr. Walter someone else will, sooner or later. If it's got back to me it'll be all round the place. Stands to reason it must, if they're going to places like dance halls. And then it'll lose him his job and maybe lose mine too.'

'Yours?' she said, startled.

Partridge shook his head with a bitter little smile. 'I know Walter. I've known him for thirty years. You're all right with him if you *are* all right, but if you aren't . . .' He shrugged.

Mrs. Partridge had gone very pale. After a moment she said: 'I think I'd better try to talk to Jack. I don't reckon he understands—and of course he gets angry with you. But if I was to talk to him I think I could get him to promise to—to stop it so that there won't be any more trouble.'

Joe Partridge slowly slit open the envelope that con-tained his football coupon. 'Ah,' he said. 'I reckon he'll promise you anything, mother.'

XI

JACK was in the canteen drinking a cup of tea and talking to Mac about the Cup Final when Fred Boxall passed on his way out. Fred said: 'What-o, Jacko. How's the car running?'

He looked up and said stupidly: 'What car?' Fred Boxall grinned and made a gesture with his fingers and went on. Jack felt his face go hot. He turned to Mac. Mac was grinning too. Jack said: 'What the hell's he talking about—"car"?'

Mac stopped grinning and said very solemnly indeed: '*I* don't know what he's talking about. Doesn't make any sense to me.'

Later on Jack got hold of Fred Boxall and said: 'What was that you said in the canteen—about a car?'

Fred Boxall said in a very refined way: 'Haven't you ever heard that expression before? "How's the car running?" It means how are you? How's tricks? See?'

He said: 'Oh—I get it,' rather lamely.

Fred Boxall grinned and said: 'What else could it mean? You haven't got a car, have you? Or have you?'

'No,' he said, 'I haven't got a car.'

'That's what I thought,' said Fred Boxall. 'Somebody was saying the other day you had, and I said I didn't reckon so.'

'*Who* said so?'

Fred Boxall's forehead puckered up in an intense effort of memory. 'Ah,' he said with regret, 'now *that* I can't recall. Maybe it was Mac. Or somebody else.'

Ted Chalmers and Harry had come up without his having noticed them. Ted chipped in and said: 'What you're thinking of is *I* said he *ought* to have one.'

Fred Boxall was one thing, but Ted Chalmers had a loose mouth and spots, and wasn't one of the gang. Jack turned round and said to Ted Chalmers: 'An' just why d'you think that?'

Ted Chalmers took a step back and grinned nervously and said: 'Well, so you ought. And all the rest of us. We should have if we was in America.'

Fred Boxall and Harry burst into a roar of laughter. As Jack turned away Fred Boxall stopped laughing and said in a worried way: 'We haven't said anything *wrong*, have we, Jacko?'

There was still ten minutes before the bell would go. He went out into the road and walked along it for a few hundred yards and back. There was nothing in it. They hadn't said anything. But he knew that game. He had played it too often himself to mistake it. They might not know it was her—most likely they didn't. But they knew something. It wasn't surprising, if it had got back to his father; but there was a cold, heavy sick feeling in his belly.

*   *   *   *   *

Sir Francis's house overlooked Regent's Park. The drawing-room was on the first floor and very big. It made Sir Francis look smaller and more bird-like than ever.

Sir Francis said: 'I thought we'd dine here if you don't mind, rather than go to the club. And I haven't asked anyone in to meet you. I find the only place where one can talk without being interrupted or having to apologise to somebody, is alone and over one's own dinner table. You don't mind?'

Lang said: 'Not at all.'

Sir Francis walked over and pressed a bell. 'Do you mind a glass of champagne as an aperitif? I never drink champagne with a meal but I do like a glass beforehand. Something else if you prefer it?'

'Champagne for me, please.' Lang glanced round the big room. Something in one of the pictures was vaguely familiar, and he stepped over and read the signature. Renoir. Of course it was a picture by Renoir that Henry Spellman was so proud of, and it was the same sort of colouring. It was very important to remember that Henry Spellman was a friend of Proudfoot's.

'How's old Henry?' said Sir Francis at that moment.

Lang smiled and said: 'Oh—he's much as usual.' He took his champagne from the manservant.

'Lazy old thing,' said Sir Francis. 'Frankly I was rather surprised when you elected him Chairman. When your brother died I imagined you'd take it on.'

'Well, somebody's got to be Chairman,' said Lang.

'Yes. I think I see the position,' said Sir Francis with his rather thin smile. 'Of course Henry would make an excellent figurehead. A very massive one too.'

He sipped his drink. 'How d'you find young Lawrence?'

Lang hesitated.

'I think you said you found that he had an excellent war record?' said Sir Francis calmly.

Lang smiled. 'That's about it.'

'I thought so. He was offered to me, you know.'

'I never knew that?'

'Oh yes. At the end of the war. So I said to his father: "Henry, I already have in my organisation several hundred young men with excellent war records. What I now need is a large number of people with excellent peace records, to keep the ex-officers in the style to which they have become accustomed. I run a business, not an armoured division".'

Lang said: 'Of course the war did unsettle a lot of these boys.'

'It's a very difficult problem,' said Sir Francis pensively. 'It's the same in every business. The war came. Some people went away and went into the services. Others stayed in their jobs. Five years later the soldiers, sailor and airmen came back, probably having done a magnificent job, but by that time hopelessly out of touch with their former work. Having lost, in fact, five years of their business lives. Yet they expect, not unnaturally, at least the same standing as their contemporaries who stayed with the business.' He frowned. 'One can see both parties' point of view. The ex-service people say: "We went and risked our lives while you stayed in a cushy job in safety. But for us there wouldn't *be* a business." To which the others reply: "You went away and were colourful heroes while we stuck to the dull old ship and pulled her through a difficult time. *We* haven't a chest full of medals, but by this time we know the job, whereas you don't. . . ."'

They sat at one end of the huge mahogany table, which seemed to stretch away out of the range of the candle-light.

'I don't know why it is,' said Sir Francis, 'that no Italian food or drink ever tastes good outside Italy. The wine's notorious, of course. But why ordinary arti-chokes . . . ?'

Lang said : 'I don't know Italy at all.'

'A ridiculous country,' said Sir Francis promptly. 'Nothing whatever to do with real life. At least—it is important to think so. . . .' He paused for a moment and stared moodily at the shadowy outline of the picture that some experts thought was a Ghirlandaio. Then he turned with the watered-milk smile and said : 'I'm afraid I have some rather bad news for you about steel supplies. Falk tells me that he doesn't see how he can carry on with this arrangement he made with your people.'

'That's very serious from our point of view,' said Lang glumly.

'Well, we shall have to see what we can do. In the meantime I wonder if you could put me straight over one or two things. What proportion of your business is affected by this steel problem?'

At half-past ten Sir Francis gave a little start, rose, and poured Lang out another brandy. 'That's all extra-ordinarily interesting,' he said. 'Of course, between our-selves Henry Spellman, though a dear old boy in many ways, knows more about French painting than he does about business. A scheme like yours would frighten the life out of him.'

Lang smiled. 'Of course with a thing like that, it's so very easy for anybody to say that what you're sug-gesting is airy-fairy and impractical. . . .'

'Yes, yes. All the usual plain-men's arguments. But plain-men don't build businesses. It's the dreamers who do that.' Sir Francis smiled at his glass. 'I've suffered

a good deal from plain-men with hard commonsense in
my time.   But I've usually contrived to be in a position
to say : "Gentlemen, I am interested to hear your views.
But here is my decision".'

Lang said : 'That's exactly the position I should like
to be in.   But as I say, you immediately get a cry of
"Dictator !" from all the scared sheep.'

Sir Francis frowned.   'Yes,' he said thoughtfully.   'I
must confess that I hadn't realised you had *that* problem.
When your brother died, I naturally thought the controlling interest would pass to you—or at least that you
would buy it from his estate.'

'Frankly,' said Lang, 'I don't see what Henry's getting
at.   If he's got to sell . . .'

Sir Francis suddenly sat forward in his chair with a
mischievous grin.   'Look here,' he said, 'this is probably
a ridiculous idea, but . . . How many of these shares
are there ?'

'Eighty thousand.   Forty per cent of the ordinary
capital.'

'And you have thirty per cent ?'

'Yes.'

'Well, then,' said Sir Francis slowly, 'what happens
if *I* buy your brother's shares ?'

'You ?' said Lang startled.

'Yes.   Why not ?   Henry's got to sell them.   Presumably they'll be sold at a valuation which makes them a
reasonable investment.   Nobody knows of this conversation.   It would look like a perfectly ordinary deal by
my group.'

'Ah, but if Lang's were bought up by your group . . .'

'It wouldn't be bought up.   We should have no control, owning only forty per cent of the equity.   *But* . . .'
Sir Francis smiled.   'But with that forty and your thirty,
then seventy per cent of the shares would be owned by
people with—shall we say—similar views about business.'
There was a long silence.   'Of course, you may not like
the idea,' said Sir Francis.   'I know a lot of people have
the old-fashioned fears of having anything to do with a
large group.   But I must say I find it rather attractive.
After all, your big problem is going to be how to make

this changeover from mainly fabricating to your own products, without going through some very difficult years. Now a group the size of ours has a lot of fabricating work and a number of fabricating plants. We could put just the amount into your place necessary to keep you going, and withdraw it as and when it becomes less necessary.'

'Yes,' said Lang slowly. 'I see that . . . Of course there'll be a sizeable capital investment in plant. . . .'

'Well . . .?' said Sir Francis with a smile.

'. . . but I think the company could finance that itself.'

'So much the better.'

'The other problem's going to be raw materials. And if Falk is as tight for steel as he says . . .'

They looked at one another for a moment and both laughed. 'Falk,' said Sir Francis, 'is an excellent business man who stoutly looks after my interests when he feels that I'm too easy-going to look after them myself. Do you mind touching that bell? I think this calls for a whisky-and-soda and a little thought.'

'Mind you,' said Lang, 'I'm not at all sure that if Henry knew about this talk he'd sell them to you. He's bent on stopping me from doing this job.'

'My dear man,' said Sir Francis, 'if I bought these shares, I should do so as an investment. Thereafter, how I voted them would be nothing to do with Henry. He might easily sell them to someone else, and find that the man was your most ardent supporter.' He took his whisky-and-soda and smiled at it thoughtfully. 'Nobody can stop a good man,' he said gently. 'People may do their best to hinder those of us with progressive ideas, but there's always a way round.' He raised his glass. 'Here's to an interesting thought, anyhow.'

They drank it in silence. Sir Francis said: 'You met my man Winter, didn't you? What did you think of him?'

'I thought he was first-rate.'

'How'd you like to have him for a bit?'

'You mean to work?'

'Yes. I was just thinking that if we did go through with this idea, presumably I should be allowed to nominate somebody for the Board. Now Winter's just the

sort of chap you want to work with you. He's a go-getter
and he really *knows* modern production. . . .' He broke
off and waved a hand. 'But I'm going altogether too fast.'

There was a moment's pause.

'I'm not at all sure that you are,' said Lang thoughtfully. 'I'm just losing my production director, and a
chap like Winter . . .'

* * * * *

Lawrence said : 'We could knock down the wall of
the spare room and throw it into ours and turn the
dressing-room into a bathroom.'

'We could do that,' said Laura. 'What we couldn't
do is pay for it. And anyhow it's at the other end that
we need another bathroom.'

'I'm very tired of this house,' said Lawrence moodily.
'Let's go and live in a caravan. Or on a boat. I should
like to live on a boat.'

He got up, wandered over to the window and stood
staring out at the lawn.

Laura said : 'Are you going to London this week ?'

He grinned without turning and said gently : 'No,
dear. A week of toil and domesticity.'

Mrs. Ryle came in and said : 'There's a Mr. and Mrs.
Pinner to see you, Mr. Spellman.'

'Pinner ? Don't know anybody named Pinner. Did
they say what they want ?'

'No. Just said they wanted to see you.'

'Well, well,' said Lawrence. 'They shall have audience. Pinner . . .?'

Mr. and Mrs. Pinner were standing in the hall. Mrs.
Pinner was a bulky woman with a red face. Her mouth
was tremulous, and she looked as though she had been
crying. Mr. Pinner was a wiry, sandy little man with a
black shade over one eye, which made him look peculiarly
terrier-like. He was wearing a hard white collar several
sizes too big for him and a black suit, and he carried a
grey trilby hat. They were clearly not his usual clothes.

Lawrence smiled and said : 'Good evening. . . .'

Mrs. Pinner sniffed and looked nervously at her husband. Mr. Pinner said : 'Mr. Spellman—you're Mr.

Spellman? Want to talk to you, my wife and I we want to talk to you.'

'Well, certainly,' said Lawrence with his best human-factor cordiality. 'What about?'

'Private,' said Mr. Pinner.

'I beg your pardon?'

'Private. My wife and me want to talk to you private.'

'Oh—I see. All right—then let's go in here, shall we?' Lawrence led them into the morning-room. 'Do sit down. Cigarette?'

'No. I don't smoke. We come for an explanation.' In the brighter light of the morning room Mr. Pinner appeared to be rather pale, and he was quivering slightly.

'Explanation?' said Lawrence, startled. 'What about?'

'About my daughter Hilda. Hilda Pinner. My daughter.'

Lawrence frowned. 'I'm sorry,' he said politely. 'But I don't think I know anybody named Hilda Pinner. . . .'

Mrs. Pinner gave a faint moan and turned her head away.

'Oh, don't you . . .!' said Mr. Pinner dangerously.

'Unless she's at the Works—at Lang's . . .?'

'Yes she is, and you took her in your car. Two days ago. In your car. My daughter Hilda. Two days ago it was.'

'Oh, *I* know,' said Lawrence. 'I didn't know her name was Hilda. I thought . . . Yes. That's right. I gave her a lift from the Works to Market Cross.'

'He gave her a lift,' said Mrs. Pinner bitterly, to nobody in particular.

'Well, what about it?' said Lawrence shortly.

'What I want's your explanation. That's what I want.'

'*He* knows,' said Mrs. Pinner.

Mr. Pinner said: 'I want your explanation. Your explanation of what you did to my daughter.'

There was a moment's pause. 'Oh,' said Lawrence softly. 'I see. Why? Does she say I did something to her?'

'What's the use of his denying it?' said Mrs. Pinner.

'Come home like that after a day's work,' said Mr. Pinner trembling, 'and find the girl and my wife all upset. After a day's work. You ought to be ashamed of yourself.'

Lawrence said politely: 'Will you excuse me for just a moment?' He went quickly back to the drawing-room. Laura was fiddling with the radio. He said: 'Darling, d'you mind coming? I think you'd better be in on this.'

'On what?'

'I'm not absolutely sure. They're a bit incoherent. But I rather *think* I'm being accused of rape.'

'Rape?' said Laura. 'Well, well.'

They went back to the morning-room. The Pinners were talking in low voices. They separated quickly as the Spellmans entered. Lawrence said: 'Mr. and Mrs. Pinner. My wife. Now please go on, Mr. Pinner. I gather your daughter Hilda has told you I did something to her when I gave her a lift the other day?'

Mr. Pinner said: 'D'you deny it?'

'You haven't told me yet what I'm supposed to have done.'

'He knows,' said Mrs. Pinner.

'Interfered with her,' said Mr. Pinner reluctantly. 'A bit of a girl like that. I've come for your explanation. That's what I want.'

Laura said: 'When is all this supposed to have happened?'

'A couple of days ago, darling. I gave her a lift from the Works down to town.' Lawrence picked up a cigarette and lit it. His hands were usually very shaky, but they were steady now. 'Look, Mr. Pinner,' he said gently, 'I can only assure you that nothing of the sort happened. Your daughter was walking home from the Works. I passed with the car, and as I frequently do with anybody I see walking home, gave her a lift. I think she said her bicycle had a puncture or something. I drove her in to Market Cross, which is more or less on my way home. On the way we chatted about this and that, but she's a shy girl and we didn't even talk much. At Market Cross I stopped and she thanked me and got out. That's all.'

Mrs. Pinner snorted slightly and looked at her husband.

Mr. Pinner said quickly : 'You don't deny that you took her in the car with you?'

'Of course not.'

'Because there's witnesses that you did,' said Mr. Pinner triumphantly. 'Her aunt Marjorie or what we call her aunt saw her get out.'

'Very likely. I've told you I gave her a lift.'

'And you say you never did anything?'

'Certainly I didn't.'

Mr. and Mrs. Pinner exchanged glances.

Mr. Pinner said : 'Then why should she say you did? I want your explanation of that.'

Mrs. Pinner said : 'Of course he'd *say* . . .'

'You be quiet,' said Mr. Pinner sharply. 'I want his explanation.'

Lawrence shrugged his shoulders. 'There you have me. I can only tell you what happened. Young girls do sometimes say these things, but I must say I'm surprised if your daughter's done so. She seemed a very nice quiet girl.'

Mrs. Pinner suddenly said very loudly : 'She's a decent girl that's been properly brought up to fear God,' and burst into tears.

'Just a minute,' said Laura. 'When did your daughter tell you about this?'

Mr. Pinner hesitated. 'This evening,' he said reluctantly.

'What? Two days after it's supposed to have happened? Why didn't she tell you at once?'

Mr. Pinner said : 'She was afraid.'

'What of?'

'She wasn't afraid for herself,' said Mrs. Pinner chokily. 'She was afraid for him—that he'd get into trouble. And it played on her mind knowing it was wrong and then she came and told her mother. . . .' She wept again.

Mr. Pinner said : 'Come home after a day's work and find that. After a day's work . . .' The thought that it was after a day's work, or the sight of his wife's tears made him angrier than ever. He said : 'I want your explanation, and if I don't get it, then it'll have to be reported. Reported. I'll show you up. Report it.'

'It's no good keeping on saying you want my explanation,' said Lawrence irritably. 'I've given you the only explanation I can, which is that it's all nonsense and no such thing ever happened.'

Mrs. Pinner said : 'Of course he'd say that.'

'The only thing that I can think of,' said Lawrence, 'is for me to see the girl with you, and make her repeat what she said in front of me.'

The Pinners exchanged glances.

'She's not fit for any games of that sort,' said Mr. Pinner. 'She's all upset. Bit of a girl like that. . . .'

'Then I'm very sorry,' said Lawrence shortly, 'but I can't do any more to help you. If your daughter wants to accuse me, then she must do it to my face and in front of witnesses, and I must be allowed to question her about it. Otherwise I shall ignore the whole thing.'

Mr. Pinner said : 'Oh, you'll ignore it, will you?' and said : 'Come on,' to his wife and went out. The front door banged behind them.

Laura and Lawrence walked slowly back to the drawing-room in silence. Laura said : 'I want your explanation. . . .' They looked at one another and suddenly burst into a simultaneous giggle.

'I dare say,' said Lawrence, 'but this is damned awkward. . . .'

'It certainly is, darling.'

'But why on earth should the little fool go and say a thing like that ? And why pick on me ? I thought it was only elderly clergymen of impeccable character that this happened to.'

Laura said : 'Do I know her ?'

'I shouldn't think so. Pretty little thing. Blonde. I danced with her at the party.'

'Ah, yes,' said Laura. She turned away and lit a cigarette. 'You know,' she said, staring at him thoughtfully, 'you know, I think you'd better take some action about this, darling. Those characters are out for blood.'

Lawrence said : 'I know. But what can I do ?'

'Think they'll go to the police ?'

'Heaven knows. It rather depends what she's accusing me of. Pa and Ma were so modest I still don't know whether I'm supposed to have kissed her or to have raped her.'

Laura said: 'I don't think they notice little distinctions like that. There was a case the other day where a girl complained to the police that somebody whistled at her in the street. Did you stop the car at any point?'

'Only when I dropped her.'

'It was moving all the time she was in it?'

'Of course. I was just driving home.'

Laura said: 'Well then, there isn't such a hell of a lot you *could* have done. Apart from what I believe are usually known as Certain Suggestions. Even so, I think I'd ring Tony Lampard up in the morning. Solicitors like to be in on things early.'

'Yes. I'll do that.' He went across to a cupboard. 'What I need at the moment is a drink. For you?'

'Yes, please.' Laura gazed thoughtfully at his back. 'The other person I should certainly get hold of,' she said, 'is your Papa.'

'Why Papa?'

'Because if they don't go to the police they'll certainly go and kick up a fuss at Lang's. Which might be almost equally awkward.'

'It would certainly give pleasure in some quarters,' said Lawrence bitterly.

'If it's coming to Papa at all, it would be better if it came from you.'

'Yes.' Lawrence sipped his drink. 'It's damned unfair this, you know,' he said moodily. 'I've often thought so when I've seen cases in the papers. Some hysterical kid has only to say a thing like that about a man, and whether it's true or not, he's got no defence. The law won't usually convict him just on a girl's say so. But everybody else will say what those people did: "Why should she say it if it isn't true?"'

'Moreover,' said Laura slowly, 'let's face it, darling —you haven't exactly got a reputation for . . .'

Lawrence said: 'I have a reputation as a skirt-chaser that it has taken me years to cultivate.'

'Quite.'

F

'That's what's so irritating, to be quite frank. As a man with no particular morals and rather low tastes, it's maddening if on one of the few occasions when you *do* act in pure good nature . . .'

'Yes,' said Laura gently, staring at her cigarette end. 'It's very hard.'

Lawrence looked at her sharply. After a moment's pause he leant forward and said: 'Look, darling . . . just let's be clear about one thing. You don't by any chance believe this kid's telling the truth, do you? Because . . .'

Laura raised the lovely green eyes and smiled at him brightly. 'Darling,' she said, 'I don't think you're a paragon of virtue, but I don't imagine you've reached the stage of "interfering" with little factory girls in motor-cars. At least I trust not.'

Lawrence grinned. 'Not quite, anyhow.'

Laura stubbed out her cigarette. She said: 'I think if I were you I should go and ring up your father right away.'

XII

MISS BELL looked at her notes and said: 'There was just the question of whether it ought to be the Works Committee on the platform, or just the Directors, and Mr. Ryan representing the works side. You see there are the two presentations, Mr. Walter. One from the Directors and one from the rest of us.'

Lang said: 'Does it matter?'

'Works Committee,' said Ryan briefly. 'Makes it more representative of everybody.'

'Anyhow, is there anybody on the Board who's not on the Works Committee?'

Miss Bell hesitated. 'Only Mr. Lawrence and Mr. Talbot-Rees.'

'Oh well,' said Lang, 'make it the Works Committee. I don't suppose Mr. Lawrence or Mr. Talbot-Rees will mind not sitting on the platform.'

Miss Bell said: 'Then I thought if you were to say a few words about Mr. Martin's services . . .'

'Why me? Why not the Chairman?'

'The Chairman's going to make the presentation on behalf of the Directors. After you, I thought Mr. Martin might reply. Then the Chairman make the Directors' presentation and Mr. Ryan the Works' presentation. Then perhaps Mr. Martin will want to say a few words of thanks. . . .'

Lang shifted impatiently and said: 'Oh, draw it mild. We don't want this to go on all night. Why not let George speak *after* the presentations?'

'It won't really take long, Mr. Walter. Then I'd asked Mr. Gage to have a few members of the Choral Society sitting together so that they could lead in singing "For He's a Jolly Good Fellow," because it's so awful if it's just ragged. . . .'

'And after that,' said Lang moodily, 'George Martin can go home and we have to manage without him.'

Miss Bell said: 'I didn't think we needed votes of thanks to the Chairman for presiding or anything like that.'

'No.' Lang sat in silence for a moment. 'Be funny without him, won't it?' he said to Ryan.

'You won't get a better man, Mr. Walter. You could always talk straight to George Martin.'

Miss Bell said: 'I've put down a few notes on—on Mr. Martin's career with the company if you'd like to have them. . . .'

'Good,' said Lang. He took the sheet of paper and glanced at it. It was headed:

> '**RETIREMENT OF MR. MARTIN**'
> *George Martin joined the company*
> *as an apprentice in* 1904 . . .

Lang said, almost to himself: 'I wonder what he'll do with his time? He'll be miserable. . . .' He got up and said: 'Well, that's that. Five o'clock?'

'That's right, Mr. Walter.' Ryan and Miss Bell exchanged glances. Neither rose. Ryan said: 'There's one other thing, Mr. Walter. . . .'

'Oh, sorry,' said Lang. 'Go ahead.'

'Rather unpleasant thing, but we reckoned you ought to know.' Ryan hesitated. 'There's a girl in Assembly named Hilda Pinner. Well, her father came up here while you were away asking for Miss Bell, and Miss Bell sent for me. . . .'

*   *   *   *   *

North put the letter down and rubbed his nose. Henry Spellman said: 'What d'you think of that?'

North said: 'Well, it's a bolt from the blue, isn't it, Mr. Spellman?'

'I suppose there's no *legal* reason why we shouldn't sell to him if we want to?'

'Not that I can see, Mr. Spellman.'

'Question is whether we want to. Any ideas about that?'

North considered. 'Well, there's a lot to be said on both sides, isn't there, Mr. Spellman?'

Henry sighed: 'You're a helpful chap, aren't you, North?'

North smiled. 'You see, Mr. Spellman, I was only appointed an executor because of—of the legal side and so on. I mean I don't want to sway your mind. . . .' He paused and cocked an eye at Spellman from over his glasses. 'I don't know what—what Mr. Walter'll think . . .?'

'It doesn't matter what Mr. Walter'll think,' said Henry curtly. 'Our job is to do the best for the estate and for the business. Here's a straight offer for the shares, and a good one. But it means tying up with a very big organisation. Do we want to do that?'

'That's really the question, isn't it?'

'As Proudfoot says, it might be to our mutual advantage. But . . .' Henry paused and shook his head.

North said: 'I understand how you feel, Mr. Spellman.'

'If it meant selling him control I wouldn't look at it. But it doesn't.'

North placed a finger on one side of his nose and pressed it grotesquely out of the straight. 'Of course,' he said thoughtfully, 'it would overcome *one* problem, wouldn't it?'

'You mean about Walter getting control?'

'Well, Mr. Spellman . . .'

Henry frowned. 'Yes. But we don't want to jump out of the frying-pan into the fire. Because we don't want to sell to Walter, it doesn't mean that we've got to sell to Proudfoot.'

'Of course not, Mr. Spellman.'

*　　　*　　　*　　　*　　　*

Lang sat for a while in silence staring straight in front of him. Miss Bell was looking down at the desk with an expression of pain.

Lang said: 'Have you talked to anybody about this?'

Ryan said: 'No. Not anybody.'

'Seen the girl herself?'

'No. See, we didn't want . . .'

'Or to Mr. Lawrence. Or his father?'

'No.'

Miss Bell said: 'I thought perhaps we ought to go to the Chairman, but Mr. Ryan . . .'

'Well, it struck *me*,' said Ryan, 'that this was a thing you'd got to be mighty careful about.'

Lang nodded. 'Agree.'

'After all, it could be a pretty serious thing. And if there was a court case . . .'

Lang said: 'What sort of girl is she?'

'Very decent girl, I should say, wouldn't you, Miss Bell?'

'Yes, **Mr.** Walter. Very nice quiet girl. Not at all the sort . . . well, you know . . .'

'Only their having come to see us,' said Ryan, 'and my having been brought in officially as it were, I don't see how we can just take no notice. Besides, as you know, Mr. Walter, a thing like that—you can't keep it quiet. It'll be all round, however much you try to stop it.'

'Oh, we can't possibly just let it go,' said Lang with finality. 'It wouldn't be fair to anybody, including Lawrence. You say her parents saw him?'

'Yes, Mr. Walter.'

'And he denied it?'

'Just said he gave her a lift and that the rest was all lies.'

Lang and Ryan stared steadily and expressionlessly at one another for a moment. Then Lang pursed his lips and turned away. 'Well, we can't leave it at that,' he said curtly. 'I'd better have a word with the Chairman—and probably with Mr. Lawrence. Thank you for telling me.'

As they rose Ryan said: 'There's just one thing, Mr. Walter. . . .'

'Yes?'

'If there's going to be some sort of inquiry, I reckon I shall have to come into it somewhere—as Chief Shop Steward. See, a thing like this that's been brought to my notice officially . . . Otherwise what's going to be said is that it'll be hushed up, and because he's a director and the Chairman's son and she's only a girl out of Assembly . . .'

Lang hesitated and said: 'We don't want to shout it around the place, of course. But I see what you mean. Anyhow—I'll have a talk with the Chairman.'

*   *   *   *   *

The specially made, inscribed gold watch from the Directors, and the extremely expensive Hardy fly rod and reel from the Works, lay on the table before him. George Martin rose and stood looking round him as the applause went rattling on. His hands were trembling, and when the audience would let him speak his voice hardly carried to the back of the big canteen room. 'I'm not going to make a long speech,' he said with his gentle smile, 'some of you will be wanting to get home to your teas. . . .' Through the laughter Miss Bell turned to Jack and said: 'That's so like George—so like him to think of that. . . .' Her eyes were full of tears. They had been full of tears throughout the ceremony. Jack nodded rather vaguely and glanced at the clock on the end wall. He had said he would be out there by half-past six, and that would be all right if old George didn't go on too long. But the thing was whether to tell her that people knew about it, and that he was having his leg pulled. Because she never seemed to think of that —about being seen. But they were on to it, some of the boys were, though they didn't seem to know it was her. . . .

'Mr. Walter's told you I came here in 1904. That's more than a world away—it's two worlds away. Because that's ten years before the First World War, and thirty-five years before the last one. . . .' He looked slowly round. 'I don't think there's anybody here who was here when I came. . . .' 'Yes, there is,' said a voice loudly. 'No, there isn't,' said Martin, as the heads turned. He smiled towards the back of the hall. 'I came in September, Joe Wells, and you didn't come till after Christmas. . . .'

Lang took a slip of paper from his pocket and scribbled on it: 'I should like to see you for a few minutes after this, if you can manage it.' He passed it on to Henry Spellman, who was sitting staring at Martin's back with an expression of goodwill and amusement frozen on his face. Henry read the note, glanced at him and nodded. The benign expression had disappeared for a moment and he carefully replaced it.

Martin was saying: 'I can well remember my first day. I was an apprentice and very frightened, and I was having the sort of time from other chaps that new apprentices did have. And I expect still do. . . . And a young gentleman came along and he said to me: "What's your name?" I said: "Martin, sir." He put out his hand and shook hands with me and said: "Well, you're welcome, Martin. I hope you enjoy it here. Don't take too much notice of these chaps. They're all right when you get to know them." He turned round and gave one of them a punch in the chest and smiled and off he went. So I said to the others: "Who's that?" And they said: "Oh, that's young Mr. Gustavus. . . ."' Martin's voice wavered for a moment. 'That was the first time I saw Mr. Gustavus,' he added quietly. 'And it was a word and a smile and a handshake for a kid. . . . And for forty-eight years, that was the spirit he gave us. . . .'

Talbot-Rees leaned over and whispered: 'I don't think this is up to George's usual standard of tact. Observe our Walter's face.'

Lawrence said: 'Oh, he won't worry about what George says now. George is dead, from his point of view. He'll be working out how to make life a misery for Barker.'

'And about this time there came a young gentleman to the office side. Very slim he was. I didn't see much of him but I was told his name was Mr. Spellman. . . .' Henry laughed with the laughter. His paunch shook. His thighs shook. His chair creaked.

'And sometimes when Mr. William Lang's carriage would come for him, there'd be a little boy in knicker-bockers with it named Walter. . . .' Martin turned slowly and smiled at Lang. Amidst the delighted roar of laughter he shook his head. 'I little knew then,' he said ruefully.

'This is all very well,' said Lawrence to Talbot-Rees, 'but we're still in 1904, and some of us will be wanting to get home to our teas.'

*　　　*　　　*　　　*　　　*

Martin had sat through the speeches and the presentations, but it was too much to go on sitting on the platform right through 'For He's a Jolly Good Fellow.' He made a dive for the wings, and only Henry Spellman's touch on the arm reminded him to take the watch and the rod.

As the platform party rose to follow him Lang said: 'You can spare a minute now?'

Henry said: 'Surely. Your office or mine? Make it mine. Got something to show you.'

When they reached the office building Henry jerked his head towards Martin's office. 'D'you want to go and have a last word with George before he goes off?'

'George?' said Lang abstractedly. 'Oh . . . no . . . I won't bother him now. I expect there'll be a crowd up there.'

Henry sat down at his desk and said: 'Before we talk about anything else . . .' He took a letter out of a file, looked at it for a moment and handed it to Lang. 'What d'you make of that? Francis Proudfoot.'

Lang read the letter slowly. When he looked up his face was quite expressionless. 'Well,' he said, 'what are you going to do about it?'

'I don't know yet. What d'you say, Walter?'

'Nothing to do with me,' said Lang coldly. 'It's up to you and North.'

Henry shifted uneasily. 'Quite. But I thought you ought to see it.'

'Yes. I appreciate that. Well—it's a good offer. The only person likely to make you a better one was me, and if I'm excluded because of some private talk between you and Gustavus . . .'

Henry said: 'What I wanted to know was whether you were opposed in principle to selling the shares to a big outfit like that. Of course it doesn't give him control and the tie-up might be useful to us. . . .'

'Look, Henry,' said Lang curtly, 'I told you what I thought might be done with these shares, and made you an offer. You wouldn't have it. You told me I'd got no standing in the matter at all. After that, you can't expect me to advise you. You're in charge. You must make your own decision and take the responsibility. I only come in as a member of the Board.'

Henry shrugged. 'All right, Walter.' He said rather coldly: 'That's fair enough. I only didn't want you to feel that I'd done anything behind your back.'

'Oh no,' said Lang with a slight smile, 'I'll absolve you of that, Henry. If you sell to Proudfoot it won't be behind my back.' He watched with enjoyment as Henry replaced the letter in the file, obviously rather disconcerted. 'Now then—what I wanted a word with you about. Has anybody told you about this trouble with Lawrence?'

'You mean about this girl?' said Henry heavily. 'Yes. He told me about it.'

     *   *   *   *   *

The inscribed gold watch and the rod and reel lay on Martin's desk. It was after seven, and they had all been and gone. Miss Bell had cried and Lawrence and Talbot-Rees had brought in a bottle of champagne and drunk it while he was drinking his first half glass, and North had offered a damp limp handshake, and Ryan a much too firm one. There was only one thing to wait for, and even that didn't really matter, of course. Martin took up the telephone and dialled Lang's office again. Lang's secretary said: 'I'm sorry, Mr. Martin. I think he's still with Mr. Spellman. Shall I take a note in to him and tell him . . .?' Martin said: 'No, no. It doesn't matter. It's not important. . . .' He put the receiver down and looked slowly round the room. His IN tray was empty, but there were some duplicated sheets of figures in his OUT tray. Martin picked them up and looked at them idly for a moment and then put them back in the tray and rose. He took the gold hunter watch out of its leather fob. The inscription said: 'Presented to George Martin by the Directors of William

Lang Sons & Horseman Ltd. 1904-1953.' He put it
back in its fob and put it carefully in his waistcoat pocket,
put on his hat and raincoat and picked up the fishing rod.
He looked round for the last time. There was a tobacco
tin on the mantelpiece, but when he shook it it was empty.
He pitched it into the waste-paper basket and went out,
closing the door behind him.

*   *   *   *   *

Henry said: 'I took the view that it's nothing to do
with the company at all.'

'How d'you make that out?'

'It didn't happen on the company's premises or in the
company's time.'

Lang frowned irritably. 'Oh come! He's a director
here and the girl works here. That's how he knows her.
It's just splitting hairs to say it's no concern of ours.'

'That was my opinion,' said Henry doggedly.

'Then you really mean you think we could just let it
go? After her parents have come and complained to
Miss Bell and Ryan?'

'As far as I can see it's up to the girl and her parents
to go to the police if they've got a complaint. Not to
come babbling to people here.'

'But don't you see, Henry—Ryan was saying to-
day—this is bound to get round the place. If we
don't do something it'll be said that we wanted to hush
it up. . . .'

'Well, *you* certainly don't seem to want to, Walter,'
said Spellman bitterly.

Lang said: 'No, I don't. Not if Lawrence is going
to go on working here.'

There was a moment's pause. Henry said: 'What
d'you want then? A sort of court martial? That's going
to be pretty, isn't it?'

'I think Lawrence has got to be given a chance to
explain. In fairness to himself.'

'How can he explain?' said Henry, flicking his spectacles irritably away from him. 'The girl says one thing.
He says she's a liar. If you're going to take the word of
some hysterical kid against one of our own directors . . .'

'It's not a question of taking anybody's word. What I want's the truth.'

'Well, I can tell you the truth,' said Henry angrily. 'Lawrence is a damned young fool in some ways, but he's not such a fool as that. And you know it. If it were anybody else you'd be all for keeping out of it. But because you happen to dislike Lawrence, you think you see a way of working him out.'

There was a moment's pause.

'Well, if we're going to talk like that,' said Lang very calmly, 'I don't mind telling you that if Lawrence hadn't been your son, he would have been out of this business years ago. He's been let get away with murder as it is. But this time he's gone too far.'

Henry hesitated for a moment, and then nodded. 'All right,' he said. 'I see. Then if that's how you want it, we'd better get him in and talk to him.' He picked up the telephone.

Lang said: 'He'll have gone an hour ago.'

'Then he can come back,' said Henry.

*　　*　　*　　*　　*

George Martin gazed into the fire. 'I'd like you to have heard Mr. Walter,' he said a smile. 'You know he's not one to say much. . . .'

'No,' said Clarice, 'he isn't.'

Martin looked up at the curious edge in her voice, but she had turned away and was getting out the table-cloth.

George said: 'I know you reckon he was a hard man to work for, and so he was of course. But he always trusted me.'

'Did he have any reason not to?'

He smiled. 'Maybe not. But he's a grand man, Mr. Walter, with all his faults.'

Clarice said: 'You always say he's a grand man. You tell me what's grand about him? I've always wanted to know.'

'I don't know,' said George simply. 'But we always got on. And old Henry Spellman too. Always very good to me.'

Clarice said harshly: 'And now they've given you a nice gold watch and you can go.' She turned her head quickly away.

'Here,' said George in surprise. 'What's the matter with you, Clarry? I'm retiring of my own accord. I've got a pension, haven't I? You've got nothing against Lang's or anybody there.'

'Forty-eight years,' she said in a low voice, 'forty-eight years you've worked and slaved. . . .'

George shook his head. 'I don't see what you're saying,' he said. 'I've done a good job and I've been well treated, and they've given me a grand send off, so what is there to feel like that about?'

She turned to him and said furiously: 'Oh you're an old *fool* . . .!' and burst into tears.

George said: 'Hey, Clarry . . .!' He got up and put his arm round her. 'What is it, dear?'

She choked out: 'You only live once and then it's over and you're old and . . .' She tore herself suddenly away from him and snatched up the watch and said: 'I hate them—the whole lot of them. . . .'

He caught her wrist and said: 'Clarry' very gently, and took the watch out of her hands. She stood stiffly for a moment and then suddenly slackened and dropped her head on his shoulder. She said in a half-whisper: 'I'm sorry, George. I don't know what came over me. . . .'

He gently stroked her wisps of grey hair into place and said: 'Upsetting yourself like that, and all about nothing. . . .'

After a while she slowly drew away and patted at her hair. She pointed to the reel and said: 'That's a lovely made thing. Is that the sort you told me about?'

'That's it,' he said. 'One of Hardy's. I've always wanted one.'

She smiled and said: 'Well, now you'll have time to go fishing properly, instead of just a fortnight a year.'

* * * * *

Lawrence took out a cigarette, patted his pockets, smiled round at Lang and Henry, and said: 'Has anyone a match?'

His father took a box of matches out of his pocket and
tossed it across in silence. Lawrence lit the cigarette and
carefully removed a shred of tobacco from his tongue.
His face was very pale. 'In principle,' he said, 'I agree
with Walter. A Royal Commission is obviously desir-
able.' He smiled at Lang. 'In the interests of justice,
purity, decency and all the other virtues.'

'I'm thinking of your own interests,' said Lang
calmly.

'I know you are, Walter, and I'm grateful. What
form do you think it ought to take? A public trial in the
canteen?'

Henry frowned. 'I think we'd better get a legal
opinion on the whole thing,' he said to Lang. 'Otherwise
I'm not quite sure where you're landing yourself.'

'The same thought occurred to me,' said Lawrence
gently. 'You see, Walter, if, in safeguarding my interests,
your Royal Commission happened to say or imply something about me that it couldn't prove, then that might
be slander or libel or something else fruity. If she takes
the thing to Court, then there's no need for your inquiry.
If she doesn't, I think you've got to be rather careful over
trying the case yourself.'

Henry said: 'You think they'll take it to Court?'

'I've no idea. I sincerely hope so.'

Lang frowned and shifted irritably in his chair. 'This
is all very fine and large,' he said, 'but neither of you
seems to understand what I'm after. Nobody here's got
the right to "try" you. You can just tell us all to mind
our own business. But in that case I think the Board
would be justified in asking for your resignation. I'm
not interested in your morals. But I *am* interested in
what's being said about a director of this company and
his behaviour to a young employee. This girl's accused
you. Either she's a dirty little liar, in which case we must
get rid of her, or else she's telling the truth. . . .'

'In which case you must get rid of me?'

'Yes. You know as well as I do that if a story like
this gets about, everybody will believe it unless it's nailed.
If you and your father think I'm using this as an excuse
to get rid of you, I can't stop you. But what I'm really

offering you is a chance to clear yourself—you don't have to take it if you don't want to. But it *can't* just be left as it is.'

Lawrence said: 'In other words, ask for an inquiry or resign, eh?'

'Well, is that unfair? After all, you've got nothing to hide if the girl's a liar.'

Lawrence smiled slightly. Old Henry said: 'I think you'd better have a word with your solicitor before . . .'

'What for?' said Lawrence wearily. 'Anyhow I'd rather like to be told what I did to her. I'm interested.' He turned to Lang. 'All right, Walter. Who's going to do the inquiring? You?'

Lang said: 'No. I don't want to have anything to do with it.' He glanced at Henry. 'I should think we want Ryan to represent the Works side, and perhaps Miss Bell, and somebody from the Board.'

Lawrence said: 'Well, if that isn't either of you two or me, it leaves North and Jim Talbot-Rees and Barker. I shouldn't think it's a job for Barker, and if it's all the same to everybody I'd rather not Jim, Amy being a weeny bit talkative.'

Henry said: 'If you must have somebody, North's the obvious man. And he'll help you to keep straight legally.'

'Agree, Walter?'

Lang nodded in silence.

'Right,' said Lawrence briskly. 'Then if one of you will tell those three, I'm ready to answer any questions they like. Whom do they report to?'

'The Board,' said Lang briefly.

Lawrence glanced at his watch. 'Well,' he said with his brightest smile, 'having been committed for trial, can I go now? I've got a date.'

XIII

ROSAMUND tied a piece of cotton round the stems
of the bunch of primroses and said: 'I never know
why one picks them. They look so much prettier just
growing.'

Jack said: 'Stop doing that and lie back comfortable.'
He threw his cigarette end away and stretched out an
arm. Rosamund leaned back and wriggled her head into
a comfortable position against his shoulder.

She said: 'I'm surprised you don't know this place.
Mummy and I always used to come here primroseing.'
She gave a slight giggle. 'I remember once we had a
great argument before we came, about whether we should
bunch them as we picked, or take them back in a basket
and bunch them up at home. When we got here there
were hardly any. We only got about half a dozen. After
that "bunching them up" was always a family joke.'

He chuckled and the hand that was on her breast
tightened slightly.

'That's funny!' said Rosamund. 'Do it again—
chortle like that. It sounds awfully queer when I've got
my ear against you.'

He leant over so that his face was against her hair,
and closed his eyes. 'Darling Rosey,' he said sleepily.

She heaved a sigh and said: 'Oh God, this is
nice . . .!'

After a while Rosamund sat up and clasped her hands
round her knees. People had been cutting the underwood
and the opened spaces were a mass of spring flowers.
She said: 'I don't know why there aren't any people
about. Usually on Sunday this place is swarming.'

'I can do without them.' He sat up too and lit another
cigarette, frowning at the bright flower carpet.

After a while Rosamund said: 'You're very quiet.
Anything up?'

176

'No,' he said slowly, 'I wouldn't say there was anything *up*. But there's something I reckon I ought to tell you about. . . .' He hesitated. 'Some of the boys—Mac and Fred Boxall and some of them—they know I been going out with you. Least, I don't reckon they know it's you, but they know I've been going out with a girl with a car. Getting my leg pulled about it all right.'

Rosamund continued to gaze straight ahead in silence.

'See, somebody saw us that night when we went to the Birdwood, and you know how things get round. . . .'

She said: 'Do you mind?'

'Me?' he said stoutly. 'Why should I? But I reckon you'd get a spanking if your father ever heard.'

There was a long pause. Rosamund said in a low voice: 'I never think about it. I don't know why, but I just never do.'

'Where does he think you are?'

'To-day? Oh—I told him I was going over to some friends of ours at Charfont. . . .' She shook her head. 'I just tell him lies,' she said simply. 'And I don't mind that either, for some reason. It—it just feels all right.'

Jack took her hand and gazed at it rather moodily. 'Still,' he said, 'I reckon we ought to be careful. I mean he *would* be mad with you, wouldn't he?'

'Oh, yes. I should think so. I don't really see why, but I'm sure he would.'

'Well, that's easy,' said Jack with a bitter little smile. 'He wouldn't want his daughter going round with one of his press hands.'

'That's what's so damned silly,' said Rosamund crossly. She thought for a moment and then added: 'Though I don't think it would only be that. I don't believe he'd like me to—to have anybody, really. He's always very frightened that I—I should want to go away.'

'Anyhow, if he didn't do anything else he'd stop you seeing me.'

She looked at him for a moment in silence, and then slowly turned her eyes away. 'What frightens me,' she said slowly, 'is how it's ever going to get any better. We

can't go on and on not being able to see one another
because of . . .'

Jack said: 'That'll settle itself, Rosey.'

'How?'

He smiled wryly. 'You'll go away and fall in love,
and marry somebody of your own sort and . . .'

She turned angrily. 'I shan't! I don't *want* anybody
else. You know I don't. . . .'

Her eyes filled with tears. He said: 'Ah, Rosey . . .'
and put his arms round her.

'I hate it when you say that,' she said in a low voice.
'It frightens me. I . . .'

'Look, girl,' he said gently, 'don't let's be kidding
ourselves. I've told you—I never meant to fall for you
like this, nor you for me. It just happened. But I
wouldn't do for you, not in the long run.'

'Why not?'

''Cause I can't give you the things you'd want.'

'I don't want anything except to be with you.'

He shook his head. 'Maybe not now, Rosey. But
you would.'

She suddenly threw her arms round his neck and
began to kiss him passionately. After a moment he said:
'All right,' rather breathlessly. 'All right, Rosey darling.'

*   *   *   *   *

'Well, what I heard,' said Mac, 'was that she was
taking him to court.'

'What for?' said Fred Boxall.

'She's not . . .' he hesitated and glanced at Jack.
'Not in the family way?'

'No. For assault.'

'So I should bloody well think,' said Jack. His face
was sullen and angry. 'Bloody skirt-chaser. Got a wife
of his own and can't keep his hands off . . .'

Fred Boxall said: 'Well, you remember what I told
you our Nell told me? That time in the stores . . .'

Jack said: 'I'd like to go and knock his teeth in.
Decent kid like that.'

'I suppose he'll have to go from here?' said Mac.
'Whatever happens?'

'Not if he's found Not Guilty,' said Harry. 'They couldn't dismiss him if he was found Not Guilty.'

'Not Guilty my foot!' said Fred Boxall. 'Why should she say that if he never did it?'

'You got to prove things,' said Harry dubiously. 'Before you can get a conviction.'

Fred Boxall said: 'Well, if they've got any doubt about it, they'd better ask our Nell.'

'Start asking your Nell things,' said Mac with a grin, 'and . . .'

'And what?' said Fred Boxall sharply.

'Nothing.'

'What you want to say about our Nell?'

'I wasn't saying anything, Fred.' Mac added hurriedly: 'Does he get sent to clink for that?'

'Depends what he did,' said Harry, the legal expert. 'Most likely not if he's a first offender.'

There was a roar of laughter. Jack snorted and turned away. They looked after him with interest. 'Now that's a bit awkward for Jacko, see,' said Mac solemnly. 'Not being able to make up his mind whether she's his girl or whether she just was once.'

'He dropped her like a hot brick, didn't he?'

Mac said: 'He says she's a decent kid. And if anybody knows, he ought.'

'Maybe that's what he's mad about,' said Harry. 'Maybe Lawrence got more than he did.'

A delighted grin had spread slowly over Fred Boxall's face. He held up a hand. 'Mates—they got it all wrong. See what happened? It wasn't Lawrence's car she was in—it was *Jacko's* car. . . .'

Jack heard the delighted howl of laughter in the distance just as Ryan was saying: 'She's your girl, isn't she?'

Jack hesitated: 'I wouldn't say she was my girl, but we been out a lot, and a nicer kid you wouldn't find. Anyhow, what does it matter whose girl she is? I reckon the Works Committee . . .'

Ryan shook his head and frowned. 'That's not a thing for the Works Committee.'

'Well, I reckon it is, and if nobody else . . .'

Ryan hesitated. 'Look, Jack,' he said, 'if you can keep your mouth shut, I can tell you. It's all being taken care of.'

'How?'

'There's going to be a proper inquiry. Mr. North and Miss Bell and me—we've been told to go into it. Proper impartial inquiry. Then we report to the Board.'

'And then they'll hush it up,' said Jack contemptuously. 'With his father . . .'

'No, they won't. You bet Mr. Walter'll see to that. *He's* no friend of Lawrence.'

'Who is?' said Jack. 'The . . .'

Ryan raised a hand. 'Ah, now wait a minute. We got to be just. It's got to be proved, a thing like this, whoever it is.'

'Well, when's it going to happen?'

'Mr. North reckons we got to give it a few days to see if there's going to be police proceedings, because if there is, that makes a different thing, see. But after that . . .'

Going back to the press-shop after the dinner-break he met her face to face coming round the corner of the corridor. Hilda looked pale and there were dark circles under her eyes. He smiled and said: 'Hallo, Hilda girl,' very gently, and half stopped. It was the first time he had spoken to her for a fortnight. She didn't smile, but just looked at him with eyes that seemed troubled and frightened, and said: 'Hallo, Jack,' in a low voice and slipped by him. He felt a sudden surge of anger, and for a moment he had a wild vision of walking into Lawrence's office and giving him what he deserved. But Harry came along and started talking about motor-bikes, and the feeling passed.

Usually Hilda's assembly team made a noise like the parrot-house, because 'Rene and Jean never stopped talking even if the others did occasionally. But it was very quiet now, and nobody talked at all except for a word every now and again. It got on her nerves that they didn't talk because she knew why. It was because they

wanted to talk about that, and couldn't because she was
there. She knew everybody was talking about it, because
several times when she passed other groups at the dinner-
break, or went through the shop, she would hear them,
and hear what they were saying. And then they would
stop when they saw her, and she could feel their eyes on
her, and then the talking would start again as soon as
she had passed. She could hear the mutter of it starting
again behind her.

She was doing Number Four and that wasn't an
accident either, because Number Four on that job was
the easiest; and yesterday she had done Number Two
and that was the easiest on that job. They were giving
her all the easiest jobs ever since it got about, and everyone was calling her 'Duck,' and even Miss Carter, who
was a terror, said: 'Hilda, dear,' when they were team-
ing up in the morning. And it was why Jack had smiled
like that. . . .

The Judge was wearing a red robe and a wig, but
she was all in black with a veil. They asked her to lift
her veil and as she did so, revealing the lovely face lined
with suffering, a murmur of sympathy went through the
crowded courtroom. Lawrence was standing there handcuffed to two policemen, only younger and in uniform
like he'd been that time in the war. She looked across
at him and there was no anger in the lovely eyes. Only
pity. His eyes met hers for a moment and then his head
slowly sank in shame. He said in a low voice: 'I cannot
look her in the face. I am guilty. . . .'

There was a buzz of excitement in court, but she held up
her hand and there was instant silence. She turned to the
Judge and said: 'Judge—I don't want this man punished.
He has done me wrong, but I forgive him as I hope to be
forgiven. . . .'

She had missed one and said: 'Oh, I'm sorry.' But
Jean, doing Number Five, said: 'All right, Duck. I got it.'

*   *   *   *   *

'Whereupon,' said Lang, 'I get this from Henry.' He
handed Rosamund the memorandum sheet and sat back
and watched her with a broad grin. The memorandum

said: 'W.L.—Following our talk, I went up to London over the week-end and saw Proudfoot. After some discussions, I told him that the trustees were inclined to accept his offer, viz. £2 : 5s. a share for eighty thousand shares, legal charges to be apportioned between vendor and purchaser as set out in his letter. He asks to be allowed to nominate one director to represent his interests on the Board and suggests Winter, whom I think you met when they came here. I said I thought this was reasonable and that I should be prepared to recommend the Board to agree to co-opt Winter or some other nominee— H.S.'

Rosamund said: 'So he's sold Uncle Gus's shares to Sir Francis?'

'Well, if he hasn't, he's going to. Thereby thinking that he's by-passed me.'

'But surely you . . .?'

Lang smiled: 'That's the cream of the joke. He doesn't know that Proudfoot and I fixed up the whole thing. Or that the whole idea of sending Winter is to help me carry the reconstruction idea through.'

Rosamund frowned. 'Uncle Henry seems to be being very silly. And rather beastly. Supposing you *hadn't* known about it and—and had minded?'

Lang shrugged. 'I don't think he would have worried much about that.' He got up and walked over to the french window. 'You've got to realise, Roz, that the Spellman family have been doing all they can to spike my guns for a long time. This is all part of the scrap— and this is Henry thinking he's being clever.' Lang lowered his head in the curious bull-like gesture. 'Well, we'll see what happens now—and whose guns get spiked.'

He pushed the french window open and for a moment she hoped that he was going out in the garden. But he swung round and said: 'I made Henry Chairman, and ever since then he's done nothing but obstruct me. I took Lawrence on because nobody else would give him a job, and he's been nothing but a darn nuisance. It's time the whole lot were cleared out. And I'll clear them out. I'll break the pair of them. . . .' His voice had risen and his face was dark and angry. This was the thing she hated most.

She looked away and said: 'Is Winter the one who came to dinner?'

'Yes.'

'I didn't like him much. At least, I thought he was a bit heavy in the hand. I liked Sir Francis, though.'

Lang said: 'Winter's a damned good man. If I get him here we'll scare the pants off some of these people.' He pointed a warning finger. 'Mind you, Roz, you mustn't say a word of this to anyone outside—and particularly not to any of the Spellman lot, Laura or any of them.'

'Of course I shan't,' said Rosamund wearily. 'I never see any of them now, anyhow.'

'Yes, but you know how it is. You go there to tea or something and . . .'

'But I don't,' she said shortly. 'You told me not to. She asked me twice and I didn't go, so now she's given up.' Rosamund's lips trembled slightly. 'It's a pity you've got to quarrel with them,' she said rather bitterly. 'I like Uncle Henry and I like Lawrence, and Laura's always been very nice to me. After all, they were about the only friends we'd got. . . .'

'I daresay,' said Lang, 'but it's not my fault if they try to do me dirt, is it?'

'But what *have* they done to you?' she said with a sudden flash of rebellion. 'You're always against Lawrence, but I don't see that he's done anything. . . .'

Lang looked at her for a moment in startled silence. 'Lawrence?' he said. 'The least said about him the better, my dear.'

'But *why*?'

'Never you mind. But I can tell you for your private information that I don't think he'll be with us much longer, and it'll be nobody's fault but his own.'

'You mean you're going to sack him?' she said very quietly.

'If he's asked to resign it'll be nothing to do with me. It'll be a decision taken by people who are quite impartial.' He saw her face and added quietly: 'Look,

Roz—Lawrence has been riding for a fall for a long while. This time he's gone too far. That's all.'

'I suppose he's got drunk or something,' she said drearily.

'That's beside the point. But I don't want you to think that if he does have to go, it's something that I've engineered. I've put up with more from Lawrence than you know—partly for his father's sake and partly because you and your mother liked him. I don't want to be told now that I've been unfair to him.'

She turned her head away and said: 'I didn't say you had, Daddy. I don't know anything about it.'

There was a long silence. Lang was fiddling with a matchbox. Once or twice he glanced in a worried way at her averted face. 'I'm sorry, my dear,' he said in a low voice. 'I oughtn't to tell you about these things. I can't tell you the whole story and if I don't you—you're bound to get the wrong impressions. Anyhow, it must be very boring for you.'

'It isn't,' said Rosamund with an attempt at a smile. 'It's just . . .'

'But there comes a time,' he said with quiet bitterness, 'when you've got to talk to *somebody*. Or go off your head.' He got up, went through the open french window and walked slowly across the big lawn.

When he had gone Rosamund took out her handkerchief and allowed herself to cry for a few moments, without troubling to decide exactly what she was crying about. Then she blew her nose vigorously, went up to her room, and repaired the damage to her face, which was not great. For a while she seriously considered ringing up Laura and warning her. But it would be a fantastically disloyal thing to do, and anyhow, what could the warning be about? 'I don't know if Lawrence knows, but Daddy's very angry about something he's done and thinks he may have to resign and—and well, look out in case Lawrence *doesn't* know. . . .' She gave a sudden little sob of misery and anger and then threw herself on the bed. Oh God, if only there were still somebody to smile at him and say: 'Don't be an old *silly*, Walter. . . .' And he would whip round looking angry and then slowly the anger would go out of his face and he would grin that rather sheepish, charming grin. . . . But one couldn't do it—one couldn't. Because one wasn't really his person. Not like she had been.

When she went downstairs again he was still walking up and down the lawn, with his head sunk low between his shoulders. She went out to him and was only a couple of yards away when he saw her. He smiled and said: 'Hallo, sweetheart. . . .' and put an arm round her. As they walked slowly on Rosamund said: 'You know, those tulips are going to be good.'

*   *   *   *   *

The Honourable Amy Talbot-Rees's horse-like face became even more horse-like when she ate, so that Laura found herself resisting an impulse to put a lump of sugar flat on the palm of her hand and offer it to her.

The Honourable Amy said: 'The general idea is to fly the car over, stay a few days with the Legreurs in Paris and then go on to the Château at leisure. The Prince is a dear old thing, but one can have too much of him. And of the Loire. At least, so I always feel.'

Laura said: 'I've never had enough of it to feel like that. Have a bun?' The Honourable Amy bit deeply into a piece of puff pastry which disintegrated messily. 'Bless my soul!' she said mildly, brushing the crumbs on to the floor. 'Of course all this is dependent on there being no major crisis to prevent Jim from getting away.' She smiled at Laura blandly.

'As far as I can see,' said Laura, 'there's always a crisis at Lang's. At least, in Walter's view.'

'I gather from Jim that the little boys are squabbling amongst themselves as usual?'

'I expect they are.'

'When you come to think of it,' said the Honourable Amy, 'men are impossible creatures. I can't think why sane women like you and I put up with them. I mean—take Jim. I realise that I've much to be thankful for compared with some poor devils of women. He doesn't . . . well, he doesn't do the—the *ultimately* humiliating things. But . . .'

Laura said : 'I should have thought Jim was the ideal husband.' There was a pause. 'Isn't he?' she added gently.

'Oh, Jim's all right,' said the Honourable Amy shortly.

Laura looked at her with slightly raised eyebrows. 'Only you said men were impossible creatures . . .?' she said invitingly.

'Well, don't you agree, my dear?'

'Oh, in general, yes,' said Laura, smiling. 'But I was hoping perhaps Jim had done something *awful*. I'm always agog for a nice bit of scandal. More tea?'

By a quarter-past five the Honourable Amy's wrist was beginning to tire perceptibly. She was an enthusia- astic rather than skilful fencer. At half-past five she finally laid down her foil and picked up the sabre. 'Laura dear, I haven't known whether to mention this or not, but what is this *ridiculous* story that's going round about Lawrence? Jim's frightfully worried about it. Of course he didn't tell me any *details*. He's always very discreet. But as soon as I heard I thought: "Well, if *anything* like that's happening I must go round and see Laura and see if there's anything one can *do*".'

Laura said : 'That was very kind of you.'

'But what I heard was a *nonsensical* yarn . . .?'

'Well,' said Laura calmly, 'it depends what you heard, of course . . .?'

'Well, my dear—frankly—it was that some girl from the factory was accusing Lawrence of messing her about in a car.'

'I don't think the actual expression was "Messing her about" . . .' said Laura. She diverted her eyes from the horse-like face with a supreme effort and lit a cigarette.

'Well, you know what I mean, Laura. I've never heard anything so ridiculous in my life.'

'Oh, I don't know,' said Laura calmly. 'Men have been known to make passes at girls in motor-cars.'

'They may in the Sunday papers, my dear,' said the Honourable Amy firmly. 'But surely not amongst people like ourselves?'

'I shouldn't think so.'

'But what a horrible thing for Lawrence—and for you. A man's so defenceless against a charge like that. I mean—how can he possibly prove it's a lie?'

'I don't see how he can,' said Laura. She smiled slightly. 'But normally of course, when people make accusations *they* have to prove that they are true.'

'Exactly. It's mainly a question of Lawrence's friends standing by him and refusing to believe it. As of course any real friend will do.' The Honourable Amy frowned. 'Who *is* this girl? Is it that rather pretty blonde that Lawrence danced with at the Party?'

'I believe so.'

'Then that'll be what put it into her mind.' The Honourable Amy shook her head. 'Dear old Lawrence, of course he's so open-hearted and—and *friendly* with everybody that he lays himself open to that sort of horrible person. I mean, it's so like him to bother to give her a lift at all. Jim says that he never *will* give a lift to a woman, precisely because of this sort of thing.'

There was a moment's silence. 'But the thing that puzzles *me*,' said the Honourable Amy, 'is what can have induced her to tell this story? Mad? Blackmail? Or what?'

'I don't know,' said Laura. 'People do these things at times. See *A Passage to India*.'

'I don't quite understand, dear?'

'A book,' said Laura, 'in which something rather similar happens.' She stood up, glancing at her watch. 'Sorry, but I'm going to have to throw you out,' she said shortly. 'I've got to go and meet Lawrence in the town.'

The Honourable Amy got up rather reluctantly. 'Ah,' she said, 'he's not coming straight here? Well—give him my love. And if you get a chance, do make him realise that people like Jim and I are all behind him.'

Laura opened the door. 'I think he can feel that you are,' she said with a smile.

XIV

MR. HERBERT WINTER'S eyebrows seemed more improbably black and his nose more pugilistic than ever. As he took the place Lang indicated on his right, Lawrence murmured under his breath to Talbot-Rees: 'Quite a pair, aren't they? And not what you'd like to meet on a dark night.'

Henry Spellman looked round and said: 'I think you all know the circumstances in which Mr. Winter has come to join us, gentlemen. It only remains for me to welcome him on your behalf and my own. Mr. Winter has had wide experience of the problems of businesses like our own, and I know we are all looking forward to —to getting a lot of help from him.'

'Hear, hear,' said Talbot-Rees. Lang grunted. There was a general murmur of approval.

Winter gave a little stiff half-bow, half-nod and said: 'Thank you, Mr. Chairman,' very quietly and without smiling.

'The general idea,' said Henry, 'is that Mr. Winter will work as a director without portfolio, so to speak, immediately under the Managing Director, on—on certain special problems; leaving Mr. Barker free to concentrate on the day-to-day running of the factory.' He glanced quickly at Barker, but the pale young man went on staring at his blotting-paper without raising his head.

'May I take it, Mr. Chairman,' said Talbot-Rees with flowing courtesy, 'that I shall be free to ask Mr. Winter's advice on certain sales problems of which he may have knowledge?'

'Anybody's free to ask him anything,' said Henry. 'As long as it doesn't interfere with—with the usual chain of responsibility.'

Barker suddenly swallowed hard, raised his head and said: 'I hope nobody will misunderstand me, Mr.

Spellman, but will Mr. Winter have any—any executive responsibility on the production side?' His usually pale face had gone bright scarlet with embarrassment. There was a moment's pause. Lang was frowning. Barker said apologetically: 'I only want the position to be clear. Only it isn't easy to—to separate everyday work from development work. Not entirely.'

Henry hesitated. 'Well, as I understand it,' he said, 'the answer is "No". For the present, at least. After all, it's bound to take Mr. Winter a little while to—to find his feet. . . .'

Lang said: 'I shall be issuing a notice in a few days setting out Mr. Winter's responsibilities. Hadn't we better leave it till then, Mr. Chairman?'

'I think so,' said Henry with relief. He picked up his Agenda paper. 'Right then—Item one: Profit Statement for Period Four. Will you go ahead, Walter?'

Under cover of the general rustle of papers, Lawrence murmured: 'Not exactly the worm *turning*, but it gave a definite wriggle, didn't it?'

* * * * *

Lang and Winter walked back from the board-room to Lang's office in silence. Lang rang the bell for his secretary and said curtly: 'I don't want to be disturbed.' He pitched his papers into his OUT tray and said: 'Sit down and make yourself comfortable, Winter. Shan't be a moment.'

Winter lowered himself into the big arm-chair. The pale blue eyes followed Lang expressionlessly as he glanced through the papers on his desk. 'Help yourself to a cigarette,' said Lang without looking up.

'Pipe if you don't mind,' said Winter laconically. He took out his pipe, filled it and lit it, all without ceasing to stare at Lang's abstracted face.

Lang put the last of his papers aside, and leant back in his chair. 'Well,' he said with a wry smile, 'you see the sort of thing we're up against.'

Winter bent his head slightly in silence.

'I don't want to say anything against my colleagues, but nobody could pretend they're a very impressive bunch.

By far the best of the lot was George Martin, the Production Director, and he's just retired.'

Winter said : 'I met him.' His voice was flat, with a strange absence of inflection, like a deaf man's.

'Of course you did. Well, he was an old stick-in-the-mud, but he was a darned good man for all that. Now he's gone and we've got this lad Barker . . .' Lang spread out his fingers. 'Well—of course . . .'

'What's his background?' said Winter. 'Home grown?'

'Yes. Been here since he was fifteen.'

Winter nodded again. After a moment he said : 'He's right about what he says. He'll have to know where he stands with me.'

Lang smiled. 'Well, from what I can see of you and from what I know of Barker, I should think that'll work itself out pretty quickly.'

Winter's mouth gave a slight twitch, which was the movement that he used instead of a smile. He said : 'Probably better that way than a lot of formal instructions. May be a good enough assistant to somebody.'

'Yes. Of course if we'd known you were coming we should never have put him on the Board.'

'Man in the double-breasted waistcoat with a double-breasted name,' said Winter after a moment's pause. 'Talbot what?'

'Talbot-Rees.'

'Sales Director?'

'Yes. Very good at it in his way. And more—more progressive than most of them.'

'I should say so,' said Winter in his noncommittal voice.

'Well now,' said Lang briskly. 'What I thought I'd better do is to give you an outline of what I've got in mind to do with the place, and then I'll give you a memorandum I wrote not long ago which puts the thing out in more detail, and you can take it away and mull it over and let me have your ideas. Has Sir Francis told you anything about it?'

Winter shook his head slowly. 'No,' he said. 'Nothing to speak of. And anyhow I'd like to hear it from you.'

'Well,' said Lang, 'the basic idea is to get away from this damned contract work and to concentrate on our own finished products. . . .'

An hour later Lang leaned back in his chair and said: 'Well—you're a good listener.'

'There's a lot to listen to,' said Winter, speaking for the first time in the whole recital, and still seeming to do so with reluctance.

'Well, what d'you think of it?'

Winter hesitated. 'You won't expect me to be able to talk about it before I've read your memorandum and thought it over?'

'Of course not,' said Lang with a touch of impatience. 'But d'you feel the general principle is right?'

They stared at one another in silence for a few seconds. Then Winter took his pipe out of his mouth and tapped it out into the ashtray. 'It depends what you're in business *for*,' he said briefly. 'I always have to start there, being a slow thinker.'

'I don't quite see what you're getting at,' said Lang.

'Anyhow,' said Winter, 'you've made what you're after perfectly clear. You've thought about it and I haven't.'

Lang's face cleared. 'Exactly,' he said. 'I've got plenty of people here who'll argue the toss about what we ought to do. But now that George Martin's gone there's nobody I can rely on to get things *done*.'

'Oh, I can get things done,' said Winter in his flat voice.

'Well, you stick to the principles I've outlined,' said Lang, 'and I'll see you get all the backing you want.'

Winter slowly bowed his head. 'Fine,' he said. 'Fine.'

*   *   *   *   *

'My information,' said North, 'is that there will be no police action. So that leaves us free to go ahead, doesn't it?'

'I don't know about anybody else,' said Miss Bell, 'but I feel, when I hear that, that it puts us in—in a rather awkward position. If the police aren't going to

act, it rather suggests that—that they don't believe he's
guilty and . . .'

'No, no,' said North through his chronic catarrh. 'If
you'll pardon me, Miss Bell—not at all. It's more likely
that they feel there's no corroboration, and so they
wouldn't be likely to get a conviction.'

'But doesn't it come to the same thing? If there's
no proof . . .?'

'It's a different thing,' said Ryan impatiently. 'We
haven't got to prove anything. All we've got to do is
to form an honest opinion and report to the Board.'

North said: 'Perhaps I'd better read our terms of
reference. . . .'

'We've all got them in front of us. Thing is—how
we going to work it? Hear the girl first and then Lawrence?'

'I should think so.'

'Are we all going to ask questions?' said Miss Bell.
'Or are we to leave it to Mr. North?'

'Let anybody ask,' said Ryan decisively.

North said: 'I don't know how well we're all ac-
quainted with the rules of evidence. But there are certain
questions that are usually considered. . . .'

'You mean leading and so on?' said Miss Bell briskly.
'Well, you must stop us if we do that. Who's going to
take notes? Somebody ought to.'

'I'll deal with that,' said North. He looked round.
'I think if we were to sit on this side of the table, and the
examinee were to sit *there* . . .'

She could feel her legs shaking under her as they
went along the corridor. Miss Bell said gently: 'There's
nothing to be afraid of, dear. Just answer the questions
you're asked, and if you don't know or can't remember
anything, just say so.'

Miss Bell opened the door and they went into the
office. Mr. North and Ryan were there. They stopped
talking. Miss Bell smiled and said: 'Here's Hilda.'
Mr. North said: 'Good morning,' and Ryan said:
'Hullo, Hilda,' rather gruffly.

Miss Bell said: 'Now if you sit here, dear . . .' and

then went round and sat on the other side of the desk, beside Mr. North, so that she was left alone, facing all three of them.

Mr. North made a sniffing noise and took his handkerchief out, but instead of blowing his nose he put his handkerchief back and said : 'Well, Miss Pinner, I think you know why we've sent for you . . .?'

She said : 'Yes,' with her lips, without making any sound.

'What we want you to do,' said Mr. North, 'is just to tell us in your own words what happened that evening when Mr. Lawrence gave you a lift in his car. Now you just tell us what happened, and we'll stop you if there's anything we want to ask.'

Mr. North's spectacles magnified his eyes, which were a sort of watery dark grey. They were waiting for her to say something, so she clutched her handkerchief in a ball in her right hand and said : 'He asked me if I wanted a lift. . . .'

Mr. North said : 'Just a moment. Start a little further back. What day was it?'

'Friday, sir.'

'A fortnight ago last Friday?'

'Yes.'

Mr. North wrote something down and said : 'That'll have been the third. What time was it?'

'When I was leaving in the evening.'

Ryan said : 'So there'll have been a lot of people about going home?'

'Well, no, Mr. Ryan, because I hadn't got my bicycle because it had a puncture, but I'd forgotten I hadn't got it and I went all out to the shed before I remembered I hadn't got it because of the puncture and I'd been a bit late anyhow so when I got out there weren't many people, not like it is just after the bell.'

Miss Bell said : 'It does clear very quickly.'

'Very well,' said Mr. North. 'And you started to walk home?'

'No, only up to the bus-stop.'

'Yes, of course. And then what happened?'

She pushed the hard ball of the handkerchief into the palm of her left hand and said : 'Well, I was walking

G

along the road and Mr. Lawrence came behind in his
car and went just past me and then stopped and called
to me . . .' She hesitated.

'What did he call?'

'He called . . . "Hallo, 'Rene."'

Ryan frowned and said: ''Rene?' Why'd he call
you that? You're not called 'Rene, are you?'

'No, Mr. Ryan.'

'Did he think you were somebody else?'

'I don't think so, Mr. Ryan. He—he does call me
'Rene.'

There was a moment's pause.

'*Does* call you 'Rene?' said Ryan sharply. 'You mean
you've talked to Mr. Lawrence before?'

'Once or twice I have. In the works.'

Miss Bell said: 'And he danced with you at the Party,
didn't he?'

She said: 'That's right, Miss Bell.' She had gone
very red.

Mr. North said: 'So you know Mr. Lawrence to
talk to?'

'Not really. But I had talked to him once or twice.'

Ryan said curtly: 'Have you been in his car before?'

'No, Mr. Ryan,' she said in a half-whisper.

Mr. North said: 'Well now—he called "Hallo, 'Rene."
Then what happened?'

'Well, I stopped and he asked me if I wanted a lift
and—and I said up to the bus-stop and then he asked
me where I lived and I said Greengates and he said that
was on his way home, at least that Market Cross was,
and he'd take me.' Hilda paused.

'Yes?' Mr. North waited and then said: 'So you
got into his car . . .?'

Her lips said: 'Yes,' silently.

After a moment Miss Bell said gently: 'Tell us what
happened in the car, Hilda. Don't be frightened. It
isn't your fault.'

She turned her eyes to Miss Bell but her lips were
quivering and they wouldn't form any words.

Ryan frowned and said rather impatiently: 'Well, come
on. What happened? Did he kiss you or something?'

Mr. North turned to Ryan and said: 'I don't think perhaps we should . . .'

Ryan said: 'Well, we can't get any further unless she can tell us . . .'

Hilda said: 'No. He didn't.' Her eyes were full of tears so that the faces were all blurred. She blinked hard to get rid of them.

Miss Bell said quickly: 'It is difficult for her. Mr. North—I wonder . . .?' She leant over and the three of them talked together in low voices for a bit and then Mr. North nodded and Miss Bell got up and smiled at her and said: 'Look, Hilda—let you and me go into my room for a minute. That'll be easier, won't it . . .?'

*　　*　　*　　*　　*

Ryan said: 'I'd forgotten about that, but I remember now seeing them at the Party. Of course by then he'd got a few drinks in him and he was dancing with her.' He shook his head. 'That's the trouble, see. He goes round being familiar with these girls and they don't know any better, or don't want to, and . . .'

North took out his handkerchief, brought it to within an inch of his nose, put it away again and gave a loud sniff. He said: 'It's difficult to judge, but she doesn't seem the sort of girl who'd encourage that sort of thing, does she?'

'No,' said Ryan drily. 'But I've known plenty who couldn't say boo to a goose who were little devils.'

Miss Bell came in and said: 'I think I've got all she can tell me. You don't want her again, do you?'

Ryan said: 'Might want to ask her some questions.'

'We can do that to-morrow if you do. I've sent her off now. She's a bit upset.'

Miss Bell sat down and glanced at some notes. Ryan said: 'What did she say in the end?'

'Legally, of course,' said North doubtfully, 'this is all quite irregular, taking her evidence like this. But perhaps . . .'

'Well,' said Miss Bell with a half-sigh, 'there isn't really much to it, for all the fuss. But of course if it's true, it's serious in the circumstances. Hilda says that after they'd been driving for a few minutes he started to talk to her in a familiar way—a way he shouldn't—and to pass remarks about her legs and—and her figure. And then apparently he put his hand over while he was still driving and—and her . . .' Miss Bell looked up with a wry smile. 'It's rather awkward to put into words,' she said, 'even for me. I will if you like, but I don't think it's necessary, is it?'

'Not for me,' said Ryan with a sort of embarrassed contempt. 'As long as you know it wasn't decent behaviour.'

'Well, it certainly wasn't the way a gentleman and a married man ought to act towards a decent young girl.'

'All right. Well, what did she do?'

'She says she asked him to stop and pulled away as far as she could, and he just laughed and said she was . . .' Miss Bell frowned at her notes '. . . said she was prissy. It's a slang word for prudish. Anyhow he wouldn't stop, though she tried to push his hand away. Then they began to get into town and he stopped doing it. Just before they got to Market Cross he asked her if she'd come out with him one night and she said no, and he just laughed and said she wasn't half a girl, and that when she was his age she'd have learned that . . .' Miss Bell peered again. 'Oh, she couldn't remember this properly. It was something about kissing something as it flies. Or so she thought. Anyhow, then he stopped and she got out.'

North said : 'And apparently said nothing to anybody for several days. Did you ask her why?'

'Yes. She says she was frightened that her father would be angry. She seems very scared of her father. And she didn't want to get Mr. Lawrence into trouble.'

'Then why did she tell her mother in the end?'

'She went to church,' said Miss Bell simply.

'Church?' said Ryan. 'What's that got . . .? Oh —I see."

They sat in silence for a moment and then Ryan said moodily : 'Well, it's a lot of bloody fuss about not much, isn't it? If she'd given him a good slap across the face and kept her mouth shut, it would have saved everybody a lot of trouble.'

Miss Bell said: 'Well, yes. But I'm afraid we can't very well look at it like that, can we? If it had been some boy out of the factory—well, we're all people of the world and we know these things happen. But with a director of the company and . . .'

North gave a loud sniff and said: 'If I might be allowed to say so, the view to be taken of the offence, if offence there was, is nothing to do with us. Nothing at all. All we have to do is to report to the Board what, in our opinion, took place. Isn't it?'

'Well, there doesn't seem to me much doubt about *that*,' said Ryan.

North held up a hand. 'Oh, wait a minute, Mr. Ryan. We've only heard one side yet. It's quite astonishing sometimes how different a case sounds when you hear both sides of it. Of course it *is* open to us to say at this point that there's no case to answer, but I take it you would feel . . .?'

Ryan said: 'Let's get Lawrence in and hear what he says.'

In the long, rather dispirited pause, Lawrence leant back and lit a cigarette. His face remained rather unnaturally serious but completely calm.

North said: 'Then really, Mr. Lawrence, there's no dispute about the facts except the—the actual words and actions between the time you picked her up and put her down at Market Cross?'

'No,' said Lawrence. 'There never has been. I've always agreed that I gave her a lift. I'm always giving people lifts.'

'Girls out of the factory?'

'Certainly. Anybody I know. And sometimes people that I don't.'

Ryan said: 'Mr. Lawrence—the girl says you told her you'd take her to Market Cross instead of putting her on the bus, because it was on your way home. I wouldn't have thought it *is* on your way, is it?'

'It's not directly on my way home, but it's directly

on my way to the County Hotel, where I was going.' He smiled. 'It's only fair to say that I may very well have *said* "on my way home".'

'As far as you know, the girl'd got nothing against you?'

'Certainly not. As I've told you, I'd only spoken to her a couple of times before. I didn't even know her name.'

'See, what I'm trying to get at,' said Ryan, 'is why she should make up a story like that?'

Lawrence smiled wryly. 'I wish I knew.' There was another long pause. Lawrence said: 'I'm afraid you're in the difficulty that—that you were always bound to be in. The girl tells this story. I say it's completely untrue. Nobody can prove which of us is telling the truth, because nobody else was there.' He waved a hand towards North. 'If somebody made the same charge against you, you couldn't *prove* it wasn't true. You could only appeal to people's commonsense. . . .' He glanced at their faces and smiled slightly. 'You probably don't think that's a very good parallel, because North's a more respectable citizen than I am. That's quite true. I don't suggest for a moment that I'm incapable of—of making a fool of myself. But I'm not mad and I wasn't drunk. And I should have to have been one or the other to act like that in those circumstances.'

'But why should she say so, Mr. Lawrence?' said Ryan doggedly.

'I tell you I don't know—except that there are cases in the papers every day of girls making charges of that sort against men. If it comes to that, why didn't she complain until several days after?'

Miss Bell said: 'I think I can understand that, Mr. Lawrence.'

Lawrence shrugged: 'So can I, Miss Bell. But then if it comes to that I can understand, in a way, how girls come to make these things up. Can't you?'

She hesitated. 'I suppose so really. Of course girls of that age are very imaginative. . . .'

North pushed his nose out of the straight with one finger. 'And you don't feel, Mr. Lawrence, that it's possible that she might have misunderstood anything you said or did, as I suggested before?'

'I suppose it's *possible*. But I don't see how. I can't remember every word we said, but it was certainly a very ordinary conversation. And as for actions, I don't think I ever touched her, even when she got in and out of the car.'

Miss Bell shook her head and said decidedly: 'No—this wasn't anything she'd misunderstood like that.'

Ryan sat back in his chair, looked at North and shrugged his shoulders. 'Well, there we are at a dead end then,' he said shortly.

Miss Bell looked up from her notes and said: Mr. Lawrence, does kissing something as it flies bring anything to your mind?'

Lawrence frowned. 'Kissing something as it flies? Yes. Kissing the joy as it flies. Blake. It . . .' He paused.

'Is it a quotation or something?'

Lawrence hesitated. 'Yes,' he said slowly. 'It's a quotation from Blake.'

'Kissing the joy as it flies?'

'No.'

> '"*But he who kisses the joy as it flies*
> *Lives in eternity's sun rise.*"'

He paused. 'Why, Miss Bell?'

'Because you see Hilda said that just before she got out you asked her to go out with you and when she said no, you said she wasn't half a girl and—and something about kissing something as it flies. So I wondered . . .?'

There was a moment's silence. 'What does it mean, anyhow?' said Ryan without much interest.

Lawrence was still looking at Miss Bell. 'It means,' he said slowly, 'roughly speaking, that you shouldn't try to keep your pleasures in cages.'

> '"*He who binds to himself a joy,*
> *Does the winged life destroy* . . ."'

He smiled at Miss Bell rather wryly. 'But that isn't quite the point, is it?'

Miss Bell hesitated. 'No. . . .' She turned to the others. 'You see, Mr. North, it's not a—a thing she could have made up and . . .'

'What Miss Bell's trying to say,' said Lawrence quickly, 'is that Hilda pretty certainly doesn't know her Blake and couldn't very well have made that up. Whereas it's a perfectly probable thing for me to have said, if her story is true.'

North said : 'Yes. Yes. I quite see . . .' He turned to Ryan. 'You get Mr. Lawrence's point ?'

'Yes,' said Ryan briefly.

North sniffed and said : 'Well—do you remember saying it to her, Mr. Lawrence ?'

Lawrence shook his head. 'No. I don't. It's quite likely that I did though, because it's rather a favourite quotation of mine. But I can't for the life of me think what I can have said it *about*.'

Miss Bell said : 'Only you see, it fits in with her story.'

'I do, indeed,' said Lawrence briefly.

There was a long silence. North looked round and said : 'Well . . . is there anything else anybody would like to ask . . . ?'

Ryan said : 'I'd like to ask one thing . . . Mr. Lawrence, would you agree with me that Hilda Pinner's a decent, respectable sort of girl ?'

'Completely, as far as I can judge. Rather shyer than most.'

'Not the sort that'd give a man encouragement to—to make advances to her ?'

'Certainly not.' Lawrence frowned. 'I don't think anybody's suggested that she is or that she did, have they ?'

'No,' said Ryan in his dogged way. 'But I just wanted to ask. . . . And you'd agree that any man who assaulted a girl like that was a pretty rotten sort of man ?'

Lawrence's lips tightened. 'I'm not really very good at moral judgments,' he said with a cold little smile. 'But I shouldn't think it's a thing anyone would be very proud of. . . . Why ?' he added gently.

Ryan said: 'I just wanted to ask, that's all.' He waved a hand to dismiss the matter and then, throwing back his head, gazed up at the ceiling. Lawrence looked at him for a moment and then, with a faint lift of one eyebrow, turned back to North.

North said rather helplessly: 'And there's nothing else you can think of that might—might clear this unfortunate business up, Mr. Lawrence?'

'Certainly. I think I should see the girl in the presence of all of you. So far all this has come to me at second-hand, first from her parents and now from you. I want her to say it to my face, so that I can ask her questions. Surely that's only reasonable?'

North hesitated. 'She's a very shy girl,' said Miss Bell doubtfully. 'And of course this is all very painful to her. . . .'

Lawrence said: 'Well, it isn't so very much fun for me, is it?'

'I think Mr. Lawrence is right,' said Ryan unexpectedly. 'It's all very well to say she's shy, but she's not so shy she can't answer questions if he wants to ask her anything.'

'Is she available?' said North.

Miss Bell said: 'I've sent her home. She was in rather a state. But of course we could see her to-morrow if you like.'

'That suits me,' said Lawrence. 'I don't want to embarrass the girl. But I do want to be able to talk to her, if only to see if I can get any idea why she's telling this yarn.'

North said: 'Then shall we adjourn until to-morrow morning? Thank you very much, Mr. Lawrence. . . .'

When Lawrence had gone Miss Bell said: 'I rather doubt if she *will* be able to answer questions. I'm afraid she'll just break down.'

'Doesn't matter if she does,' said Ryan grimly. 'Let's see them together. I reckon you'll see who's telling the truth fast enough then—if you don't know now.'

North looked at his notes and said: 'I just want to be sure I've got this right: 'But he who kisses joy as it flies . . .'

'*The* joy,' said Miss Bell.

'Ah, yes.   *The* joy.'

*   *   *   *   *

As soon as Rosamund saw the Hastings postmark she
knew it was Jo Clay, and as soon as she remembered Jo
Clay she thought of the plan.   Lang was out to dinner,
and she ate sandwiches and an orange and thought about
it, so that by the time he came home it was complete in
every detail.   She made him a last cup of tea and while
he was drinking it she said casually: 'I had a letter from
Jo Clay this morning. . . .'

Lang said: 'Jo Clay . . .?   Oh yes.   Jo Clay.'

'She wants to know if I'll go and stay with them.'

'Oh,' said Lang without enthusiasm.   He always hated
her to go away.   'I can't remember where they live?
Brighton or some seaside place, isn't it?'

'Near Hastings.'

'Well, why shouldn't you?' said Lang heavily.   'Good
for you.'

'Would you mind being left?   It would only be for a
fortnight or so . . .?'

'Of course not, darling.   When?'

'I'm not quite sure.   Probably some time next month.'
He had grumbled about it—about having to take his
holiday so early.   But he hadn't told her the date.

Lang said: 'Well, that's all right, darling.   You go.
Time you had a change.'

Jack seemed rather dubious about it and she was hurt
and said: 'Well, of course we don't have to do it if you
don't want to.   I only thought . . .'

He said: 'Of course I want to, Rosey.   But . . .
well—supposing your father was to ring them up and
find you weren't there . . .?'

'He can't.   They're not on the telephone.   Anyhow
he wouldn't.   He never telephones or writes when I'm
away.'   Rosamund gave a slightly hysterical giggle.
'We could go to Eastbourne or somewhere and I could
get myself a Woolworth wedding ring and we could be
Mr. and Mrs. Shoehorn or something. . . .'

'You are a little devil, aren't you?' he said with a grim smile. He thought for a while and said: 'Anyhow, I don't see why I shouldn't come down that way if you're going to be there. . . .'

'You see I could *really* go and stay with Jo. For a few days, and perhaps go there again at the end, so that if he ever *did* happen to ask, I should have been there. And you could either stay in Hastings or one of the other places along the coast. Probably better not Hastings itself, because the Clays are always going there and it would be a bit awkward if we bumped into them. But there are lots of smaller places around there, and I could drive down so that we had the car. . . .' They looked at one another for a moment in silence. 'It would be awful fun,' said Rosamund with a tentative grin. 'At least it would for me. . . .'

XV

WINTER leant back and began to stuff the tobacco into his pipe. 'Well, there are the figures,' he said. 'There are half a dozen press jobs where the men are taking home over twice the basic rate.'

Ryan said: 'If you're going to start talking about cutting rates, Mr. Winter . . .'

'I'm not. I'm talking about getting the rates right. There are a lot of other jobs where the men can't even earn their money.'

'That's what I was going to say.'

'Right. Well, that's no good to anybody. With the short runs you get here the job's over before you can get the rate right. You know the place and I don't. What would you do about it?'

'What should I do about it?' said Ryan, slightly startled.

'Yes?'

Ryan hesitated. 'Well . . . usually if a rate's wrong I have a word with Mr. Walter, and we argue the toss a bit and then . . .'

'Why do you have to argue the toss?' said Winter in his flat voice. 'You're a responsible man. You've been here twenty-five years. You're not likely to do the company down, are you?'

'No, of course not, but . . .' Ryan smiled. 'Of course, Mr. Walter, he's a tough nut. You have to stand up to him.'

Winter said: 'Well, where I come from we don't have any of that. Every job's properly time-studied as soon as it gets into the place. The conditions and fatigue allowances and so on are agreed beforehand. When the study's finished it's approved by the management and the Chief Steward and there's the rate and no argument about it.'

'Ah, I dare say. That may be all right in some places,

Mr. Winter. But you couldn't do that here. Not have
somebody standing over the men clicking a watch.'

'Why not?'

Ryan shook his head. 'I don't reckon the men'd
like it. First thing they'd say is: "Hallo—what's this?
Somebody trying to put the screw on us."'

'Of course they would,' said Winter calmly. 'But
that's where you come in, isn't it?'

'How, Mr. Winter?'

'You're there to see they get a square deal. It's your
job to explain that time-studies are as much for their
benefit as for the management's.'

Ryan grinned. 'Well—are they?'

Winter glanced at a piece of paper. 'In the group
I'm concerned with,' he said, 'there are four press-shops
doing work like yours. They've all got proper time-study
and in every one of them their average earnings are at
least ten per cent higher than they are here.'

'Ten per cent *higher*?'

'Yes. There's not so much talk about the workers'
rights, but there's more in the pay packet.' Winter put
a match to his pipe. 'Look here, Ryan—this is off the
record, but I know I can talk straight to you. This is a
family firm and it's got its own ways. I don't doubt
some of them were very good ways at one time—when
there was the boss on one side and the individual worker
on the other. But that was before the days of Unions.
As far as I can see, this place is full of committees and so
on, where anybody can talk about anything, whether he
knows about it or not. Now, to me, the proper people
to speak for the workers are the Shop Stewards, and the
Chief Steward ought to be the key man of the place.
Somebody to be *consulted*, not somebody to be treated as
a nuisance and argued with every time he raises a
point. . . .'

Ryan nodded vigorously. 'Well, of course, Mr.
Winter, that's what I've said always. But between our-
selves, Mr. Gustavus, he liked a lot of people to talk, and
Mr. Walter—he likes to *tell* you, see, not ask you.'

'Well, I can't work that way,' said Winter shortly.
'Take this time-study business. We don't want it just

imposed by the management or settled by a popular vote.
The proper way is for you and me to agree what we think's
necessary. Then you talk to your people, I'll talk to
Mr. Lang and there we are.'

There was a moment's pause.

'I'd like to think about it a bit, Mr. Winter,' said
Ryan rather doubtfully. ''Course you're quite right.
That's the way things ought to be done, as I've always
said. But this is a new thing, see. . . .'

'All right,' said Winter. 'You think it over, and if
you agree with me then we ought to make an experiment
with it. I take it you've got enough influence in the
place to put it over?'

'Aye,' said Ryan modestly. 'I reckon I have. After
twenty-five years. But it needs thinking about, Mr. Winter.'

'Of course it does. Anyhow, you may want to have a
word with your Mr. Lewin at Union Headquarters.'

'You know Arthur Lewin?'

The corners of Winter's mouth twitched into his
epileptic smile. 'Oh, yes,' he said. 'We've had a lot of
contact. Lewin's got his head screwed on right. Why
not have a chat with him?'

*   *   *   *   *

He wasn't handcuffed to two policemen. He was just
sitting there with his legs crossed smoking a cigarette.
He stubbed it out as Miss Bell brought her in.

Miss Bell said: 'Mr. Lawrence wants to ask you some
questions. Just sit down there and answer them, dear.
There's nothing to be frightened of.'

Lawrence leant forward and said quietly: 'Hilda—I
want you to look at me if you will. . . .' His eyes were
grey and they had brown flecks in them, which was queer
because she had always thought his eyes were brown.
They were sort of smiling at her, though the rest of his
face wasn't. When she looked at him he didn't turn
his eyes away or drop his head, but just went on looking
for what seemed a long time without saying anything.
She could feel the other three looking too, and several
times her eyes flickered away from his, but she made
them come back and look at him.

'Now,' said Lawrence, in the same gentle voice, 'I want you to be sure that you understand what you're doing. You told your mother, and you told Miss Bell, that when I was taking you home in the car I said things to you and did things that were horrid for you and frightened you. That's what you told them, isn't it?'

She said: 'Yes,' soundlessly.

'Well now, if people believe that, it will get me into a lot of trouble. It may even mean that I shall have to leave here, and leave my house and all sorts of things. Now I don't believe you want that to happen to me, do you?'

She gulped and said: 'No.' This time it came out loud.

'Then you must tell the truth and say it didn't happen. I know it's difficult when you've said it did. But you must be brave and tell the truth. Nobody will be angry with you if you do that.' The grey eyes were very gentle and friendly. She was staring into them, and now she couldn't look away even if she wanted to. Everything was a muddle, and when he spoke again she wasn't listening and had to say: 'Pardon?' Lawrence said: 'I said this story of yours isn't true, is it? Nothing at all like that happened in the car, did it?'

She hesitated and then her voice said: 'Yes.'

'Yes it did or yes it didn't?'

'Pardon?' she said helplessly.

He smiled at her and this time all his face smiled. 'Listen, Hilda—I didn't touch you while we were in the car, did I?'

Her eyes filled with tears so that his face was a blur, but there was that other inescapable, indelible face turned towards her as he drove the car. Her lips framed: 'Yes.'

Mr. North said: 'I didn't catch that?'

She turned away from the misty face at last and looked towards North and said: 'Yes, sir. It did. Did happen. Like I said.'

There was a long silence. She looked back at Lawrence and then down at the floor. The grey eyes were no longer smiling. 'Why are you telling this story?' he said slowly, without seeming to expect an answer. She said nothing and after a while Lawrence said in a different sort of voice: 'When we got to Market Cross you got out and said: "Thank you," didn't you?'

'Yes.'

'Why did you do that if I'd done horrid things to you and frightened you?'

It was a muddle and though her lips moved no sound came. 'You went home and said nothing to anybody for nearly three days. Why was that?'

Miss Bell said: 'It was because you didn't want to make trouble, wasn't it? And you thought your father . . .'

'Don't prompt her, please,' said Lawrence curtly. 'Let her answer.'

Hilda nodded towards Miss Bell and said: 'That's right, Miss Bell.'

Lawrence said: 'Then why, if you didn't want to cause trouble, did you go and tell her three days later?'

They were all looking at her and it had been going to Early Service and that smell that there was in St. Thomas's and the singing and saying her prayers and she had felt bad and had to come out and cried and her mother knowing there was something. But it was all a muddle and suddenly she felt loneliness and utter despair and she turned her head away and started to cry properly so that her nose ran.

Miss Bell got up and said: 'I don't think . . .?'

Lawrence shrugged his shoulders and sat back in his chair and said bitterly: 'All right.'

Mr. North said: 'There's nothing else you want to ask her, Mr. Lawrence?'

'No, thank you,' he said curtly.

She had to go past him as Miss Bell took her out but he did not look at her. He had taken a cigarette out and was just putting it in his mouth, staring straight in front of him.

Mr. North said: 'Well, thank you, Mr. Lawrence. I don't think there's anything more. . . .'

Miss Bell came back and said: 'She's all right. Poor child. I really thought she did very well.'

Ryan said: 'He couldn't shake her.'

North took out his handkerchief, thought about it, blew his nose and said: 'Now how do we proceed? I don't think there's any point in seeing any more witnesses because there's really nothing they could add. I suppose the next thing is to decide on our views and—and prepare something for the Board.'

Ryan lit his pipe and tossed the match-box on the table. 'Well, you know what *I* think,' he said decidedly. 'And seeing them together hasn't altered it. I reckon he did it. I don't think the girl need have made a fuss. Better if she'd kept her mouth shut. But I reckon she's telling the truth all right.'

North nodded without comment and said: 'Miss Bell?'

'Well, I don't like to say so, **Mr.** North, but I must say I rather agree with Mr. Ryan. I think she's a truthful girl and I don't think she'd make up a story like that —particularly what she told me about going to church and so on. And then the quotation. She couldn't have known that and he did. And if nothing had been going on, why should he say a thing like that to her?'

Ryan said: 'Yes. He caught himself out, there.'

'I don't think I'm as certain about it as Mr. Ryan,' said Miss Bell rather miserably. 'But if I *had* to say what I thought . . .'

North tapped his dentures very gently with the end of his pencil. 'Of course there's no *proof*,' he said, 'not of the sort that would be accepted in a court of law. It's purely the girl's unsupported testimony.' He shook his head dubiously. 'After all, the proper principle is that it's far better for a hundred guilty people to escape than for one to be wrongly convicted. And since the Board will presumably act on our findings . . .'

'But look here,' said Ryan impatiently. 'What are we really talking about? If we say we're doubtful and the Board lets him get away with it, there isn't a man or woman in the factory who'll believe he didn't do it.'

North said: 'That's nothing to do with us. Our duty . . .'

'Maybe it isn't anything to do with us. But it's what matters.' He shook his head and frowned. 'By far the best thing would be if he resigned of his own accord. I don't see why he hasn't.'

Miss Bell said: 'That would practically be admitting it.'

'Not necessarily. And it'd be the best way out for everybody.'

There was a long pause.

North said: 'Well, I certainly don't feel that we should be too—*too* positive in our findings.'

'That's what I feel, Mr. Ryan,' said Miss Bell. 'It would be too awful if . . .'

'Well, we've got to say *something*, haven't we?'

Miss Bell said: 'Couldn't we say that—that there's no proof, but that nothing we've heard shows that the girl's story isn't true.'

'Something on those lines,' said North. 'Not Proven, in fact.'

'Yes. And leave it to the Board.'

'But where does that get anybody?' said Ryan impatiently.

North said: 'I don't think we need necessarily feel that we *must* get somewhere. After all—we might get to the wrong place.' He smiled with mild satisfaction. 'Well, suppose I were to attempt to draft something on those lines and submit it to you . . .?'

*　　　*　　　*　　　*　　　*

There was a lot of traffic and it was seven o'clock before Laura reached home. Lawrence was sitting in the drawing-room with the drinks tray beside him. He looked as though he had been there some time, and the extra little shove that he gave himself as he rose confirmed it. He said: 'Hallo, darling. Have a drink?'

Laura said: 'Just a small one. Sorry I wasn't here when you got in.'

'Oh, that's all right. I left my place of employment rather early this evening. I didn't feel much like trying to buy Walter leather washers to-night.' He shook his head solemnly. 'Not keen, young Spellman. No real interest in the job.' He poured out her drink.

Laura said: 'Hey—woa!'

'You're behind the party, darling. Substantially behind it.'

Laura sat down and lit a cigarette and said : 'Well— how did it go?'

'The case of Rex v. Spellman? In the High Court of Justice, before North, J., Ryan, J., and Bell, J.? Oh, it was a lovely three-ring circus.' He waved a hand. 'I had her in. I explained what it meant to me. I asked her point-blank to tell the truth . . . and she stuck to the story like a leech.'

Laura said : 'I always thought she would. What else could she do?'

Lawrence threw himself into a chair. 'But it was a most extraordinary sensation, darling. I can't convey . . .' He shook his head. 'I opened my eyes very wide. I spoke quietly and gently. With pathos. Definitely with pathos, as I sketched for her how she might be blighting my life. I even made touching references to my unborn children. . . .'

'*Darling* . . .!'

Lawrence shook his head again and took a sip of his drink. 'And that little so-and-so,' he said moodily, 'sat there staring at me with those big, innocent blue eyes full of tears, and said I was a liar. Honestly, there was a moment when I almost believed it myself.'

Laura was looking at the end of her cigarette. 'Do you think *they* believed her?'

'Heaven knows. I think I should have, if I'd been in their place. But then I should probably have believed me too. I was very sincere, darling. A most impressive witness. Quietly impressive.' He smiled at his glass.

Laura said : 'What happens now?'

'God knows. Presumably the Royal Commission will report. Though what it's going to report that everybody didn't know before, I can't think. If it comes down to votes, my guess would be that Jim Ryan will be for me because we get on together, Miss Bell will be against me because she thinks young girls ought to be protected, and anyhow this girl goes to church. And North will sit on the fence, because that's his normal position.' He suddenly frowned and said : 'I'm uncommonly tired of it all, darling. One does get tired of protesting one's essential chastity to people like Shop Stewards.' He finished his drink and pushed his glass away from him irritably.

Laura said : ' I think some food might be a good thing.'

' Plenty of time,' said Lawrence. ' It's early yet.' He lay back in his chair and closed his eyes. ' What I wanted to ask you,' he said after a pause, ' is whether you think it might be better and more dignified just to resign. After all, it would please Walter, and I would like to do something to please Walter, never having succeeded in doing so in any other way. "Nothing in his life," in fact, "became him like the leaving of it."'

Laura was gazing into the fire.

He opened his eyes and said : ' What d'you think, sweetheart? You've got to remember that in a thing like this, you're guilty unless you can prove that you're innocent. And I can't prove it.'

Laura went on looking at the fire and slowly shook her head. She said : ' No—I don't think you should resign. I don't think you *can*, as a matter of principle. If somebody accuses you of something and it isn't true, you mustn't let them get the same results as though it *was* true. Not if you can prevent it.'

' I'm not sure that I can.'

' That doesn't matter. If you tell the truth and they don't believe you and fire you, that's their responsibility. But you must give them a *chance* to be right.'

' On the ethics of the thing,' said Lawrence rather bitterly, ' I bow to your opinion. But it won't be very pleasant for you if they *do* fire me.'

' It won't be very pleasant if you resign, for that matter.' Laura smiled. ' And anyhow, darling, what we're after isn't a pleasant time for me but a reasonably square deal for you. "Father—I bloody well *didn't* chop the cherry-tree."'

' Even though I am a bit of a cherry-tree chopper as a rule?'

' Exactly.'

Lawrence said : ' You're a very sweet person, darling, and I love you.' He leant back and closed his eyes again.

'D'you know what *really* surprises me about all this'? he said with a frown.

'What?'

'That you believe me.' He opened his eyes and stared at her slightly glassily.

'Does it?' said Laura, smiling.

'Yes. I would have bet a fiver that you would have said: "Of course he did it. He can never keep his hands off any pretty girl".'

Laura got up and kissed him on the forehead as she passed. She said: 'I'm going to see about food.'

XVI

R YAN said: 'I never knew such a lot for crying out before you're hurt. Why can't you wait and see what happens?'

'We're not crying out before we're hurt,' said Herbage, 'we're crying out so that we don't *get* hurt.'

Marks said: 'It's the thin end of the wedge. You once let the sweaters in and what you going to do?'

Ryan wheeled round on him. 'Well, what are *you* going to do, Ikey?'

'Never you mind what I'd do,' said Marks darkly.

'Ah, of course you and your pals,' said Ryan with contempt, 'you *like* trouble, don't you?'

Jack said: 'I reckon it's a thing for the Works Committee.'

Ryan took his pipe out of his mouth and spat. 'Look here,' he said, 'it's time some of you learnt some sense. The Works Committee's nothing to do with wage rates, and never has been. This has been told to me first, in the proper way. All it is so far is that Winter's told Mr. Walter some of the rates are way out and ought to be studied. . . .'

'Ah,' said Herbage cynically, 'that's all it is *so* far. . . .'

'And after proper consideration and consultation,' said Ryan with dignity, 'I've agreed with Mr. Walter that a few rates shall be time-studied as an experiment.'

'Well, why's this ever come up?' said Jack. 'That's what I want to know.'

'You know as well as I do there's rates that's too tight, and some that are easy money. Never been altered since the new blanks service came in.'

'That's so,' said Matt Wright. 'That was Mr. Gustavus. He wouldn't have them altered. Said if people could make a bit extra . . .'

'All right,' said Ryan, 'well, that was all very fine and

large, but Mr. Gustavus is gone, see? And what's more, Winter's come. I been in touch with Headquarters and maybe I know more about *why* he's come and what's going on than you do, see?'

Jack said: 'Well, why has he come? Is Barker going to run the place or him or what?'

'Never you mind. You'll know soon enough. But I can tell you this—it's got to be watched pretty close.'

'That's what I'm telling you,' said Marks eagerly. 'You once get the sweaters in and . . .'

'And what's more,' said Ryan, glancing at him, 'if you need help it won't be the Commies or the Works Committee or any of it that'll help you. It'll be the Union.'

'So it will,' said Herbage.

'Right. And that's why I got to be careful. If I start making a fuss just because they want to study a few wrong rates, who's going to back me up? There's nothing new about rate setting with a watch, is there? I don't want chaps about clicking stop-watches any more than you do. I've said so. But if they want to go on with it, you can't stop them. Because it's nothing that's not common practice up and down the country, even if we haven't had it before.'

Marks said: 'Well, I reckon you could stop 'em fast enough?'

'How? You tell me?'

Marks hesitated. 'Say the workers won't have it.'

'What he means,' said Ryan, 'is threaten to make a striking issue of it. Only he hasn't got the guts to say so. Well, let me tell you—if you listen to Ikey and his pals you'll land yourself in a lot of trouble.'

'Striking's silly talk,' said Herbage. 'But I don't like it for all that, Jim.'

Jack said: 'Nor do I. I reckon we ought to go and see Mr. Walter.'

Ryan flushed. 'All right,' he said. 'You go, Jack. You're a clever boy and maybe you can do better than I can. I only knew Mr. Walter a few years before you were born. Stands to reason he'll listen to you more than to me.'

There was a discouraged silence. Old Matt Wright
squeaked out: 'Well, I told you, didn't I? When I was
talking to you and Ikey. I said you'd soon be wishing
Mr. Gustavus was back. . . .'

Herbage said: 'Oh, hold your noise.'

'Well, what are you going to do?' said Jack sullenly.
'Nothing?'

'No,' said Ryan. 'But what I'm not going to do is to
overplay my hand. They're within their rights. Let
them make their time-studies. *But . . .*' he smiled
triumphantly, 'it's a rule of the company that no rate
can be altered without I'm consulted. See?'

There was a pause. Jack said: 'And what if Walter
wants to cut a rate and you don't agree and he says he's
going on?'

'Well, I've been working with Mr. Walter for twenty-
five years,' said Ryan quietly. 'And I never knew anything we couldn't settle between us in the end.'

'Ah,' said Matt Wright, 'but he knew he had Mr.
Gustavus near him and . . .'

'Oh, hold your noise,' said Herbage.

*   *   *   *   *

Lang turned over the sixth and last page of the
document. 'The matter therefore becomes one of judgment rather than of fact,' it ran, 'and the Committee
does not feel that it is within its province to express a
positive opinion as to the relative truthfulness of the two
parties, both of whom have been consistent in their
opposing stories, where such an opinion is not supported
by facts. It is only fair to Miss P. to say that nothing
has emerged which suggests that she is not a witness of
truth. On the other hand, it is difficult to see how
Mr. L.S. could have disproved her story, were it untrue.

'The Committee therefore respectfully suggests that it
is for the Board to decide whether a girl of excellent
character would invent such a story, and would particularly draw attention, in this connection to para. (3) (*a*)
—where a quotation which she could hardly know and
which she says was used, fits quite well with her story,
but less well with that of Mr. L.S. On the other hand,

it is equally for the Board to decide whether one of its colleagues, whose qualities will be known even better to the Board than to the Committee, is likely to have behaved in the way alleged.'

The three signatures followed.

Lang put the document down and said: 'Well, there we are, Henry. I'm sorry.'

'What about?' said Henry shortly.

Lang shrugged. 'It's pretty conclusive.'

'I don't see anything conclusive about it. They simply say there's no proof one way or the other and chuck the whole thing back to the Board. What else can they do?'

'Oh come!' said Lang. 'You can hardly expect them to come slap out in the open and say they believe the girl. But surely there's no doubt what they think?'

'You can read it that way if you want to. And the other way if you don't.'

'Well, I'm afraid there's no doubt which way the Board will read it.'

'The Board,' said Henry. He took off his spectacles, put them on the desk, and goaded them like a cat goading a moribund mouse. 'The Board consists of Barker, who won't have an opinion; and North who's said he doesn't know; and Winter who knows nothing about it; and you and me.'

'And Jim Talbot-Rees.'

'And Jim Talbot-Rees. Well—we all know about Jim.'

Lang smiled. 'I seem to remember you telling me the other day that it was no good having a Board unless it acted like one.' He leant forward. 'Look, Henry—I understand from Ryan that there's pretty strong feeling in the factory about this. If we could have cleared Lawrence, well and good. But we can't. So . . .'

'So what?'

'I think he ought to resign. It's the only decent thing he can do in everybody's interest. And if he doesn't, then I think the Board ought to ask for his resignation.'

'Well, that's asking for mine too, isn't it?'

'I don't see why. I hope you won't feel that.'

Old Henry gave a sudden snort of anger, heaved

himself out of his chair and walked over to the window. After a while he said: 'I was a friend of your father's for a good many years. I was a friend of Gus's all his life. I've tried to be a friend of yours. But you've no friendship in you.'

'This is not a matter of friendship,' said Lang coldly.

'No,' said Henry. 'It isn't. It's a matter of cold vindictiveness, Walter. You've always been out to get rid of Lawrence, because he laughs at you and isn't afraid of you. But all the same, if I'd been prepared to sell you control of the company, we shouldn't have heard any more about this.'

Lang got up and said: 'I don't think this sort of thing helps anybody. I've told you my opinion. I think the Board will feel as I do. It's up to you to give Lawrence what advice you think fit.'

Old Henry looked at him for a moment in silence. 'Like a kid,' he said, almost to himself, 'like a kid saying, "I'm stronger than you. I can push you into the ditch. . . ."' He sighed. 'All right, Walter. I've no more to say. When d'you want to bring this up?'

'The Committee's report will be circulated to the Board and it'll have to come up next Tuesday. Unless, of course, Lawrence chooses to resign before then, in which case there'll be no need to discuss it.'

'Fine,' said Henry. 'Tuesday.'

It was only just four o'clock but Barker was waiting in the outer office. He was a stickler for accuracy. Lang said: 'Oh, here you are, Barker. Come in. Get us some tea, Miss Mays, will you?' He waved vaguely at Barker. 'Sit down.' There was only one arm-chair in Lang's office. Whether one sat in it or not was a point of fine social distinction. Barker drew up a straight chair without hesitation. His face was paler than ever.

Lang glanced at him with a slight frown and a tiny compression of the lips. The man was bright enough, and George Martin had thought highly of him, but there was no doubt that he was a bit of a weed. Lang made himself smile and said: 'Well, now—what was it?'

Barker raised the pale face and said rather breathlessly: 'Mr. Walter—I feel that I must ask for my position to be clarified *vis-à-vis* Mr. Winter.'

Lang smiled inwardly at the prepared opening. 'Oh?' he said. 'Why? What's Mr. Winter been up to?'

'I don't want to criticise Mr. Winter. He's obviously a—a very experienced man. But some of the inquiries he's making—well, you see, Mr. Walter, they're not always made through me, and naturally people come to ask me if—if it's all right and sometimes I know nothing about it. It makes it difficult to know where one is.'

'I see,' said Lang. He frowned thoughtfully. 'Well, of course that's all wrong. These things ought to be done through you if you're in charge. . . . Of course it's a matter of degree. Winter must be able to make contact with people. . . .'

Barker hesitated. 'You see, sometimes I don't even know if these things are—are done with your authority. Take this time-study business. The first I heard of that was from Ryan, who'd apparently discussed it with you and Mr. Winter. Well . . . nobody's said anything to me. So of course I went straight to Mr. Winter and asked him about it, and he said, oh yes, it was being done on your instructions, and I said, well, I'm surprised Mr. Walter hasn't informed me. . . .'

Barker's voice had taken on a tone of mournful reproach. Lang said: 'But I sent you a note about it.'

'Yes, Mr. Walter. But that was after.'

'Oh, well then, that was a slip-up on my part,' said Lang shortly. 'I'm sorry.'

'Of course it didn't *matter*, Mr. Walter, but you see . . .'

'Yes, yes,' said Lang impatiently. 'I see and I apologise.' The words seemed strangely incongruous when used to Barker. Lang said rather coldly: 'I think you can take it that Mr. Winter won't do anything without my authority. I must try to keep you informed, of course. But in the meantime I think you'd be wise to try to work *with* him—and learn as much as you can from him. He's a very able man.'

'Yes,' said Barker, without enthusiasm. 'Of course
. . . he's used to a very different sort of place . . .'

'You mean a more efficient one?' said Lang bluntly.

Barker hesitated and then said quietly: 'I don't know
about efficiency, Mr. Walter. But I think I ought to tell
you that Mr. Winter is not making himself *liked*.'

'Why not?'

'Well . . . he's not used to our ways, of course, and
he has a—a rather hard way of speaking. . . . I've nothing *against* Mr. Winter, you understand. I'm merely
giving you my impressions.'

'You mean he's too tough for our people?'

'Slightly.'

Lang smiled grimly. 'Well, that may not be a bad
thing. I often used to tell George Martin that he was
too soft.'

Barker's face took on a faint tinge of pink. 'Mr.
Martin,' he said carefully, 'was worth any six of Mr.
Winter.'

Lang looked at him in surprise. The face was half
defiant, half frightened. He smiled at it with genuine
pleasure for the first time and said: 'Maybe you're right
there, Barker.'

The young man smiled back with relief and said: 'I
suppose I *should* think so, having worked with Mr. Martin
so long. . . .'

'Yes.' Lang got up. 'Well, now you've got to work
with someone quite different, and the only thing to do
is to get the best you can out of him. I'll try to see that
we don't slip up again about keeping you informed.
Anyhow, Winter won't be having much to do with the
factory from now on. He'll be busy on stuff for me that
won't concern you.'

When the door had closed Lang sat for a few moments
in silence. His face was slightly worried. Taking a
piece of paper he began to scribble rapidly: 'Mr. H.
Winter *from* Managing Director. Whilst I have agreed
to go forward with experimental time-studies in the press-
shop, and think they may be of value, I should make it
clear that I do not want you to spend your time primarily
on matters of this kind. Apart from the fact that there

is some danger of crossing wires with Barker, I am anxious
to get on with the plans for re-organisation set out in the
memorandum that I gave you, and on which I have not
yet received your comments. . . .'

*   *   *   *   *

Jack said : 'Mean to say you hadn't heard about
it?'

'Of course I hadn't,' said Rosamund. 'How should
I?' She took her hand away from his and sat staring
straight ahead. 'I think it's perfectly beastly.'

'Well, he's had it coming to him.'

'How d'you mean?'

'Everybody knows he's a chaser. Fred Boxall's sister
Nell . . .'

Rosamund said coldly : 'I don't want to hear about
any dirty little bits of gossip.'

'Well, all right,' said Jack in surprise. 'It's not my
fault, is it?'

'No. It's not your fault. But I must say you seem
very pleased about it.'

'If you want it like that,' he said, 'I *am* pleased about
it and I don't care who knows it.'

'Why? What harm's Lawrence ever done you?'

'He? He's never had the chance. But to go messing
about with a bit of a kid like that . . .'

'In a motor car?'

He stopped and looked at her sharply. Rosamund
leant forward and wiped a spot off the windscreen with
elaborate care. Jack said : 'Listen—are you trying to
make a thing out of this? Because . . .'

She suddenly banged her clenched fist on her knee
and said : 'Oh, you're all so beastly and unfair and
hypocritical about Lawrence. You all hate him and—
—and want to hurt him. Just because he's a—a bit silly,
you all seize on anything he does and . . .'

'I see,' said Jack coldly. 'So I'm unfair, am I?'

'Yes, you are. You say you're glad he's in trouble
and—and you're against him, and you don't even know
that it's true.' She turned on him. 'How would you
like it if it were you?'

'I didn't know he was such a pal of yours,' said Jack sarcastically.'

'Well then, you know now! I like him and I always have. He's kind and—and I don't care what he's done.'

Jack said: 'Well, when it comes to treating a nice kid . . .'

'Oh a nice kid—a nice kid! You keep on saying that. How do you know she's a nice kid? Do you know her?'

'Yes,' he said. 'I know her very well. And if you must know, I used to go out with her.'

'Then,' said Rosamund, raising her eyebrows and gazing innocently down the road, 'I must say I'm surprised that this all came as such a shock to her.'

He looked at her supercilious profile for a moment, his face slowly reddening. Then he turned suddenly, got out of the car, and walked away without a word. Rosamund opened her mouth to say something, closed it again, and sat looking after him with set lips.

She wanted her behind smacking when she came that game, and if it hadn't been eight miles away and Sunday and no buses he would have gone home and left her to sweat for it. As it was, he took no notice when he heard the car behind, and didn't look at it as it passed. She went on quite a way, for a moment he thought she was going on and leaving him to walk. But she stopped some way on and when he came up, still taking no notice, there she was leaning out of the window very solemn and she said: 'Do you want a lift home? Or perhaps you'd better not in case you say after that I made passes at you.' The way she did it, he had to grin, and then she gave that giggle that was like something being poured out of a bottle and put her hand out and grabbed his and put it to her mouth and bit his thumb hard. He said: 'Hey—you little devil. . . .'

On the way home he said: 'Why should I care? Nothing to do with me, is it? There was no call for taking me up like that.'

'Well, I didn't know she'd been your girl. I suppose

that makes a difference. Though I don't see much why
it should, if you say she isn't now. Anyhow, let's forget
it.' Rosamund sighed. 'Oh God, we've got the Talbot-
Reeses coming to dinner. That means I shall have to
talk to her.'

Jack said : 'She looks a dame all right.'

'She is. She's the person I've always thought I should
hate to meet when—when we're out.' Rosamund suddenly gave a little bounce. 'Golly—I am so looking
forward to Hastings. Are you?'

He took his eyes off the road long enough to glance at
the beaming face. 'You bet, Rosey.'

*   *   *   *   *

The lights in St. Thomas's were made so that they
still looked like candles. But of course they weren't
candles but electric, and when Mr. Greaves got up into
the pulpit to preach the sermon they dimmed the lights
down so that it was nearly dark in the congregation and
only the light on him, almost like at the pictures. The
light was down on the top of the pulpit so that his face
was lit from below, and when he held his face up and
looked out at the congregation it made shadows on his
face, and with his big hooked nose he looked almost
fierce, though he was very nice really.

Mr. Greaves climbed up into the pulpit and put his
sermon on it, and then stood looking at the congregation
while the hymn was ending. It always seemed to Hilda
that he was looking at her, but it might be that he was
looking at her mother, because her mother always sang
out loud in the hymns. When it was finished he said :
'In the name of the Father . . . and of the Son . . .
and of the Holy Ghost . . . Amen,' very slowly, and with
a big gap between each. Then everybody sat down, and
it was then that the lights went down.

'The twelfth chapter of St. Matthew's Gospel, the
seventh verse : "I will have mercy, and not sacrifice."'
Mr. Greaves paused for a long time and looked round
the church. '"I will have mercy,"' he said reflectively,
'"and not sacrifice. . . ."' He smiled suddenly—an
almost deprecating smile. 'To most of us,' he said in

that quiet voice, as though he was talking to you, but that carried so that you never missed a word, 'brought up in the Christian religion, the idea of mercy—of love— as the supreme virtue is an accustomed one. But to a Jew of Christ's own day, the emphasis on love and compassion, rather than on mere retributive justice, will have seemed dangerous, if not positively blasphemous. For society was, and to some extent remains to-day, based on the idea that sin must and should be punished; and that such punishment, even when carrying out the man-made law of society itself, is pleasing to God.'

Her mother had placed her feet on a hassock and settled herself in a corner of the pew. Her eyes were closed. If you went on staring at Mr. Greaves's face very hard for a long time without blinking, it went all funny, and you could see a sort of coloured circle round where the light was, like a rainbow but round.

*   *   *   *   *

Rosamund had forgotten about its being Sunday, and it was only late on Saturday afternoon that she had discovered that there wasn't any more sherry. She had had to dash and get some from the grocer's, and though they had said it was very nice, it looked rather like cough mixture instead of being gold colour. She watched the Honourable Amy take her first sip rather anxiously, and sure enough, up went the eyebrows and she put the glass down and didn't drink any more. Rosamund took a sip of her own, trying to do it in a way that implied that it was supposed to taste like that. But it was very difficult to put that into a sip, and anyhow there was undoubtedly something in what the Honourable Amy's eyebrows said. It reminded Rosamund of the sherry they gave you at the bar of the dirt-track, but it was nastier.

The Honourable Amy nodded at Rosamund's frock and said: 'We're very demure this evening, aren't we?' She was wearing a black frock too, but it wasn't one that she had had two years and then had dyed. The Honourable Amy said: 'We seem to have the same ideas about these things. Last time we met, at the Party, we were the only two thoroughly over-dressed and overexposed women in the room. I remember how my heart warmed to you when I saw you.'

Rosamund said: 'Oh, that was that *awful* dress. I bought it in a hurry.'

'I remember you told me it came from Beale's, and poor Laura insisted that she bought all *her* clothes there.' The Honourable Amy smiled. 'Never mind. You looked very nice. That's the great advantage of being young. You can wear practically *anything* and get away with it.'

Lang was saying '. . . without seeming to realise that the real capital employed in a business like ours has gone up three hundred per cent.' He had drunk his sherry but Talbot-Rees's glass was still full. Rosamund said confidentially: 'Do you think I'd better give Daddy another glass of this *awful* sherry, or is it kinder not to?'

'Awful?' said the Honourable Amy. 'My dear, it's delicious. A little sweet for my taste perhaps, but I'm not a sherry connoisseur. Are you?'

'No,' said Rosamund. 'No. I'm not.'

'Jim is,' said the Honourable Amy, glancing at her husband's glass. 'We'll ask him about it in a moment.'

*   *   *   *   *

'The list is a long one. The woman taken in adultery. The publican who beat his breast as he prayed. The thief on the cross. And last of all, those who had worked and tortured and sacrificed Him. "Father forgive them. They know not what they do." Forgiveness. Mercy. It is always the theme. "Judge not, that ye be not judged." "Forgive us our debts, as we forgive our debtors . . ." Love, our Lord seems to say, is the attribute of God towards which we all can and must aspire. But Justice—ah, that is another thing—a divine mystery reserved by God to Himself. We can all know love. We can all feel kindness and generosity and forgiveness. But to think we know justice is dangerous. For justice is a judgment of others, and it is precisely this setting of ourself up in judgment, against which we are explicitly warned. "Judge not, that ye be not judged".' Judge, I don't want this man punished. . . . But it hadn't been like that, really more as though she had done something

H

to *him* and he was being nice about it, so that there wasn't
ever a chance. . . . 'Nor must we make the mistake,'
said Mr. Greaves, 'of making the act of love and forgiveness into a matter of pride and self-esteem. "In forgiving his enemy," says that worldly man Francis Bacon,
"a man is superior. For it is a Prince's part to pardon."
A Prince—yes. But not a worldly Prince. Not a Prince
pardoning the suppliant kneeling at His feet. But a
Prince hanging dying on the Cross, pardoning and loving
those who nailed Him there.'

*   *   *   *   *

The ladies had gone and were now talking by themselves in the drawing-room instead of talking by themselves in the dining-room. Talbot-Rees waved his cigar
and said: 'I entirely agree, Walter. One is sorry for
Lawrence, and of course Amy's heartbroken for poor
Laura. But it's not a matter where one can let friendship
stand in the way. If people do these things, they must
take the consequences.'

Lang said: 'Henry's made it pretty clear that if
Lawrence goes he goes too.'

'Well . . .' Talbot-Rees shrugged his shoulders and
smiled. 'That would be—regrettable. But . . .' He
knocked the ash off his cigar. 'That man Winter—now
that's an able man. I was talking to him the other day.
I was impressed.'

Lang said: 'Yes. He is good.'

'From what he was saying there ought not to be any
difficulty in filling the press-shop with work from the rest
of their group, which would save an enormous amount
of my time in touting round for contracts. Next time I'm
in London he's going to introduce me to Proudfoot and
some of their top people. Be a good thing to go in and
show the flag, don't you think?'

'Possibly,' said Lang without enthusiasm. 'Though
mind you—I don't want us to get *too* mixed up with
them. Winter's job is to help with the changeover to
our own products, not to make us into one of their
fabricating plants.'

Talbot-Rees looked at him for a moment in silence

'Oh, yes,' he said. 'Of course.' He gazed thoughtfully at the end of the cigar. 'I take it you've had a word with him about this Lawrence business?'

'Why? Winter?'

'Yes.'

'Why should I? It's nothing to do with him. It's a purely domestic matter. And anyhow he doesn't know the—the people or the circumstances or . . .'

'Of course not,' said Talbot-Rees. 'But—well—as a director, and representing Proudfoot, he'll presumably have a vote, if it came to that. And since Proudfoot is a buddy of old Henry's . . .'

Lang frowned. 'Look,' he said. 'Don't misunderstand the situation. Proudfoot may have bought a block of shares, but there's no question of Proudfoot or Winter or anybody else interfering with the running of the company—and certainly not in a thing like this. Winter's here purely as my assistant—and between ourselves he came here at my suggestion.'

'Oh . . .? I didn't realise that.'

'Nobody does,' said Lang, smiling. 'And I'd much prefer that they didn't. But you can take it from me that whether Proudfoot happens to know Henry or not, he and I understand one another.'

'Ah!' said Talbot-Rees. 'I begin to see. I couldn't quite understand. . . . Frankly, Walter, I was rather assuming that this deal between Henry and Proudfoot, and Winter's coming and so on had been—well—rather forced on you. But . . .'

'That's exactly what you were intended to think.'

Talbot-Rees shook his head admiringly. 'You're a deep one, Walter,' he said solemnly. 'A very deep one.'

'You're quite right, my dear,' said the Honourable Amy coldly. 'And anyhow it isn't a very pleasant subject for a young girl.'

Rosamund said: 'From what little I've heard, it isn't a pleasant subject for anybody.'

'Of course to me the tragedy is poor Laura. It's completely broken her up.'

Rosamund said: 'Have some more coffee?'

'I don't think I will, thank you. Do you find it terribly difficult to get decent coffee nowadays?'

*   *   *   *   *

'. . . and in that last extremity showed us that love is not just a general vague benevolence—and absence of hate—a few good intentions; but that it is a *positive* thing. A willingness to sacrifice oneself for others—to accept pain and mortification and ridicule and loss in the name of love, as He accepted them for us.'

The lights went up and because they had been dimmed before they seemed brighter than usual. The hymn was 'Love Divine All Loves Excelling.' It was one of her mother's favourite hymns, and her mother sang it very loudly in her strong voice. Hilda did not sing, but she looked at her book, and the print was small and it blurred because of the tears in her eyes. But they were only there because she was so warm and happy inside; and when they came to the end, and the choir had gone out and you just knelt down for a moment and then went, she forgot that there wasn't really time to pray properly and went on kneeling there till her mother nudged her to get up. And then they were out in the street walking home and her mother was saying something, but she did not hear what it was, because she was in the garden of Gethsemane, knowing the end, and alone, and afraid, and utterly exalted.

XVII

THERE was the usual file of papers in his IN tray, varying from the last period's profit estimate to a request for a subscription to the Engineers' Representatives' Benevolent Society. Lang settled down to his slow methodical Monday morning reading. It always took most of the morning, for it involved, as a matter of principle, reading and annotating not only what other people had said to him and he had said to other people, but large quantities of carbon copies of what other people had said to one another. 'To Mr. J. Barker *from* L. Spellman. Sorry, but this is a Purchasing Department, not the Oxford Street Woolworths. L.S. Copy to Managing Director.' '*To* Company Chairman *from* Secretary. In accordance with your instructions the meeting of the Social Club Committee has been cancelled. J. North. Copy to Managing Director.'

Lawrence had once remarked that there was only one sort of paper used in the place of which the Managing Director did not insist on having a copy.

It was half-past ten before Lang had worked his way far enough down the pile to come to Winter's note. It said: 'In view of our recent talks, I have asked our Longwood factory to lend me a young man named John L. Parkes who is a first-rate Time-Study man. He begins work next week.'

Lang stared at the note, frowned, placed a large question mark beside it, and put it aside on the small pile needing attention. But after it, routine exchanges between Talbot-Rees and Barker seemed unimportant. He picked the note up, read it again, and pressed the bell.

Winter either did not know or did not mind about the subtle significance of the arm-chair, and he settled down in it comfortably and took out his pipe, which, at the moment, was as wrong in its way as Barker's nervous perching. Lang said curtly: 'What's this note of yours about a Time-Study man?'

Winter said: 'Oh that? He's a good boy. Just the man.'

'But you had no right to go and ask for him without consulting me.'

Winter raised his eyebrows. 'I'm sorry,' he said mildly. 'But it seemed to me that since we'd agreed to do some Time-Studies we obviously needed a Time-Study man. Parkes has worked with me before and . . .'

'I dare say he has. But I'm not at all sure that I want somebody from your Longwood place here.'

'Why not?'

Lang hesitated. 'Because I might or might not think he was suitable.'

'I assure you that he's an excellent man.'

Lang glanced at him but Winter's face was quite expressionless. 'Moreover,' he said tonelessly, 'since a substantial amount of fabricating may be coming here from Longwood, it might be helpful . . .'

'Who says it will?' said Lang sharply.

Winter spread out his hands. 'I understood that that had been more or less agreed?'

'Well, it hasn't,' said Lang bluntly. 'All that's been agreed is that we might take on some work for Longwood if it suited our plans. Anyhow, there was nothing at all as definite as you seem to think.'

'I see. But I think it might be an excellent idea, don't you?' said Winter gently. 'I talked to your Sales Director and he seemed very relieved at the prospect . . .'

'I don't care what he seemed,' said Lang rudely. 'If you want to talk to anybody about these things, talk to me.'

'I'm sorry. He wanted to talk to me, and I understood from the Board that that was in order.'

Lang got up and stalked angrily over to the window. Winter's eyes followed him with calm interest. Lang turned and said: 'I think there's some danger of a mis-understanding, Winter. You were sent here as the result of an arrangement between Sir Francis Proudfoot and myself, to assist me in making certain changes—not to go playing about in the press-shop, nor to manage the place. I've already told you what I want you to do is to stop messing about with these details and upsetting the management, and to get on with the plan outlined in my memorandum.'

'It's difficult to consider re-organising your business until your plant's running efficiently. Regarding your memorandum, I sent you my comments.'

'Well, I haven't seen them.'

'Perhaps they're in your tray now?' said Winter helpfully. He leant back and began to fill his pipe slowly and with great care.

It was nearly at the bottom of the pile, and it consisted of one and a half quarto pages of typing.

Winter looked up and said: 'Yes—that's it. You might care to read it now. It's not very long.' Lang's face had flushed dark red as he saw the document. He looked at it for a moment and then flicked over the page and read the last sentence. 'In the circumstances,' it ran, 'I can see no justification, from a normal business standpoint, in discarding a sound, profitable business, and incurring heavy capital expenditure, in pursuit of something which must be highly speculative.' Lang put the paper down. 'I see,' he said very quietly. 'And that's all you have to say?'

'I think so,' said Winter meditatively. 'As I told you before, it's really a question of what you're in business for. If it's a—a sort of game, then I don't doubt what you propose would make it more colourful and exciting. But if you're in business to make money, then it's completely out of court under present conditions. And as an employee, I have to assume that the important thing is the Profit and Loss account.'

Lang said: 'Well, if you feel like that you're quite useless to me.'

'I can only give you an honest opinion from a strictly limited business point of view. I think your proposal is attractive but not very practical.'

'You were sent here to implement my policy, not to criticise it.' Lang lowered his head till practically only his forehead was visible. 'I shall ask for your withdrawal at once.'

Winter nodded. 'I'm sorry about that,' he said calmly. 'I really think something might have been done with that press-shop.'

* * * * *

Miss Bell's first thought was that the strain of it all had sent the girl mad. But though Hilda looked pale and slightly odd altogether, she seemed sane enough, if utterly unhelpful. Yes, she was quite sure she knew what she was saying. No, nothing had happened in the car—nothing at all. Mr. Lawrence had just picked her up and taken her home like he said. Had she thought she was telling the truth before? She wasn't sure. And finally why, oh why had she done it, and told all these lies? She didn't know.

In the end even Miss Bell grew impatient and rather flustered. 'Well, I don't know, Hilda—I think you must have been out of your mind. I'm sure I don't know what everybody will say now, after all the to-do you've made. . . .'

In the end she was left alone in the Welfare Room while Miss Bell hurried away to find North and Ryan. There was no doubt that the revilings and persecutions had begun, even if gently.

Lang stared round at the deputation with a frown. 'You mean she just takes it all back?' he said sharply.

'Yes, Mr. Walter. Just says it was all a lie.'

There was a moment's silence. 'It was always a possibility,' said North. 'As we pointed out in our report . . .'

'Well, I don't believe it,' said Ryan bluntly. 'Why should she tell a yarn like that if it wasn't true? I reckon it's *now* she's telling lies.'

Miss Bell said: 'But why should she? After all, she knows it'll get her into trouble now.'

Lang was staring at Ryan. After a while he turned away with a grunt and said: 'Well, you may be right, but it doesn't help much, does it?'

The deputation looked inquiring. 'What I mean is,' said Lang, 'you can no more prove she's lying now than

you could prove it before. If he says he didn't do it and
she says he didn't, there's an end of it, isn't it?'

'It's a mercy she *has* owned up to its being a lie,' said
Miss Bell. 'Because, though of course it couldn't be
proved, there was no other way in which Mr. Lawrence
could really clear himself, and it would have been awful
if . . .'

'Well, I'd like to have a word with her, Mr. Walter,'
said Ryan suddenly.

Lang stared again at him for a moment and then
said: 'I think we all would.'

She had never spoken to Mr. Walter before. He was
very big and he looked and sounded angry, but she was
not afraid, and her voice worked properly, and she didn't
want to cry.

He said in a cold voice: 'I understand that you made
certain charges against Mr. Lawrence Spellman, and now
you say that they are untrue. Is that so?'

'Yes, sir.'

'You now say that nothing of the sort happened?'

'No, sir.'

'Then why did you ever say it did?'

'I don't know, sir.'

'Oh come!' said Lang irritably. 'You must know.'

She knew no reply to that and made none.

'You realise that what you've done is very serious?
That you've caused a lot of trouble and—and unhappi-
ness?'

'Yes, sir. I'm sorry.'

'And that you may be punished for it.'

'Yes, sir.' Her eyes were very bright.

Ryan glanced inquiringly at Lang. Lang nodded and
threw himself back in his chair impatiently. Ryan said:
'Look, Hilda—has anybody talked to you about this
except Mr. North, Miss Bell and me?'

'No, Mr. Ryan.'

'You sure?'

'Only Mr. Lawrence.'

Ryan sat forward. 'Mr. Lawrence? When was
that?'

'When . . .'—she looked round—'when you were all there.'

Ryan grunted in disappointment. 'No other time?'

'No, Mr. Ryan.'

'Well, look here,' said Ryan almost angrily. 'What I want to know's this. If this is the truth you're telling now, why d'you suddenly want to tell it when you didn't before? Is it that you don't want to get Mr. Lawrence in trouble, like when you didn't tell your mother in the first place?'

It was too long a question and she didn't know quite what he meant, but there was a trap somewhere—something that he wanted her to say. She said: 'I don't know, Mr. Ryan.'

'But you didn't want to get Mr. Lawrence into trouble, did you?'

She hesitated and said: 'No, Mr. Ryan.'

'And that's why you're saying this now?'

They were all staring at her. Hilda said: 'Because it's true and I—I didn't feel right. . . .'

Miss Bell said: Have you told your father and mother about this yet, Hilda?'

It was the moment when the curtain in the courtroom was drawn back and the rack, the thumbscrews and the boot were revealed, lying there ready for unco-operative prisoners. The martyr faltered for a moment before the horror of it. Then the blue eyes came up shining more brightly than ever. 'No, Miss Bell,' she said steadily.

After the door had closed there was silence for a while. Then Lang said: 'Well, there you are. Nothing to be done about that.'

Miss Bell said: 'I do think, Mr. Walter, that in justice to Mr. Lawrence she ought to be made to withdraw what she said *in front* of him, and to say she's sorry.'

'What's the good of that?'

'Well—I don't know. . . . If you think not. . . . And then there's another thing. Of course this is all round the factory. I think we shall have to do something to—to make it clear that she's admitted it was a lie. Perhaps a notice . . . ?'

'Going to be a pretty funny notice,' said Ryan. 'You

can't start putting up notices saying Mr. Spellman hasn't assaulted Hilda Pinner. Supposing somebody reads that and hasn't heard anything about it?'

Miss Bell said : 'We needn't do it like that. We could just say it was known that rumours were circulating about a director of the company . . . we did something like that once in Mr. Gustavus's time. Everybody understood.'

'Well, if you start saying that any rumours circulating about a director of the company are untrue you'll have to be pretty careful,' said Lang with a grim smile. He shook his head. 'We don't want any fuss of that kind. Do more harm than good. I'll see Mr. Lawrence and tell him. We'll get rid of the girl, and there it is. Least said soonest mended.'

'It'll soon get round,' said Ryan. 'You and I can see to that, Miss Bell. Doesn't take long for anything to get round this place—even if you don't want it to.'

'Well, as you think, Mr. Walter,' said Miss Bell rather doubtfully. 'I only felt that this has—has reflected on Mr. Lawrence's reputation, and that we ought to do all we can . . .'

Lang said : 'I don't think Mr. Lawrence will worry much about that.'

Neither of the Spellmans was very helpful. Lang went to see Henry only half an hour after the deputation had left him, but it was fairly obvious that Henry knew already. He listened impassively while Lang told him what had happened, showed neither surprise nor pleasure, and asked no questions. At the end he merely nodded and said : 'I see. Well, you'd better get Lawrence in and tell him, hadn't you?'

Lawrence didn't know. When Lang went drily and curtly to the point he went very white and leaned forward in his chair with a curious half-smile on his face. Lang was an honest man and he was neither graceful nor comfortable. When he had finished there was a long silence. Then Lawrence leaned back in his chair and said : 'Well, well, well . . . !' very quietly. 'How very oddly people behave.'

Lang said: 'I think she must be off her head.' He
hesitated. 'Miss Bell wanted to make her tell you herself
and put up a notice about it and God knows what. But
I said I didn't think you'd want anything of that kind.'

'No,' said Lawrence. 'No. I can do without it.'

'It seems to me the best way is simply to get rid of
the girl and otherwise ignore the whole thing.'

'Do you have to get rid of her?'

Old Henry said: 'Oh, she'll have to go, of course.'

Lawrence shrugged his shoulders. 'Well, that's up to
you. If she must go in the interests of—of public morality
and so on, then she must. I only meant she needn't as
far as I am concerned. I'm all in favour of Walter's idea
of ignoring the whole thing.' He paused for a fraction
of a second and added gently: 'I always was.' Silence
again. Lang glanced quickly from one of them to the
other. They were both looking at him, Henry with an
expressionless rather tired stare, Lawrence with a half
smile. His face was still pale.

Lang said uncomfortably: 'Well, I'm very glad it's
cleared up. It's been a lot of fuss about nothing.'

Old Henry suddenly took off his glasses, put them on
the desk, flicked them away from him with his fingers
and thumb and sat looking at them with dislike. Lawrence nodded solemnly. After a while Lawrence said:
'Then I take it you're now satisfied, Walter? You don't
feel that there ought to be a Committee to consider whether
she's lying this time?'

Lang's lips tightened. 'No,' he said curtly.

'In that case,' said Lawrence, rising, 'I don't think
there's anything else, is there?'

He went out, closing the door very gently behind him.
Old Henry was still staring at his glasses. His face,
without them, looked unusually tired.

Lang said: 'I feel that both you and Lawrence think
I was wrong to insist on having this thrashed out. I'm
sorry if you do. But I don't see what else there was to
be done.'

Henry said: 'I don't know what Lawrence thinks.
We haven't discussed it. But I know what I should think
in his place, Walter.'

Lang shrugged his shoulders. 'I dare say. But I can't help it. He's your son, so of course you thought he was right. But to an objective observer it didn't look like it at one time.'

'You being the objective observer?' said Henry with a wry smile.

'Why not?' Lang frowned and shook his head. 'I don't know where you get this idea of my—my wanting trouble with you and Lawrence. I admit I'm critical of Lawrence. I've never disguised it. But you and I . . . after all, Henry, we've got to work together.'

Henry put his glasses on. 'Have we?' he said.

'Of course we have. And what's more it looks as though we shall have to close our ranks and stop squabbling amongst ourselves.'

'Why?'

'I've had a talk with Winter this morning and I've fired him.'

'*Fired* him?'

'Well—I've told him that I shall ask for him to be withdrawn.'

'Oh . . . !' said Henry. 'Oh—I *see*. . . .'

'He's not co-operative and he's causing trouble in the place. I don't know quite what's happened, but either he's misunderstood his brief or else he's got a swollen head. Anyhow, I won't have a man like that about.'

Henry shook his head thoughtfully. 'That's a bit awkward, Walter. I'm not sure . . . after all, Proudfoot's got the right to nominate a director. I'm not sure that we can stop him from nominating whoever he likes.'

'Oh, bunkum!' said Lang shortly. 'It's obviously got to be somebody acceptable.'

'To whom?'

'To the—the management here. The arrangement was that Winter should come here as my assistant. I'm not going to have a man like that pushed on me.'

Henry said nothing. He was looking straight in front of him with the same weary stare.

'From the way he's behaved,' said Lang, 'I should think there's been some mistake in briefing him. Perhaps Proudfoot . . .'

Old Henry gave a sudden little grunt. 'Look here, Walter,' he said, 'I've known Francis Proudfoot longer than you have, and he doesn't make that sort of mistake.'

'What d'you mean?'

'I don't know what Winter's doing or not doing. But you can be pretty sure it's what he's been told to do.'

'Well, if that's so,' said Lang angrily, 'it's about time we went and saw Proudfoot and told him where he got off. He may have bought a block of shares in the business but he doesn't own it.'

Spellman glanced at him sharply and hesitated. 'He's the biggest single shareholder.'

'Maybe. But no bigger than you and me added together. And you always get proxies for old Mrs. Horseman. If it came to a showdown we've got him.'

'*We've* got him . . .?' Old Henry was staring at him now with a strange expression of almost startled interest. 'You mean,' he said gently, 'if Lawrence and I supported you . . .?'

Lang said: 'Oh, I don't imagine it'll come to that for a moment. As a matter of fact, I did have a word with Proudfoot when he bought the shares . . .'

'Yes,' said Henry colourlessly.

'Yes. One time when I was down in London. I think we understood one another.'

Henry shook his head. 'Well, if you understand little Francis, you're a better man than I am, Walter.'

Lang smiled. 'I don't say I understand him. But I do know he's a business man who knows which side his bread's buttered.' He rose. 'Anyhow, I think the best way would be to run up to London and see him and get it straight. I don't think it'll be very difficult.'

As he reached the door Spellman said: 'Walter . . .?'

'Yes?'

'I'd avoid—making a showdown of this.'

'Of course. If I can. But if . . .'

Spellman was not looking at him. He said: 'Proudfoot's a tough customer. Tougher than he looks. Don't start anything you can't finish. That's my advice.'

Lang smiled. 'Why should I—if he's reasonable?'

When he had gone Henry Spellman leaned back in

his chair, passed a hand over his eyes and sat gazing out of the window. His face was worried, and he looked very old.

* * * * *

She said: 'I don't know.' She was saying that to everything now. She would have said it if they had asked her her name. It was the one refuge left.

'She doesn't know,' said Mrs. Pinner sarcastically to the standard lamp.

Mr. Pinner said: 'A pack o' lies. My daughter. Nothing but a pack o' lies. . . .' There was a small fleck of foam at the corner of his mouth. He turned to his wife. 'Didn't I tell you? But oh, no. Hilda was this and Hilda was that. Lying little trollop. I'll be bound she wanted he *had* interfered with her. Dirty little . . .'

Mrs. Pinner said: 'Oh, Hilda . . .' and started to cry again.

Mr. Pinner said: 'Come home here after a day's work and find the pair of you crying and blubbing about a fine tale like that. A pack of lies. . . .' His voice rose to a shout. 'Fine fool you made me look, didn't you? Eh?'

He stopped in front of her as if there was an answer. She half whispered: 'I'm sorry. I never meant . . .'

'She never meant . . .!' said Mrs. Pinner.

'And saying it was going to church and not feeling right and all so good and la-di-da. . . .'

The fleck of foam was increasing. Oh God, let it come now. Let it come now. . . .

* * * * *

Laura snapped off the radio and said: 'Hallo, darling.'

He said: 'Hallo,' and came across and kissed her.

'What sort of a day?'

'Oh, not bad,' said Lawrence almost casually. He went across to the cupboard, got out the drinks and mixed two gins and french with more than usual care. He said: 'I think we need a small amount of lemon peel. . . .'

'I don't think there's lemon in the place, darling. Sorry.'

'In that case,' said Lawrence precisely, 'we will manage without it.' He handed Laura her drink, sat down, and lit a cigarette, steadying the match with both hands.

'Well?' said Laura quietly.

'You will be interested to hear,' said Lawrence, smiling at his glass, 'that the great Dreyfus case is at an end.'

'The Dreyfus case . . .?'

'Yes. Esterhazy has shot himself, the colonel has owned up (or was it the colonel who shot himself?) . . . anyhow, Dreyfus has now been released from Devil's Island and the only way now is to ignore the whole thing.'

'Darling, what *is* all this?'

Lawrence took a drink and went on smiling at his glass. 'Miss Hilda Pinner,' he said with a slight crack in his voice, 'has now admitted that everything she has said before is quite untrue, and that nothing whatever happened to her in my car.'

Laura sat up sharply. '*What?* You really mean . . .?'

'Just came clean about the whole thing. Admitted that she made it all up.'

There was a moment's silence. Laura said: 'Well, thank God for that . . .!' She leant forward and took his hand. 'Darling . . .'

Lawrence patted her hand with his free one and then gently removed it. 'Yes,' he said. 'As you say—thank God for that.'

'But why on earth . . .?'

'It's no good asking me why anything. I no more know why she did this than why she ever spun the yarn in the first place.' Lawrence shook his head and stared into the fire. 'The ways of the human race are beyond me.'

'Did you see her? Talk to her?'

'No, darling. Walter didn't think that was necessary.'

'What the hell has it to do with him?'

'My dear, Walter's in rather a spot. After all, he was the Grand Inquisitor who made all the fuss. He thought he'd got me where he wanted me, and he'd gone after it hard. And now he had the pleasant job of explaining that he'd made a fool of himself.' Lawrence smiled. 'Poor old Walter. I wish you'd heard him doing it. He's not exactly a good loser, and it was so obvious that he was bitterly disappointed. I felt quite sorry for the man. Papa and I just sat and looked at him and he went floundering on. . . .'

'Didn't he apologise?'

'What for? He'd already explained that he was really only insisting on an inquiry for my benefit. I should think he quite probably believes it. He's capable of believing almost anything if he wants to.'

'What did your father say?'

'I didn't see him except with Walter. But he was rather terrifying. He really is hopping mad with Walter about the whole thing—madder than I think I've ever known him.' Lawrence shook his head. 'I don't fancy our Walter's done himself a lot of good over this. Papa hardly ever gets angry with people, but when he does he *stays* angry.'

'Like all good pachyderms.'

'Yes.' Lawrence smiled wryly. 'Of course, Walter now feels that the less publicity there is the better. No question of doing anything to let people know that she's withdrawn her story or anything of that kind, of course.'

Laura said: 'My God, that man . . .! Why doesn't somebody take a hatchet to him?'

'Darling—I tell you—the ways of the human race are beyond me. Anyhow, Walter's proposing to sack the girl and leave it at that.' He stared into the fire for a moment rather moodily. 'I don't really see any point in sacking her myself. You can't—can't punish people for things like that. But I don't suppose it matters much. She'll find somebody else easily enough who'll let her come and plug away all day at some bloody soul-destroying job for four quid a week. . . .'

* * * * *

The one eye was staring at her, very bloodshot now. She had a peculiar feeling that she could see the other staring at her too, through the black patch. He had

stopped shouting at her and was talking in almost a low
voice, but very thick and with the words funny. Once
she glanced away for a moment and saw her mother's
face and her mother was sitting quite still staring at them
both, with a queer look, not crying or anything, but
just queer.

He said: '*My* daughter . . .!' again and looked at
her for a long time without saying anything else, and she
looked back because his face was so close there wasn't
anywhere else to look.

He said: 'Now you say this after me. "I told a pack
of dirty lies." Go on—say it.'

'I told a pack of dirty lies.'

'And I'm a deceitful dirty little trollop what's no good
to anybody.'

'And I'm a deceitful dirty little trollop . . .' She
stopped because it sounded queer. He struck at her
blindly, but his hand only brushed the top of her head
as she ducked. He shouted: 'Go on, you . . .'

'What's no good to anybody.'

'No. And no more you are. "And what I'm going
to get is no more than I deserve." Go on. Say it.'

'And what I'm going to get is no more than I deserve.'
In the silence she could hear his heavy breathing.

'Right, my lady,' he said hoarsely. 'An' now I'll
show you . . . My daughter . . .!' He moved suddenly and she ducked again, but he was only pointing
and shouting: 'Get upstairs.'

It had not failed her, and she knew it would not fail
her now. All through, with them at the factory, and all
the time he had been at her, it had been with her and
made it almost easy, like it hadn't really mattered. She
went into her box of a room and stood there waiting.
Her body was trembling all over, but she knew that was
only because she was going to get a hiding and she always
trembled like that when she was waiting. It was because
it was going to hurt and she was frightened. But there
was the other thing underneath that he couldn't get at
and frighten, and so it didn't matter what he did nor if
she trembled.

She heard him shouting at her mother downstairs and
that would be because her mother had said he didn't
ought to beat her. Her mother always did that when it
came to it, but it never made any difference except to
make him angrier, and usually she prayed that her mother
wouldn't do it. But this time she didn't care, because
she knew the more he beat her the more she would feel
the other thing and the more like Him it would be.

She thought of Him hanging there on the Cross and
them sticking spears into Him and forthwith there came
forth blood and water, and yet saying that and forgiving
them and she wondered whether He was frightened beforehand, but probably not, being God really. The door
at the bottom of the stairs opened and she heard her
father coming up. Her whole body was shaking now so
that she could hardly stand up, and as she turned round
to face the door she sort of saw him quite plain, like he
had been in the thing she had had at work about the
switchback, younger than now, and in uniform like during
the war.

* * * * *

About eleven o'clock Laura said: 'Darling—hadn't
you better pack it in? I don't want to spoil sport, but
you've had rather an odd mixture . . .'

'Nonsense,' said Lawrence with immense good humour.
'I'll bet old Dreyfus knocked it back the day *he* was
released from what's-its-name.'

'I was only thinking of to-morrow morning.'

'I never knew such a girl for thinking about to-morrow
morning. Don't you know you should take no thought
for to-morrow? What ye shall eat or what ye shall drink?
Ah well . . .' Lawrence picked up his whisky, which he
had just poured out, and tipped it carefully into a vase
of flowers. 'There,' he said. 'I wonder whether it'll
pep them up? I never heard of drunk flowers. . . .'
He rose rather unsteadily, came over, and sat down at
her feet. 'Kiss me, Laura,' he said, almost as though
he thought she would refuse. She kissed him gently and
stroked his hair. They sat for a while in silence looking
at the fire. Lawrence said suddenly, in a completely

different voice : 'If she was going to do that, why couldn't she do it when she was talking to me ? I gave her every chance. I thought I could probably make her. But no . . .' He looked up at Laura. 'It's all very well,' he said urgently, 'but it's not satisfactory. I must know what—what went on in her mind. I'm like Mr. Pinner. I want her explanation. She's not very bright, of course. But what the hell . . .?'

Laura said : 'I very much doubt if she knows herself.'

'Oh yes, she does,' said Lawrence decidedly. 'She may not have before, but she knows this time. Because . . .' He stopped. 'This is a difficult conversation to carry on in the circumstances,' he said curtly.

'Never mind,' said Laura gently. 'Why not push it along and come to bed?'

'Bed?' said Lawrence. 'Sure. And not worry, eh?' He scrambled to his feet. 'The poor little devil,' he said suddenly, 'the poor little devil. With everybody badgering her. And me in particular. Oh Christ, what will they do to her . . .?' His voice cracked and he turned away.

Laura got up and put her arms round him and said : 'Darling, they won't do anything to her—except sack her, which as you say doesn't matter a damn. . . .'

'No?' he said bitterly. 'Not those nice characters who came here?'

'I don't expect so. Anyhow she'll be all right now she's got it off her chest.'

'Got it off her chest?' Lawrence's eyes were shut and his face twisted with pain. 'Oh God, haven't you got any eyes or ears or—or nerves?' He pulled himself away sharply and stood staring at her.

Laura said : 'Yes.'

'No, you haven't, or you'd have realised . . .'

'I did realise,' she said quickly.

He looked at her for a moment in astonishment. He said : 'You *did* . . .? Then why on earth . . .?'

'Darling,' she said gently, 'what d'you think I am?'

He suddenly started half to laugh and half to cry. He said : 'Oh you *bloody* liar, Laura. Oh, you deceitful, two-timing little baggage. And I honestly thought you were being dumb and trusting and . . .'

She pulled his head down on her shoulder and said: 'What, *me*? You should have known better. You know I haven't got a nice nature.'

XVIII

THERE wasn't really room in the canteen when it was a wet day. If it was fine, a lot went home to dinner, and a lot more brought their dinners and sat outside in the sun and ate them. But on a wet day they all came crowding in, and you couldn't get your grub into your mouth because somebody's elbow kept catching yours. Mac had got there early and kept places for Fred Boxall and Harry.

Fred Boxall plonked the plate of meat pie and potatoes down in his place and said: 'Where's Jacko to-day, then?'

'South o' France,' said Mac with his mouth full.

''Course—yes. He's gone off. *Where* is it?'

'Jacko's touring the South Coast,' said Harry solemnly, 'an' therefore unable to leave an address.'

Fred Boxall looked out at the pouring rain and said: 'Reckon he'll need the hood up, you.'

'I asked him if he was taking the car,' said Harry, 'but he didn't hear me.'

'South o' France,' said Mac. 'That's what it is. He told me so himself. With the Duchess of Plushbottom. An' all expenses paid.'

'What did he want to go *now* for?'

'He didn't want to. He just came up for now in the draw.'

Fred Boxall said: 'I reckon Jacko'll be mad over Lawrence getting away with it. Be something to come back and find Hilda gone.'

'He won't miss her,' said Mac. 'Hell, that was a long time ago—before motor cars were invented.'

Ted Chalmers leant across from the other side of the table and said: ''Course, you know who that is?' His mouth was very loose and his face was spottier than ever. He was not one of them, and they looked at him coldly.

Mac said: 'Who what is?'

'Jacko's.'

'The motor car?'

'Yes.'

Fred Boxall said loftily: 'Don't know it's anything to do with anybody *who* it is.'

Ted Chalmers grinned and said: 'Well *I* do. 'Cause Henry Wright and me see Jacko with her out in Lingwood last Sunday. I didn't know who she was but Henry did.'

'Oh, Henry Wright,' said Mac. 'He knows everything.' It was a brave attempt to attack in a difficult tactical situation.

Ted Chalmers went on grinning. 'Oh well, if you don't know, maybe it's best you shouldn't.' He went back to his food.

If it had been anyone else they might have asked, but not Ted Chalmers. Fred Boxall turned to Mac and said: 'You got the sweaters in this week, haven't you?' thereby making it clear that they were not interested.

Somebody got up from behind and nudged Mac's elbow just as he was putting something in his mouth. The food fell off his fork and he said: 'Damn . . . Yes. So I heard.'

Harry suddenly said in a low voice: 'Hey—you see that?'

'What?'

'That was Jacko's old man got up right behind you. Been sitting there nearly touching you. There he is going now.'

There was a moment's pause. 'Well, what about it?' said Mac uneasily. 'We haven't said anything, have we?'

*   *   *   *   *

It was a long train and quite a lot of people got off at Hastings. For a while she could not see him and began to think he hadn't come. Then she saw him get out, right at the back of the train. He was wearing a blue overcoat and a muffler and no hat even in the pouring rain, and he carried one rather old fibre suitcase. He saw her as he came through the barrier and grinned his usual rather shy grin of greeting and said: 'Hallo, Rosey.' He did not offer to kiss her.

Rosamund said: 'Hullo. Good journey?'

'All right. Nice sort of weather for a holiday, eh? Bit of bathing, anyway.'

When they got out to the car she said: 'Want to drive?'

'No. I don't know my way about. You better.'

'All right. What would you like to do?'

'You tell me,' he said resignedly. 'I expect you got it all worked out.' He yawned and closed his eyes rather wearily for a moment.

'Well, I've got to get back to the Clays' by about half-past six because they've got some people coming in. So unless you want to go and find your digs right away, I thought we might have tea together and then I could drop you there on my way out.'

He said: 'Just as you like.'

'Unless you're tired and . . .?'

'I'm fine. You do just what you like.'

It was all rather like that through tea, which wasn't a very good tea anyhow. Afterwards they drove along the front. There was a lot of wind and big waves were sending spray all over the road. The front was very empty. They sat in the car and looked at the sea for a while in silence, but you had to keep the windscreen wipers going all the time to see anything. After a while he took her hand and that made it better, but he was still very silent.

Rosamund said: 'We've got to get fixed what we're going to do. I've told the Clays that I shall probably have to go over to Rye to see my aunt. But of course we don't have to go there if you'd rather go somewhere else.'

Jack said: 'You mean—go somewhere and—and stay there?'

'Yes.' She hesitated. 'That's what we said.'

After a moment he said: 'Of course staying somewhere's a different thing . . .'

'Different from what?'

'Different to—to what we been doing.'

She said: 'I don't see why. . . . But of course we don't have to if you'd rather not. I just thought it would be fun.'

'Of course I want to, Rosey. But . . .' he paused and then added rather helplessly: 'I'm never sure you know what you're doing.'

She turned the big grey eyes on him in mild surprise. 'Of course I do,' she said, 'I—I just want to be with you for—for longer at a time than we've had. At home we never see each other for more than a few hours and it's horrid having to leave you after that. Don't you hate it?'

'Of course I do,' he said hoarsely. 'Christ . . .!'

'Well then . . .?'

He suddenly said angrily: 'What are you trying on? What's the good of it? Why can't you be like other girls and . . . and . . .?'

'What d'you mean?'

'I can't give you things. I can't even talk to you. Christ, how often do I have to tell you I only picked you up for a bet . . .'

Rosamund smiled and said: 'Well, what about it? You won, didn't you?'

'Yes, but . . .'

Rosamund said: 'We don't want all that over again. We're on holiday, see? And we're going to have a lovely time and be together and not worry about anything. . . .'

He said: 'Oh God, Rosey, I love you,' and ducked his face quickly into her hair.

'Well, why shouldn't you?' said Rosamund, smiling at the empty sea-front. 'I never knew anybody who made such a *fuss* about things.'

* * * * *

Lang's appointment was at Tideway House, and he knew that Tideway House was a big new block of office buildings on the Embankment; but somehow Lang had always seen the interview as taking place in Proudfoot's private house—probably over dinner in the big, candle-lit dining-room. All the way down in the train he had been seeing it so. It wouldn't take long—the main item. He could explain the situation in half a dozen sentences, punctuated by that quick, bird-like nod of comprehension. Then Proudfoot would say: 'I see' (and one would know

that he *did* see—that he had grasped it all, at once).
'Well, in that case we clearly need another man. . . .'

Beside this easy understanding, the reality was slightly
irritating. Tideway House was a vast place with a very
complicated system of automatic lifts which seemed designed to prevent anyone from going anywhere. The
commissionaire at the inquiry desk on the seventh floor
said 'Good morning' politely, but when Lang gave his
name and mentioned his appointment he merely said:
'Will-you-take-a-seat-in-the-waiting-room,' and went on
studying a timetable. It was some minutes later that
Lang heard him telephoning the news of his arrival, and
quite ten minutes before a smart girl arrived and said:
'Mr. Lang? Would you come up, please?' After an
unsuccessful joust with the lifts she suggested that they
should walk up to the next floor, and then merely showed
Lang into yet another waiting-room and said that Sir
Francis would only keep him a few minutes.

After all this, Sir Francis himself was mildly reassuring.
His office was not as intimate a place as a candle-lit
dining-room, but it was not enormous or particularly
designed to impress, and he jumped up and said: 'Hallo
there!' and shook hands warmly. Best of all, the bird-
like face was as quick and intelligent as one had remembered.

While the secretary was bringing coffee Lang said
something about the lifts.

'Ah!' said Sir Francis. 'But you don't understand
about our lifts. They're like that because they're so
modern and safe. I'm assured that they're the safest lifts
in the world. In fact they're so safe that nobody can ever
get into them, so there's no chance of anybody falling out.'
He sipped his coffee and leant back in his chair. 'Righto.
Now you've got something you want to discuss? All right
—then you talk and I'll listen.'

It went very well. In practice it took a bit longer
than half a dozen crisp sentences, but it was duly punctuated by the quick little nod. 'In view of that,' Lang
concluded, 'I felt there might be a misunderstanding
somewhere, either on Winter's own part or in how he

was briefed, and I thought I'd better have a chat with you and clear it up. The man I really want would . . .'

'Just a moment,' said Sir Francis. 'You said he was upsetting the management. In what way is he doing that?'

'Well, he's rather getting across my man Barker who's running the place.'

'But I thought you'd just lost your able man?' said Sir Francis with a slightly puzzled frown. 'Wasn't that rather the point. You needed somebody of ability?'

Lang said: 'Yes. But . . .'

'Because Winter's very able. He's a man of great experience.'

'I dare say he is,' said Lang shortly. 'But he mustn't go striking out these lines of his own and ignoring my policy.'

Sir Francis shook his head. 'Well, of course, that's the trouble with able men. They do tend to have views of their own.' He frowned. 'I'm sorry you should have had this trouble with Winter. He struck me as the ideal man for the job.'

'I dare say he would be if he'd remember he's there to assist me, and not to run the place.'

'You mean he's too strong a character?'

'I think he's got completely the wrong idea of the job. Possibly he was wrongly briefed.'

Sir Francis smiled. 'Well, I briefed him myself, so that was my fault.'

Lang said: 'You see, all this business in the press-shop —time-studies and so on. It's all very well but it isn't the—the direction in which we want to go. He seems to be thinking purely about the fabricating side, when . . .'

'Ah!' said Sir Francis, 'but you can see why that is. He's thinking of the overall requirements of the group.'

'What group?' said Lang shortly.

Sir Francis raised his eyebrows. 'Of the group which, after all, is employing him.'

'Well, since Lang's isn't part of any group,' said Lang, 'I'd rather not have any man in my factory who has to think as though it was. I think what you've said is quite true. And it's precisely because it's true that I am asking you to withdraw Winter.'

There was a moment's silence. Then Sir Francis

shook his head. 'You're making it rather difficult for me,' he said unhappily.

Lang said: 'I'm sorry about that. But if Winter's thinking . . .'

'You see, on what you've told me,' said Sir Francis, 'there's hardly a case for withdrawing him.'

Lang's chin came slowly down towards his chest. He said: 'The case for withdrawing him is that I want him withdrawn.'

'Precisely,' said Sir Francis at once. 'Well, of course that's very important. But . . .'

They looked at one another in silence for a moment. Lang made a curious little noise in his throat and said very calmly: 'Let's understand one another. Are you refusing to withdraw Winter?'

'Not at all. He may not be the right man. I merely feel that the case for withdrawing him is not made out. Why not give it a few months and see if you—settle down together?'

Lang said: 'You realise that this is directly contrary to the promise you made me?'

'I don't quite understand. I'm not aware that I made you any promise.'

'You said that you didn't want to interfere with the running of the place. . . .'

'Well, bless my soul,' said Sir Francis rather irritably, 'I don't. The last thing I want to do is to spend my time discussing the details of your business. All I've done is to send you an able and experienced man to help you.'

'Who immediately starts to treat the business as part of your group?'

'You can take it that any advice Winter has given you will be entirely honest and based on a lot of experience,' said Sir Francis shortly. 'And I think you would be foolish to quarrel with him.'

Lang smiled contemptuously. 'I see. In other words you think you can impose anyone you like on us whether we want him or not? Well, we can stop you.'

'We?' said Sir Francis mildly.

'You're a minority shareholder. If it comes to a show-

down, we can outvote you. Henry Spellman and I and
—and others hold . . .'

Sir Francis sighed. 'Henry Spellman,' he said, 'is an
old friend of mine.'

Lang hesitated for a moment. 'And you think
he'll . . .?'

Sir Francis held up a hand. He said : 'Just a moment.
There may be developments that—that you ought to
know about before . . .' He stopped and gazed out of
the window. His face was unhappy. 'Henry Spellman
is getting on in years,' he said slowly. 'He's been talking
about retiring for some time. I was surprised that he
was willing to take on the Chairmanship when your
brother died. . . .' He paused again.

Lang said : 'Well?' His throat had suddenly gone
very dry.

'When I bought your brother's shares,' said Sir
Francis, 'I made Henry an offer for his own. At that
time he refused. Two or three days ago he rang up and
said that he proposed to retire forthwith. . . .' Sir
Francis brought his eyes from the window to Lang's face.
'I didn't go into it, but I gathered there had been some
friction . . .?'

Lang made no reply.

'Anyhow,' said Sir Francis simply, 'I took an option
to buy the Spellman family's shares when Henry retires.
Which . . .' he hesitated, 'which affects the argument
you were putting forward.'

Lang said : 'You bloody pair of swindlers.'

Sir Francis frowned. 'Oh come,' he said, 'what's the
use of being abusive? I should never have raised this
ridiculous question of exactly how many shares people
hold if you hadn't. All I'm telling you is that if you
want your own way in this matter you'll have to get it
by reasonable argument and not just by ukase.'

'You promised me . . .'

'Mr. Lang,' said Sir Francis, closing his eyes, 'I
promised you nothing.'

'You said you didn't want control. You know damned
well that if I'd known what you were after I would never
have agreed . . .'

'To what?' said Sir Francis. He shrugged his shoulders.
'As far as I am concerned I bought eighty thousand shares
in your family concern because they seemed to me a good
investment. I have now bought an option on another
twenty-two thousand or twenty-four thousand or something, for the same reason. As far as I know there was
nothing for you to agree or disagree about. I don't want
to run your business. I have plenty to do without that.
But having invested about a quarter of a million pounds
I must protect it. That's all. And it has nothing to do
with being a swindler, bloody or otherwise.'

There was a long silence. Lang said hoarsely: 'My
father built that business. My brother and I made it
what it is to-day. You may buy control of it, but you
no more understand the sort of place it is or how to run
it than . . . It's not like your other places with their
Winters and their time-study and . . .'

'Ah,' said Sir Francis. 'Now you're talking. You
might easily be right there. It's essentially a family
business, and that's why I think it would be a great pity
if we were to quarrel.'

'You'd like it to stay a family business as long as you
have the last say?' said Lang bitterly.

Sir Francis looked at him for a moment and then gazed
moodily out of the window. 'I don't understand you,'
he said. 'I understood your brother and respected him.
I heard him speak a number of times, and his views were
always interesting, even if I personally didn't share them.
He saw a business as—as a group of individual men and
women of whom he was a sort of benevolent father.' Sir
Francis sighed. 'Now I, on the other hand, am not
interested in business at all, from that point of view. I
am interested in a number of other things—medical re-
search, Renaissance painting, juvenile crime, and so on.
Business simply gives me the—the resources with which
to pursue these interests. Both of these approaches I can
understand. What I can't understand is yours, which
seems to me neither quite idealistic nor quite practical.'

Lang stood up abruptly and said with great care: 'I
don't think I want to go into the philosophy of business
just now. As you probably realise, I've been kept entirely

in the dark about this latest deal of yours. I shall have
to think the whole thing over and—and to reconsider
my position.'

'I quite agree,' said Sir Francis cordially. 'The only
thing I ask you is to think it over calmly and—and not
reach any hasty decision. I should be extremely sorry if
anything were to interfere with—with our relationship.'

* * * * *

He did not feel like food, so instead of lunching he
walked slowly all the way to the station. It was obviously something that needed thinking over very carefully
and very calmly. The important thing was not to be
angry, because to be angry would be to play right into
their hands. One must accept that one was dealing with
people without honour, without scruple, without decency
—people who would smile in your face and stab you the
moment your back was turned—people who would pose
as your friend for thirty years and then . . . But the
important thing was not to allow oneself to be angry, but
to look at the facts calmly and make a cold, calculated
decision.

It was a two and a half hour journey back from London
and Lang decided that the two and a half hours would be
an excellent chance to think. But somehow it was not
possible to start while the train was still fussing through
the suburbs of London, so he read the evening paper for
a while. He was still doing so when the attendant came
to announce tea, and he realised that in a different compartment, over a cup of tea and a cigarette, it would be
easier, so he went along to the dining car.

The train was travelling fast and rocking a good deal,
so that most of the tea slopped into the saucer. The man
opposite put his spoon into his cup and left it there, and
after that his tea did not slop over. Lang remembered
being told that this was so, but he had never seen it done
before, and he spent some time trying to work out the
mechanics of the thing. After a time he realised that
this was quite irrelevant, and stared out of the window
and tried to get started. But attendants kept coming
along and offering toast and tea-cake and heaven knows

what, and he soon gave it up and decided that he would have to wait until he got back to his own compartment.

Two of the men in the compartment were asleep and the other was reading a magazine with a picture of a girl on the cover. The girl was rather like Rosamund. It was all very well to say one must think, but when one came down to it the thoughts tended to go in a circle. The essential fact was that Proudfoot hadn't bought Spellman's shares. He only had an option on them when Spellman retired. So as long as Spellman didn't retire there was still a majority against Proudfoot, and Spellman would surely see that to hand over control to Proudfoot was a thing no decent man could do.

But on the other hand Spellman had rung Proudfoot behind his back and given him the option. And that meant that he was in the other camp, and even if he didn't retire he was an enemy. One could not work with Spellman after that, so he must go. But if he went . . . It was not so much a circle, as a sort of map of Mercator's projection. You started off from Australia at one end and travelled East, and then just as you thought you were getting somewhere you came on Australia again at the other end.

It was vitally important to get it sorted out, but you needed to be fresh to do it, and the compartment was stuffy and smoky and he could hardly keep his eyes open. At Banbury he settled back in the corner and closed his eyes to see if that would help him to concentrate. When he woke up the train was already slowing to pull in to his station.

It was only when she did not come into the hall to greet him that he remembered that Rosamund was on holiday. He felt a sharp spasm of anger with her and of pity for himself as he looked moodily round the empty drawing-room. It was all part of the same thing. Messing about with a girl friend was more important to her than the fact that he needed her. . . . There was something coldly terrifying about that though, because it carried with it the final loneliness. He shied away from it sharply and thought of Rosamund and her grin and the grey eyes, warmly and gently. Dear Roz, and he hoped she was having a nice time. But the bitterness was there all the same. Mrs. Dart had switched on the electric fire and put the sherry out. In a way it would have been better if she hadn't, so that the cold unwelcomeness would have been complete. But the sherry was undrinkably sweet and unpleasant anyhow. He suddenly realised that he didn't want that muck. What he wanted was a whisky and soda. But he never drank whisky before dinner, and his lips curled at the thought of being the sort of man who had to have a whisky and soda as soon as something was slightly wrong. What was needed wasn't whisky but some good hard thinking. He put the undrinkable sherry down beside him and glanced at his watch. It was only half-past six, and there was a good hour and a half before dinner.

* * * * *

When Mrs. Dart came in and told him that Mr. Partridge wanted to see him, Lang thought at first that it was the Rector, and sighed and said: 'Oh God—all right. Show him in.'

Joe Partridge came in. He was still in his working clothes and carried his cap. Lang was startled and for a moment he could only say: 'Oh—hallo, Joe. It's *you* . . .'

Joe Partridge said in a quick low voice: 'I'm sorry, Mr. Walter. I went along to your office and they said you was away but that you'd be home about six, so I came straight out because otherwise I thought you might be having your supper and . . .'

Lang said: 'That's all right, Joe. Sit down. What's the trouble?'

Partridge hesitated and then sat down on the edge of a chair and put his cap carefully on his knees. He said: 'Well, Mr. Walter, I reckoned I ought to see you about something I reckoned you didn't know, and ought to, because I don't reckon it ought to be let to go on without your knowing. . . .'

'Something among the men?' said Lang quickly and almost hopefully. If Winter had started something . . .

I

Joe said: 'No, Mr. Walter. . . .' He looked down at his cap and put it a little farther on his knee and looked up with worried eyes. He said: 'You know my boy Jack?'

'Yes?'

'Well—far as I can see, Mr. Walter, he's been running after—after Miss Lang.'

'Running after . . .?'

'Your Miss Rosamund, Mr. Walter. Leastways, taking her out and such things.'

Lang said: 'Joe—what the hell are you talking about?'

'It's true, Mr. Walter. That's why I'm telling you, because I don't reckon you knew, and I thought it wasn't right that . . .'

Lang said slowly: 'You say that Jack's been taking my daughter out?'

'That's right, Mr. Walter.'

There was a long silence.

'How long's this being going on?' Lang said.

'I first heard of it a couple of months ago, Mr. Walter.'

'Well, why the devil didn't you tell me at once?'

Joe hesitated. 'I didn't hardly like to, Mr. Walter. I did my best. I talked to him and told him it wasn't right or proper and that he was a young fool. And his mother made him promise he wouldn't. So we thought it was all over, see. But now . . . well, it seems it isn't.' Joe paused. 'Mind you, I'm not saying that there's any *harm*,' he said anxiously. 'But I didn't reckon you'd like it and . . .'

'Well, you were right there,' said Lang grimly. 'I think I'd better have a talk to Master Jack. The impudent young . . .'

Joe shifted uneasily. 'Mind you, Mr. Walter, you got to be fair. 'Course he oughtn't to have done it, but . . . well—I mean it's her car they been going out in and so on . . .'

'Her car?' said Lang foolishly. 'She hasn't got a car.'

'Well, the car she drives, Mr. Walter.'

'What's that got to do with it?'

'Well—she didn't *have* to go with him, not if . . .'

Lang whipped round and said: 'Look here, Partridge.

My daughter's a child of eighteen. There's no excuse for some young blackguard . . .'

Joe Partridge stiffened slightly. 'I'm not trying to excuse anybody, Mr. Walter,' he said with quiet dignity. 'I'm just telling you what I think you ought to know.'

Lang stared at him for a moment and then nodded. 'Yes,' he said rather vaguely. 'Yes. I see that. Well, I'd better have a talk to your boy. Is he at home now? Because if so . . .'

'No—he's on his holidays, Mr. Walter. . . . That was partly it, see. . . .'

'Partly what?'

'Why I came to see you. We don't rightly know where he is. Somewhere down the South Coast way. He wouldn't tell us the address because he said he was going to be moving about.'

Lang said: 'The South Coast . . .?'

'Main reason why I come to see you,' said Joe unhappily, 'was on account of some talk I overheard yesterday among some of Jack's pals, about his having gone off like that . . . and—and being with somebody with a car. . . . It did just flash through my mind . . .'

Lang rose slowly to his feet. His head was sunk low between his shoulders. He said: 'What were they saying?'

'They weren't saying much, but it was something about Jack and a car and . . .' Joe looked up suddenly and said bluntly: 'I take it Miss Rosamund's here with you, Mr. Walter?'

There was a moment's silence. 'No,' said Lang. 'No. Miss Rosamund is away.'

XIX

FOR a long time he could not even remember the people's name, or where they lived, except that it was near Hastings. After a while he remembered that the girl was called Jo, and what she looked like, but though he went through the alphabet time and again, he could not get the other name. In desperation he started to read through the names in the telephone directory, but that was hopeless, and it was ten o'clock, when he had given up for a moment from sheer exhaustion, that he remembered the name 'Clay' and at the same time Lime Cross, because he had thought of 'Clay' and 'Lime.'

Mrs. Dart came in again looking frightened, and said something about dinner, but he brushed past her and went to the telephone. There were no Clays on the telephone in Hastings, and though there were several in the district there were none at Lime Cross, though there was such a place. He sent a telegram saying: 'Is Rosamund with you wire reply,' addressing it simply to 'Clay, Lime Cross, Hastings,' and went and sat down. But it wouldn't do, and at eleven o'clock he got the car out and went. He had gone ten miles on the London road before he realised that he had not even told the Darts where he was going.

It was about four hours to London, and, he guessed, about another three to Hastings. That meant that he would get there about six o'clock. What he would do in Hastings at six o'clock in the morning was not yet quite clear. The main point was to get there, and he settled down grimly to make it half-past five. It had been going on for months—matter of common talk in the Canteen between boys with loose mouths and dirty grins. Taken about and mauled over by hands with permanent black grime in the cracks and nails—by that snubby-faced young bounder who was too big for his boots. . . . He had a sudden vision of her standing there, and her breasts

in the green silk frock, and the black hair just below the
level of his eyes and the tiny bit of tongue protruding
as she tied his tie. He groaned aloud and his body gave
a convulsive heave, so that his hands wrenched at the
steering wheel and the car swerved sharply. He remembered coming in a few hours before and refusing to let
himself be angry because she was not there—thinking of
her kindly and with love, even though she had gone
away and he needed her. And yet it was all a sham
and a treachery. Yes, darling. No, darling. The kiss
in the hall, and the big grey eyes. The Judas kiss. Something behind it. Double meaning. Double edged.
Double dealing, where one had no reason to fear—no
reason to suspect, and came in simple faith. Like Henry
Spellman and . . .

It came again, the cold panic fear, because if that
were so, if that were Roz, what would there be left? He
said aloud: 'She's eighteen. Eighteen. The dirty blackguard. Eighteen. My little Roz.' It helped a little, if
only a little, and he gritted his teeth and went on saying
it till his eyes filled with tears, and the cold fear thawed
away in his fury and pity for all betrayed.

South of Aylesbury the main London road swung
sharply to the right. He was dozing, and saw the corner
very late, but with all the acuteness of a waking man,
and he just managed to pull the car round with its tyres
squealing and two wheels on the grass. After that he
drove more slowly, and when just out of London a front
tyre burst and the car went mad for a moment, he held
it calmly to a standstill, accepted without emotion that
he had no jack, and set off walking in search of help
without really interrupting the train of thought. It was
after seven the next morning when he passed the signpost
saying: 'Hastings 10 miles.' He was feeling rather
strange, and realised for the first time that he had not
eaten for nearly twenty-four hours.

* * * * *

Lawrence said: 'O.K. Well, give me a ring when
he comes in, will you?' and put the receiver down. It was
a slight anticlimax that Walter was not in, but it was

merely a pleasure postponed. He reflected that in any case the thing would have to be put formally on paper, and with a little smile he picked up a scribbling pad and a pencil. 'Dear Walter: I have felt for some time that my work here has given little satisfaction to either of us, and have frequently considered offering you my resignation. Recent events have confirmed this impression. I could hardly resign until the unfortunate *affaire* Pinner was settled, but now that it is satisfactorily disposed of, I hasten to ask you to release me. An opportunity has arisen for me to take a partnership in . . .' Lawrence paused and grinned happily at the paper. What would it be . . .? He wrote: '. . . in a firm of cheesemongers' sundriesmen . . .' and then regretfully crossed it out. It was perhaps better to be dignified and just to stop at 'release me.'

He tore the sheet off the scribbling block, took it into the outer office and handed it to May, saying: 'Get this typed for me, will you?' He watched her face with interest as she read it. There was no flicker of expression. She said: 'Yes, Mr. Lawrence,' and put it down beside her and went rattling on with what she was doing. He smiled to himself all the way down the corridor and hoped she could still read the bit about the cheesemongers' sundriesmen, though it was crossed out.

The sun was shining as he crossed the yard. He looked at the buildings and realised that they really were a very odd shape—so odd that he began to laugh quietly to himself. 'And you come here every day?' Humphrey Peart had asked, incredulously. He was not going anywhere in particular, and at first he went towards the press-shop. But he did not want to wander amongst all that rumbling and crunching, and he turned away and hesitated. Matt Wright was going across the yard, and as soon as he saw Matt Wright he knew, and followed him across towards the foundry, hoping they might be pouring. For just a moment there was that queer tingling in his feet and the faint sickness, but he laughed and went in as Matt held the door open for him. They were pouring a line of moulds close to the door. The coloured flames were still round some of them, and the tiny rivulets of spilt metal were still red. He looked at them and smiled as he walked slowly along the narrow gangway. 'Yes,' she had said, 'yes. You can resign now. Go to sleep, darling.'

* * * * *

Lime Cross consisted of only about a dozen houses, and it took some time to find, but once he had found it there was only one house that could be the Clays'. As Lang rang the bell it occurred to him that Rosamund might be there after all, and the whole thing a wild-goose chase. But he never really believed it, and when the lanky girl explained that Rosamund had gone over to Rye to see her aunt, he nodded and said: 'Oh, I see,' exactly as though Rosamund had such an aunt. He even realised that the lanky girl was Jo Clay, grown a foot taller. They told him that Rosamund might be back that evening or she might be staying the night at Rye. It only took five minutes to get away, but it seemed much longer.

He was feeling very tired and his brain was not working properly, for he drove half the way to Rye before he realised that there was no reason at all to suppose that Rosamund had gone there, and that even if she had, it was no good going and inquiring where somebody lived who didn't exist. There was a sign by the side of the road that said: 'Mole's Café,' and he pulled up there behind several lorries, and drank some coffee and ate half a cheese roll. But by that time it was after eleven o'clock, and he left the other half of the roll and got back into the car rather stiffly and drove towards Rye, because that was the way the car was pointing.

* * * * *

Rosamund drove out past the golf course and on for a while, and then left the car by the side of the road and led the way up the sand dunes. She got to the top first and said: 'Oh hell—the tide's out. You have to walk nearly to France if you want to bathe when it's like this.'

'Bathe?' said Jack, 'crikey . . .!' The sun was bright, but there was a strong cold wind blowing.

Rosamund said: 'Why didn't I wear slacks? The

thing to do is to get down in one of the hollows, out of the wind.'

The sand in the hollow was warm from the sun, and if you looked up you could see the wind whipping the sand about above you. Rosamund lay down and closed her eyes and said : 'Oh gosh—this is lovely. . . .'

After a while Jack said : 'This is a rum place. What's all this wire?'

'Put there during the war,' said Rosamund sleepily. There was silence for a few moments except for the wind and a very distinct hiss from the waves, and then she heard a scrambling sound and opened her eyes. He was standing on top of the bank looking out at the sea. His hair was very black against the blue sky and he looked very big standing up there like that. It was silly that he had to wear a blue suit to come on a picnic, and an open-neck shirt didn't look right with it. But his neck was thick and brown and strong. She said : 'Come back.' But he said : 'Half a mo'. What's *that* there?' and disappeared over the edge, and she sighed and closed her eyes again.

The lunch wasn't very good because whatever you did things got sand in them, and she could never drink out of a bottle because her tongue got in the way, or else the stuff just poured out and went all over everything. Rosamund collected up the paper and put it in the bag and said : 'Well, I shall have about four pounds a week, so that would make it twelve pounds, which isn't bad.'

'Four pounds a week?' he said. 'What for?'

'Uncle Gustavus left it to me. Twelve pounds would be all right. We only give Mrs. Dart ten pounds a week housekeeping and that's for four.'

'Yes,' he said irritably, 'but that's only for grub. Hell, you'd get a long way on twelve quid a week, you would. Nowadays. Run a lot of motor cars on that.'

'I don't see that we need a motor car. You were going to get a motor bike.'

He stared out to sea for a long time in silence. 'Well, of course people *do* manage,' he said. 'And I don't reckon to go on earning eight quid for the rest of me natural. If I can't do better at Lang's in a while, then I'll go somewhere else. I'm not going to stick about all my life and end up with about ten pounds a week like Dad. But . . .' he paused and shook his head. 'It wouldn't ever be what you'd like,' he said sombrely. 'Not whatever I could do. No training, see. Now if you're a proper engineer . . .'

Rosamund said: 'Can't you be one? You're not very old.'

'You mean night courses and things?' He shrugged his shoulders. 'Might find out. But . . .'

There was a long silence. Rosamund said: 'Of course, I don't get my money till I'm twenty-one—only the four pounds a week. After that it's five thousand. But it's only just over two years. Anyhow, you can do what you like when you're twenty-one, can't you? I mean they can't stop you getting married or . . .?'

He turned and looked at her. 'Married?' he said with a grin. 'I never knew such a girl for getting married. How d'you know I want to marry *you*?'

She blushed hotly and said: 'I don't know . . . I always think . . .'

He put his arm round her and said: 'Ah, Rosey . . . I was only pulling your leg. . . .'

She said: 'Well, if you don't want to I'd much rather you said so, because . . .'

'Sure we'll get married,' he said, gently kissing her cheek. 'An' have fourteen kids. All on eight quid a week.'

'Twelve,' she said with a grin. 'Twelve children and twelve quid. A quid each. Plenty.'

*   *   *   *   *

It had been clear enough during the long drive through the night, but after he had left the Clays' it had become more and more vague and muddled, and Lang was driving now merely because to be in the moving car gave him a sense of purpose, which was missing when he sat and drank cups of coffee. His back was aching dully from sitting in the driving position, and his eyes felt hot and stiff. He knew he really ought to sleep, and several times he had stopped within sight of the sea to rest, only to find that it was more restful to be moving. He had been along the coast to Dymchurch and to Folkestone and to Dover, but though he had stopped the car in all of them for a few minutes, he had never driven round them as he had in Rye, and it was only the fact that he had lost his way in Dover that turned him round and sent him back along the road by which he had come, with too little energy to turn round and go on farther east. Indeed, since about three o'clock he had not thought much about why he was there or where he was going, being fully occupied by a scheme for bringing an injunction against Henry Spellman which would prevent him from selling his shares to Sir Francis; the alternative being to get George Martin, and go and set up a place of his own to make the sprayer. There would be difficulties about the steel, but he was fairly sure that with his connections they could be overcome. At about half-past four he ran out of petrol. It took him some time to realise why the engine should have stopped, and by that time the car had coasted some thirty yards to some petrol pumps. There were only five pounds in his wallet, which was peculiar, because he had drawn fifteen that morning. Then he remembered that that was before he went to London. But it was disturbing only to have five pounds, and he found that his hands shook as he paid for the petrol.

The Morris by the side of the road was vaguely familiar, but he was busy thinking, and he drove past it and on for fifty yards before something made him stop and look back at it. Even then he was not at all sure, for he had never remembered the number of any car since CR 1121, which was the Humber he had had in 1927. But he backed up to it and got out and looked through the side windows, and saw a scarf of his own on the floor in the back of the car. It was a nice scarf, and his first emotion was anger that Rosamund should take it and then leave it on the floor of the car to get filthy.

He passed a hand over his eyes and stood and looked up at the sand dunes. They seemed to stretch away for miles, looking very big and empty, and for a moment he felt utter despair at the prospect of looking for Rosa-

mund in a place like that. But then he realised that
she was bound to come back to the car in the end, if he
just waited, so he got into his own car again and shut his
eyes and started to wonder whether it would be any good
to ask them all to a dinner—Sir Francis and the Spellmans
and Winter and the whole lot—and just put his cards on
the table quite frankly. 'Gentlemen, you can probably
run this place without me, but you can run it a damned
sight better *with* me. After all, we're in business. . . .'

He must have dozed for a while, because when he
looked at his watch it was quarter-past five. For a
moment he was afraid she might have come back while
he was asleep, and gone and left him. But the Morris
was still standing there, and the sand hills still stretched
away solitary and empty. The sun had made the inside
of the car very hot. He was sweating, his back was
aching and he was intolerably uncomfortable, so he got
out of the car and started to walk across the sand to the
foot of the dunes.

The sand was loose and deep. Even on the level it
was an effort to lift his feet clear of it, and as soon as he
came to the steep slope, he slid back almost as much as
he went forward. He knew that the way to get up was
to take quick short steps, but he was very tired, and his
legs would only move slowly and heavily. He stopped
after a while, panting. His heart was pounding so that
his whole chest seemed to quiver, and his shirt was wet
through with sweat. Looking back, he found that he
had only climbed the first thirty yards of the slope, and
was only now reaching the steepest part. Yet even as
he stood, the sand was sliding away under his feet, and
he was slipping very slowly backward. When he saw
that, he made a tremendous effort and started to plough
forward and up in a sort of frenzy. He gained a few yards,
and then the effort faded. For a few seconds he was
stationary, still floundering desperately like an exhausted
pony in a moorland bog. Then he lost his balance and
fell forward on to the sand, cutting his hand slightly on
a piece of broken glass as he flung it out to save himself.
For a moment he saw the top of the dune sharply yellow
against the blue sky, thirty yards above him, and as

remote as the last two thousand feet of Everest. Then everything was a peculiar green colour, and he closed his eyes and lay there gasping for breath, and feeling the trickle of the sand under his fingers as his body began to slip almost imperceptibly back down the slope.

When they got to the top of the ridge and could see the road Rosamund stopped short and said blankly: 'Where on earth's the car? It's gone.'

Jack looked and said: 'No, it isn't. There it is, right along there.' It was a good half-mile along to the left, though they were sure that they had crossed the dunes both times in the same place. The sun was low now, but it was still warm, and the cold wind from the sea had dropped. They walked slowly along the ridge in silence looking at the sea, until they were nearly opposite the car. Rosamund said: 'Well, if I'm going back to Lime Cross to-night I shall have to go soon.'

He did not answer the question in her voice, but went on gazing moodily at the sea. After a moment Rosamund said brightly: 'I'm going to run down. Come on.' She took his hand and started down the slope. Jack said: 'Break your neck,' but he let her pull him after her, and once on the slope there was nothing to do but run and slither, until Rosamund suddenly gave a wild squeal and sat down with a bang, and went shooting on in a sitting position in the sliding sand, nearly to the bottom. She got up covered in sand and said: 'It's absolutely gorgeous tobogganing down like that. I'm going up and going to do it again. You try.'

He laughed and said: 'Mind yourself on the wire. There's a lot about.'

They were about fifty yards from the car when Rosamund suddenly let go his hand and stopped dead and said: 'Hey . . .!'

He looked at her in surprise and said: 'What's up?'

She was staring at the other car which stood a few yards from their own. After a moment she said very quietly: 'That's the Daimler,' and started to walk slowly towards it.

'What Daimler?'

'Ours. Daddy's.'

'Don't be silly,' he said uneasily. 'How can it be?'

'Well, it is,' she said. 'At least I think so. . . .' She hesitated and then walked in a wide semi-circle to the front of it, as though it was a dangerous animal, so that she could see the number plate. She nodded briefly and said: 'Yes. It is,' and turned and faced him. They looked at one another for a moment. 'Well, Christ . . . !' said Jack in sudden panic. She said quickly: 'He'll have seen the car but he hasn't seen you. You'd better . . .' His eyes were on something behind her, and at that moment Lang called her name. When she turned he was only a hundred yards away, ploughing through the sand in a queer half-run.

His face was running with sweat and he was panting heavily as he came blundering through the deep sand. Rosamund took a couple of steps forward and said: 'Hallo, Daddy,' quietly, but he ignored her and went on towards Jack as though he was going to trample over him, and then stopped short and panted out: 'You dirty young blackguard . . . !' Jack had stepped backwards so that he was almost against the front of the car. His face was white and scared.

Rosamund said: 'Now steady, darling . . . !' Lang turned to her and said: 'Get into the car.'

Rosamund said: 'It's not his fault at all. It was entirely my idea. He didn't even want to come. . . .'

Lang shouted: 'Will you do as I tell you, Rosamund, and get into that car?'

Rosamund hesitated and then said: 'No, I won't— not if you're going to be silly. . . .'

Lang stood and panted for a moment and then said: 'All right. Then stay and hear it. . . .' He took a step towards Jack and said quietly and breathlessly: 'Now —I want to know what you're doing here with my daughter?'

Jack said in a low voice: 'We haven't been doing anything. Only . . .'

'You've been going out with her before, haven't you?'

'Yes, Mr. Walter.'

'Behind my back? You've been taking her out? That's so, isn't it?'

'Yes. We . . .'

'Do you know how old she is?'

Jack's eyes flickered helplessly towards Rosamund. 'Near nineteen.'

'Eighteen,' said Lang. 'She's eighteen . . .' He stared at Jack with exhausted, bloodshot eyes. He said: 'Do you know what you are?'

Rosamund stepped forward and said: 'Daddy, for goodness' sake don't *do* it. . . .'

'Well, I'll tell you,' said Lang in the same quiet voice. 'You're a dirty skulking young blackguard who ought to be given a damn good hiding. . . .' His voice rose: 'Who the devil do you think you are, leading my daughter into this sort of dirty . . .'

'Well, she didn't have to go with me, did she?' said Jack with a sudden flicker of anger.

'My God!' said Lang furiously. 'And now I suppose you're going to throw the blame . . .!'

Rosamund said: 'Daddy, will you kindly *listen*? There's no question of Jack having led me into anything. If you must get into a rage with somebody, it's me. *I* suggested . . .'

Lang gave her no more than a quick glance. 'You?' he said contemptuously. 'You little fool.' He turned back to Jack and said breathlessly: 'The trouble with you, my boy, is that you've got a swollen head.' His voice was rising. 'But I'll show you your place. I'll break you for this. Yes—you and your whole damn family . . .'

'What's my family got to do with it?' said Jack quietly. He had moved a little from the front of the car now. His face was whiter than ever, but it was no longer frightened.

Lang said: 'I won't have any of you near the place. I'll put the whole lot of you in the gutter.' His face was a curious dark, muddy purple and he spoke in gasping jerks.

'Oh ah!' said Jack contemptuously. 'You're the big

boss, aren't you? Fire people out of your bloody factory's all you can do.'

Rosamund said: 'Jack . . .' quietly.

He swung round on her and said: 'Well, so it is all he can do. All he's fit for. Come down here calling me names and talking as though I was dirt. . . .' His eyes were full of tears.

Lang said: 'You are dirt, you . . .'

Jack moved forward a trifle. 'Oh, am I, mate? Well, I'm no more dirt than you are My father was as good a man as yours except that yours made a bit of money. Christ, anybody'd think you was Royalty, talking about *your* daughter. . . . An' you keep her there by herself and never give a damn about her. . . .'

Lang gave an inarticulate grunt and lunged forward. Rosamund said: 'Daddy . . .!' and grabbed at him. But Jack had flung up his hands defensively and seized Lang's arms just above the elbows. 'Steady, now!' he said breathlessly, 'steady! We don't want . . .'

He was a big powerful young man, and for a moment he held Lang helpless, struggling impotently to free his arms, like a child in a rage. Then with the last strength of pride Lang wrenched himself free. He saw the half-frightened face staring at him as though he saw it through moving water, and tried to launch himself at it again. But though the top part of his body moved, his legs would not, and the face vanished above him into darkness.

He was lying on the sand and there was some grit in one of his eyes. Rosamund was looking down at him. She had a handkerchief in her hand. He put up his hand to get the grit out of his eye and she said: 'Lie still, darling. It's all right,' and dabbed at the side of his head with the handkerchief. It stung. 'Don't do that,' he said irritably. 'It hurts.' He turned his head away and said: 'Have I done something to myself?'

'You've given your head a biff on the bumper of the car. Just keep quiet, darling. The doctor's coming to have a look at you in a minute.'

He remembered and said: 'Where's that bloody young . . .' and half raised himself. But an intolerable pain shot through his head as soon as he raised it. He heard her say: 'He's getting the doctor.' After that the only other thing was seeing her again quite suddenly, but inside now. He said very carefully: 'Now, you will come straight home to-night, Roz. No nonsense, mind,' and she smiled and said: 'All right, darling,' and that was all.

XX

IT was only half-past nine, and the milk-bar on the front did not seem to be quite sure whether it was open or not. It had given Jack coffee, but was still washing the floor rather resentfully round his feet.

He looked up as Rosamund came in and said: 'Hallo,' and then looked away again and went on staring out of the window at the sea.

Rosamund said: 'Well—he's more or less all right. He's got some concussion, but there's no fracture or anything like that, thank goodness.'

Jack nodded and said: 'Oh,' and went on looking at the sea.

Rosamund looked at him for a moment in silence. 'But of course it will be several days before we can get him home. . . .' She moved towards the counter for some coffee.

Jack fumbled in his pocket, produced a stub of cigarette, lit it, and went sullenly back to his seascape, all without looking at her.

After a moment she said: 'I don't think I have to tell you how sorry I am for—for all this. I . . .'

'That's all right,' he said. 'What's there to be sorry for? Had your bit of fun, haven't you?'

'Fun . . .!'

'I told you,' he said bitterly, 'right from the start— that he'd get on to it. But no. You knew better.' He shrugged. 'Well . . .'

Rosamund said: 'But I *still* don't see how he can have got to know. Or even if he did, how he can have found us out there. . . .'

'Doesn't matter, does it. I say you've had your bit of fun. . . .' He dropped the stub on the floor and crushed it under his heel.

Rosamund said quietly: 'I think you're being rather unfair. I know it was my fault, but . . .'

He turned and looked at her for the first time. 'Fair!' he said, 'that's good. I lose my job, and maybe dad loses his and all because of a silly little fool . . .'

'Stop it!' she said rather sharply.

They stared at one another for a moment. Jack gave a slight shrug and looked sullenly away again.

Rosamund said: 'I've told you I'm sorry. That's all I *can* do. But I'll tell you something else. . . .' She hesitated.

'Well?'

'I love you,' she said quietly. 'And when I've—I've got him home and he's better, I'll—come away with you if you like. Whatever anybody says. . . .'

'Oh Christ . . .!' he said with weary disgust.

'Why? Don't you . . .?'

He said: 'You don't know what you're talking about. Don't know the first thing about anything. Always talking about "going away" and "getting married" and so on. You're just a play-acting kid.' He was staring at her contemptuously. Rosamund had gone very white, and her lips were trembling. He saw this and raised his voice. 'What you think I'm going to do now? I s'pose you never thought of that? This is my holiday, see? I get a fortnight a year and this is it. Doesn't mean anything to you of course, yours all being holiday . . .'

He turned quickly away and she suddenly realised that his eyes were full of tears. After a moment she said: 'I'm terribly sorry, Jack. It's quite true. I—I hadn't thought of that. I . . .'

'I'll lay you hadn't,' he said bitterly. 'Why should you anyway?'

'What *will* you do?' she said after a moment's pause. 'Only you see . . . I rather have to be at the nursing home most of the time, and then in a few days I shall have to take him home. . . . Will you . . .?'

'That's my affair,' he said curtly. 'Don't you worry about me. You go and look after your Dad.' He got up abruptly and waited for her to do so.

As they came out on to the front Rosamund said in a low voice: 'And saying I'm sorry's no good?'

'You don't need to,' he said more quietly. 'You don't

want to worry about it. Truth of it is, if you make a fool
of yourself like I have, you got to pay for it.' He half
turned away.

Rosamund said: 'And I shall see you when—when
we get back?'

'Sure,' he said vaguely. 'Sure. Take care of yourself.'

The front was very long and empty and it was only
when she was almost at the end of it that she turned and
looked back. Right down at the other end somebody
was leaning on the rail looking out to sea, but it was too
far away to be sure.

     *   *   *   *   *

Henry said: 'I don't really know. His daughter rang
up, but I was out and she spoke to my secretary. All
we know is that he's had some sort of accident and that
he's in a nursing home with concussion.'

Ryan said: 'Is it serious, Mr. Spellman?'

'Not very, I gather.' Henry frowned. 'I can't ring
up because I don't even know exactly where he is, except
that it's somewhere on the South Coast. Heaven knows
what he was doing down there. They don't seem to know
anything about it at the house.'

Winter said: 'I understand that he was going to
London to see . . .'

'He did that and saw Francis. I had a telephone
call about that.' Spellman and Winter looked at
one another for a moment in silence. 'This seems to
have happened the next day,' said Henry colourlessly.
'Anyhow, it seems likely that he'll be off for some time.'
He removed his spectacles and looked at them with ill-
focussed, unhappy eyes. 'I've called a Board for to-
morrow to decide how we'd better—arrange things. But
I thought I'd better let you know in case anything was
being held up. . . .' He stood for a moment in silence,
staring moodily out of the window. Then he said: 'Well,
there it is,' put on his spectacles and lumbered heavily
away.

After a pause Ryan said: 'Well, I suppose it's no good
talking about this if Mr. Walter's away?'

'Why?' said Winter. 'He's agreed to the studies being made. We want to get on now we've got Parkes here.'

'You reckon that'll be all right?' said Ryan doubtfully.

'Why not? If he's going to be away for some time, we can't hold everything up.'

'I suppose not,' said Ryan, and hesitated.

'What's on your mind?' said Winter gently.

Ryan said: 'I don't know whether I got the right to ask this, Mr. Winter. . . .'

'You've got the right to ask anything you like.'

'Well, there's a rumour going round that Lang's is being sold. On account of Mr. Gustavus dying and so on. Can you tell me if that's so?'

Winter stared at him for a moment. 'Ah—that's rather a tricky one,' he said in the queer flat voice. 'That's finance, and I'm not a financial man. . . .'

'Only if it *was*, see—well, there's some old ones here who'd wonder what was going to happen. You know what they are. Think the world's coming to an end if there's anything new.'

Winter said: 'Well, I can't answer your question in so many words, but . . .' His mouth twitched into an almost recognisable smile.

'Anyhow, Mr. Walter—he'll be carrying on when he comes back?'

'You know as much about that as I do.'

There was a long silence. Ryan said slowly: 'Of course, Mr. Walter did a lot for the place. But he wasn't ever an easy man to work with. Different stamp of man from Mr. Gustavus altogether.'

John L. Parkes was a shock-headed young man with a broad, beaming smile. He was twenty-seven, but he looked younger. Nine years' experience of time-study had left him still feeling that it was a delightful and fascinating game. He was a good technician, but his main use was in places where the introduction of time-study might be regarded as an organised attempt to cut wages. John L. Parkes was so obviously not an organised attempt at anything.

Winter said: 'Well, there you are, Parkes. You can get going as soon as you like. You've seen Ryan?'

'Yes, Mr. Winter.'

'I don't think you'll have any trouble with him.'

'He seems very co-operative, Mr. Winter.'

'Yes. I've talked to him and so has his Headquarters.' Winter reflected for a moment. 'Go easy and don't rush it. Keep it on the generous side, and mind you carry Ryan with you. You've got to remember that it's an old family firm and all that sort of thing. I doubt if most of them have ever seen a stop-watch before.'

John L. smiled. 'I understand, Mr. Winter. I'm used to that.'

'Yes.' Winter frowned thoughtfully. 'As a matter of fact,' he said, 'I should be very surprised if there was any trouble. There's the usual talk about the family and their traditions and their particular way of doing things, but when you come down to brass tacks there's nothing much to it. Of course, the old man they really liked is dead.'

* * * * *

On the third day Lang informed the nursing home that he was now quite well, and would be going that evening. On the fifth Rosamund went to the doctor and said: 'I think you'll have to let him go home soon, or he'll go mad.'

The doctor sighed and said: 'Yes. He is restless. What I call an im-patient.' He smiled and Rosamund smiled politely too. He was a rather good-looking youngish man with a confidential manner. He said: 'Concussion's always a thing to be treated seriously . . .'

'The question is,' said Rosamund, 'whether you won't do him more harm by keeping him here fussing, than by letting him go home.' ('Always remember, darling,' her mother had said, 'if a doctor starts curing you of something, he'll go on and cure you of it if it kills you, unless you stop him.')

'Precisely the thought that had occurred to me,' said the doctor, nodding wisely. 'Mentally, of course, he's rather upset, and sometimes home—the familiar background . . .'

'It isn't as though he had to go by train. We could make him comfortable in the back of the car and I could take him straight home.'

'How far is it?'

'About four or five hours.'

'Five hours. . . .' The doctor considered. 'Well, it's not really *advisable*, but if he's anxious to get home. . . . Of course as soon as he gets there he must go straight to bed and stay there until—until your own doctor gives him permission to get up. Even slight concussion . . .'

When he had been in bed he had seemed fairly well except for times when he became very tired. But when they brought him down to the car he looked very pale and tottery, and Rosamund half wished she had made him stay. They made him as comfortable as they could in the back of the Daimler and gave her a letter to Doc Stevens, and explained to her about the dressing on his temple.

It was very odd to be sitting in the front driving, with him in the back, but luckily he seemed sleepy and said very little. Once he said: 'What have you done about the other car, Roz?' but she was ready for that and said: 'Oh, I arranged to have it driven home.'

Lang said: 'Oh, yes.' After that he seemed to go to sleep and did not speak again until she was through London and heading for Aylesbury. Then he said suddenly: 'You drive too fast. Like your mother.'

She smiled at him in the mirror and said: 'Who's driving this car, anyway?'

After a while he said: 'Roz . . .'

'Yes, darling?'

'I don't want you to feel that—that this has done anything to you and me. I can quite see how it happened, and it's probably partly my fault anyhow.'

She was being forgiven and there was nothing to be done about it. She changed down and kept the car moving through a round-about and said: 'Don't be silly, darling. Of course it wasn't.'

Lang said: 'I was bound to be angry that it should be a—a fellow like that. But it's all over now and I just want you to forget it. . . .'

Rosamund glanced in the mirror. He was leaning back in the corner with his eyes closed. His face was very pale and drawn. She said: 'Are you all right, darling, or would you like to stop for a bit?'

He muttered: 'No—no. Let's get on home . . .' without opening his eyes. A minute or so later he said: 'I think anybody could have felt the same. But I wouldn't like you to think I was angry with you.'

She said: 'No. Of course not. Try and go to sleep for a bit, darling, and by the time you wake up we'll be home.' Maddeningly, she felt her eyes filling with tears at the hopeless, agonising unfairness of it all, and for a moment she could not see properly. But you couldn't possibly burst into tears when driving a motor car at sixty miles an hour, so she kept her foot right down and blinked hard, and the blur soon cleared.

*　　*　　*　　*　　*

He was quite well now except for those occasional violent headaches, and it was nonsense to keep him in bed and fuss about the curtains being drawn, and to stop him from reading. Once he lost his temper with Rosamund and told her he supposed that she wanted to keep him in bed so that she could go out without his knowing. But most of the time he hadn't the energy to argue, and lay there in a sort of half-sleep, only waking up properly when they brought him meals. Once or twice he decided that this was really an admirable chance for the hard thinking that had to be done. But as soon as he really settled down to it, his head would start up again; and as soon as that went away he would go to sleep, so that it never got anywhere.

But this morning he had slept very well, and when he woke there was no trace of the headache. He knew he had been asleep a long time, and for a moment he was afraid it might be late. But his watch said seven o'clock, which was the time when he always woke up. He lay for those last few luxurious moments and then got out of bed and stretched and yawned. It made his head spin so that he had to lean against the wall for a moment. The dizziness soon disappeared, but it left a curious, rather pleasant feeling of lightness. He looked round for his clothes, but they were nowhere to be seen, and after a puzzled moment he remembered what he was up against, and that they were trying to keep him at home while Spellman and Proudfoot fixed everything.

He sat down on the bed and considered. There could be no question of bathing and going down to breakfast in the ordinary way, because they would spot what he was after at once and stop him. It was necessary to get out of the house as quietly and as quickly as possible, and be in his office when people arrived. The idea of having to slip out of his own house like that made him smile grimly. But it was necessary to remember what he was up against. It was failure to realise it before that had been the mistake.

He found his clothes and a clean shirt without difficulty, but he could not decide about a tie. He stood and stared at the rack for a long time in helpless indecision. But in the end he shut his eyes and took one at random, and after that dressing was easy.

He came silently out on to the landing and stood for a moment listening. There was no sound in the house at all. It was a quarter-past seven, and the Darts would certainly be up and about in the kitchen, but Rosamund would still be in bed. As long as the door of the corridor leading to the kitchen was shut, there was nothing to stop him from walking quietly through the hall and out of the front door. They might possibly hear the car start. But the garage was a long way from the kitchen, and by then it would be too late anyhow.

Everything went well. The door was shut. As he crept past it he could hear the Darts talking in the kitchen, and smiled quietly to himself. He had reached the front door before he realised that he had not got his brief-case with all his papers. It was somewhere in the house, but he could not remember where he had had it last, and it was too dangerous to go and look for it.

The first thing that told him something was wrong was that the garage doors were open and the Morris was not there. His first thought was that Rosamund had got up early and gone off somewhere behind his back again. But there was something wrong about the light and the feel of everything, and it came to him quite suddenly and clearly that it was not the morning now, and that he had slept right through till the evening. It was a tremendous blow, and for a moment he slumped against the car at the impact of it, and closed his eyes and nearly gave up. But he looked at his watch, and it was still only twenty-past seven, and there was a chance—just a chance—that they would be working late and still be there. He had no real hope, but there was nothing else left to hope for, and he got into the car and started the engine.

*   *   *   *   *

Piker wasn't the youngest of the apprentices, being older than both Les Gordon and Micky. But he was the smallest, and he looked young, and that was enough for everybody, so he was always picked on as the kid, and laughed at if he smoked or anything. It was because they laughed at him about smoking and said he wouldn't grow, that had really started him on it, and that was how he came to make his petrol lighter on the Q.T., and started making things altogether. He had made a lot of things now, and never been caught taking the stuff out, and now he'd got a hacksaw and a file at home, so that he could do some of it there, without having to watch all the time for the foreman coming round.

Piker knew exactly what he wanted, having marked it down when he went through the press-shop that day. They were just ordinary small pressings, only about four inches across, that looked like an end-cap to go on something. But if you could get four of them and slot them out to fit through the spokes, and polish them up or give them a lick of aluminium paint, they would look like brake-drums, like the expensive bikes had. He knew there would be plenty lying about on the stillages in the press-shop. It was only a matter of getting in without the watchman seeing, and Piker knew all about getting into Lang's. He came to where the wall ended and the railings began, and slowed down to a casual stroll. The slightly bent bar was about twenty yards away, right

down at the other end. All you had to do was to turn
yourself sideways, and once you had your head through
it was easy, if you were small.

*   *   *   *   *

The gates were locked, and though of course they
would be, Lang knew instinctively that none of them
would be there. But there was no going back now, and
when Ted Heath came out and peered through the gate
at the car, he called : 'Open up, will you, Ted?' in an
ordinary way, and waved a hand and smiled when Ted
swung the gate open and touched his cap.

There were no cars in the park, and if he was too
late and they had all gone, it was a little difficult to
know what to do. He sat for a while in the car and
thought about it, but then Ted came up and said : 'You
want to get into your office, Mr. Walter?' and he said :
'Yes,' and followed Ted in.

The light was going fast now. He went through the
outer office and noticed the cover on his secretary's type-
writer, and wondered vaguely what on earth she had
found to do with herself while he had been away. He
went into his office and switched on the light. Suddenly
realising that he was very cold, he put on the electric fire
too, and stood and looked round him. The office was
safe and reassuring, and with relief he sat down at his
desk and closed his eyes. It was very quiet, and he remembered noticing several times that though you didn't
hear the distant rumble of the factory when it was working, you noticed the silence when it was not.

After a while Lang opened his eyes and turned almost
mechanically to his IN tray. There was the usual big
pile of stuff in it, and he decided that since he was there
he might as well run through some of it and get a clear
desk. It would take some time, and after that one would
have to do some hard thinking before they came back.
There was a sealed envelope on top of the pile, marked
'Private.' He opened it and read : 'Dear Walter : I
have felt for some time that my work here has given
little satisfaction to either of us . . .' He was horrified

for a moment, because he knew that if once Spellman resigned, Proudfoot had the option on his shares and it was all up. Then he realised that it was not Henry Spellman but Lawrence Spellman, and laughed, because the sooner young Lawrence got out, the better he would be pleased. But it was possible that they had sent in their resignations together, and if so Henry's would be somewhere in the pile. He hunted feverishly through, but it was not there, so there was still a chance.

As soon as he looked down to read anything, he had a feeling that they were all sitting there looking at him. Not doing anything—just sitting and waiting. Old Henry, and Lawrence with that supercilious grin on his face, and Proudfoot nodding and pecking, and Winter. . . .

He said : 'Gentlemen—let's put our cards on the table. You can probably run this business without me, but you can run it a damned sight better *with* me.' He lowered his head and looked round the office and said angrily : 'It seems to have been conveniently forgotten, but I'll remind you that when I took over the managing directorship, the place had a turnover of about a third of its present size and was barely breaking even. Its present position is not due to a lot of pious talk and high-flown ideals, but to my hard work and initiative. Some of you may remember the fight I had to get the new press-shop built. I had to fight my way through against every sort of opposition and obstruction from people who . . .' He stopped short and jumped up and shouted : 'Get to hell out of my factory, the lot of you . . .' and stood there erect and powerful and dominant. But the silence swung back into place as though he had struck a velvet curtain, and after a while he sank back into his chair and said wearily : 'Very well. If that's the general view, I'll go.'

* * * * *

Piker had not thought the press-shop would be all locked up, because what did they think, that somebody would come and steal a press ? But it was, and he was near giving up when he saw the window a bit open. Piker hesitated, because somehow getting through the window wasn't like just slipping through the fence. But

he thought of the brake-drums all polished up, and put
his hand in and unlatched the window so that he could
swing up and get through. It was only half light inside
the shop, and very quiet with all the presses standing
there so still, as though they were waiting, and for a
moment he was frightened of it. But he set his teeth
and made himself go into the gangway and walk down it
toward the end with the small presses, where he had seen
Reg Hathaway and the German chap working on the
things that would do for brake-drums.

They were all right, like he'd known they'd be. A
whole stillage of them. Piker had picked up three and
was looking for a fourth one with a proper smooth edge,
when he heard the voices. He only had time to slip
round behind one of the presses, leaving the caps out in
the gangway, before there was the key in the lock and
he heard the door open. Piker was crouching down
behind one of the small presses and he couldn't see, but
Ted Heath said : 'You'll want a light on,' and somebody
else said something he didn't hear. Ted Heath said :
'All right, Mr. Walter. You let me know when you're
going, see, and I'll lock up after you.' Then the door
shut and it was all quiet. Piker thought they had gone
away again, being so quiet and no light on, and after a
bit he half stood up ; but he bobbed down again mighty
sharp, because there was Mr. Walter Lang standing not
five yards away in the gangway, and if there'd been a light
on he couldn't have missed seeing him. Piker moved just
an inch or two so that he could see, and Mr. Walter was
standing there quite still, staring down the press-shop.
After a bit he moved on till he was right in front of the
little press that Piker was behind, so close that Piker
could almost have touched him, and in the half dark like
that he looked ten foot high. Piker's heart was beating
so that he was sure Mr. Walter would hear it and spot
him. But Mr. Walter went on down the gangway,
walking very slowly and turning his head from side to
side and sort of peering at the presses. What bit of light
there was left was on his face and it was queer and sort
of twitching about as though he was going to sneeze.
There was a click as he kicked something, and it was

the caps left out in the gangway, and that gave Piker a
nasty turn again. But Mr. Walter bent down and picked
them up and looked at them for a long time and felt
them as though he was looking for ones with smooth
edges too. Then he went over slowly and put them on
the stillage with the others, except for one that he kept,
and went on down the gangway with, still looking at it
and stroking his hand over it.

It was a long gangway right down the length of the
shop with smaller ones going off each side, and it was
getting darker all the time. By the time Mr. Walter was
right down the other end by the two biggest presses they
called Goliath and Carnera, Piker couldn't see him
properly when he was in the shadow. Mr. Walter stood
so still and quiet down there that once Piker thought he
must be gone and was just going to come out. Then he
heard a bit of a sound as though Mr. Walter was coughing
to himself, but very quietly; and when Piker stared hard
he could just see a shadow as if he was leaning up against
the wall by the big presses. Its being so dark by then,
Piker didn't actually see him go, but after a long while
he thought he saw something move, and then the coughing
had stopped and he couldn't see the shadow any more,
so he reckoned Mr. Walter was gone all right, and very
cautiously got up.